PHOENIX FLOWER

J T HARPER

Dr Al,
I can only hope that
my descriptions live
up to your teaching.

JH

Daugherty
PUBLICATIONS

ACKNOWLEDGMENTS

I wish to thank the following people who played an important role in the creation of this book:

Every professor who said anything to me about writing, especially Timons, The Goat, Dr. Al W, Scott, and everyone I am likely to forget to mention.

I wish to thank Frank Cook for his encouragement,

Leslie Petersen for her magic,

and a special thanks, hugs, and kisses to my wife Sue. She let me do this. And I will never forget it.

CHAPTER ONE

President Hsieh
9 May 2249
Office of the president
Barca City
GPS: 37°33′57.884″N 122°11′38.62″W
Outside Conditions: light fog, temp 22.22
Sustainability Factor: -14 (viral saturation)
Interior Conditions: all systems functioning at peak

IT FELT LIKE I WAS STANDING ON SOME ASTRAL PLATEAU, hovering out over what was still one of the most breathtaking views on the planet Earth—north over the San Francisco Bay. I could experience, at least visually, the Bay Area at almost any point in modern time. It never got old. I often scanned through the menu of available views, showing the evolution of the Bay Area over the past two centuries. Anything looked better than the stripped, flattened hills of the East Bay now devoid of human life, hilltops scarred by our mining, muddy waters of the bay now a dumping ground for the byproducts of silica production.

The peninsula wasn't any better, with its ghostlike remnants of what were once homes, teetering skyscraper skeletons, and rotted and disfigured signs of all forms of transportation methods rambling out toward San Francisco. The airport was now used as storage for weapons from the final solution—the Great Purge. Amphibious troop transports, laser cannons, missile haulers all stood as reminders of the awesome power that had once been needed to restrain the populations. Physical control no longer an issue, they sat rusting like so many of the remnants of twenty-second-century life.

For my own reasons, these weapons and what they'd once represented filled me with pride and a sense of great power.

Directly following the Purge, many had thought of the Out and seen death and destruction. Those thoughts had slowly faded away as new generations, born and raised inside the benevolent Barca City, grew up with no concept of the previous world. They only knew Barca—and what we allowed them to think about. Of course, there had been legends of a different life that might exist outside the confines of Barca City, but these myths were fading, no longer something people talked about. Most Barcans saw only life as they knew it.

For my part, I chose to see progress—the evidence of my successful enterprises and the culmination of man's dominance over man—determined by one thing: who had the most money held the most power. I held sixty-seven percent ownership in Barca, which made me the one in charge. The one in control of the money also controlled the people. That had never changed.

I stood at the pinnacle of the most advanced self-contained ecosystem ever created: Barca City. Many would fault us for our tightly sealed world, the inability to leave the environment and venture outside into what was oddly called the "natural world." But what good was nature that took away life? That was the reality for those inside our city. For any of us to go into the Out without hazard clothing and safety gear, with no breathing apparatus, would be suicide. Nothing natural there. Who needed nature when we could create our own world that fulfilled our every need: food, shelter, air that didn't kill us? Those who might leave would never leave. We knew that, and we provided for their living, asking only a fair share of work from them for the privilege of living here in Barca City.

"Scan sectors."

As expected, I was soon soaring over the Barca City superstructure, hovering over each sector long enough to get a reading on that sector's production and activity monitors. I scanned from one hologram to the next until I had a clear idea of the status of each production center in the city.

"Out status."

I found myself projected skyward, flying as if a god surveying his domain. Virtual projection traveling was more than a necessary tool. It was also one hell of a lot of fun, at least in the beginning.

From the first time I'd fired the system up, I found it exciting, even intoxicating, to travel in real time to any place within my purview. Just mentioning a location would cause the system to teleport me right to that location as if I was really there, even though it was through the magic of technology and not actually happening. Nonetheless, it felt real and was energizing.

Now, years after that first experience, I went through the motions of holographic travel as something I now had to do, no longer something I necessarily wanted to do. The newness had worn off, and the excitement was dulled a bit.

To add a slice of intrigue, I had set the system to a randomized trip from one Out station to the next, hoping to avoid the casual attitude that was often the result of boredom. Boredom led to apathy, led to sloppiness, which led to mistakes. I didn't tolerate mistakes in anyone, much less in myself.

This morning, as I flew over the lower reaches of Sonoma Sector, an aberration caught my eye. Observing northward toward the Santa Rosa ruins, the sky took on a red glow, an indication of a pending alarm situation. The system had picked up some form of life, or undetermined energy, that indicated there could be humans in the area.

"End scan." Instantly, I was standing on the floor of my office, staring out the wall-to-wall, floor-to-ceiling windows. *What the fuck was that?*

∼

TESS

A time and place seen only by the Great Ones

I AWOKE IN THE PRESENCE OF HER GLORY. WAKAN TANKA, the Great One—the total of all the powers of the world as a single presence, who showed herself as woman to me. I felt a warmth of love and power surge through my spirit as I opened my eyes to her greatness.

"We welcome you, Tess, child of our design, woman of spirit."

I lowered my eyes and bowed, feeling so small in the light of this power.

"Dear one, the world is again in terrible need of the White Buffalo and her teachings. As before, people have been led to a dark place. This evil takes the form of a dominating society called Barca. The powerful have enslaved the meek.

"There are those who have not yet been devoured by the devil of greed. These people, descended from those who left their society years before it began to crumble. The evil ones have become aware of their existence and would destroy them, if they could find them. The evil ones will do all they can to destroy the tribal people."

"Shall I destroy the evil ones?"

"In a way, yes, but not directly. That would only leave a hole that could easily be filled by the next greed-filled people, who would simply pick up where the others were stopped."

"I see." But I didn't see at all. I needed to tell her, but I was afraid she would think I was not smart enough to handle what she asked of me. I forgot, for the moment, that Wakan Tanka knows everything.

"No, dear one, we don't think that at all," she said in response to my unspoken thoughts. *"Of course, you don't know everything unless we tell you."* She smiled at me. *"You are right to question."*

"Then I need to know: why me, and how can I help the world this time?"

"These people, the ones who left their society in hope of a life in nature, this community of people who only wish to live simply, are not yet a tribe as we know it. They're more like a herd, a flock of sheep, but without a shepherd. This flock is surrounded by hungry wolves, ready to devour all unprotected sheep. These people are powerless against the evil ones. Worse, they're unaware of the danger.

"Imagine a tribe without a purpose, a flock without a shepherd. They're little more than slaves waiting to be enslaved. Sheep ready for the wolf."

"So, if I'm not to destroy the evil ones myself, then I have to teach the flock to protect themselves?"

"Again, yes, but not you directly. There is one whom we have chosen among these people. You must teach this chosen one to be a leader. That is all I will say. How and when is for you to determine. The Great Ones will never take direct action in the affairs of the people. But we will provide, through spirits like you, guidance and love. The people must then guide themselves and be ready to face the result of their free will. Go, then, with our love, and give hope for the future of the world. It is yours to pass to the people."

Then she was gone.

CHAPTER TWO

Ranza

   23 April 2249
   Somewhere west of the Santa Rosa Ruins (former California)

I SIGHTED DOWN THE ARROW TO THE TIP WHERE THE SHARP blade sat, tied tightly with rabbit-gut strings. From the tip, I followed across the distance to the heart of the boar, where my arrow would do the job it had been created to do. My muscles tight, my focus steady, I drew in a deep breath, then let some of it escape. Staring into the eyes of the animal, I wished its spirit peace, and I thanked it for its sacrifice.

Neither of my parents were hunters. Dad was a farmer and Mom was a tribal council member. But here I was, at the age of seventeen, about to qualify as a primary hunter, the youngest ever to be given that honor. All I had to do now was take down this wild boar, skin and dress it, present it to the tribal council, and I was in. My body shook with excitement.

I'd tracked the pig for more than an hour, looking for the best opportunity to take the fatal shot. Now, here we were in the dark cave, the boar trapped under a rock outcropping, hoping it was crouched low enough and that the cave was dark enough I wouldn't see it.

Sorry, pig. No such luck.

Connell, my master trainer, stood close behind me—so close I could feel his breath on my neck. He wanted to watch every move. Did I remember the steps? Would I take any shortcuts?

Steps. I could imagine Connell's curt tone every time he demanded I both act out and recite them for every kill.

One: load and nock arrow.

Two: draw and hold.

Three: sight the arrow.

Four: tense only the firing muscles.

Five: take a deep breath in, let it out a bit, and hold.

Six: look into the soul of the prey and give thanks.

Seven: loose the arrow.

Missing the target was never acceptable, so Connell just assumed the prey was dead. A final step went unsaid, but we learned early to *Eight: dress and pack* the carcass, leaving the remnants in the open for the cleanup crew of turkey buzzards that followed hunting teams everywhere.

At this point in my life as a hunter, I was running on instinct. Didn't have to think about the steps. They just happened.

I released the bowstring.

I couldn't explain what happened next. My arrow clacked uselessly against the cave wall above the pig.

What the . . . ? Can't be. I never miss.

I quickly drew another arrow, but too late. The pig, sensing a reprieve, leapt to its hooves. Or to its . . . feet?

No, wait . . . pigs don't have feet! My heart skipped as I realized that what I had been certain was a wild boar had somehow changed, before my eyes, into a girl—a young girl about my own age. *But . . . This can't be. How can a pig become a human? How could I be so wrong to track a girl, thinking she was a boar, and almost put an arrow in her heart? None of this makes sense. I can't make a mistake like this*. My mind grew hazy, and I was sure my brain would shut down, making me pass out.

In a heartbeat, Connell reached out to grab the girl. He scooped her into his arms and held her as she kicked and screamed to be set free.

Truly this is a girl. Not a pig. What the hell happened?

"Easy, girlie. Not gonna hurt you. Settle down." Connell's eyes grew large as he obviously tried to wrap his mind around what he had just seen. "I mean, really, settle down. You have some talking to do, little girl."

All I could do was stand there, my mouth hanging open, my brain swimming, still holding my bow, arrow drawn and ready, although I had no idea I was still about to shoot. I was all mixed up, couldn't focus even if I tried. I stared at the two of them, waiting for I don't know what to happen next.

The girl suddenly stopped fighting. Bowing low at the waist and opening her arms to the side, she began to hum—a low, soft sound that filled the cave.

Connell was probably as confused as I was. He must have relaxed his grip on the girl for an instant, as she took a step back from him while the hum continued. I expected her to run, but she just stood there, totally still for a time before she raised her head, lowered her arms, and looked first into Connell's eyes and then into mine. As her eyes met mine, an unfamiliar feeling came over me—somewhat warm and comforting, yet a feeling I'd never known before. Her eyes seemed to speak without words, as if to look inside my thoughts. Then, as quickly as the feeling came, it left and the humming stopped.

Again, I became aware of the bow in my hands, arrow still nocked, still pointed in her direction. I was horrified. It only made me feel more that I had almost killed a girl.

As though she sensed my thoughts, she looked right at me, the hunter holding an arrow at full draw, ready to fire, and she just smiled.

Connell moved to jump between the two of us, reaching out

as though to guide the girl out of the way, but somehow, he was unable to. I watched as he tried to step toward her yet his feet remained planted. A look of panic crossed his face. "No," was all he said.

The girl looked toward him again, smiled, and said, "It's alright."

She turned to me again. Maybe she was about to do something to me. I knew I could defend myself, but I didn't want things to get worse than they were.

No time to think. I lowered the arrow and ran toward her, hoping she wouldn't think I would hurt her. When I was close, I fell to my knees and held the bow and arrow out to her in an offer of peace.

"Please, take these. I mean no harm. I just . . . You were . . . You were a boar, and now you're a girl. I thought . . ."

"Do I look like a boar?"

"No, I'm sorry. I didn't mean . . ." I stared into her face. What I saw scared the life out of me. They were the same eyes I'd thought I'd seen in the boar.

But how can that be?

As I gazed at her, transfixed, I felt a strange sensation. My knees were shaking, and I felt weak. Was it fear?

"Relax, Ranza. I was teasing you. It's dark in here. It was easy for you to mistake me for a boar. It probably was a boar that you tracked. I think I saw a large animal race past me when you came into the cave."

"What? This is crazy. You aren't a boar. You're a girl, like me. And how do you know my name?" I shook my head. "But . . . You *were* a boar. I didn't make that up. I saw. I'd never shoot a girl, but I did try to kill the boar . . ." I paused again, dizzy with the effort of trying to figure out what was happening. "*How do you know my name?*"

"Well, since you asked twice, and since you shouted the second time, I'm going to answer the name question first. But you won't like the answer till you know more. For now, under-

stand that I know more than your name. I know *you*. I was sent
here for you, and we will get to know each other very well,
Rannie."

"You even know my nickname? C'mon. Who's been talking
to you? Tooren? Juvie?"

"I don't know those names. For the moment, just know this
—there is a time to know, and a time to wonder. This is a time to
wait. Answers will come when it's time to know."

"No more of this game." I peered at Connell, stuck in
midstride. He looked frustrated yet somehow comical. I looked
to the girl. "What did you do to him? You put some kind of spell
on my friend, my teacher. I don't trust you. I think everything
you say is a lie." I backed away from this girl—if she even was a
girl.

"I understand. I might feel the same if I were you. In time
you'll come to trust me. We'll be friends."

"You're pretty sure of yourself. Now you say we'll have some
sort of friendship? In time I'll trust you? Sorry, I don't know you,
and I *don't* trust you. Whatever you did to Connell is more than
enough to make me distrust you. I think I'd prefer that you just
leave us alone."

The girl turned toward Connell and held her hand up toward
him where he stood as if his feet were locked in place. She closed
her eyes and softly hummed a tune I'd never heard before. I
watched closely to see what she was doing.

If she hurts him more, I'm gonna grab that bow and—

What I saw shook me. A soft glow settled down over
Connell. As it covered him, I could see his face begin to soften,
like he was no longer fighting to move. He wasn't as rigid. He
actually started walk toward me—only a few steps, but it was
movement nonetheless. He smiled at the girl.

"By the gods . . ."

"That's exactly right, Rannie. By the gods. Or as we say,
thanks to Wakan Tanka."

"What the hell does that mean?"

"Soon. This is a time to wait."

Connell was rubbing his legs, probably to see if they were really okay. "What happened to me? Why did my legs lock up, and what did you do to make it stop?"

"I have no idea what you are talking about, Connell. Did something happen to your legs?" She turned to me and smiled an odd kind of smile. "Maybe the planets lined up to create magic?"

"You talk funny. Now I have questions. Who are you, where do you come from, and why are you here? Those will do for starters. After that, start explaining whatever this is that you called magic." I slowly picked up my bow, hoping not to alarm her.

"You'll soon know who I am, Ranza. You feel my spirit, so you know I'm not going to harm you. I can see into your spirit, as you can see into mine. Before, when you looked into my eyes, you felt strange, didn't you?"

"Yes, but there was a lot going on then."

"I'm called Tess in your language. I'll tell you what you need to know, but we need to know each other first. About saying that we'll be friends—I hope that will be possible. I would like to stay here in your community for a time. I'm drawn to live among those who have chosen the natural, simple life. If you feel I'm asking too much of your tribe, then I'll respect your wishes and just move on. I leave that to you to decide. But I've seen you, and you've seen me. We're close in age, and, I believe, in our spirit—who and what we are. You and I can learn so much from each other. But I need to know if you'd be willing to allow me to stay among your people."

"Don't you have a home? A family?"

The world is my home, Ranza. All people are my family."

"You see, that's what makes me not so willing to trust you. You say very strange things like that that make no sense at all. Everyone has a home, some family, even if they're no longer alive. Are yours passed on?"

"Alright. Actually, it's very simple. I'm what might be called a wanderer. A traveler. I have no real home, never wanted to be tied down. As for family, I have no memory of a time I might have known someone to call family. I've always been on my own, alone, free to go anywhere and do what I wish."

"You call that simple? How can that be? How does a child go anywhere and do whatever without any parents or other family to protect them—provide for them?"

"I never said I had no one to protect or provide for me. I've always had the Great One, Wakan Tanka, with me, just as she is with me now. And you will come to know Wakan Tanka as I do, as we come to understand her plan for us."

"There you go again."

"I'm sorry, Ranza. Please, try to trust me, or at least try to wait. You will soon come to understand."

Something in her voice, and the sincerity in her face, touched my spirit, and I felt there was something in this girl that I wanted to know. She was, in some way I couldn't yet figure out, special. I wanted to understand her.

"Yes, I'll help you stay among us." As I spoke, I felt a slight shiver come over me.

"Thank you, Rannie. That means the world to me."

Connell was concerned and cautioned me even though it wasn't his place to advise me on anything but hunting. "Ranza, you don't even know her. I advise you to take Tess to your parents, let them help make any decisions like this one. I know she seems good of heart, but you just met her. Your mom and dad should be a part of this decision."

What he said made sense.

"Yeah. I suppose you are right. Tess, I will take you home with me to meet my family. That is if you'll agree."

"Of course. I'd be happy to meet them."

We left the cave and headed toward the Santa Rosa Nomás village. Connell walked behind Tess and me, as if to be ready to protect me. I needed no protection from this newcomer.

CHAPTER THREE

Tess
Santa Rosa Nomás village
Santa Rosa Ruins
Early morning
Light fog

I FELT THE EARLY MORNING GROUND FOG WASH OVER THE camp like a giant wet feather—a dampness that chilled me to the bone.

Sitting on a log at the edge of the well, I was half concealed from sight by the bushes that Marlon, Ranza's dad, had planted to hide the well from those who might harm them. Pretty easy to tell how important secrecy was to the Nomás. All I had to do was look around, knowing that this was home to an entire community of people, yet I was unable to see any sign that there was any life around except the incredible variety of wild animals, birds, and reptiles that wandered the area fearlessly.

My energy came alive with the sights, smells, and sounds of the morning. The sweet-bitter smell of the olallieberries mixed with the heady aroma of dusty ground below my feet. I couldn't help but laugh at the harsh chatter of the clownish grackles, odd birds whose tails looked as though they were attached sideways, lending an awkward appearance as they flew from one crumbling building to the next. They seemed to be searching for a place from where they could spot a careless lizard as it poked its head out from under a rock to nab an equally errant bug.

The nature of it all, I thought. *One dies to feed another, an unending chain of life and death.*

I was too aware that nature had been perfectly designed, balanced, until humanity found so many ways to disrupt the cycles, putting Earth at the brink of ruin. I was reminded of my purpose and how important my newly forming friendship with Ranza and the Nomás might be.

I recalled what Wakan Tanka told me. *"Tess, you and Ranza share a common spirit."*

"I get it, so far, but I'm confused by the phrase 'common spirit.'"

I believed I could hear the voice of the Great One reminding me of my own words to Ranza: *"A time to know, and a time to wonder . . . This is a time to wait."*

Ranza and her family had prepared a place for me to stay—a small building that was well hidden by overgrown bushes and trees. It was small but comfortable, as they had provided a bed made of tree branches woven into a platform and covered with an animal-skin padding filled with some dried vegetation, probably pine leaves. A warm hide blanket protected me from the cold night air, and there was a pail I used to wash myself and cups for drinking. I didn't mind sleeping alone; the freedom allowed me to explore the area when I wanted.

I had met many of the Nomás people on my walks—a friendly, helpful tribe. Even though they had no idea of who I was and why I was there, all welcomed me as a friend. Their trust and willingness to make me feel at home was refreshing. Also, I'd been able to get to know Ranza better during this time.

"Morning, Tess." I turned toward the sound to see Ranza as

she led Whisper into the open area, tying her rope to the low branches of the nearby tree.

"Hi, Rannie. Beautiful morning, huh?"

"Yeah. It's my favorite season. This fog'll burn off soon, then we'll be able to see for miles. And also, I have good news to share: Connell certified me last night. You're looking at the youngest lead hunter ever for the Nomás. Tooren, Juvie, and I are going to celebrate with a new-team hunt today."

"Oh. I'm happy for you. You have a team. They seemed like nice guys when I met them, and I'm sure you'll be a great leader."

"What are you planning for the day?"

"Really, nothing. I'll probably just go on a walkabout to learn more about the area, maybe introduce myself to some more of the folks. Then I should spend some time praying to Wakan Tanka."

The mention of Wakan Tanka caught Ranza off guard. Her eyes widened in a look of surprise.

"Wakan who? I'm sure I never heard that name, yet it has a slightly familiar sound. Tell me about it."

"Wakan Tanka is the name you heard me call the Great One."

"Oh. Some sort of god?"

"Not quite. Not just a god, but the combined spirit of all gods. She is all power."

Ranza paused, seeming to want to understand. The sudden shriek of a grackle startled her so that she leapt to her feet, ready to fight whatever needed to be fought. But there was nothing. Just a clown-bird. Finally, pressured by her fear, she sat back down, shoulders sloped, head down, not looking at me.

"Ranza, what's wrong?"

"I'm just on edge lately, that's all. So, about my plans for the day. Wanna come? It'll give you a chance to see what I do for my keep."

"No, I'd only slow you down. I don't know anything about hunting."

"Oh, you won't slow us. You'll see. It'll be good, and it can give us more time together."

I paused, trying to feel her thoughts. She was sincere, her eyes direct and open. I could also tell she was intent on getting her way.

"Well, maybe it'd be good. We have so much to talk about. I think it's time we start to become friends and open up to what's coming for us."

"'Become' friends? I thought that's what we were doing, becoming friends."

"We are. That's for certain. But we'll become very close, Rannie. We have work, important work, to do."

"What are you babbling on about? Work? I have work—hunter work."

"Work that's more than you can imagine. Work for the future and for Wakan Tanka. Work that we must do to save your people and all others in the Nomás world."

I knew this was sure to shake her up, so I tried to leave it there.

"What? Tess, you can't just clam up. I need answers. What are you going on about? 'Save your people'?" Ranza was almost speechless.

"I will tell you more when it's time. There is a time to know, and a time to wonder. This is a time to wait." I spoke the words, knowing their effect. It was now the third time I'd told her this.

Ranza gazed directly at me, as if she could see right through me, if only for a second. She was clearly trying to process what I was telling her. She tried to speak. Her mouth opened slightly, but nothing would come. It was a good thing, too, because at that very moment Tooren rode into the clearing, jumped from his horse, pulled off his hat, then bowed.

"Good day, ladies. The great Tooren, master hunter, at your service."

I scanned from Tooren to Ranza. She seemed to be slowly regaining her composure.

"Hi, Tooren. It's good to see you again." I walked to him and reached out my hand.

Tooren met my handshake. "Yeah. I was hoping to see you this morning. Rannie keeps talking about you, and I pretty much felt that I knew you when we met the other day, but she never told me how pretty you were."

Ranza jumped into the fray before any trouble could start. "Tooren's a great hunter, but he has a lot to learn about people." She stepped between Tooren and me, and the look on her face told Tooren everything he needed to know.

"Uh, sorry, Tess. I guess I sometimes come across as a smart-ass. Didn't mean to offend."

He looked to Ranza as if to ask if that was enough falling on his sword to make up for being rude. This gave me time to more carefully size him up. I could see beneath the human wrappings and into his spiritual core. I saw a good person, a guy who didn't harbor any ill toward others, a young man who'd do whatever he could to please people around him. On the other hand, I could see he was pretty insecure about his position on the hunt team, and I could see he was crazy about Ranza.

"I don't mind. Sometimes we all need someone to say something nice to us. Thanks, Tooren. I'll take it as a compliment." I could sense his relief as Ranza backed down.

"Tooren, Tess is going with us today. She's never been on a hunt, so this one-day trip will be an education for her. Maybe you and Juvian can show her some of *your* magic." She then glanced at me. I didn't show any signs of having noticed her unfortunate choice of words, so Ranza continued. "Tooren, maybe you can explain our technique as we go along?"

"Sure, I'll be happy to. Oh, I forgot to tell you, Rannie. Juvie isn't going with us today. Shree's still pretty hurt with that wing injury, and Juvie said he isn't about to leave his friend just to go pack up a few deer. He said to say he's sorry and he'll work double the next hunt to make up for it."

"Alright, then it's just the two of us plus Tess. We can at least hope for a buck or a couple boars."

She looked at the pile of provisions she had packed for the trip, grabbed a few pieces of the hunt clothes, and walked toward me. I felt her spirit open to me, remembering the first time we met. The moment our eyes fully locked on each other's, Ranza stumbled on a rock in her path, dropping some clothes. I probed her thoughts.

"Will I ever be able to forget I nearly killed a girl? What if Tess hates me for it and is waiting to get even? What about this Wakan Tanka and the big secret mission I have agreed to although I have no idea what it is all about? Real? Not a chance."

"Rubbish," she mused out loud.

"What?" I pretended to not know what she was saying. "They might be a little dirty, but I wouldn't throw them away."

"Huh? What are you talking about?"

"The clothes you just called rubbish because they fell to the ground. Dust them off—they'll be fine."

"Oh, yeah," Ranza managed to mutter. "Actually, they're for you. These are hunting clothes. They can make it nearly impossible for the prey to see you."

"You have magic?"

"Not magic, Tess. When Barca was still active out here in the natural world, they often wore clothing that seemed to make them invisible to wild animals and people who might harm them. Nomás people found many of these articles of clothing over time and set out to understand and copy the technology for our own needs. They were able to succeed—in fact, our version is far better than the one we copied. I have no idea how it works. Mom once told me it was a result of using principles of reflection and angles that confuse the eye. That meant nothing to me, so I just like to say it works, very well."

"Yeah. I see," Tess said. "Well, I'm not going to need those."

"Huh? You think it's okay to just go on a hunt and let the prey see you as you try to kill them? I imagine you'd go hungry if left to feed yourself."

I heard her thought: *"She thinks she know everything and I'm stupid."*

"Let's get to the point, Ranza. No, I think you're very smart, not stupid. And about your other thoughts—I don't hate you, thinking you tried to kill me. You tried to kill your prey, what you thought was a boar. If you tried to kill me, actually knew it was me, then it'd be different. But I'd have done the same if I were in your place."

With a frown, she began walking toward where her horse stood. "Tess, is it always going to be like this? Are you always going to look inside my head? Can't I even have any private thoughts again?"

I avoided the answer. Of course, it was always going to be like this. "Be right back. I'll get my horse, then we can go. And just so you know, I saw you in the cave when you took a shot at me. Did you have the hunting clothes on then?"

She watched me leave.

~

RANZA
Left alone with her thoughts

As I watched Tess leave the area, my thoughts took me back to the cave. It was looking more like I'd imagined the boar. *"'What you thought was a boar,'"* she'd said. How could I have been so wrong?"

"Rannie? Are you feeling alright? What's wrong? You seem nervous." Tooren stood beside me.

"Huh? Oh, yeah. I'm fine. I was just daydreaming. So, what do you q about Tess?"

The question left Tooren speechless for a time. It was a simple query, but I knew there was a certain uneasiness about me that Tooren had never seen before. It showed in the way I acted around Tess.

Uneasy? Hell. I didn't just look nervous—I *was* nervous. I'd tripped over a rock, mumbled out loud, daydreamed. Damn! I was daydreaming now. And all this stuff about Wakan Tanka? What the hell?

And I knew for certain Tooren was worried. There was nothing he wouldn't do to protect me. This newcomer concerned him.

"Yeah. She's nice. More than a little weird, though. She turned down the hiding clothes for no reason? Maybe she doesn't understand how dangerous that can be." Now he became a little secretive, leaning in to lower his voice, looking around to see if Tess had returned. "I don't really know her yet. But you do. So, what do *you* think about Tess?"

There was just no way I was going to tell him what I really thought. He'd call me crazy. "I like her. She's different, what you called 'weird,' but she's a good person. I think I can trust her. I had some concerns in the beginning. I wasn't sure about her motives. I mean, who is this girl—where'd she come from? But I've gotten to know her pretty well, and I've come to believe that these things aren't so important. What counts is what's in her spirit. I've seen her spirit, and I believe she's all about good things. Good for me, good for the Nomás people, and actually good for Earth."

I was trying to convince myself.

"Rannie, I'm listening to my best friend prattle on about how this girl that she met only recently is good for the Nomás people and good for the whole world. I can feel the hairs on the back of my neck stand up." His fingers tensed and his eyes squinted involuntarily, sure signs he was worried. "You've 'seen her spirit'? What does that even mean?"

"Uh, never mind. It's just an expression."

Not even a heartbeat later, without warning, a mountain lion sprang from behind the low berry bushes and pounced on me.

"Niamh, where've you been?" I pulled on my cat's ears and jumped on her back as if to wrestle this monster to the ground. It had no effect on her, as she simply sat on her haunches. The result sent me rolling off to the side, where Tooren reached down to give me a hand up. I tousled Niamh's head roughly. "Happy you could make it to the hunt, young lady."

"Is it safe to come back into the plaza?" Tess led her horse into the common area.

"Sure is," said Tooren. "We're just waiting for you to load your bags with the food and hiding clothes we're going to need, then off we go."

"Fine. But I told you, I won't need the clothes. I'm pretty good at hiding."

CHAPTER FOUR

Tess
  Alone with Tooren while Ranza scouts ahead
  Somewhere outside Santa Rosa Ruins

"Well, Tess, Rannie just told us all we need to know for now, so let's go." Tooren led the way.

"Yeah. I pretty much get what she was saying. So maybe we can just spend the ride getting to know each other, find some common ground that's a little friendlier than the one we seem to have now? I'll start."

Tooren nodded. We rode slowly and carefully, aiming the horse's hooves onto the edges of the dusty path to avoid leaving tracks as much as possible.

"I can see how important Ranza is to you, Tooren, and I imagine I might look like a threat to your relationship. Well, you're right. I might be a threat, but not for the reasons you think."

"Good start, Tess. First, you can tell me how the blazes you think it's okay to talk about my and Ranza's relationship. Second, you don't even know me, so what makes you an expert on what I think—ever? Last, you sure are way too self-centered to even think I would see you as a threat to me. So, Tess, we're sure on better footing now, aren't we? I'm glad we had this little talk."

He gave his horse, Santo, a snap with the reins. "Let's go." He resumed the lead, and we moved a little faster.

I studied him from behind for a bit. I saw the way he leaned on the horse, a kind of haughty attitude, the way he refused to look back, just assuming I'd followed. *Lots of bravado*, I thought. Adding things up, I figured Tooren was a man-child. He had the physical prowess of a fully grown hunter, but he was still filled with childish insecurities. I wanted to remember to keep this in mind when trying to deal with him. It might call for some less threatening posturing. *Time to try again*, I thought.

"Tooren, wait up. Please, I need to explain. Please. It's important." I picked up the pace a bit to allow my horse to catch up with his. As I came alongside, he suddenly reined in, stopped, and looked at me in an accusatory way.

"Let's hear it. I really enjoy how someone is a threat to me. And I really want to hear what you think you could do that actually would threaten me in the first place. Rannie is my friend. Has been for a long time. Try to come between us, and you'll learn a lesson in how to get the hell out of here."

I softened my look and lowered my shoulders—a sign of submission. Then I gave him a broad, sincere smile, gazing into his eyes. The effort was not lost on the boy. I looked into his spirit while giving him a glimpse into mine, opening just a bit and only for a second, enough to convince him that I was a friend and not his enemy. It happened in a flash, without him being the least bit aware of the connection I had just made. But it had the needed effect. He knew enough of me to help us get over the tension and form a friendship—at least a start.

"So, as I said, I'm sure we'll get to be great friends, you and I." I turned and continued off in the direction Ranza had gone.

"What the hell? Hey, Tess," he called. "I . . . um . . . What just happened?"

"Hmm? Not sure what you're talking about." I gave him a blank stare and didn't say another word.

"Uh . . . Yeah. Never mind. I was kind of daydreaming, is all."

We rode on until we came across Whisper, standing alone in a glen. There was no sign of Ranza.

"Tess? What do you think happened here?" Tooren went up to Whisper, standing free next to the emptied-out contents of Ranza's bags, carelessly strewn on the ground near the horse. "I hope nothing bad happened to her."

"Oh, I'm sure it hasn't. She's fine and is probably having a laugh at our expense."

"Maybe, but this is so not like her. Ranza would never leave Whisper out here alone like this." He leaned down to pick up the bag's contents.

From her hiding spot, I heard Ranza let out a loud whistle command that apparently told Whisper to raise on her back haunches above the boy. The horse began churning the air with her front hooves, a frightening sight. Tooren began to spin away from her at the same moment Ranza gave a second whistle command. The horse lowered herself downward, her chest pushing into Torren's back, forcing him to face-plant on the ground.

Laughing out loud, Ranza emerged from her hiding place and reached down to offer him a hand up. He refused, struggling to his own feet, his face red with anger.

"Happy to be here, Tooren? I noticed you kissing the ground."

"I should have left you behind when I saw Whisper without her rider. Maybe I will next time."

"Yeah, that would make for a successful hunt, wouldn't it? You stalking wild beasts alone. Huh? C'mon. You know you need me."

"And you know you need me. There's nobody better at

finding and herding deer toward you so you can look good when you get a clean kill. So I'm going to go ahead and do just that. At least I'll be able to feel like I'm doing a good thing." Tooren jumped onto Santo and raced away, embarrassed.

Ranza called after him. "Just be sure to head them in the right direction. I'd hate to have you miss and drive the deer into Tess instead."

"That would never happen," I stated flatly. "You don't need to worry about me. Just hunt as normal."

Ranza seemed puzzled. She waited for me to finish the thought, but when I didn't fill in the blanks, she watched as I mounted my horse and waited for her to do the same. I heard her thoughts. *"Wow. Cocky times two. No hiding clothes, 'I can take care of myself' . . . She might be in for a big surprise when the going gets tough out here."*

I wondered what she would do differently if she knew I could read her mind.

We headed out at a slow pace to give Tooren time to locate and cull the herd. This was shaping up to be one of those special days in Nomás territory. The fog was showing signs of lifting. A soft breeze carried the chirping songs of the warblers across the fields and into the forests.

I could tell Ranza was feeling pretty good about it too. "This kind of day always makes me get lost in the beauty of it. The rain on the redwood bark gives off a musty smell that takes me back to when I was a kid."

"Ranza?" I came alongside her.

"Yeah?"

"Does Tooren ever tell you how it bothers him that you seem to enjoy reminding him of your superiority? I mean, does he ever complain?"

"What do you mean, 'superiority'?"

"I mean you're stronger and cleverer than he is, and you didn't hesitate to remind him of that back at the clearing."

"I'm not sure I like where this is going. Yeah, I played a trick on him. We often play tricks like this at the start of a hunt. Keeps us sharp and gets the energy flowing. Hunting isn't like anything else, Tess."

"Sorry. I don't mean to put myself where I don't have a right to be. I just happened to see how embarrassed and angry he was after you made him look foolish. You weren't paying attention, but I saw his face, felt his anger."

"He's not a child, Tess. Tooren is one of the best I have on the team. If he can't take a joke, then I might have misread him. Maybe he isn't as strong as I thought."

"It's not just what you did, it's more that it was *you* who did it to him. He admires you, Ranza. To him, you're what he strives to become—a leader. When you put him down like that, it's as if you're proving to him and to everyone else that he's nowhere close to becoming like you."

"Huh. To me it's just a game."

"A game that you might let him win once in a while. When people are respected, made to feel proud, they have more room to respect others. When you're a leader of your people, you'll know that respect and obedience can't come from fear. When you make people feel good to be themselves, they'll respect you. They'll want to be near you, and they'll be ready to do what you need from them."

"Tess, why do you feel it's your right to tell me how to live my life, how to treat my hunters? I don't mean to call you out, but you only met Tooren recently, and this morning is the first time you ever really spoke with him. Now you feel right telling me how I should treat him? I don't get it. What's up?"

This made me stop in my tracks. I pulled up on the reins and turned sideways to face Ranza full on. "Ranza, you are destined to be the leader of your people. Not just a leader, but *the* leader. You have so much to learn before then." As I said this, I wanted to pull it back in. Too much, too soon.

"You don't know me, and you don't know my people. What

makes you think I'll be their leader, and why do you think I would even believe you, a newcomer, in matters like these?"

I'm sorry. There'll be a time to know. This is a time to—"

"—wait? Yeah, here we go again, Tess. You're coming very close to being a real pain. All the drama and mystery doesn't win you any friends."

"Rannie, I'm sorry. I overstepped. I took advantage of our friendship. I just wanted to help. Sometimes we can see things in others that we can't see in ourselves, and—"

"That may be, but I don't remember asking you to judge my leadership skills. I know I'm new at it, but please, let me do it my way. If I need advice, I'll be sure to ask for it."

I lowered my eyes, hoping to show her some respect. "I understand, Ranza. I'll try not to butt in with my advice unless you ask for it. You're in charge, and I'll listen to you so I can learn. Please accept my apology."

Ranza thought about it for a moment, then she smiled and nodded. I dismounted and waited for her to follow. At first, she was hesitant. "We need to keep going until we find Tooren and the herd."

"But," I warned cautiously, "we've found them. You should be down here with me." I pointed down the trail.

The way I said it caught Ranza's attention. She didn't even think to argue. Without question, she dismounted, grabbed her bow and quiver, and quickly moved away from Whisper to get a full view of the path as it curved away from us. Not forty steps down the trail stood a huge culled buck. The beast was panting heavily, fully aware that Tooren was on its trail. Ranza turned back to me as I stood on the path behind her.

"No hiding clothes?" she hissed in disapproval.

Knowing that any further movement or sound she might make to warn me would spook the animal, Ranza froze in place to see what the buck might do next. Then she cautiously slid an arrow from the quiver, preparing to take the animal down the instant it took flight. She knew Tooren saw her and knew she was in killing range, so there was no need to roust the buck.

She was wrong.

Tooren whistled and shouted toward the buck, startling it, causing the animal to leap forward and run full speed toward Ranza. Since the bushes hid her, it couldn't yet see her, but bushes wouldn't be much protection when the two hundred-plus pounds of deadly antler-carrying death came around the curve and ran right over her.

Her instinct had the arrow nocked and drawn up to her chin. But instead of shooting, she turned toward me, shouting a warning. "*Tess*!" And then, having used up all the time she might have had to take the buck down, Ranza watched as I seemed to vanish.

Intent on escape, the buck didn't even notice and headed right for Ranza. But Ranza gaped at where I'd stood. Then, desperately, she turned back toward the animal, hoping her well-honed instincts would find a last-minute escape from the certain impact she knew would kill her. The buck headed directly toward her, with Tooren screaming at it from behind.

But I hadn't disappeared. Instead, I'd moved from one pace to another so fast no one could see. I gave no warning, no hint of where I'd come from, as I now appeared between the beast and Ranza, calling the beast's ancient name in spirit-speak, my hands raised in protest. The thundering buck slammed to a full stop, panting feverishly as it stared wild eyed into my spirit. I walked up to stand directly in front of the animal, put my face next to his, placed my hand over his forehead, and spoke in an almost whisper to his soul: "Spirit of the hunt, we thank you for this." I removed my hand and smiled into the deer's eyes.

The buck gently lowered to the ground and died.

Total silence overtook the trail as Ranza, her arrow still nocked, her bowstring pulled taut against her face and her breathing all but stopped, stood motionless. "Well, that's it. It's magic, and nothing else. And it came through you."

I turned to face her, bowed my head in honor, and said, "Ranza, I'm sorry, but you must forget what you think you just saw." I raised my hand in her direction.

Ranza stood transfixed.

"I'm sorry I've frightened you, but understand that I'm here for you. We have so much to talk about, and we need to prepare for what's to come. But this is not a time to know. It is time to wait."

I turned next toward Tooren, who stood slack jawed, his feet planted, unable to react. I smiled at the boy, waved toward him, and he froze.

Ranza was shaking. She tried to control it, but she was obviously frightened like never before. She glanced over at the dead buck. She had just watched as I simply touched it and the animal died. She was not about to argue with someone who had that much power.

But now, as I again gestured toward her, that memory was lost to her.

Eyes wide, Ranza startled into movement. "What . . . How did . . . A dead buck? What happened to it?"

"You don't remember? Tooren and the buck collided when he jumped between you and the animal, saving your life. The buck would have run right over you. If not for the spear Tooren held that hit just the right spot in the animal's chest when the two of them collided, we might all be dead." As I said this, I surreptitiously made sure a deep stab wound emerged from the animal's chest. The most effective magic was the magic no one saw happening.

I moved closer to Ranza and put my hands on her shoulders to comfort her, waiting until she seemed to gather herself. Soon, she was able to slow her breathing and relax her shoulders—part of her training as a hunter.

"Ranza, this is a time to forget." As I said this, she closed then reopened her eyes.

"What's wrong with Tooren?"

"He was so brave," I told her. I turned toward Tooren and touched his shoulder. He shook his head a few times, then rubbed his eyes.

"What's going on?" he mumbled.

"You were great, Tooren. You dove in front of the deer, putting yourself between those antlers and Ranza. You saved her life."

"I did what?"

"The impact was so strong that you've been unconscious for some time. We were getting worried."

"Yes. Uh . . . ," Ranza said, not really understanding but going along anyway. "Thank you, Tooren. I am so grateful to you." She drew her knife. "Maybe you should take a rest while Tess and I dress the buck."

We quickly dressed and packed the meat for the trip home.

It was while Ranza loaded the bundles that a soft hum, coming from nowhere, caught my attention. None of us had ever heard such a sound before—not quite a sound a living thing could make, nor any sound from nature. It was a buzz that might come from inside our own heads, but we knew it was an outside noise. Frightening, unknown, yet somehow awesome.

The noise grew louder, and soon something appeared from beyond the trees. It looked like a strange bird, flying in weird patterns across the horizon. Ranza drew an arrow. "Tooren, what is that bird?"

Before he could answer, I reached out toward the approaching bird as it rounded the stand of trees, heading straight toward us. While my friends were both distracted by the object, I lifted my finger to point at the bird. As I did, it dove hard and crashed into a tree before dropping to the ground, now silent.

"What's that?" shouted Tooren.

We went to investigate. A pile of debris lay on the ground. It didn't look like any bird we'd ever seen. It didn't even seem like it had ever been alive. There was only metal and some glass parts, like the pieces of broken window back in the ruins. We could find no head, no wings, and no signs of any internal organs. More important, I felt no soul, no spirit. This thing had never lived. I saw the evil in it, and I knew we were in very real trouble.

"This is a thing of evil, Ranza. We need to get out of here before those who sent it come to find us."

Tooren stood still, mouth agape. I sensed that he was searching his thoughts to come up with an explanation for something that couldn't be explained.

"*We're in danger.*"

Ranza heard the urgency in my voice. Quickly, we grabbed the packs of deer meat and finished loading the horses, then mounted and headed toward home as quietly as possible. I heard Ranza's mind racing with fear.

"*What does Tess know that she isn't telling me? What was that not-living thing that flew at us, that thing Tess called 'evil'?*"

I was on alert, expecting that we might soon be attacked, but I said nothing. Ranza would make it her mission to find out what I was thinking at this moment, but she'd have to wait for a better time to interrogate me. Now was a time to wonder, and a time to get the hell out of that place.

CHAPTER FIVE

President Hsieh
   9 May 2249
   Office of the president
   Barca City
   GPS: 37° 33' 57.884" N 122° 11' 38.62" W
   Outside Conditions: light fog, temp 22.22
   Sustainability Factor: -14 (viral saturation)
   Interior Conditions: all systems functioning at peak

STILL SIMULATION-HOVERING OVER THE SANTA ROSA terrain, my instinct was to back away for a wider scan, hoping to gain a clearer perspective of the red glow coming from the ruins.

"Full view."

Immediately the end-to-end windows of the main office disappeared and I stood over an unimpeded view of everything from San Mateo north to the San Francisco ruins to my left and Hayward through old Oakland to my right.

"Mr. President, please pardon the intrusion." Goh stood in front of me, awaiting acknowledgment.

"Pause, Goh." I quickly turned back to the Bay viewing, but the mood had already broken. "Full view off. Yes, Goh. Proceed."

"Sir, you have instructed me to alert you in the event any anomalies came up in the Out that might need your attention."

Goh, my Personal Artificially Intelligent Assistant (PAIA), again waited for my response.

"Yes. Goh, continue," I answered him grudgingly, knowing that his last five so-called alerts had been nothing more than wild-goose chases. One had been a rabid raccoon that one of the Out Security details mistook for a human. Another had been the feeble attempt of an outcast to strike back at Barca in whatever way he could as his miserable life abandoned him. He'd tried to throw a large rock at the detail. It landed three feet away from where he took his last pitiful breath, and he fell to the ground in a decaying mass of former humanity. I had used the Out detail record of the event for playback on the Barca City News later that evening. Great propaganda.

"President Hsieh, the North Bay Security team has reported a sighting that might indicate human activity in the area of the Sonoma hills. They have forwarded a video. Would you care to see it?"

"Yes, Goh. Please project." *I was right to suspect.*

The hologram that represented Goh vanished and was replaced by a life-sized hologram of the Out detail providing me with a review of the events of the morning in the Sonoma wilderness.

"Replay proceed."

The quality of the playback was excellent, almost as clear as if I had been there right beside the Security team. The voice-over identified the video:

9 May 2249
  GPS Coordinates: 38° 27' 36.148" N 122° 42' 0.428" W
  Santa Rosa Ruins

North Bay Out Security Detail encounter 3 hours 14 minutes prior

"THIS IS LIEUTENANT MALLOY. I HAVE LED MY TEAM TO WITHIN *a couple of kilometers of the suspected Outdwellers. Sensors indicate that we might have found solid proof of tribal dwellers in the area of Sonoma. I have ordered that this transmission be delivered directly to President Hsieh under extreme confidentiality. What follows is a recording of the events of this morning in the previously identified sector."*

The playback framed on another detail member.

"Yes, sir. The drone detected some movement in that direction. No telling what it is. Do you want me to send it back there for some visual?"

"Yes, Sergeant Rodriguez," Lieutenant Malloy said. *"Let's find out whatever it is out there."*

"Yes, sir. Pauling, you heard the lieutenant. Make it happen." The drone jumped to life and raced skyward. *"It's on its way, Lieutenant. Pauling, let me know as soon as the drone has located the source of that movement."*

"Okay, Sarge."

Malloy interrupted. *"I don't think we should wait for the report back. Just tell us what direction, and we'll head there while the drone is searching. I'd hate to miss anything for the sake of a little detail."*

Pauling studied the screen as he spoke. *"The last hit on the sensors showed the disturbance at 1.5 kilometers heading northwest of our current position, Sarge."*

Malloy pushed the sergeant out of the way to get a clear view of the screen.

Pauling studied the screen. After a pause, he continued, now addressing the lieutenant directly. *"There seems to be a problem, Lieutenant. A moment ago, the drone captured an image that appeared to indicate two young females and one male, along with horses, all standing at the location in question."*

Malloy barked, *"Let me see the scan."*

"I'm sorry, Lieutenant. It appears that before the drone could focus in, one of the females either pointed at it or threw something, and the image

just stopped transmitting. I am pretty sure that whatever it is, it has disabled the drone. I'm unable to get it to respond to hand controls at all, and the visual is now gone."

"Dammit . . . Thank you, Pauling. Rodriguez, call the order."

"Yes, sir. Moderate speed . . . Keep the motors silent. No talking, and keep eyes out for anything unexpected. Ready . . . hut." The team mounted their speedcycles, and Rodriguez took the lead. The rest followed.

"Malloy, again. End of transmission."

I wasn't sure what I had just watched, but it was something alarming, and it put me on alert. *Two females, one male, horses at their side . . . It's been a long time since I heard such strong evidence of Outdwellers.*

The hologram projection returned to the image of Goh.

I could feel the tension as the back of my neck tightened like airlock doors, and I knew the headache and vision issues would follow. I closed my eyes and tried my hardest to slow my breathing. The last time I'd had such a feeling was the week the workers in the San Jose 12 Fabrication Pod decided to stage a pitiful uprising.

That day had started with signs that something was out of place. Workers showed up late for their shifts, attendance at morning meal was low, and a generally foul mood was evident as most of the workers were unable to hide their anxiety. The tension was palpable; it showed on many faces. My neck had tightened just like it was doing now.

The incident hadn't had a great outcome. By the end of the week, a full-on rebellion had been launched. Work pods were destroyed, and Barcan management was forced to vaporize more than half of the workers in San Jose before they were convinced that their feeble bid for freedom would only gain them either immediate death or a slow miserable decay from viral infections a week or two after they were exiled to the Out. I was reminded, *We did the right thing. Often, it's necessary to take drastic action in order to maintain the status quo.*

"Do you have any instructions, sir?"

My eyes popped open. "Yes, Goh. Forward a confidential link for this scene to the board and a separate link to Tom Sands with my attached comments that you will now record."

"I am ready, Mr. President." Goh had already activated his recording function, and a soft spotlight opened on me.

"Tom, I need your immediate attention on this issue. If there's any truth that some Outdwellers exist in that area, I'm ordering you to seek and capture several so we can interrogate them quickly. Exterminate any others on sight. I don't need any controversies getting in the way of our coming negotiations with Toyokohama."

Just the mention of the Japanese corporation, the current target of our takeover strategy, reminded me of how much was at stake. "As you know, Tom, this is highly sensitive, so keep your mouth shut about this."

After a pause, Goh must have assumed I'd finished.

"Will that be all, sir?"

"Yes, it will. Keep me informed of any changes or additional information."

CHAPTER SIX

RANZA
Santa Rosa Nomás village
Santa Rosa Ruins
Early evening
Clear sky

THE SUN HAD STARTED TO SET, AND I WATCHED THE SHADOWS as their drifting, twisting shapes were light-painted on the wall across from the hidden window. My mind was pulled back to the day's happenings.

I need to talk to Dad.

He had just returned from his new-crop fields, the place where he grew the crops he'd developed with his experiments. Dad was the best at what he did. Some called it amazing, the way he'd doubled the size of his crops just by making small changes to the things he added to the soil around the plants. And the taste—even the kids liked to eat his vegetables and fruit. I couldn't say I'd rather bite off a bunch of broccoli than cut into one of Mom's meat pies, but it was pretty close. Dad was a vegetable wizard. He even knew what herbs and plants to use for medicine. He was the one all the tribe came to for healing.

He also happened to be a great thinker. The way he could understand a problem and come up with a solution was amazing. And it was that magic I needed from him now.

"Hi, Rannie. How was the hunt?"

"Hi, Dad. Good." I just sat there, like I was in trouble. I hadn't done anything wrong this time, so why did this feel like I was about to get a lecture? I guessed I was afraid to tell him about the incident with Tess, Tooren, and the dead buck. But I had to talk to someone, and I knew he would give me real ideas, not just casual head nods. He would really think about it and would give me some logical feedback. So why did I feel like I had done something wrong? It was that the whole thing felt unreal— like it had never really happened, although we'd brought back a full pack of meat.

He sat patiently waiting for me to say something. After all, I had asked him if we could spend some time together as I had something I needed to talk over. But when it came down to it, I couldn't even find the words to begin. If I just told him what happened, he might think I'd lost my mind. On the other hand, if I didn't tell him everything, he might not be able to help me understand what was happening. My heart wanted to shout about magic, about Tess, about the evil flying thing.

"Rannie? What's wrong?"

I decided to just tell him small bits. Maybe I wouldn't have to come right out with the magic part. "Yeah. I'm fine. Well, actually I need to ask you about something. Stuff happened on the hunt today that left me confused, even scared." *This is going to be harder than I imagined.* "So, Tess, Tooren, and I went on a local hunt today, hoping for a buck or some pigs, and things got off to a kind of weird start. Tess seemed to think it would be okay to give me some lessons in how to lead my team, particularly Tooren. She didn't like that I played a joke on him . . . seemed to think I was somehow putting him down by tricking him."

"Well, were you putting him down?"

"No. Of course not. It's just a thing we do on hunt days. We try to trick each other, and have a good laugh in the process. Gets the energy rolling, and it's a good way to ramp up the competition. But that's not the point, Dad. The point is that it wasn't her place to judge me. She's not the lead hunter. She isn't even any kind of hunter. I'm the leader, not her."

"She was judging you?"

"Of course. She even tried to tell me how I was wrong."

After a long pause, he spoke. "Well, Rannie, maybe she wasn't judging you at all. Sometimes we can see things in others that they might not be seeing in themselves. Maybe she saw how Tooren reacted to your trickery, and she wanted to let you know what she saw. I also sometimes try to get you to see things from a different perspective. It helps when we kind of step outside ourselves for a moment."

"Yeah, maybe. But I didn't like it. Who does she think she is?"

That didn't work the way I hoped it would. No more excuses. I have to do this.

"Dad, Tess scares me, and I don't think I'm imagining what I feel."

He peered at me, then stood. "Okay, hold that thought for a moment. Mom can help us figure things out." He went out back to where he knew Mom was packing some vegetables for storage and returned with her in tow. When they were seated, I took a breath and began again.

"Mom, I need to figure out how I feel about something, but I need you two to listen and trust that I'm not losing my mind. Just listen and tell me what to do, okay?"

"Yes," Mom said. "And you promise to not hold anything back."

"Yeah. I promise, but it's gonna to be hard." I closed my eyes, hoping to gain even a tiny bit calm before opening up. Then, letting out my breath, I just blurted it out. "Some things have happened that I can't explain, and they scare the daylight out of me. Remember, you promised not to think I've lost my mind?"

They both just smiled and nodded.

"Mom, Dad, I'm afraid Tess is some sort of magical creature. She says she talks to someone called Wakan Tanka, someone she says is the Great One—all gods rolled into one. And she might have even done some magic today."

Dad seemed to drift off, like he was daydreaming, and Mom sat there and smiled. I kept going.

"So, a few things happened today that I can't understand. Tess and I met at the well, and we were waiting for Tooren and Juvie to go on a local hunt."

Dad refocused. I just gave him a look to tell him he wasn't taking this as seriously as I needed. He sat back and waited for me.

"Well, the day started out fine, just sitting and talking, waiting for the guys to show for the hunt. I invited Tess to come along for the ride, and she agreed. She'd already met Tooren, so I figured it would be good for them to spend time today. She could use more friends here than just me. Well, right away problems started. I pulled one of my jokes on Tooren, and Tess accused me of putting Tooren down. She said I was acting superior to him— but I already told you that part."

"Rannie, why not just get to the point," Mom urged. "I'm guessing this much drama isn't over something like a trick you played on Tooren."

Now it's all going to come out, and there's nothing I can do to stop it.

"Tess said I have to learn to be a leader. She said that I'd be called on by the Nomás to lead all of our people. Me? I'm not even old enough. And that was just the start. Next, Tooren accidentally set a huge buck charging toward us. I shouted to Tess, knowing she had no idea what to do, but before I could do anything, the buck was a few jumps away from driving me into the sky at the end of his antlers."

I paused, steeling myself to continue. "Then everything was a blur for a moment. Next thing I knew, I was standing next to Tess. The buck was lying there, dead, and Tooren was nearby, and he was out cold. I didn't kill the buck. Tess sure didn't kill it. And Tooren was unconscious, so probably not him either. When I wondered out loud what had happened, Tess made up some story about Tooren jumping in front of me with his spear, and said he'd killed the buck on the spot when it slammed him to the ground. Sounded great, but that's not at all what I have running around in my head every time I think of it."

Dad took a deep breath. "Tell me what you think happened."

"Okay. Here's the part where you'll think I'm out of my mind. When I go over it, like right now, it plays in my mind like it's happening through a fog. I see the buck racing toward me. I see Tess step in front of me and hold up her hand. The buck stops, she whispers something to the animal, it lowers to the ground, and it just dies. Tess turns to me and says something— I'm not sure what—and then I feel the fog lift, and I'm standing there, dead buck, unconscious Tooren, all just like I described it."

Dad looked at Mom, then at me. "Are you sure it isn't just your imagination?"

"There's more, Dad. When Tooren woke up, Tess tried to get me to back up her story, as if I really believed it myself. And for some reason I can't figure out . . . I did. She told Tooren about how he'd saved my life and killed the buck, then she got me to agree that it happened like she said, even though I didn't really believe it fully myself. But I backed her up anyway."

Dad's eyes looked worried. "Rannie, I'm sure Tess is a nice person. But I want you to be careful and not just believe what someone tells you unless you have good reason."

"Dad, we aren't serious friends yet. I don't believe Tooren killed the buck, and I am not about to believe everything she tells me. I'm afraid of her. And I'm not done telling everything. There's more, and this is the scariest part. As I was loading the deer meat onto the horses, a weird sound came to us from beyond the trees. We all looked up at the same time to see a strange-looking bird round the stand above us. It was different from any bird I'd ever seen. It started turning toward us, like it was gonna attack. I reached for my bow and was ready to loose an arrow at this thing when Tess reached out and pointed her finger at it. She didn't think I saw, but it was clear that she pointed at it at the same moment the bird suddenly dove into a tree, crashed, and fell to the ground in a pile of metal and glass. I wanted to ask her what it was, but Tess took on a totally different manner. Her face looked pale, and she whispered that the bird thing was evil and we needed to get out of there before its owners came looking for it. She called it a machine, not a bird. Evil, Dad. She said it was evil."

"So why do you just take her word for it? Maybe she's just saying things to impress you. Maybe she has no idea about these things. And, Rannie, maybe you're taking this all too far, and there's nothing to worry about."

I thought about it a few moments. He might be right. I ran the scenario through my mind every way possible, trying to imagine Tess was no more than a girl like me and that she was making this stuff up to impress me. But when I got close to buying this theory, my mind suddenly flashed onto the sounds and sights in my somewhat foggy memory. Then my heart nearly pounded out of my chest as the image of the boar I'd almost killed came into my thoughts—the boar that had turned into a girl. Into Tess. I held that part back, but Dad could easily tell I was frightened, possibly more than he'd ever seen me. "Dad, I think Tess has great magic. And then this stuff about Wakan Tanka . . ."

Dad now turned to Mom. "Lora, what do you think?"

Mom was even better at figuring things out than Dad, if that was possible. I started to feel better about Mom being a part of this, but I was still drowning in anxiety over the whole thing.

She turned to me. "Rannie, would you help us understand just what you mean by 'magic'?"

Now I knew for sure it was time to be blunt. There was nothing to be gained by softening the blow. Once started, I was ready to pour it all out. The words spilled out of me like a waterfall. "Well, remember the first time I met Tess? Connor and I were on a training hunt. I had tracked a boar into a cave, shot an arrow at it, and it shifted its shape into Tess. She tried to say that wasn't what happened, but I know what I saw. And she has powers to kill a buck just by touching it, she—"

"Rannie," Mom said, "take a breath. You say she changed from a boar to a human? Then she killed a deer with a touch, a few words?"

"Yes, Mom. I saw the whole thing. She held out her hand, walked to the animal, whispered to it, put her hand over its eyes, and it fell over dead." Tears were running down my cheeks. I had no idea why. I wasn't sad. I just felt so many emotions at once. Mom came over to sit next to me, comforting me.

"What do you think about all this, Rannie?"

"I don't know, Mom. I can't figure it out. Tess said that I'll be the one called on to lead the Nomás one day—all Nomás. After she told me that, I had a dream. I haven't told anyone about this, not even Tess. In the dream, I heard a voice—a woman's voice coming from everywhere, like I was inside the sound of it. She told me I must lead our people, and unless we take control over the Earth, Barca will destroy it and every living thing on it. She said that Nomás is a threat to Barca, but she didn't say why. I asked her why I'd be called on, but she was gone by then." I shrugged helplessly. "I don't know what to think."

Mom took a long time to answer. I could tell she was struggling to say the right thing to me. She closed her eyes as if thinking deeply, her brow all wrinkled as she rocked softly in her chair. Finally, she glanced at Dad, then looked down for a moment. "Marlon, I need to say things that you don't yet know about. Please forgive my secrecy, but I needed to understand them for myself before I could share them."

Dad smiled at her. I didn't get it. I'd just naturally thought they knew everything about each other. *This can't be good.*

"Ranza, I've known since I met her that Tess has powers. You don't know this, but sometimes I can see things that others can't. For instance, I can see a glow that surrounds each person. I believe it's the life force in each of us—some call it the soul. I've always been able to see these. Sorry to say, I can't turn it off when it happens. It's not always a good thing. Sometimes, when someone approaches and their glow is dark, I see that as a sign they aren't to be trusted. But they may also have a dark glow because they are in pain. Do you see?"

I had no idea what she was talking about, but Dad nodded, so I just shut up.

"So, I try to not make judgments on this glow. With Tess, judgment couldn't be helped. When I met Tess, she radiated the most brilliant rainbow-colored glow I'd ever seen. It was obvious to me that she was no ordinary person. I knew she was someone special."

Dad sat forward. "Lora, just like you say it is not fair to judge someone based on having a dark glow, isn't it also unreasonable to say someone with a brilliant glow is special? Is good?"

I saw he was trying to grapple with this new side to Mom—seemed to want to be included somehow. I guessed he wasn't having a good time with this new realization.

"I suppose it would be, if these were ordinary differences. But you haven't seen this glow on Tess. She carries a life force that's not of this world. I'm not talking about simply different colors and brightness. I'm talking about colors and brilliance that I've never seen. I believe Ranza's right. Tess is in touch with powers beyond our world, possibly even with a god."

I was dumbstruck. The room grew silent again. Nobody moved for a time. Then Dad lifted Mom's hands into his own, pressed them to his forehead, and just stayed like that for the longest time, not moving. It was as if they were talking without words. When he was ready, Dad looked up at me.

"Rannie, you'll have to decide for yourself. Do you believe Tess? Do you intend to take on what she's told you is your destiny? This is an important decision. I don't envy you, but I'll tell you that Mom and I will always be here for you. No matter what you decide."

What? They're dumping all of this back on me? Am I really hearing this? I need to get out of this room, now.

I jumped to my feet. "I need to think. I'm going for a run with Niamh. I'll be back."

My heart was pounding, ears ringing, and it was all I could do to get my feet to push the rest of my body out the door.

CHAPTER SEVEN

Ranza
Mourning Feast—Nomás tribal gathering
Ruins identified by old broken signage as Sonoma State University
Early evening—sun has not set
Chilly, light fog

DEEP AND THROATY, THERE WAS NO MISTAKING THE SOUND OF a wood flute in the hands of an expert player. The echoes and long, slow vibrations hugged the air and wrapped each of us in an otherworldly, unending tone that reminded me of the dying bleat of a desperately wounded bull moose as its life slipped away. When a single note, played without stop for five long minutes by the Nomás, heralded the start of the annual Mourning Feast, the effect struck deep into the heart of anyone in range of the ghostly sound. The ritual had begun.

Running full speed toward the Mourning Feast, I couldn't figure out why I was so anxious. After all, I'd been late for these gatherings before and gotten off with just a cross frown from Dad and raised eyebrows from Mom. Not a big deal. But I was late again.

The talk with Mom and Dad the night before came rushing into my head. Indeed, it had hardly left my thoughts all last night and today.

I wasn't paying attention to where I was running when I had to leap over a sleeping grey wolf, its rope collar marking it as a pet of one of the Nomás families. I misjudged my speed, had to make a quick turn, and slammed into the rusted hull of a twenty-second-century car near the corner. That was enough to bring me to a sandal-scraping stop.

Rannie, get it together.

After catching my breath, I walked to the rear entrance of the place known as Mus Cen, so-called for the only parts of a name that stood on a metal sign at the entrance to the great hall. I slowed down so I wouldn't show that I'd run there, then walked with a false confidence through the castle-like doors of the ancient building into the wood-filled interior, stopping just inside.

Sounds—even minor life sounds like clearing a throat, adjusting one's seat in the old wood chairs, a baby's cry—were amplified and seemed to fill the entire hall at once. It was force-ful, as if someone halfway across the hall from another could throw their voice into the chair right next to them, their whisper sounding like they meant it for the other's ears only. None of the Nomás could ever get used to this place.

Why had they ever needed such a huge hall?

I waited to gain control over my thoughts. Then, when I was confident no one would see I was on alert, I moved into the crowd.

"Stop!"

A large man with a warrior's club blocked my path. My body tripped to a stuttering halt.

"I'm sorry. I wasn't paying attention."

Eyeing at the man, I saw two more guards, poised and ready to strike, blocking the way.

"Sorry, guys." I'd forgotten to give the passphrase. "None more than all."

The guards stepped aside to allow me to pass.

My eyes scanned the room like a hunter sweeping the ground for the next victim.

"Hi, Lena," I called to the unfortunate girl who had baby duty that night. I took great care in passing the sleeping rows of kids.

"Hi, Ranza. Go ahead and make some noise. Wake these puppies up, and I'll get some relief."

"No, thanks, Lena." I recalled my own days sleeping there with the other little kids, hoping the ceremony would end soon so Mom and Dad would take us home. I stretched my frame over the legs of the sleeping kids and stepped into the great room, being careful not to disturb any of them. If I did, I'd be required to stand guard over them.

The crowd began to hum softly. I stopped walking and noticed that Elder Mother had just now taken her place on the floor of the stage. A small, leathery-skinned woman, Elder Mother closed her eyes for a moment to communicate with her own inner spirit. Her brow furrowed, she sat cross-legged in meditation, chanting, bathed in a glow from the candles that surrounded her. The low, soft moan of the crowd was joined by the distant flute music—haunting and melodic this time, not just the mourning signal. This music felt like a dream.

Elder Mother slipped into another meditation. I used this quiet moment to locate Tess, who was seated next to Mom and Dad.

What have they been talking about? I looked at Tess as if to say, "Why are you so friendly with my parents all of a sudden?"

Hoping to go unnoticed, I joined them. With a nod from Dad, I smiled at Tess and sat next to her. We pretended to medi-tate, waiting for the old woman to speak. I had never been more uncomfortable.

After a time, Elder Mother opened her eyes, smiling to us all.

She raised her head, brushing the thick black-gray hair from her eyes, signaling she was now present among us.

I leaned over. "Tess, we need to talk after the ceremony."

"Sure, Ranza."

While Elder Mother prepared, I could feel Tess study me. I even didn't have to glance at her to know she was staring at me intently. I felt it.

"Ranza, I'm concerned. Something is wrong, very wrong. I sense a darkness coming over you. I want to tell you that I feel the need to protect you.

"Yeah, well, that was out of nowhere, and that's not what I want to talk about."

Tess trembled. It felt weird. I didn't know what to make of it, so I just let it drop. Maybe Tess tended to be an alarmist.

I was aware of the voice of Elder Mother as she performed the ceremonial calling out of the spirit names of those tribal members who'd shed their human form within the past year. "Right now, we need to focus on Elder Mother."

Reciting the names, Elder Mother waved her hands in toward herself, pulling the lost spirits back to the community, a long-standing tribal custom.

"Tess, now we all do as Mother is showing. We do this as a community, all hands pulling the air and the energy from the universe back to ourselves in active prayer so that we might grab onto just a tiny particle of our lost souls."

"This is so beautiful. Why do the Nomás do this?"

"For us, for the dead. Once we leave our physical bodies, we remain in spirit long enough for the living members to pull us back into the consciousness of the community."

Tess stopped and stared at me, deeply focused. "Yes, I can actually see the lost souls as they rejoin their families and friends. I bless them to the Great One, welcoming them back into the tribe."

I thought, *Yeah, you see them. Uh-huh*. But I didn't say anything to her.

Elder Mother called on the Nomás to relax, urging us to speak out loud the names of those we were mourning.

I called out to Patrius, my first hunt teacher, who'd just left the Nomás as a spirit a week before. I could see him in my mind, smiling as he was the moment before the rattlesnake uncoiled and pushed a torrent of poison into his arm as he reached to the ground to pick up his bow and quiver. I felt the scream welling up inside me, knowing that we were too far from help. Knowing he would leave this life a victim of a momentary slip of focus, a tiny lack of concentration. As heartbroken as I was, he had taught me against this moment, telling me this was a risk that all hunters took every time we went out, knowing we might become the prey ourselves. My heart missed him as I called him back. Soft drums and gentle high-note flutes underscored the process of "calling out" to these spirits.

"I saw one named Patrius, Rannie. He came back to you, as did so many others." Tess smiled.

I was shocked. How could she have known that name? Maybe my parents?

"This ritual is hard for me, Rannie, but, I need to say something to you that has me worried. Although I'm grateful to be a part of this special ritual, I can't concentrate on the mourning. My thoughts keep drifting back to you. I feel a darkness."

My fears came to life. I saw a look on Tess's face, a look of dread. I didn't think she was in danger, but she was aware that someone known to her might be. At least that's the way it felt to me. I couldn't tell what it might mean to Tess, and I couldn't ask here, with all the people around. We'd have to wait till after the ceremony.

Elder Mother recalled the Nomás history.

"Long ago, corporation stole all power from government and placed the corporate directors in charge of all laws and their enforcement. At first this was a good thing. Barca provided for all the needs of the people—food, shelter, work and income, education, and health. They even gave an income to those who, having worked all their lives, wished to stop working and enjoy their final decades in peaceful relaxation. And still this was a good thing.

"As time passed, directors were slowly replaced. The new directors brought change, and much of it was not good. First, they simply took away nonessential benefits, like arts, culture, and travel vacations. Soon, human rights were either taken away or severely curtailed. Workers had no rights, worked longer and harder hours, and lost the privilege to marry and procreate except under the strict management of the Corporate Birth Control. And even these procreation rights were only granted to add more and more to the workforce. After some years, as children were born, they were taken from the parents and housed in compliance centers. These children were the first generation of corporate slaves.

"People longed for a time when they could make decisions about their lives. Many chose to leave the corporate life to live simply outside of Barca City. This was met with strong resistance by Barcan directors, who knew many more would follow. They first built a secure dome around the entire city, a locked world where even the air one breathed, the water one drank, and the food one ate was controlled and sterile. Once secured, no one was permitted to leave the City, as the corporation feared the loss of workers meant loss of control.

"But many did leave that place. Barca, concerned about the possibility of revolt under the leadership of then president Wallyce Tilton, launched a terrible slaughter called the Purge, seeking to eliminate any potential organized human life outside the confines of Barca City.

"But Barca did not kill all. Some had left the area before the massacre and migrated north, deep into the redwood forests, to live a simple life. They understood it would be a 'them against us' existence, and they carried that knowledge, along with whatever was valuable to them, and left in peace, seeking to live among nature and her animals rather than become enslaved. This band of people forged a simple life, hidden from the eyes of Barca. We built our new life, and we swore never to bow down to anyone. Never would we depend on anyone else. We became a part of the Earth, and we are thankful for her benevolence. Nomás will always give back to Earth. But we will never bow down. 'No más!' is the origin of our tribal name—the words for 'No more' in the language of the California ancestors."

Now, Mother called for a moment of reflection.

"We live through the spirit of giving to others. Ask the Spirit to make you a conduit through which all can pass to their own betterment. Seek to be a river through which all good can come to others. Ask nothing in return."

I couldn't help but think about how this affected me. *I need to put my people before me. Are my own thoughts too centered on myself? As a hunter, I'm often treated differently than others. It's hard to center on others when everyone's telling you how important you are to them.*

I decided to devote my meditation to becoming a better member—not just a better person, but better for all the Nomás.

Elder Mother said, "While you are deep into this meditation, ask the Great One to allow you to be ever mindful of the good of the Nomás."

The Great One? She mentioned the Great One? I've heard Elder Mother speak those words so many times, but now it has a new connection to Tess's Wakan Tanka. Has Elder Mother always meant that to mean Wakan Tanka?

The meditation continued for a time. Then Elder Mother stood. The crowd repeated "No más" several times. She raised her hands, and the room became silent.

"We promise—our community will guide us. So we wait for another year. Bless us all." That signaled the end of the ceremony.

Tess leapt to her feet and reached out her hand to me. I didn't react at first. I was still deep into my meditation, but at the same time, I felt a deep-rooted fear. When Tess nudged me, my hunter's instinct took over. Without thinking, I jumped to my feet and reached for my knife, crouched, about to fight off the beast that was surely after me.

"It's me," Tess said. "You need to stop daydreaming so much. You might have hurt me."

I returned to the moment. "Oh, Tess, I'm so sorry."

"What was that about?"

"I was in a dark place in my mind. Things were pretty scary, but the details are kind of hazy. I just know it represented something bad."

"Well," Tess said, "I'm not surprised. Actually, I've had similar feelings. We should talk it through."

"Okay. Maybe we should get some food and go over to that field where we can talk and eat."

We waited for the crowd to thin a bit then headed for the food lines. Once we were seated, I fought to avoid Tess's stare. I spooned a little of the stew into my mouth and savored the sweet taste of venison, recalling a recent hunt when the team had brought down enough deer to feed the entire tribe for this celebration. The memory made the stew taste even better.

"Ranza, tell me about your vision. What did you see that disturbed you so much?"

I wanted to avoid talking about what I now wished would fade from my thoughts. Tess just stared at me, wordlessly encouraging me to answer. She waited, silent, until I gave in to the pressure, choosing my words carefully.

"I saw myself in tribal dress, but I was returning from a hunt. This confused me because I'd never go on a hunt in full dress. I'd wear the hiding clothes so I could be invisible to the animals. Everyone knows that." I stopped there, hoping to convince Tess this was the whole story. It didn't work.

"Okay. That's a good start. Go on."

I felt I could tell Tess what I saw in a dream, but I wasn't sure I should tell her the important part of the dream.

Do I lie or trust? There were no options. I had to trust her.

"Okay. I was walking home from the hunt. My path was

blocked by a huge mountain lion. Not Niamh, but a large male lion. A fierce, giant red-tailed hawk sat on the lion's head. I gazed beyond them to the path to my home, and I saw my father. He held out his hands to me. In his hands I saw a plant he must've been cultivating. It was a bright-red color, and it seemed to be on fire. Before he could say anything to me, the lion blocked my view and said, 'We are blessed that your father is willing to sacrifice himself for the good of all.' With that, the hawk flew to my father, grabbed him with its great talons, lifted him up off the ground, and flew into the clouds. I wanted to kill the bird, but I couldn't move. The lion warned that my father would play an important role in the future of our people. He said, 'Love him while you can, for he does what he does for the good of all.'"

My heart pounded, recalling the terror of this vision. "I know, it's just a dream. Go ahead and say that. But if that's true, then why am I so frightened?"

Tess was quick—too quick, it seemed—to calm my fears.

"That's an easy one, Ranza," she said. "It's clear you were exposed to the animals as a result of not wearing the hiding clothes. They were able to see you. This frightened you, knowing they were fierce killers who'd love nothing more than to drag you off to their den. Your father, not being a hunter, was the most vulnerable. Your own fears made you invent the part about putting the tribe at risk, so he was taken away. Simple. See what I mean?"

Her words rang hollow.

"So now I feel like you're making this up. Why?"

"Because I don't know what the truth is, Ranza. I'm just as worried as you are, but the fact is I can't see the outcome of this. I haven't been shown the rest, only that there's danger ahead, and it scares me too."

I filled with dread. Tess was also worried. I started to believe this vision was no less than a true glimpse into the future.

The ceremonial bell rang, announcing the event was ending.

Time to return home for the night. My family was waiting for us near the door to Mus Cen.

"Come, Tess. Let's head home with my family."

"I think I'm going to stay behind a bit, Rannie. I need some private time so I can focus on this dream. You go on, and I'll see you in the morning."

I wanted to stay with her, but it was clear she didn't want any company on her ride home. I gave Tess a quick hug, wished her safely home, then I ran to meet up with my family.

Tess

Lagging behind
Absorbing and wondering the meaning of the vision

I stood motionless, trying to absorb the awful vision Ranza had shared moments before. I had had an instinct about such things many times in the past, and I'd almost always been right. This time, I was more worried than usual. This vision was so strong it was sure to be a warning.

I jumped when Marlon placed a hand on my shoulder and said, "Would you like to travel home with us?"

"No, thanks. I have some things I need to think about, and it'll be better for me to be alone."

"Okay, then. Safe ride."

Marlon left and rejoined his family for the ride back to Santa Rosa.

I stayed on for some time. The thought of what I'd seen ahead for my friend wouldn't leave my mind. I cared a great deal for Ranza. It was natural to care for the one Wakan Tanka itself had chosen. What would Ranza do if she knew the truth about us? Would she be able to handle what lay ahead? I meditated on these questions for a time. Then, with no answers, I headed home.

∽

LT. MALLOY
    Barca Security
    North Sector, south of Rohnert Park
    Early morning
    Full gear required—airborne contaminant level extreme

THE FOLLOWING IS A RECORD OF THE EVENTS OF THIS MORNING:
    Before daybreak, our drone, flying reconnaissance near the old school grounds, sensed recent heat and smoke from possible fires of the night before. Within a few seconds, this information was transmitted to our Out Security detail, who were headed toward Santa Rosa via the old freeway. I received an audible alert telling me I should review the data from the reconnaissance drone. We brought all speeders to a midair halt so I could closely read the data in my visor display.
    The forward drone has sensed human activity within the past day at the old university ruins in Rohnert Park. There is remnant smoke containing traces of animal fat, indicating fires were likely used for cooking. There is remnant heat-print from what appears to have been a very large gathering of humans. We need to head up there to see what we can learn. Update to follow.

"SIR, COULDN'T THIS HAVE BEEN JUST A LARGE HERD OF animals and a forest fire?" Second-in-command Sgt. Alexia Rodriguez was anxious to get home. The team had been out for three days, and she was ready to be done with this trip.

"And what if it isn't? You are aware that there has been an increase in the number of human markers found in the area.

What if it's more than a few stragglers and you didn't think it was necessary to take the trip up there just to find out?"

"Sorry, sir. I wasn't thinking . . ."

"Sergeant, you are either on my team, or I can replace you. Your choice."

"I'm with you, sir. I'm all in. Ready to do whatever you say, sir." She flipped her visor down, gripped her hand controls, and waited for the order.

"Rodriguez, lead the way to the area pinpointed by the drone."

On command, she gave the hand signal to head out, kicked her speeder into forward, and raced northward.

CHAPTER EIGHT

RANZA
Santa Rosa Nomás village
Santa Rosa Ruins
Early morning
Clear sky

MY FISTS WERE CLENCHED SO TIGHTLY THE TIPS OF MY fingers burned with a mixture of fire and thorn spikes. Pain screamed from my outstretched arms, preparing to fight off the unseen wolves that I knew were just beyond my reach, ready to make a handy meal of my small hunt team. I was certain, based on the pain, that I'd been bitten at least once in the fight.

Oh, Spirit—please don't let them be rabid.

Like the last time, these wolves were probably only driven mad with thirst and hunger. *Is it the same ones? I don't think so—we hit them pretty hard, killing the alpha, and then Niamh chased the rest of them out of sight. They won't be back.*

Wait, is this happening?

As the fog cleared, I became aware that I was lying on my own sleep mat, about to wake up from this nightmare.

Trying to clear my mind, I peeked through the wall crack to the outside and saw Niamh as she crashed through the thick brush that surrounded our home; she leapt onto the large rock near the pond and gave the alarm yowl three times. Without a word, as we'd trained every week for as long as I could remember, my family went on full alert, ready to fight whatever threat came through the brush.

Well practiced, Mom, Dad, and I jumped up and began hurriedly putting everything out of sight to make the area appear uninhabited—an abandoned, ruined neighborhood like every other one in the Santa Rosa area, dilapidated buildings nearly hidden by wild-growth trees and bushes. I pulled on hunting clothes, which would help me hide in plain sight, in case I needed to sneak up on whatever, or whoever, was the threat. Mom and Dad slipped into their own hooded garments, and they disappeared from sight. My trained eye could detect their outline, but only because I knew what to look for.

Mom took command, ordering us to our hiding positions and calling for a guard at the entrance to the camp. "Ranza," she called to me, "post Niamh outside at the gateway." I gave Niamh the hand signal, and she went right to work. I came back to stand ready just inside the building, next to the covered fire pits.

All of this was important, but the final step was critical. We each went into meditation to lower our heartbeats and slow our breathing. This was part of the training. It could mean the difference between life and death. And I was good at it. Soon, I was so relaxed my body was operating at what might be near hibernation levels.

Niamh broke the silence. Through the haze, we heard the low rumbling of her warning growl. Danger was approaching. She was in attack mode, for sure. I watched as the hairs on her back bristled and her entire body tightened as if she was ready to pounce in any direction. She froze in place, her silent watch giving me some comfort. I just hoped things wouldn't get any worse. If anyone entered the compound from the outside Niamh might go on an all-out attack. If she did, then they would fight back. This would force us out of hiding to defend ourselves.

Dad seemed to be having trouble fighting off his instinct to control the situation. He whispered in too loud a voice, "It's the Barcan patrol. I had a close call with them early this morning before you two were up, and they must have tracked me here. This is worse than anything we've ever dealt with before. They might be just outside the camp, in the clearing. We have to be ready for what can happen if they find us."

Mom was angry. "Silence."

"Dad, what do you mean 'a close call'? Did they see you?"

"No, I don't think they did. But I'll explain later. Get ready."

Mom was angrier than I had ever seen. Her body language message was clear. She wanted to scream at us to be quiet. She was probably as scared as the rest of us. It was the first time any of us had come this close to actual contact with the Barcans. From childhood, we'd all learned that these people were evil and would kill us if they found where we lived. This could get real in a hurry. We were forced into warrior mode. Problem was none of us were warriors.

I had no doubt about the actual danger we were in. I fought to keep my emotions in check the best I could. As a hunter, I'd become skilled at silence and waiting. I stayed on alert but forced myself to remain calm.

Inside every person lived a little kid. The little girl in me was scared, so scared. I wanted to be that little girl again and run to Mommy and Daddy so they could protect me.

Am I ready for this? Can I really fight if I have to? What if they hurt Mom? Dad?

Our home was covered over by thick vegetation and tall trees. To an outsider, it'd be difficult to suspect there were any humans within miles of this place.

So why are they here?

We hadn't had any fires that day that might lead them here, yet I watched as these scary people stayed focused for a long time, checking every inch of the old ruins. They were obviously not going to leave until they were satisfied there were no people in the area—or until they found us. I didn't want to think that all the way through.

I could hear them trying to whisper to each other. They weren't very good at it, or their voices were so different from Nomás voices that it made them sound louder than we would have sounded. Who knew? None of us had ever seen a Barcan. Were they even the same kind of humans as the Nomás?

I sneaked a quick glance out the wide crack in the rock wall, hoping to catch a glimpse of one of them. What I saw made me want to run away as fast as I could.

I saw two of them—couldn't tell if they were even human. They were dressed in shiny black clothes that made them stand out against the blue sky. Every inch of their bodies was covered in black. Shoes, pants, jackets, hats—or whatever they had on their heads—that made them appear almost like some sort of shiny dark fish on legs. Their faces were covered by a smooth, rounded black cover that they must have been able to see through. The effect was chilling. They were faceless.

One of them commanded the others. "Make sure you check everywhere—under bushes, in trees, everywhere."

The voice was deep and scary. It didn't sound like any person any of us had ever heard—like it was talking down into a well, a kind of strange, echoing sound. For the most part, it was understandable. They spoke our language, but their voices . . . So not like Nomás.

"And keep checking the sensors. We're getting heat signals here, so there must be something alive in the immediate area."

I don't know what these words mean. "Sensors." "Feedback." It makes no sense to me. Maybe we don't really speak the same language.

What he said next frightened me more than I could have imagined.

"Weapons at the ready."

They had to be Barcans. I'd never heard of any other people

who would want to hurt us, except maybe roaming bandits. *Weapons? Why?*

They stayed in the compound for half of the morning. At first, I was just scared—scared but ready to fight. My instincts were on fire, and my body was all wound up like never before. It felt like I would snap at any time. But I soon learned one could stay that tightly wrapped only so long before something had to happen to release the muscles before they started to cramp. I worried about Mom and Dad—how long could they take this pressure?

I glanced over at them. Mom seemed to be in control. But Dad was getting ready to blow it. He was not cut out for this, or maybe his instinct to protect Mom and me was an additional pressure that wound him even tighter. Whatever it was, I could see his knee bouncing as fast as a running jackrabbit trying to keep from becoming some coyote's meal. Mom saw it, too, because she reached over to put her hand on the "jackrabbit knee," and it seemed to comfort him.

It also comforted me, but only for a brief moment as the voices outside in the compound jolted me back to the reality of the situation.

"Sir, should we just lay down a pattern of laser fire from our weapons to see if we can drive anyone out?"

"Not yet, Sarge. We can be sure that lion we followed here is still around, and lasers might set off a brush fire that could spook it and make it harder for the drone sensors to scan the area effectively. Let's keep looking. Establish a perimeter about a half klick from this clearing and set the drones out to scan the area. We can always use the lasers if our search turns up nothing."

More "sensor" talk. "Laser fire"? And "drones"? What are drones? Do they click?

"Let's just wait and see what we can find first, Sarge. And for the rest of you, remember we're in capture mode. If we do find any Outdwellers, immobilize them and take them back to the

City. If, on the other hand they can't be captured, you have my authority to kill them where they stand."

Good. They aren't looking for Nomás. They're looking for something called "Outdwellers." But what would they do if they found us? Would they kill us too? Do they mean us? Is that what they call Nomás? Outdwellers? My heart pounded like a drum. *Guess my hibernation failed.*

"Lieutenant, I have the drones ready to scan," one of the intruders said. I looked out through the crack again and was so taken off guard that I almost cried out to Mom. *He's holding that strange bird thing that Tess made fall from the sky. That must be a drone.*

As he sent that drone into the air, it flew around quickly, but not like any real bird I'd ever seen. This drone bird flew in a straight line, stopped, floated, took off in a different direction, and turned to fly sideways to get through tight spaces. It wasn't like any living creature in the way it moved.

Barcan magic?

Just as soon as I thought that, the drone bird stopped in the air, turned, and hovered as if it was sniffing the air, then suddenly flew straight to our doorway, only partially hidden by the bushes. On instinct, I reacted too quickly. In an instant I had my bow in hand and was aiming through the wall crack, ready to send an arrow at the drone thing. The tension was too much, and I lost control. I fired at it, barely missing. The drone must have known it was almost killed, as it made loud sounds, and red flashes came from its spinning wings. The invaders saw it, and they ran toward our home with some type of weapons held out in front of them.

"Capture mode," one of them shouted.

This was too much for Niamh. Acting on her command to guard the family, she attacked them before they could reach the bushes. She grabbed one of them by the leg and began to drag it out of the clearing and into the thick growth. They fired their weapons at her—streaks of red and green brilliance leaving momentary death trails imprinted on the air—but by the time they shot, she was too deep in the thicket to be seen.

Chaos arose as the invaders rushed to save the Barcan from Niamh's attack, but I knew she'd already abandoned her victim, having seen her slink around from behind the well. They didn't notice that she went to her position and resumed guarding from there, well hidden in the tall weeds.

The Barcans soon came back to the clearing, carrying their wounded. They lifted the bleeding invader onto a small bed that unfolded from poles, placed straps around the bloodied legs and chest, then waited—for what, I couldn't tell.

"Mom," I whispered, "what do I hear? It sounds like a swarm of bees."

I'd no sooner spoken when four Barcans came flying in on what might be magical horses—headless animals that flew in unbelievable ways, changing directions as if by magic, fierce lights coming from where their heads would be if they even had heads, no feet on the ground as they somehow hovered in midair like a drone, their nonstop breathing an unearthly hum. The Barcans sat on them just like Nomás hunters sat on their horses, but these didn't walk or run—they floated, hovered, and streaked away in a brilliant flash of power.

"Flying horses without heads?" I whispered. Dad pushed his face to the wall crack to see what I was so excited about, and he nearly fell over me to tell Mom that I was right. They were indeed sitting on some form of flying creature, and they had fixed the wounded person's bed-like structure between two of them.

It was a good thing that these "horses" were buzzing so loud, or they would surely have heard us making such a racket.

Somehow, they never found the entry to our home. Maybe it had to do with Niamh's attack. But it may also have been because they didn't seem to be willing to poke their black, shiny heads into dark, overgrown weeds and bushes, not knowing what sort of wildlife might be in wait, especially after seeing Niamh's attack.

The one who was called Lieutenant walked toward our home.

I reloaded my bow to be ready just in case they found us and we had no choice but to defend. We waited, as quiet as could be, until Lieutenant picked up the drone thing, stared directly into our home, then backed away and walked back to the others and handed the drone to one of them. They mounted their horse creatures and took off in a scream of buzzing. We only started to breathe normally again when we were sure they were out of hearing range.

By the time I was ready to drop to the floor from exhaustion, Mom gave the signal to end the alert. We came out from under our cloaks. Mom said what I was thinking: "I thought we'd have to fight for our lives."

"Mom, they have floating horses, and a bird that isn't real. They called it a—"

"Drone. I saw it too. We need to tell the council about this so they can warn everyone to be on the lookout for Barcan drone spy birds."

My knees were shaking. Tears fell from my chin; I hadn't even know I was crying. Dad saw this, and he put his arm around my shoulders and comforted me.

"I'm okay, Dad." I was anything but okay, but I needed to keep my head level. I turned away and looked for some venison scraps to give to Niamh.

"I know you're okay, Rannie. We're all more than a little upset. It'll get better."

"Okay, Dad. Thanks."

I didn't want to look weak. It might make Dad take on the protector role that he sometimes tried so hard to be. I loved him, but although he was many things, a warrior wasn't one of them. Plus, I was still trying to understand why he didn't wake us as soon as he got back home after his earlier encounter with the Barcans. Maybe it had happened so fast that there was no time to awaken us. Which reminded me, we needed to thank our true hero.

"Niamh."

She came to the doorway, careful not to enter. She knew the rules. I walked out and thanked her for watching over us. I'd grabbed a large piece of venison from the food box and was hiding it behind my back. Niamh sat right down, waiting for me to offer the reward. "Well done." I tossed the meat, and Niamh went off to a place where she could eat without interruption.

I stood there watching her go, not moving for a bit even after she was out of sight. Suddenly, I felt my knees, weak and shake; my vision blurred and I was pretty sure that I was about to black out. I grabbed the nearest bush and tried to stay upright. *No. You can't lose it now. You need to be strong for Mom, for Dad, for yourself. Wakan Tanka, help me.*

I had no idea where that came from. I consciously thought it, and I may have even said it out loud.

"*I am with you.*"

I wasn't sure if I actually heard that voice or imagined it, but I was certain I felt the color return to my face. My vision cleared, and my legs regained their strength. Could this be real? I looked forward to asking Tess about this.

Now, it was time to find out what Dad knew.

Mom was there first.

"Marlon, start talking. And begin with why you thought it was okay to talk right when the Barcans were within hearing." She waited for him.

"I'm sorry—I just thought at that moment you needed to know what we were dealing with. This morning, I was off on my usual routine. I made my way down the dirt trail that leads to the grassy mesa where I usually sit early in the day. I do this every morning, before any of you wake up. I can usually sit there for a long time without worries. I never see anyone up at that time. Everything was perfect. The birds filled the area with their chirping, the fog was lifting, and the sky was green-blue—a perfect morning.

"I focused and began my chant. 'Nomás . . . Nomás . . .' Soon, I was in full meditation.

"My mind wandered to a scene I couldn't understand. I stood in front of what I somehow felt was the Barca complex, somewhere near the San Mateo Ruins. This was a place I'd never been before, yet I knew where it was. A mountain lion—not Niamh—stood facing me, and I felt like it looked deep into my soul. I heard the animal speak.

"*Marlon, Come here, to this place. Come here to find the flower.*' Then the lion moved aside to reveal an odd-looking plant with a single large flower, growing at the edge of the road near the Barca enclosure. This plant was not so unusual—unimpressive except that it glowed. More than glowed, actually. It was on fire."

I caught my breath. *This was the flower I saw in my vision.*

Dad went on.

"The lion spirit continued. '*You must bring this plant to your people. It has great powers.*'

"I asked the lion, '*Who are you, lion?*'

"'*I'm the heart of the people, the spirit of Nomás. You, Marlon, are to be the one to bring this special flower to the people. There will be a need for its power before long, and the flower must be there when it is needed. Come to this place before one week is over.*' Then the lion faded away."

Fear filled my heart. I was about to tell them about the vision I'd had at the Mourning Feast—that I knew Dad was called for this mission and that he was taking a risk. At the last moment I stopped. *What if I tell them, and what if Dad decides not to go, and my vision meant something else? He would never forgive himself. But what if my vision was right?* My thoughts spun out of control. Dad was still talking.

"I was surprised when I didn't come out of this trance state in my normal way. The sudden disappearance of the lion jolted me, and I jumped to my feet, heart pounding. I saw that the fog seemed to be clearing again, even though I knew that it had already lifted. There was a new sound I'd just become aware of. It came from a strange bird that seemed not to be alive, and it was flying toward me. It had spinning wings, red flashing eyes, and it was able to stop in midair, like a hawk, and look around in a circle.

"I dove toward the bushes surrounding the mesa without even a thought for safety. I knew that I could be ripped open by the thorns below. But if I were spotted, I was sure that this bird-like thing would cause me more pain and suffering. It was evil, that much I knew. I made an instant decision. I pulled my hood over my face, then jumped.

"My feet were the first to hit the thorny branches. I fell more than ten feet down through the covering bushes."

I guessed when these invaders had come searching for us, we all went into survival mode. Now, after the danger had passed, for the first time Mom and I saw his scratched hands and torn shirt.

"As I fell, I covered my face with these hands. My eyes were spared the sharp thorns. I looked up and saw that the evil bird was hovering above me—not far above the rock outcropping.

"*It knows*, I thought. "*Otherwise it would have moved on.* Just then, a goat jumped onto the rock and bleated loudly at the bird. After a few moments of the goat's bleating and jumping at the bird thing, it must have determined there was no human, just a goat, and it flew off in the direction of the coastline."

Dad then told us that he picked his way out of the brambles and hurried home to warn us about the bird thing. He was only a few steps from the rock when Niamh jumped in front of his path, almost knocking him off his feet. She must have been trying to force him to take a different route. He told us that he didn't get it. He was back on his original path when he heard the sound of footsteps crunching the dried twigs scattered on the ground. He didn't have a moment to waste.

"Niamh sprang into action. With a loud growl, she jumped across the path, which soon revealed a dozen people dressed in black like the invaders. I think it was the same group. She stopped right in front of them and turned to snarl at the closest one, who raised his weapon at her. One of them shouted they were not to kill the animals, only set guns to make them sleep, or something like that. While they talked, Niamh got away. I, too, saw my chance to sneak away. I made my way down the hillside and back into the compound. That's when Niamh raised the alarm and the two of you came down."

I looked at my father, and I saw the vision of the lion, the hawk, and the flower in my mind. I thought, *I can't let him go alone. I have to protect him. Niamh and I will go with him on this quest.*

CHAPTER NINE

President Hsieh
11 May 2249
Office of the president
Barca City
GPS: 37° 33' 57.884" N 122° 11' 38.62" W
Outside Conditions: clear sky, no fog, temp 25.03
Sustainability Factor: -19 (heavy viral saturation)
Interior Conditions: all systems functioning at peak

STANDING ON THE BALCONY OVERLOOK IN THE DOMED overhang of my office, peering out to the east, I was somewhat blinded by the brilliant fire-orange sun as it slowly rose up over the East Bay hills, smearing beauty all over the decrepit and mostly fallen Bay Bridge. I was impressed. *No morning fog today. Pretty rare view.*

"Goh. My office, now." *Where the hell is that damned assistant?*

His absence was just shy of technological insubordination. I needed to have that thing fine tuned. I hadn't given him any instructions yet today, so there was no reason for him to be anywhere but right here, available at all times.

Since when does a damned hologram decide to be absent from its duty station?

"Yes, Mr. President. I am here. My image was transferred to your office early this morning. I have been in standby mode ever since, and as a result, you possibly wouldn't have noticed me."

Damned hologram. Fades into the furniture when he's in standby. Terrible design. I need to fire someone over this.

"Goh, new discussion. Topic is related to the M&A files, under Threats and Barriers.

"Yes, sir. Mergers and Acquisitions, Threats and Barriers. Ready, sir."

"Mark this discussion as 'Highly Confidential: Access Only on Presidential Authority.' Also mark access authority for Tom Sands. Begin recording.

"Eleven May, 2249. With regard to the recent possible sightings in the North Bay, and given the sensitive nature of our pending discussions with the Toyokohama conglomerate in Japan, Barca Corporation is wise to take certain preventative measures. Merger discussions with Japan are at a critical point. We have thus far been able to convince the Toyokohama board that our intentions are for a mutually beneficial merger that will strengthen us individually and jointly. Our product compatibility and exclusivity make us the perfect candidates for such a merger that will leave us with a cooperative management team comprised of key players from each of our corporations."

I thought to myself, *Yeah, players from both teams—that never works in business. Smartest, fastest, hungriest fish eats the other fish. Simple as that.*

"There's no indication that anyone from Toyokohama suspects our objective. The plan, so far, is on track."

The screen over the office doorway came to life. I could see that there were two people standing outside the door. One was Tom Sands. The other was an unknown.

"Goh, pause current session and record the next meeting

with Sands." Turning to face the door, I invited the two inside. "Tom, I only have a few minutes. What is it?"

Sands stepped inside and motioned for the other to follow.

"Thank you, Mr. President. I just want to introduce you to J35 from Assembly Sector MV12. This is the young man I was telling you about. He's interested in getting on a management track, sir, climbing the corporate ladder. He and I happened to meet in the break room one evening, and we hit it off right away. I mentioned to him that we might have an opportunity opening up very soon—hope you don't mind—and it might be perfect for someone like him.

"Jude and I've become like a team, sir. Over the past few months, he's transferred into my Security detail and is currently working in undercover mode as an operating systems specialist. We can easily move him around to any sector on temporary assignment without arousing any suspicions. I've already moved him into the target sector in the Systems Testing Lab, ready to activate the plan on our signal."

Tom stepped aside so I could see the young man. Walking toward this Jude—or J35—I reached out to offer a handshake.

"Good to meet you, J35. Mr. Sands has told me good things about you. I understand that you're a dedicated company man."

"Yes, sir, Mr. President. I'm honored to meet you, sir. There's no question, sir. I've dedicated my life to Barca, and I am ready to do whatever you ask me to do. I'd love the opportunity to prove my value to the company, and to you, sir."

"Good, my friend." I paused for effect, pretending to think long and hard about what I was about to ask of this young man. *Dedicated his life? Of course he has. He doesn't have a life if not for Barca.* "Can I call you by your social name, Jude?"

"Of course, sir."

"Well, then, Jude, what if I asked you to get close to someone and to report back to us if you found him to be a threat to Barca? Would you still be willing to do whatever I asked, even if it could cost him his life, Jude?"

He must not have been ready for the suddenness of this question. He started to answer, then paused before committing. This was just the reaction I was expecting.

"Take your time, Jude. Think this through carefully."

J35 seemed to relax a bit, looking around the office in an attempt to calm his nerves. He seemed interested in the twentieth-century handgun display on the west wall. Each one was labeled with the manufacturer, type of gun, name of the former owner, and any details if the gun had been used in a significant crime. I was about to mention a few of them when he turned back to face me, a serious look on his face.

"Mr. President . . . I . . . sir . . . Yes. If he were a threat to Barca or to you, I'd hand the rat to you on a plate, sir."

"Good, then, Jude. You will hear more from Mr. Sands as the time approaches. Now, you need to know that this is classified information of the Corporate Top-Secret level. You need to be aware that should you even hint about any of this to anyone other than the three of us, you'd be tried for corporate sedition. Is that clear?"

Jude stood ramrod stiff, almost at attention. "Yes, sir. Understood."

"Very well, young man. Welcome to the team. Tom, please show our new friend out. I'll talk to you later." I turned my back on them as Goh activated the door, rotating it open. I waited until I could hear that they were gone.

"Goh, resume previous discussion. Repeat last statement."

The active-processing light above Goh's waist plate flashed red, then yellow, before turning solid green. He played back my last statement in my own voice: *There is no indication that anyone from Toyokohama suspects our true objective. The plan, so far, is on track.*

"Record. At this time, we have identified our scapegoat, one A37921, socially referred to as Andy, an inspector in Systems Testing Lab. We've selected him for a number of reasons. First, he has no known family. There'll be no reason for anyone to snoop into the circumstances of his conviction and subsequent sentencing.

"Second, we have record of him actually talking in what could be loosely interpreted as seditious terms, playing 'What if we were able to leave Barca' with his friends. Of course, this was more or less a joke among peers, but we'll make it appear more like serious plotting when it's taken out of context. We can make it as devious as we need.

"Third, he's not an essential worker. His functional area can be taken over by anyone, as the essential inspection work is done by robotics with a failure rate of near zero. In short, we don't need him.

"We've also identified the bait. This is a worker from MV12 appropriately named Judas, called Jude by his coworkers. He's been set up nicely to lead Andy down the path of self-destruction.

"Once we activate the scenario, this so-called Andy will be tried for sedition, he'll be exiled to the Out, where he will surely die a horrible death from the plague or some other viral killer, and we'll play that up to our population as if it'd be the end of the world.

"Now for history—the reason for this plan. There's been much grumbling among the workers about the potential for life in the Out. Somehow confidential information has been leaked by some rat in the search teams. Information about recent reports of sightings in the North Bay have triggered widespread rumors that life in the Out is possible, and that if so, our workers could believe they might be able to leave our environment and survive. We know this isn't true, but perception is fast becoming reality for these workers. If we were to have an even minor revolt while we're finalizing our negotiations with Toyokohama, the deal could fall apart in a heartbeat. We can't risk that. By demonstrating, in a frightening way, the reality of death by exile, it's clear that those who might rebel would see the error of such thinking, and they'd simmer down and behave like good workers should. For us to give up the lives of only two workers to save all of Barca is a small price to pay."

I paused, noticing the ancient bullet fragment on its stand on my desk. This bullet was reported to be the very same one removed from US President Andrew Jackson's chest after his death. He'd received it in a duel that ended in the death of his opponent. It had lodged deep in Jackson's chest and remained there for years.

It, along with Jackson's very own gun, was my lucky charm. *Jackson has always been an inspiration to me*, I thought.

Goh sensed that I was finished.

Would you like to review, sir?"

"No, I am satisfied. Mark and seal it."

I turned back to the observation deck and noticed the deep shadow scars the sun cast on Mt. Diablo, reminiscent of the dark days following the last volcanic belching from the Cascade Mountains in the northern sections of the former Washington State. That particular eruption had cast a dark shadow over the land for nearly two years, until the winds eventually blew the particulate crap off to the east. Eruptions, like rebellions, were never good.

CHAPTER TEN

RANZA
  Firecave
  Santa Rosa Nomás village
  Santa Rosa Ruins
  Early evening
  Chilly, moonless

THE COUNCIL REACTED QUICKLY ON HEARING OF THE CLOSE call with the Barcans. Mom alerted the members, who immediately called for a meeting to take place just before the Returning ceremony here in the Firecave.

The night was particularly dark, as the moon had yet to rise. Owls chanted their endless question of the Nomás intruders as everyone made their way to the Firecave. Footfall betrayed the dampness as sandals beat a slow, steady rhythm and dozens of feet flapped their sounds against the chirp-stream of the crickets. A natural cacophony, as Earth intended it to be.

Penetrating the hard rock face of the hill, the pursed mouth of the Firecave was an unusually small entrance that belied the massive interior main room—a room so big two could stand at opposite sides, speak to each other in normal voices, and one wouldn't be able to understand the words the other said. Maybe some of the volume was taken up to the ceiling of the cave. Who knew how high that was. Whatever the reason, just being in that cave made me feel tiny, unreal. That was good, though. It also prevented any sense of self-importance. It was said that those who entered this place would leave with a true picture of who and what they were. I always left feeling I was just one of the many, no more important than the others and no more valuable than any member of the Nomás family. I was aware we are all important, yet each no more than the other. We were just what we were—all the same.

"Tess, this is one of my favorite places: the Firecave. We've been gathering here on occasions since I can remember, sometimes as a group of neighbors to spend time with each other and relax by a warm fire that can't be seen from the outside, and sometimes for special ceremonies like tonight. But it's not just a cave. Firecave is the center of our Santa Rosa community. It's the very heart of who we are."

Viewing the deep cave, Tess seemed to be impressed.

"Tess, I'm confused. On one side, you tell me that you are from Wakan Tanka, and you do seem to have magic. On the other side, Wakan Tanka as the gathering of all Great Ones is the most powerful, all-seeing god, right?"

"Yes," she answered cautiously.

"Then how is it you don't already know all about us? Why are you surprised when I explain our customs?"

"Oh, I see. That's a fair question. I can clear this up. You see, just because I am from the Great One, it doesn't make me a great one. What I mean is I am only the servant of Wakan Tanka. She tells me only what I need to know. Remember what I keep repeating: there is a time to know, a time to wonder, and a time to wait. It's a little like that. There are things to know, things to ponder, and things to learn."

"I think I understand, but you sure have a complicated way

of explaining things. So, now, you seem to like the Firecave. What do you wonder about it?"

"It's oddly untouched. I mean that since you've been coming here for so long, and spending so much time in this cave, I might've expected it to eventually show some signs of being occupied. But there are no humanlike signs, no markings, no food residue, bones, smoke stains that I can see on the cave roof . . . nothing to hint that people ever occupied this place."

I had to think about what Tess was saying before I answered. "You're right, of course. And there are reasons for it. The darkness and color of the rocks make it nearly impossible to see smoke stains so high up on the cave ceiling. And we break down the fire ring and bury the ashes deep inside the cave every time we are here. Second, we Nomás see this as a holy place. We keep holy places as natural as possible. This is where we commit our ancestral spirits to the world and to each other. When I walked in here tonight, I felt an awesome respect come over me. It was as if I entered a place where my ancestors live forever. You remember the things we did at the Mourning Feast, right?"

"Yes, of course."

"And you remember that at one point we recalled those who had died since the previous feast, and we pulled them back into us. Remember that?"

"Yes, and I was amazed by it. It was so real for me."

"I'm glad. Tonight, you'll see just how important it is to the Nomás."

At that point, Mom and Dad returned to the fire ring area with the Nomás council, who'd been meeting in the deepest room of the cave. They walked solemnly in to stand around the fire in the center of this large open cathedral. My thoughts drifted back to the many other ceremonies I'd seen in this place. I looked upward toward the roof of the cave.

My mom, as a head councilor, was the group leader. She stood at the center of the group and led us in the ceremonial ritual. A soft, haunting melody drifted throughout the cave—a special song that seemed to call out to the ancestors, pleading that they rejoin the living to welcome the recently passed Nomás to this gathering of souls.

Mom raised an earthen pot over her head. The others followed her lead.

"This is the night," she said, "when we return our lost souls to the tribe. Here in the Firecave, as we've done for generations, we bring their humanity and their spirituality together to be joined as one with the Nomás. These pots contain their ashes, remnants of their physical being."

One by one, the elders lowered their earthen pots and withdrew large spoons from inside them. Without saying anything, each of them began a slow walk in a random pattern all over the cave. As they walked, they let the ashes fly from the spoons, like a dust storm that settled on the cave floor.

"As we bring their humanity back, we also return their spirits to the tribe." Mom turned to face us and placed her pot on the floor.

On her signal, all of the assembled walked slowly toward the fire, holding their hands out in front of them. When they had all reached the fire ring, they stopped and lowered their heads. This was a time of remembering those they had brought back to rest within them from the Mourning Feast. All sounds, including the natural sounds of the crickets, had stopped. The silence was violated only by the sound of moisture dripping off the roof somewhere nearby within the cave. It was eerie to hear it so pronounced, since we hadn't even noticed it a moment before.

Mom spoke. "We bring you back to be one with your physical selves, one with your Nomás family. Nomás," she chanted, as all joined her.

"Nomás." As one, all opened their arms outward as they chanted. "Nomás. Nomás . . ."

Although I'd experienced this magic before, it always somehow surprised me—nearly frightened me. As we chanted and I opened my arms, there was a sensation of being lifted, as if something was being pulled from within and it wanted to be free from its bonds. The sensation was intense as I watched wispy, ghostlike forms leave our bodies and rise with the smoke from the fire until they reached the roof of the cave, where they faded —a puff of smoke.

Mom recited the ritual welcoming. "We bring you out to be with us. Here in Firecave, you'll stay until the Great Ones take you to them. We welcome you home and we join with you in this sacred place of our ancestors. We rejoice in your return."

I saw that Tess was clearly enjoying this formal reverence.

After a respectful time, everyone relaxed, and the cave became a more social place. Mom and Dad spent a few moments with the rest of the council members, giving blessings and wishes for their continued health, before joining Tess and me where we sat on a rock pile in the far-left corner of the cave near a dark tunnel leading off from the main room. Others began the process of breaking down the fire ring and sweeping away their footprints from the floor.

Tess smiled. "I was happy to watch you all bring your spirits home in this place. You Nomás are the perfect example of tribal custom. Wakan Tanka is pleased. Thank you for inviting me into this." She hugged my parents and returned to sit next to me.

Dad seemed uncomfortable. His discomfort was so strong that I could feel it—a physical connection between us that made me shiver.

"Ranza," he said, "I need to tell you something." He paused for a time, maybe trying to find the right words, or perhaps to give me a chance to prepare for bad news. I couldn't tell; he wore no expression.

I looked from Dad to Mom to Tess—hoping for a sign from anyone that things were not as bad as I suspected they might be. I saw no such sign.

"Sure, Dad. But you sound so serious. No nicknames?" I tried to lighten the conversation, but it just made things go from tense to very tense. Dad folded his hands in his lap and fixed a stern look on me.

"The council has listened to my retelling of the vision I had this morning. There is some amount of concern that this could be a very risky journey, and since we have recently experienced teams of Barcan Security in our home trying to find us, this concern is even worse than it might otherwise be. It's so risky that the council has only agreed to allow me to follow the vision if I agree to take my own security with me. I have agreed to do so."

"Sure, Dad," I answered without hesitation. "When do we leave?"

Dad and Mom shared a look. Now I was really worried.

"No, you won't go with me. If I were captured, the Barcans would torture me to try to get me to tell them about the Nomás. I'd fight to the death. If you went, and they caught us both, and they tortured you in front of me, I would not be strong enough. I know for sure I'd break and give them what they wanted if it would save you." He shook his head. "The risk to the tribe is too great. And, I remind you, we Nomás understand that no one is greater than all. The Nomás must be protected at all times. My life is not as important as the safety of the community. So, the council has decided that Carter will travel with me. We can't put that responsibility on you, my daughter."

"But Carter, he doesn't even know you. Why send him?"

"That's just the point, Rannie. It lessens the emotion and increases the resolve. We might be more inclined to protect the tribe instead of each other."

"Yes," Mom said, "it is the right choice. You've been excluded from the trip. The council has studied your dad's telling of the vision. They have tested his truth, and they believe all that he has said. They've voted to send him on this trip. And Ranza, the council believes that this journey could be critical to the future of the Nomás. Even though we haven't been told what its powers are, if this flower is as powerful as the vision said it is, then there's no question about this. Your father understands just how important it is, and he is ready to meet the task, even if it means . . ."

I studied Mom, spotted a tear in her eye as she turned to Dad.

∽

Ranza
  Nomás communal well
  Later that evening
  Chilly—no fog

EVERY SHADOW HID A BLACK-UNIFORMED BARCAN KILLER. Crickets chirped a desperate warning, undertones of the evil from all over the world that had flocked to this spot to threaten me, my family, and the entire Nomás nation, every community from all parts of Northern California. Several times, I caught myself up short, certain that I saw movement from the shadows and ready to defend myself and Tess against any evil Barcan threat. Tess noticed.

"Hey, take a breath. You're jumpier than I've ever seen you. Stop. Talk to me."

I stopped walking and looked at the ground. "Tess, I don't know what to do. I can't let my dad head off with that weird Carter guy just to find a flower. I'm gonna fight it all the way." The echo of this hung out in the dank air for a while, neither of us willing to take the next step and actually look at the probable outcome of this mission. After some time, Tess was willing to start the impossible conversation.

"I know it must break your heart, but he has to do this. Ranza, this flower's going to change the world."

"How would you know? Do you even have parents? I don't

care how important this plant is to anyone. I just know how important my dad is to me. Nothing can take that from me."

Tess didn't answer. She didn't react at all. Neither of us spoke for a long time. My mind was racing.

How can I sneak away and follow them? If I'm there, I can protect him by staying just far enough back but close enough to put an arrow into any Barcan murderers. But I knew that wasn't the answer. I just had to come up with a plan.

"Ranza, I'm not your enemy. You trust me, right?"

"Yeah. I think so." I was sorry for my answer the moment I spoke it. "I mean, yeah. I trust you."

"No matter how it might hurt, you should also know that it's for the best that your father makes this sacrifice. He knows the importance of this plant. He's the expert. He can adapt it to the best use for your tribe. This isn't something he's decided without reason. This quest comes from Wakan Tanka. What he's about to do will protect the Earth herself from the evil greed of the Barcans and people like them. He has to go on this quest."

"Again, how do you know, Tess? You keep saying things are part of some plan, some mission from Wakan Tanka, whoever that is, but you don't really know that. You are just guessing. You have this belief, and you think everything is decided by this Great One god. Okay, then. Tell me so I can believe. How do you know?"

Tess hesitated. "I can't, Rannie. Not just yet. Like I said, there is a time to wonder, a time to know, and a time to wait. There are other times—a time for hope and a time for trust. I need you to trust me. I know that the vision of the flower has come directly from Wakan Tanka. And I know that she has spoken to you, and you heard her when she said she was with you."

I was surprised. "Yes. I heard her. But . . ."

"I also know that the flower is of world-changing importance to the Nomás."

"But no flower can be that important."

"I know you think that, but it's more important than you know."

"It's a flower, Tess."

"This flower has the ability to heal, to protect from Death himself. This magical power could ultimately cause the total destruction of Barca. If their people believe they can live outside the domed City, they'll have no workers to keep the corporation going. Their leaders would do everything they could to prevent their people from learning about it and about the Nomás, and to keep us from getting our hands on the flower."

"Tess, what the hell are you rambling on about? None of this makes any sense." My voice rose. "And believe me, I don't care about the Barcans or their leaders or their City or their future!"

Tess paused, and I could that she was surprised and saddened by my outburst. She whispered, "Do you think shouting at me will solve any of this?"

Helpless to understand, I broke down sobbing. Tess took my hands in her own and softly cooed like a mourning dove into the air. It was a little weird, but after a few moments, I stopped crying, my breathing slowed, and I composed myself. Back under control, I looked at Tess and said flatly, "If you tell me this is another time to wonder, I'll scream again." This set me off into a giggling jag that almost felt like sobbing. Tess laughed with me.

"But, Tess, we've never had threats from them before, so why would Barca want to destroy us now?

"Barca is a power-distribution machine. The leaders hold power over their subjects through a system of servitude; those in charge depend on the workers to create the products that they then use to create wealth. This wealth gives them worldwide power in many areas. They have to keep the people in slavery or the whole thing collapses. In order to lock them in, they threaten to exile the people to the natural world outside Barca City, where they are certain to die from diseases they have not yet developed natural defenses to. 'Either do what we command, or get out.' And to leave the compound means certain death."

Tess, how do you know all this?"

"Please stop asking that. It makes me answer the only way I can, and you must be tired of hearing it by now."

"Time to . . . ?"

Tess smiled and nodded.

"What does this have to do with a flower, or my dad?"

"Barcan government views any life outside the complex as a threat to their own corporate future. If the Barcan slave people ever learned that Nomás exists, the people would revolt against the leaders, thinking that they actually could live in the Out. This flower *can* help them live in the Out."

"And my dad?"

"He's been chosen. He understands what this can mean, and he's agreed to be the one to bring this medicine to the people."

"How does he know all this?"

"Wakan Tanka has told him through visions. And I've spoken to your father to confirm that what he sees for the future is real. I've told him all. He knows the risk, and he's prepared to take it. I've waited to tell you about this, but now is probably the right time."

"You've told him? When could you have told my dad anything? And what did you tell him?" I was ready to scream again but held it back.

"At the Mourning Feast. We were waiting for you to show up —late as usual." She smiled. "Your dad took me aside. He wanted to know about how you and I met, how I somehow killed a deer by touching it—or so you seemed to remember—and he wanted to know why I told you that you'd someday be the leader of your tribe. I know you told him these things, and that's good. He is your dad. I also told him some things that were key to the reason for the journey to get the flower. He knows why it is important, and he knows, too, that his part in this is critical. But before you ask, the answer is 'Not yet.' You will learn these things and more when it is time. For now, you need to be strong enough to allow him to fulfill his promise."

This was too much for me. I broke again. Sobs came from so deep inside that I shook all over, and tears poured from my eyes. I wanted the Earth, Tess, and her Wakan Tanka to leave us alone. I wanted to run away, but to where? I closed my eyes, trying hard to slip into meditation. It wasn't going to happen.

I thought about the tear that I'd seen from my mother's heartbreak, and I knew that Mom was feeling every bit as broken as I was. It made me ashamed to be thinking only of myself and what I wanted.

I understand, it isn't about me. It's about everyone. But I just hurt so bad.

"I know you're right. It's just that I'm so afraid for my dad. I don't know what I'd do if anything happened to him."

"Something will happen to him someday. Although we never talk about it, we are all going to someday leave this existence and travel on to the next. We don't get to know when that is. You can love your father right now and be happy in that. To worry about when his *someday* might come takes away the happiness that you can have right now."

I didn't want to hear any more. Giving into anger, I screamed at Tess. "What do you know? You show up here and tell me how to live, and you tell me that I'm being selfish? How about you? What if your Wakan Tanka was suddenly taken away and you had to find a way to live knowing that there was no one you could turn to so the world wouldn't scare you every time you opened your eyes? You'd probably be bawling like a baby."

"I do know. I know more than you can understand. I feel everything that you feel. I see everything that you see, and I hurt right along with you, as if these things were happening to me."

"Yeah, but they're not. They're not happening to you."

There was a silence all around. Profound silence. There was no frog chorus of repeated burps and chirps, no night birds like the owls on the hunt adding their melodies to the silence, and even the occasional cry of the coyote who made a successful catch of some unlucky hare seemed to have vanished for the night. My senses were on fire. I felt alone, even walking with Tess. For the first time I felt disconnected from life, as if I was in a cave of my own—a cave that was only big enough to hold me, and no one could reach me there. I was not a part of anything, no longer Ranza of the Nomás. For the moment, at least, I was just Ranza, the little girl.

CHAPTER ELEVEN

President Hsieh
  12 May 2249
  Barca City Flight Port
  Barca City
  GPS: 37°33' 57.884" N 122°11' 38.62" W
  Outside Conditions: clear sky, no fog, temp 22.33
  Sustainability Factor: -18 (heavy viral saturation)
  Interior Conditions: all systems functioning at peak

I WAS A MASTER SHOWMAN, FINDING GREAT ENJOYMENT IN grandstanding every move with the board of directors and my own management team, even though I had complete discretionary power over them all. Still, I chose to dazzle them with brilliance rather than simply handing down orders and dictating policy. Today's management meeting was no exception.

The managers were all seated in their places when I boarded the presidential VTO aircraft that would be the platform from which I would unveil my strategy for the future of Barca Corporation. I admired the smell of well-oiled leather seats, enjoyed the brilliance of hand-rubbed brass and gold ornamentation, noticed that each member appreciated the elegant seating. Some had reclined them, trying out the sleeping quarters. Others were getting used to the personal virtual-reality headsets that offered a mini experience of their destination that day: the Hawaiian Island Rest Centers. A few—those more sensitive to my extreme protocol—sat upright, waiting for their president to enter the craft. When I did, they sat more upright, stiffer.

The assembled team included critical representatives of the departments that would be important to the success of my plan. Picked for the team were Inter-Corporate Communications Officer Sean Clair, Chief Financial Officer Margaret Showalter, Compliance Chief Vonn Eriksson, Chief Technology Officer Brendan Murphy, and of course Tom Sands, my director of Security.

"Hello, Mr. President," chirped Margaret.

Damn, she's so annoying, I thought to myself. I simply nodded in her direction, eager to set the tone of the day.

"Thank you all for coming. Today's meeting will take place here in my jet as we take a brief but well-earned work-play trip to the Hawaiian Corporate Dome and Vacation Center. I'll be happy to provide the details of our trip after takeoff, but for now, sit back and enjoy the ride." Then I added, "Tom, please join me in my office suite."

Tom was on his feet and following before I even finished telling him. I motioned with a flick of my wrist to tell him to wait a moment. I was interested in seeing the reactions of the team when they experienced the transparent floor and the balancing capabilities of the newly installed gyro-levelers—the first of their kind. Currently, only my personal jet had them installed.

I pressed the command button to let the flight crew know we were ready for takeoff. At the same time, Goh appeared in the main cabin to express my wishes for a safe and enjoyable flight to Hawaii. Goh would serve as tour guide for the trip.

"Ladies and gentlemen," he said cordially, "welcome to the

Hawaiian Islands flight. As we lift straight up, you will note I'll open the floor viewing panels so you can truly experience the glory of flight as a bird would."

As he spoke, the floor of the craft became transparent, offering all an unimpeded view of the Flight Port as it grew smaller and smaller, a result of the speed at which we were rising above Barca City. Some were excited; others, not so much.

"Oooohhhh," groaned Margaret. She turned her head away to keep from passing out.

Brendan was thrilled. "What a display of twenty-third-century technology. I love it."

The others hesitated to let their feelings be known.

"You can see, as we rise above the deck," Goh continued, "a line of freight aircraft being loaded and dispatched to various destinations around the globe. They will be carrying many of our technology products, parts, and even tons of silicon from our East Bay mining operations. On the other side of the deck, notice aircraft from many other corporations delivering goods that we purchase from them to use in our own products. This is our parts supply chain.

"We will make a slow pass over the City to allow you to see all of it from the Out perspective. It is, as you will see, truly amazing." Goh paused as the aircraft moved into position. "As we pass the front of the structure, note that the building itself is nearly seven miles wide and more than sixty stories high. The entire building is wrapped in a composite glass that enables whatever solar energy is available to generate electricity, a somewhat old technology that still works well. From the inside, the glass panels are capable of projecting pleasing video images but can be muted to show the Out in all its beautiful horror. In addition, certain locations are set for virtual-reality scenic display, but those are reserved for certain confidential purposes.

"If you look directly to the left, you will see the outside of President Hsieh's upper balcony dome, where each of you have met with the president from time to time. At the roof level, note the elaborate living gardens, with trees from every sector, flowers and statuary to give a calming feeling, and reflecting pools and fountains that provide a sense of serenity to those who are lucky enough to earn family passes. Finally, before we accelerate, you can just about make out the complex structural grid that adds strength to the building and supports the transparent dome that makes it possible for all to live safely in Barca City without any risk of infection from the Out. Now, relax and enjoy the ride."

Without warning, the jets on the wings of the craft rotated to provide forward thrust. The crew ramped up speed quickly, causing a gasp to rise from the group. This was followed by more acceleration that left the craft racing forward at what would be a land speed approaching fifteen hundred miles per hour. Although they all could sense the incredible speed, it didn't seem to bother any of them. This was a result of the balanced pressure systems and the recently perfected gyro-levelers that countered any atmospheric disturbances, giving them a smooth ride. Their reaction—which was actually no reaction of note—was what I wanted to see. The engineered comfort evidently worked as planned. Tom and I headed to my office quarters.

"Tom, I think they're ready for this. We've given them a dose of wonder with the outside-in view of the City, and Goh's little tour-guide routine just now has set the mood well for what we are going to tell them. I need you to step it up and make sure they see us as capable of pulling this off. Any hesitation, any weak link in the chain, and all of it fails. You, Tom, will take the role of my enforcer. Get each one aside and try to read their minds. Are they loyal or fearful? Do they have any hesitation? First example is Showalter. I just don't like her, but I can't say I have any hard evidence that she isn't going to be a player. Get inside her head. Let me know if you think she is worth taking a risk on. Otherwise, I can just forget to bring her back from Hawaii, if you get my meaning."

"I'm with you."

I opened my communication channel to be heard and seen

throughout the cabin. "Folks, please meet me in the aft conference. Follow the lights on the ceiling. If anyone needs to take a
break, now is the time. Restrooms are located immediately
before the conference room.

The stage was set for a very different kind of meeting than
the usual facts-and-figures updates they were accustomed to.
The lights were slightly dimmed; energizing music whispered in
the background while Barcan propaganda images and videos
faded in and out from many corners of the room. Goh invited
them to take their designated seats. The meeting was about to
start.

"I'm proud to be a member of the greatest management team
the world has even seen." I walked briskly into the room and
wasted no time taking my seat in the open end of a *U*-shaped
conference table. This seat enabled me to sit closer to each team
member than I could at a rectangular table. Close equaled
control, and I'd need that control with what I was about to tell
them.

"You all know each other, so I'll dispense with the formalities. Let's just get to the point, shall we?" They all nodded in
agreement. "As you've been told, Barca Corporation is about to
take discussions with Toyokohama Corporation to a new level,
hoping to secure agreement for a merger . . . of sorts." I left that
last part hanging in the air like smoke. Nobody asked for an
explanation. They knew me well enough to know I was about to
provide all the details.

"There are mergers, alliances, acquisitions, and many other
forms of corporate cooperative agreements in the business
world. That we know. What we often lose sight of is that business has evolved over the past few generations. Business is the
new government. He who holds the purse strings controls the
people. We, as an example, are unchallenged in our hemisphere.
But it's becoming increasingly clear that we need to take steps to
guarantee our continued financial success in global business.
That success can be at risk if we aren't able to control every part

of our production. The parts supply chain is a critical part of the equation. Of all of the companies who supply our parts, Toyokohama is the most important and consequently the one that presents the greatest risk to our future success. Therefore, it's my considered opinion that a simple merger is not enough. We need to be the controlling partner in any merger, with the management of Toyokohama reporting to us."

Inter-Corporate Communications Officer Clair was the first to speak. "Mr. President. If I may?"

"Yes, Sean. Feel free to speak. This is a discussion, not an edict."

"Well, sir, as you know, I've been closest to the Toyokohama team for several years now, and I have a pretty good sense of their culture and methods. As I see them, I'm having a problem envisioning a world in which they would ever consider selling out to us. What am I missing?"

"Great question, Sean. That hits at the heart of our plan today. Hold that question for a bit if you will."

"Of course."

Margaret Showalter was next. "Sir?"

"Margaret?"

"Sir, As Barca's CFO, I have a very clear picture of our financial position relative to theirs. No disrespect to you and your management, but Toyokohama is possibly twice our size and controls more than double our financial holdings."

"Your point, Margaret?"

"We can hardly afford to pay them what their company is worth."

"Why would we do that? We're going to have them begging us to save them. Again, hold that thought. Are there any more questions?"

I could tell by the downcast eyes from the rest of the team that no one was willing to take a chance until I gave them some inkling of what I actually had in mind. I liked the results so far.

"Okay. Let's dispense with the guesswork. Here is my thinking. The next few days in Hawaii will appear to be characterized by open and mutual discussions that seek to find common ground between Barca and Toyokohama. This will be an opportunity for us to gather as much insider information as we can about the Japanese corporation. Someday in the near future we can use that information as a bargaining chip to secure dominance over them. Each of you will be called on for a specific purpose related to your skills, loyalties, and familiarity with how each company does business. Margaret, your role in this mission will be to secure and scrutinize all of Toyokohama's financial information."

Next, I turned to my technology officer. "You, Brendan, will similarly demand the details of any products that they're working on or about to release to production. Make certain to ask specific and pointed questions designed to push them toward breaching their confidentiality. Don't respect their 'corporate secrets' claim. Be as demanding as you see fit. It'll knock them off guard. Of course, they won't comply, but it will confuse them.

"Sean, it'll fall to you to smooth the waters that the other two have just disturbed. You will take a conciliatory role in this charade, smooth ruffled feathers. If and when they get pissed off at us for our tactics, I'll jump in the middle and pretend to fire one of you. Probably you, Margaret. I'll bring the order out of the chaos.

"Vonn, you'll fill two roles. First, you'll act as official as can be. Mean and intractable is better. Second, infiltrate their private meetings—you know, technologically. Listen to the things they fear, the things they are most angry about. That'll reveal their vulnerabilities."

"I believe I have the right tools for that. I'll be the fly on the wall."

"We'll learn all we need to know to take complete control over these bastards. The objective of all this is to find their Achilles heel—their weak point. Then we can devise a plan to use that weakness in pushing them over the edge, so to speak," I concluded. Then I shifted focus.

"Now, I need to bring you up to speed on another critical matter before us. Recent events in the North Counties suggests there is a possible problem that could completely shut these merger discussions down for good unless we take necessary steps to mitigate it. Let me explain. I'm speaking of the detection of possible groups of Outdweller humans by one of our Security details, the likes of which we've never seen." I waited for this to sink in. "We have, as you all know, long heard the legends of tribes of wild people living in the Out who have somehow been able to avoid the bacterial and other biological hazards that would kill us quickly. These legends have never been proven out. Sure, we've spotted several individual stragglers from time to time, and true, we've become somewhat lulled into apathy over the years of inactivity, almost believing that these indigenous people no longer exist. And we've never found any villages or seen evidence of organized tribal communities. But recent sightings might change that. Before you ask, Margaret, the board has been brought into this and are now fully aware of this problem as well as my probable solution."

The sounds of flight—the roar of engine thrust, the hiss of the interior cabin-pressure units, the various electronic beeps and whirs—filled the silence left by the team collectively holding its breath. I liked the effect. "Tom, please give us the details."

"Yes, sir." Tom stood. "Discovered and recorded by our Security team, these humans appeared on a drone screen for only a brief moment before the drone that spotted them somehow became unable to transmit. The team later located the drone, smashed to pieces on the ground. There was evidence of humanoid activity in the area. The image the team claims to have seen included three humans, possibly two female and one male, accompanied by what appeared to be horses that they rode. Unfortunately, as the drone was destroyed while filming, a permanent record was not uploaded to headquarters. There is no record. I'll turn it back over to President Hsieh. Sir?"

"Yes. Thanks, Tom. This sighting came as the team was searching in the area of a former university. Seems there were definite signs of a large gathering of humanoids, based on evidence of cooking and human body-heat signatures analyzed by the drones."

Vonn raised his hand.

"Yes, Vonn?"

"Sir, all due respect, but do we need to react? What if we just add more security?"

"Not sure how to answer that, Vonn. I feel we've settled into complacency. As long as our workers think these Outdwellers are only a myth, they won't believe life in the Out is even possible. So, if they don't think about it, then it doesn't pose any real threat to us. But we've had some leaks in the Security teams recently, so our risk factor has suddenly risen dramatically.

"Imagine the chaos that would follow in the event our workers learned that humans actually *can* live in the Out. Regardless of how that might happen, our workers might incorrectly believe that they, too, could survive out there, and they might also feel that escape is a viable plan. If history teaches us anything, it is that freedom is a powerful incendiary for those who are not free. If they feel freedom is possible, then no mere Security forces could stop them. We'd have massive attempts to breach the Portals, forcing Security to take extreme measures to prevent that, leading to the unnecessary deaths of possibly thousands or more of Barca's working class. Clearly, such chaos would be viewed as a serious risk factor to the Toyokohamans. It would represent, at the very least, a deal killer. We can't afford that."

Vonn stood. "What should we do, sir?"

"It's already in play, Vonn. As you might expect, Tom's developed a plan to set the entire population of Barca City on notice that any attempt by a citizen worker to escape would be the last decision they would make. The fear Tom can create with this simple strategy will carry us for years. Tom?"

"Thank you, Mr. President." Standing again to address the group, Tom took on an air of authority. Here he was, speaking to the most powerful corporate managers, people running the largest organization in the western hemisphere, and he almost seemed to look down on them. Maybe it was the cloak of protection that working directly under me provided, or perhaps it was just his personal confidence. Whatever it was, he was doing what I expected of him.

"Danger begets danger, lady and gentlemen. It's obvious that the risk we face if these primitive Outdwellers are discovered and the population of Barca catches wind of them could be devastating to all we do. Therefore, we'll meet danger with our own form of danger." He waited for that to sink in. "We have a three-part plan in place. First, we'll make certain that the Barcan people see the foolhardiness of an attempt to escape Barca City. Second, we'll immediately initiate a large assault team to seek and destroy these primitives wherever they live. Third, we will record the entire process for future production of a propaganda video to be shown regularly in Barca and maybe even distributed to other corporations to demonstrate our superior control over our populations. Any questions?"

"Mr. President?"

"Yes, again, Margaret." Tom stepped back as I responded.

"Sir, are you sure that there isn't a better, more humane, way to deal with these so-called 'primitives' than to just declare them as hostile and destroy them? Didn't we learn anything from the Purge?"

She must have known her words were a huge mistake but couldn't stop. At some point, her own humanity had taken over, and she must have been compelled to speak against atrocity. It was as if someone lit a fire in the middle of the table. Each one turned toward me, hoping I didn't realize the anger in her question, but knowing I did.

"Margaret, are you certain you're a team player? I haven't even told you two the three parts of this plan, and already you're questioning my instincts. Well, what's it to be? Are you in or *out?*" The pointed reference to the word *out* was not lost on anyone, least of all Showalter herself. She knew exactly what I was threatening. And she knew that none of the others would be coming to her defense.

"I'm in, sir. I've always been a loyal Barcan. I'm not about to change my loyalties. But . . ." She spoke softer now. "You know I've always advocated for mutual cooperation in our negotiations."

"Yes, Margaret. Mutual cooperation. Just like the Purge, right? Our great society was founded on the culture of domination, not some namby-pamby, happy-happy cooperation. People understand domination. They know the boundaries. Cooperation always carries a hint of 'open to discussion' that leaves too many things unresolved. Forward movement demands a clear starting line."

"Yes, I see."

"Do you, Margaret? Do all of you truly see?" I sent my gaze around the room. "We're at a moment of tremendous risk. Our profits are low, our production is dependent on the supplies from others, who are also dependent on our own products, and it's a deadly circle. The time is now for decisive and severe action. We must be strong and strike while others don't suspect. Now, since you chose to question the second of three parts, Margaret, and the security video is compelling evidence, I'll tell you what's in play for the first part: convincing the population that any attempt to escape would cost them their lives. Tom, may I?"

"Of course, sir."

"Right. Tom, here, has uncovered a plot to perform a seditious act against the corporation. In particular, he's caught one of our product inspectors trying to convince others to join with him and leave Barca City, hoping to live in the Out. This inspector is currently being interrogated. I am confident he'll break and confess his crime. Once he does, we'll place him under an Order of Banishment. He'll be exiled to the Out, and there he'll be tracked until he dies a horrible death from plague. The process will be filmed, and we'll require all people to watch it as it unfolds. The sheer threat of such a frightening death will be more than enough to dissuade everyone else from wanting to try to live out there. I'll dispense with the usual questions and answers, and I'll tell you that this strategy is already under way, and we will not back down."

Sean meekly raised his hand.

"Yes?"

"Mr. President, is the board in agreement?" It was a very dangerous question, and he knew it, but it needed to be asked.

"Please don't be concerned. I've held deep discussions about this with the board. Quite naturally, they've been informed, and all are in complete agreement."

It was another one of my skills. Truth or lie, it mattered not a whit to me. I told them what they need to hear. I didn't care that anyone believed or disbelieved me. Just as long as they did what I said.

"So, the bottom line is we'll first dissuade our own people from seeking to leave the benevolence of Barca Corporation. This will show us as a strong, united organization. Then, we'll seek out and destroy any Outdweller societies. Of course, their existence and our solution must remain under secrecy, otherwise the whole thing will blow up in our faces. Finally, we'll secure control of Toyokohama, marking Barca as the first, and only, multinational governing corporation. The actual plan details will come later on an as-needed basis, but here is the outline."

Goh understood and started the presentation on the far wall. A screen panel opened and the wall was covered with a drone-captured video of Barca City, inside and out. Background music —Wagner's *Ride of the Valkyries*—set an appropriately sophisticated mood.

I moved to the front of the room, alongside the video screen, and spoke in a loud voice. "You stand on the threshold of a new era in corporate governance. Make no mistake, the ultimate goal is world governance. Are you all clear on that?"

Almost as one, they voiced "Yes, sir," as if they'd rehearsed it. Truth was they were afraid not to show full support to me. It didn't matter that their rapid response was more out of defense than for any other reason. *Just do as I say.*

"So, here is the plan in synopsis. We will use all of our methods to learn all we can about the Toyokohama Corporation—financials, plans, and, most important, the skeletons in their closet. We will learn enough that we will then threaten to use that intel if needed to completely discredit them in the global marketplace. But we hope it won't come to that. And don't think for a moment that they have no skeletons. Our advance intelligence tells us that there are plenty. Again, no details yet, but believe me that we already have enough to use. Still, it will be better if we can gather more information against them.

"We will establish talks for a mutually beneficial merger, maybe even let them think they are the acquiring company and we plan to become a part of Toyokohama Corporation. But then we shake them to the core. We inform them of what we know, leak a tiny bit of information to the world, and let them see the financial impact of that leak. The leak should be sufficient and powerful enough that their suppliers and customers begin to scream bloody murder. At first, we change the acquisition to a mutual-benefit merger. Then we go for the throat. If we play this right, Toyokohama will be forced to sell out to us for a very low price. It had better be low, or the plan fails. Once we acquire, we replace their management with our own."

I paused, looked each of them in the eye. "Now, this plan is already in play. There will be no discussion. We are doing this."

A heaviness fell over the cabin. Goh reappeared.

"And now, off the right side of the aircraft you can just see the beautiful coastline of the Hawaiian Islands and our own private heaven." It was an odd thing for a hologram to say.

OUR MEETINGS WITH TOYOKOHAMA WERE ABOUT AS MUCH A waste of time as they could have been. President Nakayama must have sensed that our intentions were less than honorable, as indicated by how quickly his people stopped responding to our interview questions. In my desire to move things forward, I asked for and received a private one-on-one with him.

"Tatsuo, how good to see you again, old friend," I began as we sat.

"You take a great deal of liberties using my first name, President Hsieh. Let's just keep things on a formal level for now, shall we?"

I was slightly startled by his tone.

"As you wish, President Nakayama. Although I must admit to a certain level of confusion. I thought we were here for some initial talks that might lead us to a closer business relationship. Why the sudden shutdown?"

"Let's not play games, President Hsieh. You know as well as I do your team has been digging for whatever info they can get to put you in the dominant negotiating position. In short, you want to take us over, not merge as equal partners."

Based on the level of animosity I saw and heard, I knew I had to tread carefully. I leaned in, spreading my arms in a gesture of conciliation.

"Nakayama-san— Sorry, President Nakayama. I am surprised and disappointed to hear this. Have we been too detailed in our desire for information that would support our decision to merge? Perhaps we have. For that, please pardon our enthusiasm. But we have never entertained the idea of taking over the great Toyokohama Corporation. That never entered our thoughts."

"Perhaps you have, and perhaps you haven't. The single most

important reason we are concerned is the rumor that Barca has a rebellion in the making. We have sources who tell us that you are dealing with some very dangerous possibilities. Are these rumors true?"

I was dumbstruck. There was no possible way Nakayama could have heard about these things unless he had a spy on our management team. Or one of the team members I'd brought with me to this event had turned traitor. Either way, this was a personal problem, and I knew what had to happen. I would make an example of this turncoat immediately.

"I have no idea what you're talking about. Are you making this stuff up?"

"Let's just say I'm going to come down on the side of caution. For now, our discussions are finished. In the future, if things change, please contact me anew."

As if to demonstrate the finished nature of the talks, he stood up, walked out the door, and headed straight to his awaiting aircraft.

I sat quietly for a moment, absorbing what had just happened, going over the details in my mind. I quickly resolved that my first order of action would be to discover who the turncoat on our team was.

"Goh. I need some pure calculation. You have records of all that's happened since we left Barca City. I need you to apply your highest order of analysis to determine which of my team leaked the information to Nakayama. I'll need your analysis by the time we land in Barca Flight Port.

"Yes, sir. I'm on it already.

CHAPTER TWELVE

MARLON
14 May 2249
Arriving with Carter at Bodega Bay fishing village
Western Nomás Territory
Mid-morning
Warm with moderate fog—good protection

I COULD FEEL THE GHOSTS OF MY CHILDHOOD RISING UP IN ME as Carter and I approached the downhill trail leading to the beach at Bodega Bay and the fishing village where I was raised. They tugged at memories, springing them to life as if I'd never left. I imagined myself as a little boy, a young man, a father-husband, as the flashes of the past rushed to top-of-mind, an overwhelming and emotional experience. It happened every time I visited the village, which was no longer a frequent event.

We rode our horses across the old roadway, now little more than a sand trail, giving the animals a break from the harsh land they'd been traveling through in the hills surrounding Bodega Bay and the fishing village. As we crested the last hill and headed down to the beach, my excitement turned to disappointment at seeing the fog had rolled in and clung to the bay. I couldn't even see the water. Not unexpected, but still . . .

"Sorry, Carter. I was hoping to give you a special treat—your first view of Land's End, where the bay meets forever. From here, when the conditions are right, your eyes can look out past the edge of the ocean and give you a sense of the crazy power of the waves. A power that is just there, unceasing, nothing driving it. The waves simply *are*. But, as she sometimes does, nature is playing a trick on us with this fog."

"I'm sure we'll see it soon."

Wow, he sure was unimpressed. Well, that'll change as soon as I get him out on the bay in a tiny outrigger. We shall see, my friend.

We didn't need to tell the horses where to go. They knew this land well, having been born here as a part of Ardon's herd. Our Santa Rosa Nomás traded venison and fruits and vegetables with the Bodega Bay Nomás, who supplied us with several horses as needed, usually about a dozen. The Nomás way—trade one's strength with others for their strength, then each will have the best of everything.

The horses hobbled down the rock-strewn hills and onto the flatland leading to village, just this side of the beach. The closer we got, the better we could make out the large water-packed sand beach stretching out all the way to the Bodega Head cliffs. Nearer to the cliffs, we could recognize there were people tending their nets and stringing up fish to dry in the sun. *As if it could get through this fog*, I thought to myself. *Fog-dried fish is more like it.*

"Where do they live?"

"The Nomás fishing tribe lives there, in the cliffs where they've built their caves, just high enough above the water line to stay dry and low enough to be practical."

"I can't see any caves," Carter said.

"And that's the point. Just as we've disguised our homes in Santa Rosa to be invisible to outsiders, the fishing village is also hidden from view. During times like these, there's little fear that

Barca will be out looking. They don't seem to come out in the fog. Maybe they haven't developed a way to see through it yet."

Closer still, as we were spotted by villagers, people stood upright, acknowledging us with folded arms and a quick head bow before turning back to their work. We continued on to the edge of the beach. I spotted an older man come out from the cliff, probably from a cave. He waved both arms and walked toward us. I nudged Carter, and we both knelt down in the sand then prostrated ourselves in our traditional greeting when entering another tribe's camp.

"Praise and blessings, Ardon the Elder," I greeted the village leader, my friend and uncle, brother of my father. He was immediately joined by Opatama, another elder of the tribe.

"Praise and blessings, Marlon. Please, let me help you up." He reached out a hand to me, then to Carter. "We knew to expect you." He wasted no time on formalities after that simple greeting but went right to the point. "A spirit in the form of a young lady came to us yesterday evening to tell us to prepare certain things for you, that you'd be here with another." He nodded to Carter. "And that you'd need an outrigger to carry the two of you down the coast."

"Yes. That was the one called Tess. She is a friend to our people and has become a close friend to Ranza."

She is a powerful spirit."

"What do you mean 'spirit,' Ardon?" Carter said.

"Just what you might expect me to mean. *Spirit*—a spirit. Not physical but spiritual, a vision. We were at evening meal, sitting around the fire and eating, enjoying each other's company. Out from the flames came this young female spirit. She was there, and she was not really there, do you understand?"

Carter scowled. "I'm not sure I believe in such things, but I get what you're saying."

"You don't understand anything until you have seen it, experienced and questioned it.

"I do understand. You think you saw a spirit. Not surprised in all this fog."

"So, young man, you don't believe me? I'm not telling the truth?"

Carter softened a bit. "Ardon, I believe you saw what you say you saw, but there must be a logical explanation. Please describe her."

"Well, then," the old fisherman said, "she was a very pretty young woman, dressed all in white skins. Strange eyes, fiery hair, and an intense way about her. And she told us that she was from the Santa Rosa camp."

I was convinced. It sounded like Ardon was talking about Tess. "Did she tell you anything else?"

Ardon smiled, thought for a moment, then said, "No. That was everything. We did follow her instructions." He pointed to the bay where an outrigger with a removable small sail had been floated up onto the beach and was now slowly rocking with the soft waves of the rising tide. "We dug this out from the sand dune we'd covered it with, by the cliff over there," he said. He looked rather pleased with himself.

"Buried in the sand?" Carter asked.

I answered. "Yes, they do hide everything. The outriggers pose a particular problem if they're out on the beach when the fog lifts. Any Barcan Security team would easily see them, even from a distance. So they beach them up against that cliff wall then pile sand over them every time they use them."

"Seems like a lot of work. How often do you go out in these?"

"Every day. Out here we work for our living." Opatama fired a look at Carter that might be described as anger.

Ardon interrupted. "We also loaded some dried fish and water bags for you." He looked at Carter. "Now you might wonder why we did this, believing a stranger, especially a spirit. It's not so simple. First, we were quick to question her about you —" He gestured to me. "—and Lora and Ranza. She wasn't willing to tell us much, but she gave us enough detail about your quest that we decided to not take any chances. We got the boat ready, just in case." And," he added, "only a fool argues with a spirit." The last jab was directed at Carter.

"What was it she told you?" I asked.

"Only that your mission was of great importance to all Nomás. She wouldn't tell us more than that."

"And you took her at her word?" Carter asked.

"And what would it have served to deny her?" Opatama groused. "It doesn't take much to ready a canoe. Are you saying that we did wrong? When's the last time you were willing to ignore a spirit?" His smile had vanished.

I saw that Carter had been too abrupt with the old man and stepped in to calm things. "No, you did well. We're grateful for your help."

"So, then, tell me what the big quest is all about."

"My dear Uncle Ardon, I can't do that."

A wry smile came to Ardon's face. "As I suspected. Well, it was worth the try."

We embraced each other as two old friends would.

"My boy, and how is your lovely wife, Lora?"

"She's well, Uncle. She sends her love and wishes she were here to give it in person." I remembered Carter behind me. "Ardon, you have already met my friend Carter. He is to accompany me on this journey."

Carter stepped forward and extended a hand to Ardon. "I'm honored to meet you, Ardon."

"And I, you. Even though I must tell you both that although I respect the reason you, Carter, are on this journey with my nephew, in the event you are called on to carry out your purpose, it's my wish that you are seized with guilt and are unable to do what your oath calls for you to do." He flashed his most sarcastic smile.

"Uncle. Carter is here to help me retrieve something, a thing of great importance. He is an honorable man who will do what he is called on to do, assuming there is no compelling reason to hesitate. We all love the Nomás and will do whatever is in our ability to protect the tribe. And now, let's not talk about it any longer."

"As you say, nephew." He tried but wasn't able to hide his feelings about Carter. But he bowed to me, then to Carter, before turning to Opatama. "Opatama. Please join us," he said, reaching out to the old man.

I was thrilled to see the one who had taught me to navigate the waters of Bodega Bay as a child, the one who had always told me I just wasn't ready every time I begged to take the rigger out into the open ocean. Now this same man, Opatama, would be the one to give me directions and cautionary hints that would lead us eventually to the San Mateo shoreline.

If his expression was to be trusted, Carter obviously had a different view of the old man who hobbled alongside. Nevertheless, he was respectful.

"Hello, I'm Carter," he said, reaching his hand out.

"I'm not an idiot. I know exactly who and what you are," Opatama replied, ignoring the handshake offer.

We sat in a circle around a small fire that had heated some water. Ardon prepared and poured each of us a bowl of hot berry tea and offered a length of dried fish. It was tradition to conduct business over food. I took the fish, eager to taste the childhood memory. It always left me with a dry mouth, encouraging a taste of the sweet tea. As I raised the sweet-salty brew to my mouth, the sounds and sights of Bodega Bay took on fresh meaning as my senses recalled their own memories. It'd been a few years since I felt my taste buds come alive from the combination of the berry tea and the freshly heated dried fish.

Nothing like this feeling anywhere else in the world, as far as I know.

"Uncle, you know how to win me over. Dried fish and tea."

Carter didn't seem to like the salty, pungent aroma of the fish, but he was polite and simply declined the offer, claiming his stomach was a little upset from the five-hour horseback ride it took to get to the Bodega Bay village.

In every Nomás village, there was a minimal amount of authority, and each member of the tribe respected all others as equals. On the other hand, there was a natural tendency to honor certain members as having greater life experience. One was the tribal leader, in this case Ardon.

The next in line for special honors here in Bodega Bay was the navigator, Opatama. His experience and life spent navigating the coastal waters from Bodega Bay south to the rugged Half Moon Bay provided a valuable skill set for the tribe. Opatama could draw from memory the map of the coast, showing dangers to avoid, natural currents, and the best places for each variety of sea life that they might want to fish for. He could also tell where likely places were that Barcan Security might be monitoring, and other places to avoid. I wanted that information.

"Opatama, we're grateful for your knowledge. Have you been told where we need to go?"

"Yes, Marlon. Ardon has given me the understanding that you wish to travel under the old bridge in the hope that you can reach the San Mateo ruins without being discovered. Is that true?"

"Yes, that's about it."

"Then pay close attention to what I will show you."

He drew a long stick from under his tunic, swept the sand with his gnarled, bony foot to clear a space. The act of scraping sand deep enough exposed the moisture from the recent high tide. The wafting marine odors joined with the sounds of the waves that sent their rolling-thunder over the camp. I recalled that, as a child, I hardly ever noticed that the constant waves had become just another background sound.

Opatama smoothed the sand, then he began to draw. As the stick tracked through the wet, tiny-grained sand, it created a magical scraping sound, cutting a V-shaped line. I could tell Carter was fascinated at the tiny particles of damp sand that sparkled like glass as they tumbled from the top to the bottom of the furrow. They twinkled like little spirit lights, reflecting the sun that was just starting to peek through the fog.

"This is where we sit. As you see, we're at the southern tip of that place the ancestors named Bodega Bay. There is an inlet just down the coast. You can almost see it from here."

He pointed with his stick to the direction of where he was speaking. We all looked that way, but there was so much fog over the coastline south of the camp we wouldn't have been able to see it if it was fifty feet away. Carter looked as though he wanted to point this out to Opatama but didn't interrupt as the old man began writing in the sand again.

"You stay right of the inlet and follow the coastline very closely. There may be fog, and you wouldn't want to drift too far into the ocean."

Carter and I looked at each other as if to say, *Fog? Really?*

Without missing a beat, Opatama pointed to the far end of what he had drawn. "You see that the land makes a deep run to the west here. Be watchful, as it makes as sudden a turn back to the east, here."

He pointed to the natural breakwater at the end of the ancient point. The land suddenly seemed to race back, making a hard left turn, nearly heading back to the north.

"You'll know this is where you are when you see the old broken tower. It is said that this was a place of warning to ancient sailors, telling them of the danger of being too close to the shore. There must have been some light, or fire, warning ships away in the dense fog that we have come to know. You'll also know this is a place of danger for you. The Barcans often have Security watchers here to look for any that they call Outdwellers. If they are there, and they see you, your journey is over."

I remembered I'd heard them mention Outdwellers when they attacked my home.

"Thank you, Opatama."

"Listen carefully. Even though there may be evil there, you

must paddle close to the shoreline, no matter that it seems you could do well to go on a diagonal cut. There are often very strong ocean currents and waves that can drive you to the bottom of the sea in a moment. Stay up here—" He pointed inside the land curve. "—where the waves are never destructive, where the currents are slowest."

He continued his description of the sea journey, providing details and warnings as needed. It was just so much of the same thing, until he announced that at a certain point we would enter the most dangerous part of the trip: the crossing under the old bridge, where the ocean and the bay grabbed each other with force that could be a friend one moment and our worst enemy the next.

"You will do well to get inside the bay, well past the bridge structure, as soon as you can. First, the sea is stronger than the bay. Second, there are many eyes on the bridge."

"Eyes?" I asked.

"Oh, yes, the old bridge can see. Many times, when we tried to fish in the area of the bridge, we were only there but a short time before lights and sounds came from the bridge with loud explosions—things hitting our boats with such force that they tore holes in the wood. I am certain it was some form of gun. Hard to believe, though, was that there were no people manning the guns. They fired at us all by themselves. It means the bridge has a spirit. The old bridge could see us. This I know. And it told the evil ones about us. I know this because the two times we were seen by the bridge, only two of us in an outrigger, the next few days we were forced to stay in hiding here in Bodega Bay as the seal people came looking for us."

"'Seal people'?" I asked.

"Yes. They were clothed in shiny black skin, and their heads and faces were covered by tight coverings that made them look like the seals."

"Then," I asked, "how can we hope to make it to the San

Mateo ruins? If the bridge sees us, and if the guns are still there, we are stopped, one way or the other."

"You'll travel in darkness. Not in the night, but in the darkness of the fog. You'll wait right here, in this small cove," he said, pointing to the northernmost end of the bridge. "When you see a thickening of the fog, you head out under the bridge's cover. You will be able to see the base of the bridge, where the giant touches the earth, yet the fog will enshroud the bridge itself, mostly from the roadway up to the top of the towers. At that time, you can still see where you are going, but the bridge's eyes will be blinded. It will not see you. We have learned to fish in the fog, and we are no longer seen by the bridge. It is your best chance to reach the other side."

Opatama drew the lines of the bridge, then the outline of the bay. He showed where the San Francisco ruins began and ended, where the San Mateo ruins were situated. Then he drew what seemed a massive box that stretched from shore to shore and from the middle of the bay to the southernmost end. His face became expressionless.

"This," he said, pointing to the box, "is Barca City. At the closest right corner is the area known as the San Mateo Portal to Barca City. This is the location that your woman spirit said you will find what you seek. It is also the area that is usually very busy with Barca Security. I advise you to beach your boat well north of that area and walk carefully down to the location you are looking for. Stay deep in the tall tule plants."

"'Tule'?" Carter asked. "What is that?"

Ardon answered. "Some call them cattails. Tall weeds. They will hide you. Marlon knows them well."

I nodded, turned to Opatama, and smiled. "Opatama, I thank you for the great help you have given. Is there any other advice that you'd share?"

Opatama did not return the smile. "Yes," he said.

I waited for the rest of it. The old man just stared off to the south.

"Opatama?"

He turned to face me, I could tell that he was gravely concerned.

"Is there more?"

"Yes . . . go home . . . right now. No matter how much you believe in spirits, when the Barcans come, spirits won't save you."

CHAPTER THIRTEEN

Ranza
   Santa Rosa Nomás village
   Santa Rosa Ruins
   Cool temperatures and dark moonless night

TOTAL SILENCE INSIDE TOTAL DARKNESS. THERE WAS NO MOON to brighten the mood, no sounds to indicate I was awake, even alive. For all I knew, I could have been in another world, another dimension, a place that offered no sound or vision to welcome those who slept when they awakened. It was the most uncomfortable feeling I could imagine—it was what I always pictured death to be like.

It was hunt day. I knew I had to be dressed, loaded, and ready to go in a few minutes. The others were already waiting, if I guessed the time correctly. I wanted to hurry, to be there for the team. It was just that I hadn't been able to sleep well these past few days, with Dad being on his dangerous journey. And when I did fall asleep, nightmares filled my thoughts. Last night I'd had the worst. I dreamt that Carter, believing that Dad was about to be captured, killed him. Although I never screamed out loud, the screams my mind imagined in the nightmare actually woke me. I wasn't able to get back to sleep the rest of the night.

I crept silently out to the yard, washed myself at the well, and quickly returned home to change into hunting clothes. Once I'd dressed, leaving the hood down so others could see me easily, I strapped on my long knife and my sling and grabbed my quiver of arrows and bow before heading down to the family gathering room for breakfast.

Mom was already putting out the bread when she saw me.

"Good morning, Rannie."

"Hi, Mom. I didn't expect you to be up so early. What's the occasion?"

"I was just lying in bed thinking about your father and Carter. They've been gone for three days now. I was trying to imagine where they are, if they made it to San Francisco ruins yet, and what the Golden Gate looks like. We've heard of it since I was a child. The way it's described is magical. I hope your dad likes it." She sounded almost giddy, whimsical.

Yeah. I was awake too. But I was thinking about the dangerous trip they were on and wondering how I'd live if anything happened to him. "Mom, I think I want to stay home today. I can let the others go on the hunt. They can do it without me."

"Rannie, calm down. Your dad's very capable, and Carter will be there to help fight off any threats."

"But, Mom, I won't be able to focus on the hunt. I can't get him off my mind."

"And that's exactly why you need to go. Plus, you told Tess that she could go along. I know I'll feel better when Dad's home, but in the meantime, we have our responsibilities. The tribe will not go hungry because its number one hunter isn't on the hunt. And don't forget your new trainee, what's his name, is starting this morning."

"Lantana. Yeah, almost forgot about him."

I couldn't tell Mom I knew about the premonition she'd had

recently, the one she'd told Tess about. I was certain Tess had lied to me about the vision. I could tell by the way she looked at me when she tried to say that it didn't mean much of anything. I could see Tess was holding back, and the holding-back part was what was making me so afraid right now.

"I'd rather put together a team to meet Dad and Carter halfway when they return, just to make sure that he gets home alright. That would be good, Mom. Right?"

"No, dear. Your dad was definite that you're not to go. He said to tell you good luck on the hunt." Her look was final.

If I was being honest, I hadn't held out much hope that Mom wanted me to go chasing after Dad in the first place. I just figured I'd give it a try. When I saw Mom's face, and that look that told me I was about to go too far, I decided to drop it and move on with the hunt.

I kissed Mom's cheek before running out the door, grabbing my gear and gloves on the way to the horses.

"Aiyee, Ranza," came the greeting.

Aiyee," I responded. "Tooren, have you packed the horses and readied the tents?" I always asked, although I already knew the answer. Tooren never missed anything as he prepared the supplies for the hunt. He'd been my valued hunt partner for the past two years while I was in training, and I'd come to rely on him. I never had to worry; everything would just be done, and I knew it.

"Yes," he answered. "It's all ready. I can't wait for this hunt to begin." Tooren mounted his horse and came alongside the rest. "Where're we headed this time?"

"I've decided we should follow the old roadway toward Bodega Bay and see how far we can get before dark. We can camp there and send the animals out to find prey before we wake up tomorrow. Does everyone agree?" I didn't need their answer; it wasn't a democracy. Still, I wanted to make certain the team agreed at all times. There was nothing to be gained from disagreement within a hunting party. As one, they answered, "Aiyee!" and it was settled. I didn't feel the need to tell them why I wanted to head in that direction. I just had to be nearby in case Dad ran into any trouble on his own expedition.

"Has anyone seen Tess?"

"I'm right here," Tess said as she came in from behind Tooren.

Right behind Tess came the new hunter-in-training, Lantana. He was younger than the rest by a couple of years, it appeared, and looked to be pretty nervous.

I greeted him. "Welcome, Lantana. Everyone, this is the new guy I mentioned, Lantana." They all waved in greeting. Tooren opened the conversation.

"I think I've seen you before. They call you Tana, right?"

"Yeah," he replied. "But I prefer Lantana just the same."

"Then Lantana it is," I said. "So, tell us about your hunt experience."

"So, I have trained for the last half year on bow and spear. I'm a very good archer, and my prey never get past my spear. Other than that, what do you want to know?"

"Pretty full of yourself," Tooren snarled.

"Back up," I interrupted. "I remember how each of you were your first hunt. Give him some room, okay?"

Tooren nodded. "Yeah, okay. Can we just go now?"

I figured it would take a bit of time to open up to the new guy. That's just how it was.

"Aaaaoooooooo! Aaaaoooooooo!" I called the hunt animals to my side. Out of nowhere came Niamh, followed by Rouah the wolf, then Shree, who took her perch on the arm of Juvian, the falconer. When everyone was ready, I climbed on the back of Whisper, and the hunt was officially underway.

I was excited too. About the hunt, sure, but also to let Tess see how good we were at what we did. "You ready for this, Tess?"

I looked back to see her smiling. "I sure am, Ranza."

Riding alongside Juvian, I let him know we were all happy

that Shree was fully mended and ready to join the hunt. "Juvie, how is Shree's wing?"

"She's great now, Rannie. And thanks for giving her time to heal. The injury was bad enough that she might never have flown again if we'd tried to push her on it too soon. I'd have a tough time finding another hawk who could do what she does for us."

"Juvie, nice try at covering up your feelings. You and I know that if you lost her it would break your heart, like it would mine. We all care for her."

"Yeah, you're right. I feel like she's part of me, my friend, and not just a bird. She understands me, you know?"

"Yep. I do know. Like you are my friend."

For a moment, Juvie didn't respond, but he seemed to blush. Finally, after we'd ridden on a bit, he said, "You mean a lot to me, too, Rannie. I'm glad you got to be my lead hunter." Not waiting for an answer, he clucked to his horse and moved ahead in line, like he might have wanted to let that sink in before I answered.

Tess moved up beside me. "Juvian seems like a nice boy."

Trying to minimize what had happened, I just nodded. She pushed for more.

"He sure likes you. He almost giggled like a child when he told you how much you mean to him."

"No, he was just being respectful, that's all."

"Believe what you want, Ranza, but I can see you are also a bit nervous around him. You care for him, don't you?"

"Tess, stop," I protested. But she might have been right. I did feel all confused about Juvie. I felt something, but I had no idea what it was. Maybe I should just focus on Dad and the hunt for now and try to sort things with Juvie out later. "I have more important things to worry about at the moment."

Tess just smiled. I hated when she did that.

CHAPTER FOURTEEN

MARLON
14 May 2249
With Carter south of Bodega Bay village
Evening
Cold and dark with moderate fog

IN THE DARKNESS, THE SOUNDS OF THE OCEAN WERE VERY different—foreboding, an unearthly warning that some distance away lay a frightening, unknown monster, ready to grab the foolhardy who ventured too close by the ankles and drag them to a watery end. It was certain that the village's animals, pigs, horses, never stepped toward that sound after dark, except during a full moon when they could at least see how far the tide had slipped toward the village. They, by their nature, were sensible. But, I also noted, Carter was no ordinary animal.

"I'm gonna walk down to the water's edge to dip my feet and maybe see what kinds of critters come out at night—you know, crabs, turtles, things like that."

I raised an eyebrow. "Well, Carter, you might do that. I can describe the nighttime activity at the water's edge, or you can, as you say, *dip your feet*. You might want to know that the shoreline you saw during the daylight has probably moved a great deal since then. It may be much closer, or it may be much farther away. Only way to tell is to *dip your feet*. Problem is twofold. One, there are plenty of drop-offs very close to where the tide was earlier. These can be tricky either way, water filled or not. Two, this bay is known for some pretty treacherous currents when the tide shifts. Some will drag you out so far you can't possibly swim back to shore, they are that strong. Others might be deceptive, float you far to the south of where we are now and you wouldn't even know it. You'd end up having to walk a great distance to get back to where you started—that is, even if you know what direction to head. But, you're right. It would be fun to dip your feet. It's pretty dark out there, but you go ahead. I'll wait here, if you don't mind."

Carter didn't say another word, just made an about face and headed back to the fire where he sat on his blanket and resumed sipping his berry tea.

Opatama turned away to hide the slight grin that had crept onto his face. "Tell me, Carter. How did you come to select your career, if you don't mind my asking?"

Carter looked at the old man, trying to assess whether he was asking in earnest or just being an old smartass.

"Well, I've always enjoyed the combat sports. Ever since I was a kid and we had to learn to fight and battle, I just always won over all my friends. So, it made sense that I'd naturally become a community tracker when I was old enough."

"'Community tracker'? Is that what you're called? Why not just call yourselves assassins?"

Carter was ready.

"I know many think of us in that light—murderers. You have no idea the training and commitment we go through to become trackers, so it's probably easy for you to just put us in a bucket, throw some sand on us to keep us from getting our smell on the world. Call me whatever you wish. I'm used to it.

So you know, we are protectors of the innocent—ready to kill to keep people like Marlon, a good man but very gentle natured, from putting the entire tribe at risk. Would you rather send Marlon out on his own to defend against stragglers, lions, even Barcans, if it came to that? How long would he be able to keep from spilling his guts? What the hell do you know?"

Waves continued to roll their thunder onto the shore. Flames leapt from the old driftwood logs, and Carter continued to glare at Opatama.

"Carter." I broke the stalemate. "I'm sure you felt offended by what Opatama said. But I won't have you insulting a respected elder of this village. I've looked at Opatama as my revered friend all my life, and I can't have you speak to him like that."

"No, boy," Opatama said. "He is right to speak to me in any way he feels is justified. Just as I am right to speak to him as I feel, which I did. He's a grown man. If he can call himself a tracker, then that's his right. Just as it is my right to call him a murderer."

This was going downhill in a hurry. Ardon decided it was time to put the conversation on better terms.

"Marlon, I understand that you're on a journey that's very dangerous. Was there no one else to do this? Weren't there others who didn't have families—bachelors, widowers? It seems that if anything happens to you there would be at least two others who would lose a great deal. Father . . . husband. . . You're a farmer, not a warrior. Why you?"

I wasn't prepared with an answer. I'd asked myself this same question several times since we left home. *Why me?*

"Not sure I know what to say. I know I was called to this. I was given a vision. The dream told me exactly what I have to do, and I've verified that vision to my satisfaction. I trust in the wisdom of the council, and I accepted this vision as being real, a quest that had been handed to me by the Great One. Am I fearful? Of course I am. But there's no other choice, is there? I'm ready to go on this mission."

Carter and I watched as Ardon filled a long pipe with what was called the sacred plant. He handed it with formal gestures to Opatama, who accepted it, held it out in front of him, and said, "We offer to our friends this pipe, filled with cuttings from the sacred bush, a gift from our ancestors to us that we now freely offer to you." He took a burning shard from the fire and used it to light the leaves in the pipe, filling his lungs with a pungent aromatic smoke. He blew it out, lowered his eyes, passed the pipe to me, and said, "Please accept this sharing from us to you, our friend."

I accepted the offered pipe and smoked it in the same manner I'd seen Opatama do. Carter sensed the significance of this ritual, so he didn't refuse the smoke as he might have under less formal circumstances. Not understanding the principles of portion, he took in more than the usual amount of smoke in a single pull. Coughing uncontrollably, he passed it back to Opatama, who then passed it to me, again repeating the offering. I took it, smoked then passed it back to Opatama, who returned it to Ardon, who then inhaled his own share. We smoked as if we knew what we were doing, and most of us did. But not poor Carter.

The sound of the waves grew louder, more pronounced, hummed a rhythmic undertone to set the mood at a calming pace. The few stars we could see winked down on the village as if to say "We see you, we watch over you."

Carter obviously felt the effects of the smoke, turning one way and then the other, staring out into the darkness as though he heard or saw something. Perhaps the deepening call of the waves, as I did.

"What's happening?" he asked out loud to no one in particular.

Opatama quickly understood. "It is the sacred weed. You've never smoked this before?"

"No, I don't think I have. Am I insane? I see and hear things that are probably not there, only in my mind."

"These things that you see and hear. Are they as if the gods are among us?"

"Yes.

"Then," Opatama explained, "these things that you see and hear have always been here, present among the people. You've just never been aware of the magic of the Great Ones. You are not insane. In fact, the opposite is true. Your brain is no longer broken. The gods have opened it so they can speak to and through you. This is why we smoke the sacred plant."

Appearing to struggle to concentrate, Carter described his experiences. He spoke of the sounds of nature blending into a magnificent chorus of life, a symphony of heartbeats and breaths so joined that as they drifted through him he felt as if he were really out there embraced by the surface of the ocean—lifted and dropped, turned and propelled in all directions at the whim of the ocean gods. And he wasn't concerned. He told us he liked the feeling. He'd never been so happy, so much a part of the forces of life.

To me, he just sounded like a rambling fool.

Ardon acknowledged what Carter felt. "Carter," he said. "This is what people like your friend Marlon do, these farmers. They are the path through which the gods give to us these gifts. People like Marlon look at a tiny seed, like the sacred plant seed, and they see all of nature inside that tiny package. We look at it and we see a seed. That is if we see it at all. The gods speak to us through the hands and minds of farmers like Marlon. A master grower like he is can open our hearts to the Great Ones just by knowing which seeds are the pathway."

"Ummmmmmmm," Carter replied. His now fully "opened" mind was completely unable to form words. "Ummmmmmmm." It might have meant something to him, but not to the rest of us.

"I remember my own first time," I said. "It was pretty weird.

I had no idea how to control my thoughts. Uncomfortable. I'll take him in and let him sleep this off."

"Good idea," Ardon said. "We'll wait here for you."

"C'mon, Carter. Looks like it's time for a rest. Been a long day." I reached down and lifted Carter's arms up from behind, guiding him to his feet. With a lot of pushing and pulling, I managed to get him into the cave, helped him to sit on the sleep mat, covered him with a blanket, and started to leave.

"Greeb tervend, okay?"

I couldn't help but wonder what the hell Carter meant by that. I decided to ask in the morning. "Okay. I'll be back soon."

Carter had no answer to that, so I figured it would be fine to rejoin the elders at the fire. I walked out of the cave and back down to the sand. No secret that I was more than a little relieved Carter was out for the night. *That guy is way too intense.*

Feeling the sand sift through my toes as I walked back to the fire took me back to my childhood. Happy thoughts flooded my mind. I let the emotions course through me as the effects of the smoke lowered me into deep relaxation.

"How's the assassin doing?" Opatama just couldn't let go of it.

"He's out for the night. I wish you'd let up on him. He's really not a bad guy, just has an important job to do, and he's committed, from what I hear."

Ardon had been silent up to this point. This crossed the line for him.

"Marlon. Don't allow yourself to be fooled. Yes, he's a tracker, and his life is dedicated to protecting the members of the Nomás who might be at risk of harm from the outside. But what do you think he would do if you were captured by the Barcans? Think of it. The council has approved your journey to Barca. They're willing to support you in this quest, even though there's a very real possibility that you could be captured by Barcan forces. Do you follow?"

"Yes. I see."

"Then imagine that the council members, fearing your capture, acknowledged that if you were taken, it would be possible for Barcans to torture you until you were unable to hold back. Acknowledged that you might then tell the Barcans all about our existence—our locations, numbers. And that they sent Carter to make sure you could never do that." He paused, letting that sink in. "Would you call someone a good guy if they were planning to kill me? Or Opatama? Or even Ranza? Of course not. So, understand why we feel he is a bad spirit to be on guard against."

"Yes, Uncle. I get it. But I would know if the council gave Carter instructions to make sure I wouldn't be captured—maybe even to kill me. My own wife, Lora, is a respected member of the council."

"And what if they asked her to stay out of this decision for obvious reasons? Or worse, what if she agreed to it and was sworn to secrecy?"

"Bah. You know Lora. Not a chance of that."

"Just the same, Marlon, be careful."

Opatama handed me a fresh berry tea. "I'd be happy to take him out of the picture, if you asked. I don't hold this against him. There are many things we each must be prepared to do. Some of these are tasks that we find to our liking. Others are distasteful and often feared. But we never brag about the bad things. We simply do them, pray for guidance, then move on. I would pray for guidance to kill him, then the problem would be ended."

"Yeah, I see what you mean. All I can come up with is that if this is true, if he is sworn to kill me, he probably doesn't feel great about that responsibility. I've gotten to understand him. We talked about many things on the long ride here. I think the more I get to know him, the more I believe he is truly a good person."

Ardon was to the point. "That remains to be seen." Opatama nodded in agreement.

I bid them good night and walked to my cave. Once there, I found I couldn't easily sleep. I was haunted by the idea that Lora might have had to agree to allow a tracker along on my journey in case I needed to be silenced. I just couldn't bring my mind to believe that. More likely, I thought, she was excluded from the decision. But still, she'd never mentioned it to me. Maybe it had never happened and Ardon's theory was nothing more than the musings of an old man. Whatever, I found myself missing Lora and wishing I could be with her.

The thought I had been afraid to think came rushing in: *what if I never see her and Ranza again?* The idea nearly overwhelmed me. And what would that do to Ranza? What if I was captured? Would she blame herself for not coming with me? Would she hate me for being so selfish to allow myself, her dad, to be killed on the basis of a silly dream?

The many thoughts and possible scenarios played out in my mind until I thought of giving it all up and going home. Sleep must have overtaken fear, however, because I finally drifted from awakened fear to dream terror. It was a horrible night.

CHAPTER FIFTEEN

Marlon
15 May 2249
With Carter heading to Golden Gate
Coastal waters south of Bodega Bay village
Early morning
Cool and overcast with moderate fog—good protection

FOG BLENDED SO WELL WITH THE SURFACE OF THE OCEAN IT was hard for a land-locked person like Carter to figure out where fog stopped and ocean started. Sounds come from first one direction, then another—nonstop sounds Carter said he imagined were sea creatures checking us out, trying to decide if we were something good to eat.

He told me he guessed the brighter fog to our left indicated the direction of the sunrise. I told him he was right. It didn't really matter to him since I was operating the hand sail that steered the boat Ardon's people had given us for our trip, and Carter was desperate to reach the safety of dry land. Nothing else mattered to him at that moment. Not that it was totally blind fog, but there was enough of it to confuse even locals who ventured out into the bay this time of day. That only added to the concern that rapidly built in Carter.

"Marlon, you never said we would take this trip in a log." He hadn't been prepared for the tiny little dinghy they called an outrigger. It had a long pontoon, a hand-operated sail, some oars, and a few small, uncomfortable logs that we were expected to sit on. But it also had one other thing that overshadowed the rest. It had leaks. Not big ones, but enough to force us to bail out every so often.

These things almost never used to leak, I thought. *Must be really old and dry*.

"It's a good thing you grew up on the coast, Marlon. Your experience probably makes it possible for us to get where we need to go. If it was up to me, we'd be in serious trouble. And then we'd have been forced to take Opatama along to manage the navigation. He was getting pretty nasty toward the end of last night's meal, what with calling me an assassin—a murderer."

"Don't be so quick to judge. He's a respected and wise member of the tribe whose opinions are often sought. If Opatama cautions you, it would be stupid to ignore his words. As things stand now, I'm far more on alert than I was before his talks."

"If you say so. I just saw him as an old storyteller. You know how annoying they can be."

I let that go. Somebody like Carter, with his fixed ideas, might find it hard to understand the unusual ways of one like Opatama.

"How can you steer in this mess? What do you see that I don't?"

"Mostly," I replied, "I see we're approaching what looks like a man-made structure out at the end of a natural breakwater. The land seems to hook out to the right, the headlands rise so high above the sea, and there is a ramp-like path that leads down to a granite mesa that sits only slightly above the water."

"How in the world do you see that?" Carter had been bent down, bailing water.

"Well, if you look, you can see we sailed into a patch where the fog has somewhat lifted."

Directly ahead, nearly on top of us, we could see the details of a time long past. A time of ancestors. The ramp might have been an old stairway. I could make out a series of lines, tracing a raised path that mostly stepped down a long hill.

As I looked down below the mesa, I was surprised the land ended suddenly. In the distance there was more shoreline, but it was extremely far in from where we were floating.

"I think this is what Opatama warned us about. We need to head left around that tower and we should see the land again."

Soon we made the turn around the headland and headed back northeast where the ocean became calm, only a gently lapping series of waves that seemed to move the outrigger along at a steady pace. Before long, we were once again headed south, along the coastal headlands. There were no major problems for the next few hours as we made their way toward the San Francisco ruins, then on to the San Mateo Portal of Barca City.

"Marlon, what's that ahead?" Carter pointed toward a ghostly shadow that made occasional visits through the fog above us.

It was hard to make out as it was nearly completely enshrouded in fog, but my best guess was that it was some gigantic structure looming across the bay at about the same distant height as the headlands. This massive ghost stretched as far as we could see, and probably farther, as it yawned out away from us.

"I'm pretty sure that's the old bridge at the Golden Gate. Opatama said it would be here, where the 'ocean and the bay throw waves at each other.'" Looking over to the right, I saw what could fit that description, even though there wasn't anything golden about it, just a violent sea under a rusty old giant of a bridge.

Not far out from where we sat drifting in relatively calm

water, I could see that the waves were both beautiful and frightening. Frightening because the water actually boiled in front of our eyes. At that moment it was easy to believe there were giant sea creatures thrashing about just below the surface, their a random dance forming huge, narrow waves that crashed into each other with violent force.

"It looks like the timing is right for us to cross over to the San Francisco ruins," I told Carter. "The fog above us is still thick, so the bridge's eyes won't see us as we cross under. We'll need to stay to the left of the bridge line, to avoid the boiling water, but I think we can make it easily."

"I'm with you. You've done well so far, so keep going. I'll agree with whatever you say."

Every adventure seemed to have its moments—those opportunities to break the mood, lighten the tension. I saw this as one such moment.

"Keep your eyes well focused for any sign of Saltwater Dragons."

"Salt *what?*"

"Look closely over there, just under the old bridge. See how the water is boiling there, yet it's somewhat calmer here where we drift?"

Yeah. I do see that. What is it?"

"Saltwater Dragons."

"There's no such thing." His eyes told another story. They said he was *hoping* there was no such thing, but he wasn't sure.

"They go crazy when they find a group of seals. Must be what's happening there. I hope they don't smell us."

By now, Carter's head was spinning in all directions, his mouth open wide and his hands clutching his oar tightly as he strained to see a Saltwater Dragon.

When he'd turned fully away, I scooped up as much water as I could with my oar and splashed it all over Carter's back as I let out a loud cry. "Aiiieeee."

Carter screamed like a little child in the middle of a nightmare.

The sight of this big, tough tracker, clutching his oar, eyes popping out of his head, screaming like a kid was too much for me. I laughed so hard I nearly went overboard.

"You rotten leather fish." Carter sat down and tried to regain his composure.

"Sorry. I couldn't help it. We were just getting too serious. I wanted to lighten the mood."

"Well, you sure did that. In fact, I think it was pretty funny. By the way, Saltwater Dragons aren't . . ." He saw my grin. "Oh, never mind."

"Nope. Made them up."

That seemed to relax him.

We continued over to the far side of the bay entrance. I felt some apprehension as I realized the fog was starting to thin out, possibly opening the bridge's eyes to where it might see us. But eventually, we did make it to a secure little cove just before the base of the bridge, where we were able to rest, fill our empty bellies with dried fish and water, and look at the spectacular views, not the least of which was the rusty old bridge itself.

This was very definitely the most amazing man-made structure that either of us had ever seen. Although very old and likely in great need of repair, the bridge was breathtaking. It hung there, between the headlands of the north and the structures of the south, with no visible reason to stay up without crashing into the water below. Resting on a footing of land at either end, the bridge met a massive tower that held it up. Anchored below the water, towers stood like silent sentinels guarding over the suspended length of the structure. Between the towers, for nearly all of the length of the man-made monster, the bridge floated so far above the ocean that it was hard to understand the magic that kept it aloft.

Carter wasn't interested. He kept scanning the bridge for

signs of danger, back and forth, searching for what, we didn't know.

"Well." I said, "We need to go on. We still have some time before nightfall, and we should get as close as possible so we can find our target then get out early in the morning."

Using the hand sail to direct our travel, we finally made it to the other side, a natural beach where we made landfall, partially hidden from the feared bridge eyes that, no doubt, would give us away.

The first thing I noticed was that the cold had settled into our bones. But we couldn't risk a fire. We put the rigger between us and the water, hoping it would keep us at least a little protected from the cold breeze.

"Carter, I can't wait to get down there, grab the plant, and head home."

"Do you really think it'll be that easy?"

"Why? What do you mean?"

"Well, although you have an image in mind of how this flower will look, what if it's different? What if we have to search for it all day and we find the area is crawling with Barcan Security? It might be impossible to get the plant and get out quickly."

"Well, now that you've mentioned it, I'll tell you what I think we need to talk about." I paused, wanting the right words to come, wanting Carter to understand and agree.

"Carter, I know why you're here. I understand completely that we can't risk the safety of the entire tribe for one or two of us. In short, if I'm captured, you're to kill me, so I can't be tortured into telling them about the tribe. I think I've known this from the start, and I fully agree with it, up to a point." I paused to gather my thoughts. Carter made no attempt to contradict his purpose on this trip.

"As I'm led to believe, this flower's important to the tribe— so important that we shouldn't allow anything to prevent us from getting back home with it. So, here's what I'm thinking." I waited to be sure Carter was ready.

"Go on," he said.

"If you see me captured, and you're not yet discovered, I feel it best that you not give away your position by using whatever means you plan to kill me with."

"Knife," he said.

"What?"

"Knife. I'll simply throw a knife into your heart. I never miss."

"How you do it doesn't matter. What matters is that you'll be discovered. Then you'll also be captured, or you'll kill yourself, and there'll be no one left to carry the magical plant back to the tribe. Damn, man. This isn't about saving my skin. I give you my solemn oath that in the event I'm captured, I'll take my own life before I let them torture anything out of me. I swear this on my family. Think of this, Carter. If I were to give away tribal locations, I'd be telling these murderers how to go and kill my wife and daughter. How could I do that? Of course I'd take my own life to protect theirs."

Carter looked at me, expressionless. "I'll think about it."

That was probably all I could hope for.

CHAPTER SIXTEEN

MARLON
  16 May 2249
  With Carter near former Presidio area beach
  San Francisco Ruins
  Morning
  Foggy, still cold

I SLEPT ONLY HALF THE NIGHT. THE OTHER HALF I SPENT with my mind racing back and forth between Carter's knife and the way it might feel as he plunged it into my heart and the other real concern he raised last night: *What if we can't find the plant? Will this trip have been a total waste?*

I opened my eyes to a sight I hadn't thought to expect, but should have. The tide had gone out, and the 'rigger was now at least three lengths away from the water.

"Hey, Carter, wake up, sailor. We have a problem."

"Huh?"

Carter looked like something I might have dragged out of the bay—eyes squinting like they just wouldn't open, shoulders pulled up and in, trying to hold in as much heat as possible, and his pants dripping wet, as if— Well, I couldn't imagine.

"What happened there?" I asked, pointing to his wet lower extremities.

"What? Whatya mean? You think I pissed my pants? Oh, hell, no. I was closer to the water all night than you. Tide must have come in."

"Well, that must have been a very fast-changing tide. Look at the 'rigger." I pointed to the pretty far distance we were going to have to drag the boat to get it back into the water.

Carter finally fully opened his eyes to survey the problem. "Well, let me change into dry clothes, and we can drag that thing down to the bay and be on our way."

"That's fair."

After a brief wait while Carter changed his pants, we reloaded the canoe and began hefting it down to the bay. When we realized it was heavier than we had imagined, we decided to unload it and drag the empty craft close to the water before reloading and pushing it out just enough to make her float. This time, at least, Carter was smart enough to roll his pants up to his knees so they wouldn't get soaked when we had to wade in to jump into the hull.

Once underway, I waited long enough for Carter to settle in before I asked him about our talk of last night.

"Have you had time to consider what I suggested last night?" I didn't need to elaborate.

I could see he was looking at me as if wanting to read my thoughts. What I'd asked Carter to consider went against all of his training and beliefs. Against mine, too, for that matter.

"Yeah. I thought about it, but no decision yet. Time and situation will have to make the decision for me. I will say I am not totally closed to it. Now, don't ask again."

CHAPTER SEVENTEEN

President Hsieh
  16 May 2249
  Presidential terrace #2 overlooking San Francisco Ruins
  Barca City
  GPS: 37° 33' 57.884" N 122° 11' 38.62" W
  Outside Conditions: clear sky, no fog, temp 23.03
  Sustainability Factor: -19 (heavy viral saturation)
  Interior Conditions: all systems functioning at peak

I enjoyed my chair in the center of the terrace, with the expansive view of the San Francisco ruins below me. On my left, a small cocktail table held a private bottle of Hsieh-Livermore Merlot, one of the wines from grapes the Barcan farmers cultivated in our greenhouse platforms for leadership privilege. Only I had my own private stock—the finest grapes of each harvest held for my pleasure. I held a delicate plate under my chin to catch the crumbs of a flaky pastry I'd sampled from the selection on the server tray.

"Tom, come sit with me. Let's watch as our plan comes to life."

"*Your* plan, sir. You're the master planner. I'm just the one who gets to implement your brilliance." He turned down my offer of a glass of the wine, knowing that I only offered out of formality and to appear generous. He knew that if he accepted it, I'd would see it as a sign of insubordination.

The terrace was arranged for maximum effect. The entire population of Barca City would soon be looking in, and I wanted to display the most presidential image possible. It wasn't important that they like me—quite the contrary. It was crucial that they hate and fear me. The wall behind me had been staged for this purpose. Directly above and behind my head were portraits of all the past presidents of Barca Corporation. Their names and dates of their terms were printed directly below their faces. Where I was seated, behind and exactly left of my face on camera was the face of Wallyce Tilton, the first president of Barca, from 2090 to 2105. Her portrait would call to mind the Great Purge—the final solution to end government and begin corporate rule as it existed today. The stories of her ruthless destruction of all who opposed her were legendary, calling to mind the horror of a decade-long murdering spree that pretty much ended life as it was then. Wallyce Tilton had been the catalyst for world dominance. Every citizen knew her image only too well. She was a legend to be loathed. We made certain that her legacy of evil was drummed into every worker from their first formal education. The effect of seeing her portrait behind me would be chilling.

"Goh, we're ready." The holograph flashed acknowledgment, and studio lighting flooded both Tom Sands and me as cameras lit up and sound systems poured their background music into the ready space. Goh flashed twice, signaling it was time to start.

The all too familiar official voice of the electronic Barcan announcer simulation opened the proceedings. "Greetings to the people of Barca. This is a system-wide event. All workers are given permission to stop their work and be ready for what follows. All personnel and their families are ordered to pay close attention to this event." There was a momentary pause designed to give every citizen enough time to wrap up what they were doing and to focus their attention on the thousands of screens affixed everywhere in Barca City.

The cameras closed in as Goh signaled for me to begin.

"I'm sorry to tell you that one of our own, a valued employee in the Systems Testing Lab, known to the census as A37921, and known socially as A37, or Andy, has been found guilty of sedition against Barca Corporation for advocating an escape to the Out and plotting to live there without the benevolence of Barca. As you all know, that in itself is suicide. The penalty for this is, appropriately, exile to the very place he wanted to go: the Out, where he will be tracked while his body is infected by the many viral forces found there. He will be recorded as he dies a slow and frightening death. In short, we will give him what he wants: life, then death, in the Out.

"Now, let's look at the final events that led up to this harsh sentence." Screens all over Barca lit up with a close shot of a young man identified as Andy speaking with a man identified as J35/Jude.

"You want a drink?" asked Jude. "How about a coffee?"

"Sure, black's fine," said Andy.

Jude brought two cups and sat at the table opposite Andy. "So, another break today. You must be hitting on all four."

"Huh?" Andy didn't understand this phrase.

"Just an old saying that means that everything is working well. Don't know why it means that. I just heard it from my boss. Guess your job is going well. Mine is, too, so I get breaks all the time. I think the only thing that would be better is if we could break out of this fishbowl and live for ourselves."

"Yeah, me too," Andy responded. "I mean, I wouldn't really break out. I just wish we could be more independent. Wish we could make our own decisions, fend for ourselves, instead of always having to do what we're told. This sucks." He immediately regretted saying that. "Hey, I don't really mean that. I just get carried away sometimes, is all."

"Oh, no problem. I do it too. But I do dream about living on my own in the Out. You? Oh, this is yours." Jude handed Andy a slip of paper.

Andy put the paper into his back pocket without looking at it. "Yeah, I guess we all have that dream sometimes. Who wouldn't want to be in control of their own life? But it's just a daydream."

"Well, better get back to work. See ya next time, Andy."

The two of them shook hands and left for their workstations. The scene switched to Andy stepping into his workstation entry portico. The scanner clicked into action, followed by a rapid whirring sound, then a very loud alarm screamed as lights began to flash and the portico instantly sealed Andy within its security enclosure. Automatic lasers trained on him as he spun around wildly, looking for an exit, trying to escape before the guns fired and turned him into a pile of ashes.

From outside the enclosure, a voice: "A37921. You will stand at fast attention with your arms behind you. Any movement at this time will result in immediate execution. Do you understand?" Shaking heavily, Andy nodded that he did and complied.

Slowly, the portico enclosure revolved so that two armed guards could enter. They grabbed him roughly from either side, clamped his hands fast behind his back, and shoved him through the opening into the next room.

"Hey, what did I do?" he stammered.

Neither of them answered him. The guard on his left reached into Andy's back pocket and withdrew the folded paper that he had just put there in the break room.

"That's just the receipt for my coffee credits."

The guard turned toward the ceiling cameras as he carefully peeled away the top layer of the paper to reveal a handwritten note pasted underneath.

. . .

JUDE—

If you hate this place as much as we do, then join us. We are about to do something about it.

—Andy

"HEY, I DIDN'T WRITE THAT. THAT GUY JUDE GAVE IT to me."

The screen went momentarily blank, then Tom Sands and I returned to the screen.

"Tom, please tell our Barcan family what you learned after you interrogated the prisoner and the one known as Jude."

"Yes, sir. First, J35 told us under oath and electronic detection that he was returning the note to A37, who wrote it. It seems that Jude read it and decided he would not encourage such devious plans, so he gave it back. On deep interrogation, the prisoner, Andy, admitted that he had written the note after all and was trying to recruit Jude into his plan."

"Well done, and thank you, Tom. People of Barca, you have seen for yourselves. You will now see what happens to a well-treated citizen who seeks to overthrow the benevolent Barca Corporation. Security, carry out the sentence."

Screens shifted to the Palo Alto Portal. A long, vibrating noise accompanied the opening of the Portal, where the massive doors slowly revealed the wilderness outside of the Barca City Shell. Wildlife could be seen everywhere. Birds filled dead trees; wild dogs and feral cats gathered in packs as if to see the spectacle happening at the Barcan complex. At the base of the Portal lay a large pile of bones, left behind by previous exiles from Barca who were too afraid to venture far from the only home they had known their entire lives. They died desperately wishing they could just go back inside.

The irony wasn't lost on the viewing audience. Audible gasps were heard in the hallways. As the Portal gates opened wider, a rumbling sound filled the airlock chamber, a sound so loud that it forced Andy to cover his ears. The guards wore sealed helmets, so it didn't seem to bother them.

My voice rang out over the rumble.

"Prisoner A37921, you've been found guilty of sedition against the Corporation, and you have been sentenced to exile. Security, proceed."

As a unit, the eight guards surrounded Andy and used their electric prods to force him out through the gate and down the ramp to the earth below, where they zip-tied his wrist to a post, giving themselves enough time to return to the compound before he could work himself free and try to run back inside. Such desperation was always messy, and I had commanded that this exiling go without a hitch.

As the Portal gates rumbled closed, cameras zoomed in on the frightened face of Andy, trying madly to break the zip tie to free his arms. In the midst of the drama, I proclaimed in a booming voice, "Citizens of Barca, this is to be a reminder to you all. The benevolence of Barca Corporation knows no bounds —unless you seek to throw it off like a hated enemy. What you wish for will be granted you, just like our friend Andy." A final zoom to his panic-riddled face. "You will learn that it's always best to seek the good of all and to never strive for personal, selfish benefits."

Screens all over Barca went black.

Tom Sands waited for the signal that the cameras and sound were off. "Mr. President, that was brilliant."

"Yes, it was. Thank you, Tom."

"So, to satisfy my curiosity, sir, what was the outcome for Jude—J35?"

"Good question, Tom. As I'm certain you know, Barca always seeks to reward its citizens for their extra efforts."

"Of course, sir."

"We rewarded Mr. Jude with a week off in the paradise compound in Hawaii, all expenses paid. He boarded the first-class jet-copter flight this morning. I am sorry to say that for some reason, Jude used the opportunity to commit his own suicide. He opened the hatch and jumped to his death right before VTO sequence was finished and the craft was shifting to jet mode. Poor guy. He didn't survive the fall and died on impact with the bay."

Tom grinned and chuckled. "Too bad. I guess he won't be around to tell his story to anyone."

"Yes, too bad, Tom." I lit a cigar, leaned back in the recliner chair, put my feet up, and took a long, slow sip of the merlot.

CHAPTER EIGHTEEN

MARLON
  16 May 2249
  Heading south with Carter to San Mateo Ruins
  Bay waters, east of the Golden Gate
  Afternoon
  Cool and sunny—fog has lifted

PADDLING AWAY FROM THE MONSTER BRIDGE JUST BEHIND US, I was surprised to see the shoreline was relatively free of any buildings, at least down near the water. The fog was light on shore by now. Deeper inland, I could see an army of giant skeletons marching to sea—the ruined buildings were just taking shape through the mist. As the fog lifted, the ruins came to life —as much as ruins can live—and the spirits of those who used to inhabit them seemed to make their presence known in the sounds of the water lapping onshore, in the movement of birds who almost followed the fog line, and in the skeletal remains of a civilization long wasted and forgotten. It was frighteningly beautiful yet solemnly grotesque.

From here, it was possible to see more details of the bridge hanging above us. Carter looked back and pointed. Though it was far out and above, I could see the bridge was filled with countless old and rusted vehicles, whose occupants had likely been killed during the Purge. Some died in place, seated upright as if expecting to suddenly move forward. Others seemed to have tried to escape and had died lying in the middle of the roadway or hanging near the very edge of the bridge, possibly willing to jump just to get away from the firestorm on the surface. The bridge itself had decayed, leaving it drab, the color of clay. Once glorious, it now stood tattered and unwelcoming.

I looked to the south and was shaken by the largest city I had ever seen, bigger than I could have imagined—the San Francisco ruins. Onshore sat hundreds more abandoned, decaying vehicles, lined up in rows as if waiting for their owners to return and rescue them from oblivion. Just beyond these stood more skeletons of what were once large buildings. Like the inhabitants of a massive graveyard, they crumbled there, their steel bones posed as they were in life, their concrete and granite clothes dropped unceremoniously to the floor of the city in piles of rubble, where they had stayed for these many years. This was evidence of a murder. San Francisco—unashamed, naked, and dead, a rotted king holding sway over the island minions that dotted the great bay at his feet. Assassinated in his prime, left to decay, his once regal hills now no more than craters and dirt mounds peppered with partial building frames long since rusted, their limbs detached and fallen away.

At times, we were forced to skirt around submerged piles of rubble that extended out from the shore. The abandoned piers had become home for all manner of sea life. Seals, fish, and crabs all swam, slithered, and crawled about freely, as if unaware of any natural enemies. We were invading their homes, and they weren't even mindful of us.

"Hard to imagine what this must have looked like before the Purge."

Carter was dumbstruck. He didn't answer.

I tapped him on the arm. "Is this anything like you thought it would be?"

He shook his head.

At first, scanning the immense once-city, I fixed on an impression of darkness. There seemed to be nothing alive in this rotting place. San Francisco was little more than the withered mummies of ancient skyscrapers that promised to topple to the ground in honor of the next minor ground shake.

"Marlon. We're going to be pretty easy to spot if Barcans are searching for us. We should keep lookout for anything on land that's moving. We're close to Barca City, so there might be guards all over the place from here on."

"Yep. Let's hug the coastline as much as possible." I opened the small hand sail, rotating it until it billowed with the mild wind from the bay. Carter used his oar to control what direction we headed.

I kept scanning the bay waters for signs of trouble. "I think that must be the middle bridge. See how it looks like two bridges separated by that island? Hard to imagine anyone was ever safe crossing the water on that thing."

"Yeah. It's a mess. So, what's next, Marlon?"

"The old man said to hug the right coast here and ride it around to the south. That'll put us on a direct heading to Barca City. And remember, he made a strong point that we should put to shore well north of Barca City."

The breeze picked up a bit, moving us shoreward at a faster pace.

"Carter—look!" I pointed over his shoulder toward the opposite shore. "They must be mining for something over there. See how the hillsides are stepped, like they just stripped off a layer at a time."

We studied the massive equipment, the way these miners filled huge boxes on wheels then hauled the boxes to the south, offloading them into some building that belched an awful smoke into the sky.

"Marlon, pay attention. We're in the middle of the bay."

Turning my attention back to the bay, I let out an involuntary groan and froze in place. "What the fuck?"

Carter had also seen it.

A giant building, as big as the mountains, blocking everything in its path, rose up from the water to the sky. Trees and statues sprouted right out of the roofline. The building, far too large to be real, seemed to float on top of the water from shore to shore.

A platform for flying machines hung like an afterthought on one side while a massive dock rested on the other. Magnificent ships loaded and unloaded their cargo.

Adding a hint of magic to the scene, the whole structure was encased in what appeared to be a bubble.

Carter sucked in air.

Suddenly finding a monster right in front of me, I sprang to life. "Shit! We'd better get the hell out of here right now. I'm pretty sure we just found Barca City."

I folded the sail down in a hurry, not wanting it to be spotted, and we rowed ashore like two men possessed, making landfall just beyond an ancient flying-machine graveyard, where old rusted machines fell apart in pieces where they'd been left by their humans long ago. We grounded the boat and scrambled into the weeds. Carter was more than a little clumsy. His feet took him toward the shore but his face was turned away—unable to take his eyes off the huge bubble city that seemed ready to reach out and swallow us whole.

I also couldn't focus. It felt like the real world no longer existed, replaced by a new one that defied everything I had known all my life. Logic went out the window.

Carter voiced his amazement. "It floats on the water. But it's impossible to build anything on top of water. It stands as tall as it is wide and must be larger than the entire city of San Francisco might have been. *But it floats on water.*"

I was puzzled too. "If they capture me, how would I ever get out of that place? It doesn't seem to have doors. And if they capture us both, the question of killing me to protect our people becomes unnecessary—you'd have to kill yourself too. Not acceptable. Let's just find that plant and get out of here as fast as we can. Carter, you take care of the canoe. Lash it to a tree and cover it with branches. Stay with it so we can find it when we're ready to make a run for it. I think we should be glad for these tule weeds here. At least we have something to hide behind in case we need to."

Carter looked as if I was speaking another language.

"Tule, bulrushes, cattails. For the love of . . . Carter, do you not remember what Opatama and Ardon said? Have you never seen water edged by tules?" I grabbed a few and shook them to indicate what I was talking about.

"Not really. They're pretty thick, though. Whatever you call them, they should give us some good cover."

"I'm going to head down there and look for the flower." I pointed toward the right front corner of Barca City. "I'm hoping it'll find me so we can get out of here in no time."

"Hold it, Marlon. I need to stay close to you." His expression showed determination.

"Yeah, you go ahead and do that. Leave the damned canoe out in the open. No problem. Those Barcan Security guards will appreciate the help." I just kept walking. Either Carter would follow, one hand on his knife, or he would stay behind to hide the canoe. There was no time to stand there and argue. *Either he'll kill me, or he won't*

I headed right toward what was probably called a Portal, like the lion of my vision had described. It was easier than I thought, since the Barcans didn't seem to have any concern about leaving tracks wherever their feet landed. I often saw it back at home, and I could see it here—flattened ground cover, broken branches, what looks like burn marks where they might have launched those headless horse machines. They made it too easy.

It took a few minutes for my eyes to become accustomed to

the local vegetation, but I was soon able to make out what might be common local plants. From there it would just be a matter of looking for a plant that stood out from the rest—a nonregular plant, the odd one. I was pretty sure I would be able to spot it if I just looked for a plant that was on fire. That would be the strongest sign of all. But, though I covered a lot of ground quickly, no flaming plants popped to the forefront.

What started out to be a quick in-and-out mission soon became an ordeal pretty much like Carter had warned about. I climbed up hills, crossed crumbled roadways, searched inside and outside dangerous buildings that might fall in on top of me if I took a step in the wrong direction. I looked everywhere. No magic plants. And now the sun was fast dropping behind the hills above. I headed back to where I'd left Carter. As I turned the last corner toward the bay tules, I was startled to hear a low roar over my shoulder. I turned to face whatever it was that was tracking me.

It was the lion from my vision.

"Marlon. You have come as I asked. And now your people will be rewarded." He faded to a fine mist and then was gone. In his place stood the most beautiful red-orange flowering plant.

It wasn't so very different from other plants I'd seen before, except that it had a soft glow about it. I could see that a pile of ashes had built up underneath it, hinting that it might have recently ignited. I turned toward Carter, who had caught up to me.

"Do you see it? It's real. The magical plant is real."

Carter had started grinning as he saw how overwhelmed I was. His smile suddenly vanished as he dragged his hood over his head, pulled a knife out from under his hiding clothes, then dove down into the tule bushes near the canoe. I could no longer tell where he was. I waited for the inevitable, a knife to the heart. *Just don't miss, my friend*. But the knife never came.

"Don't move or you'll be killed on the spot," came the now-familiar mechanical sound of a Barcan voice. "Grab him and bind him. Jacobson, you and Rosser get that old boat thing over there and shoot some large holes in it so nobody else can use it. Leave it there for later recovery. District will want to get a good look at this."

"Sir," one replied. "There're two oars. Should we look for another Outdweller?"

"Yes. Thorough area search."

I couldn't see him in his hiding clothes, but I knew Carter was out there, making his way carefully out of the tules and heading away from the area. I was grateful for the breeze that moved the tall weeds, so his movement wouldn't give him away. It was important that he deliver the plant back to the Nomás. I only hoped that he'd be kind when telling Lora and Ranza what happened.

CHAPTER NINETEEN

MARLON
  16 May 2249
  Captured by Barcan Security near San Mateo Portal
  Barca City
  GPS: 37°33'57.884" N 122°11'38.62" W
  Outside Conditions: light fog, temp 16.67
  Sustainability Factor: -14 (viral saturation)
  Portal systems functioning normally—tracking chips recognized

"Drag his ass up here into the Portal, and make it quick. Let this one get away, and you'll be shoveling sand in Hayward for ten years."

I could hardly move after the beating these bastards had given me. One eye was closed, I was pretty sure my arm was broken, and who knows how much damage they'd done to my ribs. Those damn jackboots hurt like hell. I knew that was what they were called, since one of them had told the other to *"Shove that jackboot through his gut and out the other side."* I found out what he meant, the painful way.

I looked back to see if I could pick out Carter, but he was

either gone or well hidden. As I turned back, it seemed that they were going to just leave me here, up against a wall that was as tall as the Golden Gate headlands and covered in a mirrorlike glass.

"You expect me to climb that?"

No response.

"I'm glad we had this little chat."

Jackboot to the groin, and I was out. I came to in time to see the first twenty feet of the wall separate in the middle as we were pulled inside the City on some form of moving walkway. As soon as we were clear, the wall closed quickly behind us. The sound of the Portal closing in around me seemed final.

The walkway continued to move us along what must have been a very long walkway. Lights grew brighter along the way, and I had to squint hard to keep them from blinding me.

"Attention on deck!" one of the jackbooted monsters shouted, and the others jumped to a fully stiff standing pose, feet tight together, arms close by their sides, heads all pointed straight forward, unmoving. I was pulled roughly to my feet by what seemed to be two large men, who held me in a standing position while several others walked around me and poked me in several places until I cried out.

"Get your hands off me," I tried to yell, but it came our garbled due to my swollen face.

"Thought you said they spoke our language."

"Yes, sir. They do," one of them said. "Maybe his fall to the ground messed his face so bad he can't talk right."

The first one came close, put his face right up to the side of mine. I could see that he was clothed in what looked like a dress that ended halfway between his feet and his knees. It covered skin-tight pants and looked almost like what our women would wear to important rites, except the whole outfit was all black with gold trim, covering him all the way up to just under his chin, as if he wanted to keep the dirt from the rest of the world from contaminating him. I could hear him breathe.

"He fell? Is that what we call it now?" Then he spoke to me.

"I wouldn't want you to fall too hard. It could kill you."

I tried to break free to attack this man, but another jackboot to my groin put me out cold again. When I came to, I was strapped to some sort of tilted flatbed table, upright with my arms and legs splayed out as wide as they were meant to go. The man in the dress came up to me again.

"I am not a patient man, Outdweller. I will ask you some questions, only once. First, how many others are out there like you?" He waited.

I spit blood on his fancy dress. Without even a gesture, my legs were suddenly pulled farther apart. I screamed as pain ripped through me.

The dress-man spoke. "I am President Hsieh, leader of Barca City and the Barca Corporation. I intend to get all of the information I need from you before you die an excruciating death at the hands of my interrogators. If and when you tell me what I want to know, I will release you from the pain and give you a swift relief from the suffering. Until then, you will beg for the end."

He turned toward what appeared to be a ghost—what looked like a man, yet a man I could somehow partially see through. Dress-man spoke to it. "Goh. Have a clean uniform ready in my suite, and incinerate the one I have on after I remove it." He turned back to me. "Enjoy your pain, Outdweller." He walked to a doorway that opened without his touch, and then he was gone.

"My turn, Stinky." From the corner of the room, a large, scary bearded man walked toward me, holding out a strange device that was probably designed to cause someone intense pain. On one end it had heavy weights attached to a strap. At the other end of the strap sat a large, obviously very sharp, hook. My mind quickly turned to Lora and Ranza and our friends at home who would be at great risk if I were to give these monsters any information. I knew for certain at that moment: they would never get me to say anything to endanger my family.

Let's go, jerk, my mind screamed.

CHAPTER TWENTY

CARTER

Heading home to Santa Rosa

I HAD NO IDEA WHY I HESITATED. MY ENTIRE CAREER AS A tracker, a security provider sworn to protect the Nomás at all costs—now just a sham. The one time I'd been called on to perform my supreme duty, the first and probably last opportunity I had to show loyalty to the people of Nomás, and I'd failed miserably. I saw what they did to Marlon. And that was just for their own enjoyment. I could only imagine what they'll do when they want to get information out of him. I might have saved him from all that torture.

I failed the people, I failed Marlon, and I failed myself.

I searched frantically for the plant, the flaming flower, finding it close to where Marlon was taken. I grabbed it and, without thinking, pushed it deep into my pack.

I forced my brain to focus, knowing exactly what I had to do. *I have to get back to the tribe, or Marlon's sacrifice will mean nothing.* It was clear. The plant was everything. I had to get back and bring it to the tribe.

I've waited too long. The Security force will be back, and if I'm captured, all will be for nothing. I know in my heart this plant is magical and somehow important to our future. It might even be the Phoenix Flower of our tribal mythology. The Phoenix!

I fell to my knees, sobs welling up from my heaving chest.

This plant could change the world.

~

I WAITED THERE ALL NIGHT, AFRAID TO MOVE OR GIVE MYSELF away to the eyes of the City. It had to have eyes—it had found Marlon so easily, it must have told the Security forces where to look.

I slept on and off. At some point in the early morning, when the sky above the eastern shore began to glow faintly, I decided it was my last chance to get as far away as possible. I grabbed my bag, slung it over my shoulder, and headed north. I didn't notice that the hood from my hiding garment had fallen to the ground.

I didn't bother looking for the canoe, having heard the guns that they used to put holes in it. Instead, I decided to walk through the San Francisco ruins, hiding within the building remnants as much as possible to avoid detection. I had some training about using the direction of the sun, so unless it was hidden by the fog I could find my way back to the Golden Gate, cross the old bridge, then find my way to the Marin Nomás village I'd heard about. They might be able to provide a horse for the rest of my journey.

The walk through San Francisco was far more difficult than expected. The city must have been built on the highest hills they could find. I climbed up one monster of a rise and down to the next more times than I wanted to know. Direction was no problem—endurance was. My head buzzed, my heart pounded, and I just wanted to lie down and catch my breath.

Why in the hell would they build their homes on such hills?

The answer came as I reached the peak of one such hill and saw what looked like a giant storage building. It was filled with old-style vehicles.

The people of San Francisco didn't walk anywhere. They had machines to take them up and down these horrible hills.

These machines, lined up carefully in rows, were well protected from the elements. No sun, no rain, no wind. More than one hundred years, and they looked like they could still work.

Too bad I have no idea how to work them. I kept walking and cursing the hills of this hateful place.

Finally, I broke through a dense forest to where I could see the bridge. In reality, all I saw was the very tips of the two giant supports as they peeked through the fog; the huge bridge itself had seemingly disappeared into the white fog. The result was magical. A thick, almost solid, band of fluffy white foam stretched from where I stood all the way across the bay, resting on the far headlands like an ancient beard through which two sentinels poked their heads as they stood guard over the Golden Gate. This was man-made, but it somehow brought the Great Ones to mind—the gods of earth, sky, wind, and water. Each had had a hand in the painting of this picture.

As happens too often, fate chose the exact wrong time to test my endurance, ability, and survival skills. Out of nowhere, in the looming dark, an evil-looking pair of eyes reflected the first glimmer of sunset. At first I thought nothing of it, although I did still my movements. But then I realized: the eyes were focused on me, and they were headed my direction in a hurry. I had only a moment to wonder how whatever creature it was could see me before it became frighteningly clear that I had left part of my hunting clothes—the hood to my invisibility gear—somewhere back in San Mateo. I'd have to fight my way out of this problem.

What might have otherwise been a pet, a domestic dog,

grown larger than I had ever seen, meaner than could be expected, snarled darkly as it hunched down on very muscular legs, its teeth dripped lather from upward-curled lips. It was obviously making ready to enjoy a midday feast of human flesh—a delicacy not often found any longer, I was certain. I'd already pulled the knife from inside my waistband and now prepared to throw it into the heart of this frightening beast.

I knew that it was some form of a dog, but it was very different than I'd ever seen before. The animal's skin was without any fur, almost fog white, pulled taut over a meatless skull that held two blazing eyes above a mouth filled with blade-sharp teeth. Its frame was hunched, lower to the ground than its size would suggest, but every inch of it rippled with muscles. The dog stepped cautiously toward me, teeth bared and a low growl underscoring the menace in its eyes.

"*Stop*." What a feeble attempt to talk the beast out of attacking me.

The creature's response was a loud gurgling noise. No words, just sounds, as it launched toward my throat. The move was so sudden I had no time to throw my knife. As best I could, I lifted the tip of the blade upward and under the killer's ribs, driving it into the heart one instant before the teeth found my neck. Without even a whimper, it fell to the ground, dead. I'd hit my mark.

Wasting no time, I grabbed my knife by the hilt and pulled it out of the dead animal. Wiping the blood off on the dog's haunch, I pushed the blade back into its sheath in my waistband.

Better get moving. Might be more of these creatures around. I decided to keep my hand on the hilt, just in case.

I continued on my way, mostly downhill now that I'd reached the former military base above the Golden Gate Bridge. I'd seen the base from the water earlier that morning, and it gave me a landmark that guided me to the old bridge. I stepped onto the broken surface of the structure, ready for the trek of a lifetime, moving quietly and carefully through the dense fog that hid whatever dangerous things might be around. I tried to focus on what I'd seen the day before, heading south toward San Mateo. I couldn't help but recall the places where the bridge had crumbled—the sides no longer there to protect me from just falling over. The roadway was pocked with bomb-like craters and mountains of rusted debris. Then there were the eyes of the bridge to worry about. Would the fog protect me from the eyes?

This was the most difficult part of the journey. Although the bridge had looked very high up when we'd seen it from the water, it felt so much higher now, more frightening when I now had to walk from one end to the other. Worse than the height, many of the rusted vehicles were still occupied with what was left of their owners, some still seated where they died from corporate murder—poison gas, a hail of bullets, flames thrown from a fire vehicle, bombs . . . The road surface showed the ravages, with some craters open to the water below. Vehicles dangled halfway from the edge of the bridge in a macabre dance of death that would someday end with the vehicle, and its former owner, slipping noiselessly down to the bay.

At what might be the halfway point, I became aware of the unmistakable hum of drone engines racing toward me. I guessed the eyes of the bridge had detected my movement.

I can't be caught. No matter what, I have to get back to the tribe to tell them about the plant, or die trying.

My first instinct was to wedge my body under a rusted roadway barricade. Unless the drones had some form of magic, like life-detection scanners, I thought I might be okay. But no, "might" wasn't good enough. *I don't have the right to take any chances. Whatever I do, it has to be foolproof.*

Seeing my chance, I hopped over the side of the bridge structure and into what was surely a rickety repair-team carrier. Part of the carrier hung well under the bridge and gave enough room to hide from the drones. I squeezed into that tight space and waited for the flying machines to continue on across the bridge. I couldn't look away from the water below. Hanging so far above the bay, with nothing to grab onto in a fall, made a man imagine a frightening death. Moments turned into forever when your life was on the line.

I thought I must have been out there in the structure for an hour. In reality, it was not long at all before I heard the sound of the drones fading rapidly. Slowly, I pulled up out of the wedge I'd forced myself into and began to climb back onto the bridge itself.

It wasn't going to be as easy as it had been on the way down. I had to pull myself forward to the outer part of the rig, dangling out over the abyss, while simultaneously pulling upward toward the bridge surface—all while looking all around for any returning drones. It took all of my strength, but I did it. I was about to breathe a huge sigh of relief when I was startled to find myself facing a drone, not ten feet in front of my face, running in silent mode.

I couldn't help my instinctive reaction. But as I recoiled, I felt myself slip backward and begin to drop. Even as I realized the finality of my predicament, I was still amazed at the beauty of the bay and the shoreline below me. They would be the last things I ever saw.

Good that the view is beautiful.

But as I readied myself to die, to slam into the water below with such force as to kill me before I could drown, I was snagged in midair by something that grabbed me in a hard, painful grip. I hung, suspended in the air, well above the water. Struggling, I twisted my body enough to see above me to the bridge. I was amazed to see I had only fallen one or two body lengths. Now fully able to see around, I realized that the bridge had some form of netting below it—not rope, like a fishing net, but some form of metal wire or something like it. It was still intact in several places, and I'd happened to fall into this barricade. Now, the problem would be was I still strong enough to pull myself up and onto the bridge?

Let's find out, Carter.

It took only one single failed attempt to learn I was too broken and weak to get back up to the bridge.

Perhaps if I wait . . .

CHAPTER TWENTY-ONE

RANZA
 17 May 2249
 With Tess and the hunt team, three days into the hunt
 Old Bodega Road—halfway between Santa Rosa Ruins and Bodega Bay
 Cool temperature and bright, sunlit sky

I DRIFTED AWAKE FROM A PEACEFUL DREAM IN WHICH I WAS flying alongside Juvian's hawk, Shree, our wings beating a soft wave into the air around us as we circled high above the encampment. Suddenly, I felt a wet tongue on my cheek and a paw scratching at my shoulder; it was unrelenting. Opening my eyes, I found myself eyeball to eyeball with a huge silver wolf. The wolf's eyes glowed an eerie gold as if there were candles behind them.

"Rouah! Why'd you wake me? I was just learning to fly." Without warning, I jumped up and pounced on Rouah, turning him onto his own back and pinning him down while I teased a few bites to his cheeks.

"Glad you could make it this morning."

I looked up to find Tooren standing over me, holding my hiding clothes in his left hand and my bow in his right.

"Why don't we see about bringing some meat back to the tribe?" he said.

"Am I late?"

"Not yet, but hurry up or you will be. We have a big day ahead of us. Shree found a huge sounder of wild boar about three miles from here. She indicated at least a dozen of them are just waiting to be hunted by the best team of hunters in the Nomás world.

A dozen? I wondered, understanding that Shree had used a specific flight pattern—a series of up and down movements—to convey the number of prey. "Sounds like a competition to me. What's the bet?"

Even though I'd said this in a whisper, the others heard it. Right away, the entire team, including Tess, appeared beside us, ready to get in on the competition. Tooren came up with the bet.

"I have it: the winner doesn't have to do any meat packing after the hunt. He can just sit on his rump while all the rest of you clean and pack the meat, load it on the sled, and bury the remains."

"It sounds like you've already determined the winner. Don't think I missed the 'he' and 'his' statements. What if the winner's not a he but a she?" I loved to tease this bunch. They knew I was right too. There wasn't a hunter anywhere in Nomás who could outhunt me.

Lantana, the new kid, jumped in. "What are we betting on, Ranza?"

The winner'll be the one who takes the most wild boars today. It's a simple bet. If you want to win, then simply drop more boars than anyone else? Think you can do that?" I winked at the others. "Show us what you're made of, puppy. This is your first big hunt. Let's make it unforgettable."

He was just cocky enough to fall for the teasing. "Okay, I'm in. You think you all know everything about hunting and I don't know anything. I've taken plenty of boars on my hunts. I accept."

It was a sucker's bet. "C'mon, new boy, you don't have to prove anything." I tried to let him off the hook. "These guys are pretty good, so nobody'll think less of you if you pass on the competition first time out."

This seemed to bother him even more. "I said I'm in. Let's get to it. Or are you afraid?"

Tooren broke the tension. "I'm afraid. I'm afraid we won't have enough energy to hunt anything if we don't have our morning meal." He handed out some jerky and water to each of us before mounting his horse.

I bit off a chew of jerky, jumped on Whisper's back, clicked my tongue as I pulled left on the reins, and trotted off westward. "You can all stand around yapping like a pack of wolf pups. I'm going to get some boars." Whisper and I broke into a trot and headed off down the trail. The hunt animals followed without being told to.

THAT DAY, AS EXPECTED, I WON THE LUXURY OF SITTING ON A large flat rock and sipping berry tea from a goat-skin bag while the others first cleaned, then prepared the boars for packing and transporting back home. I watched as Tooren skillfully dressed and packed a large boar and stifled a chuckle as Lantana struggled with his first boar for more than triple the time Tooren did. His animal was eventually cleaned and ready to pack, but it looked pretty beat up, the result of a dull blade in the hands of an unskilled hunter.

"Are you finished flogging that poor animal yet, or should I begin to set up camp here so we can stay overnight?"

Lantana kept his eyes down, pretending that he didn't hear

me. His embarrassment was overwhelming. Tooren saw what was happening.

"Hey, he did kill more than anyone else except you. He just needs some practice in butchery, that's all."

I was enjoying that Tooren was defending the new kid he had made fun of earlier. *He listened*, I thought.

"Yes," I agreed. "He did kill more than you others. But it's not enough to have a steady hand and sharp vision. We also need to be prepared to do the tough work that follows. Our job is to feed the tribe. That includes making their meat ready so our families can cook it without having to spend hours butchering the catch."

"I know," said Lantana. He was almost too quiet to hear. "I'm fine with taking life from a distance. No problem. I can bring them down with the best. It's just when it gets so up close and I have to look at their faces while I . . . Well, you know, I'm just not so good at that." He looked back down to the ground.

I sat beside him and placed my hand on his shoulder, comforting him, to let him know that he was one of us. I understood my own teasing had just added to Lantana's discomfort. *Not the sign of a great leader*, I thought. *He needs to feel welcome. I need to work on my team-building skills, and I need to start right away.*

"Yeah, I do know. We all go through this. Any hunter who tries to pretend this isn't the hardest part of the process of becoming a hunter in the first place . . . Well, he's not being truthful. When I struggled with this, my leader sat with me. He explained that this part of what we do is not only necessary for the tribe, it's necessary for the animal we've just killed.

"Think of this. When we take a life, it's for a purpose—to provide food for the tribe. There's no other reason. If we just kill and we don't finish, if we simply kill and leave the animal lying there for others to finish, then we're not hunters, we're killers. There's a great difference. This difficult part—cleaning the animal —is how we honor the animal for its sacrifice. We show the animal that we're thankful. We are saying that we're not killing without reason; we're fulfilling our part in the life cycle. Yes, it's hard, but it's our obligation to our tribe and to all living things."

Tess must have liked this. "You should believe her, Lantana. Ranza is a great leader. Taking the life of a wild beast is never easy, yet it is necessary and part of the way of the world."

He took this in quietly. At last, he looked at me and spoke softly, with total conviction. "Yeah, but I hate to do it." He looked back down and focused on the work at hand.

"Well, that went well." Tooren was loading his packs onto the horses. "You're such a great teacher, Ranza." Laughing, he began to load my horse, too, with several packs of fresh boar.

When the last pack was loaded and the area was cleaned to looked as it did before we got there, we mounted and headed back home. Along the trail, I kept a lookout, half expecting to bump into Dad on his way back from the trip to the coastline. After a half day of no sign of him, I began to worry, enough to ask the team to keep lookout for him. It worried me that we hadn't seen any sign of Dad or Carter, either their tracks out to the ocean, or coming back on their return. I was certain that he wouldn't stray far from the trail. It just wasn't his way to do this.

The more I thought, the more scared I got. He could have been back by now.

Juvian tried to help. "Maybe I can send Shree up for a look around. If he's out there, she'll find him."

"Good idea. Go ahead. We can stop here to give the horses a water break."

While the rest led the horses to the water, Juvian spoke softly to his hawk. "Shree. Marlon . . . find."

He pulled the leather hood from the bird's eyes, allowing him a moment to adjust before sending him aloft. Shree climbed quickly, very high above us, and began to fly around in slow, ever-widening circles. Juvie kept his eyes fixed on the bird for a sign that he had spotted anything that might be Dad. There was no such communication.

"Shree hasn't found anything. No sign of your father. Could he have returned home already?"

"No. He'd have passed us. Even if I'd missed him, the animals, especially Niamh, would've put out the alert. I'm certain he is out there. Maybe he was under a tree and couldn't be seen from the air. Can you send Shree up again?" Although I knew Dad would return when he was finished and not in some made-up timeframe that I decided on, I worried more with the passing of time.

"Shree. Marlon . . . find."

The bird again took to the sky, repeating the pattern, calling back in his shrill *skree* every so often to tell them that although he was searching every inch, there was no sign of Marlon. After a half hour, Juvie whistled him back to the perch, and re-covered his eyes.

I turned away from the group, hoping that none of them saw the tears that began to fill my eyes. The rock I sat on felt rough, the sun began to burn my face, and the thoughts of Dad in trouble overcame me. Tess must have known what I was feeling. She joined me, and we just sat there quietly for a while.

"I wish I could say things that would take away the fear you're feeling. That might be comforting, but it wouldn't be real. No one knows what'll happen from one moment to the next. For me to tell that your dad will be fine would be something I just made up. I really don't know, and you don't know where he is. But I know that I care about you. So, if you're in pain, I want to be here to share your pain. Maybe if I share it, it'll somehow lessen it for you."

Although I was more scared by Tess's words of comfort, I reached for her to hold her close, wanting to let Tess know I was grateful. Our bond was becoming more like that of sisters. But the moment I touched her, fire and ice coursed through my body. *It feels as though she is me, and I am her,* I thought, *reaching out to myself—touching my own shoulder, arm, face.* I was shocked, but I didn't back away. Tess saw my reaction.

"You felt it, didn't you?"

She knows. "Yes. It was like we were one person. I've never felt such a feeling. What's it mean?"

"Our spirits joined as one for that moment. It's a way to share pain and to share strength. I felt your pain, and I shared my strength with you. This will come in handy soon."

I wanted to know more—this was somehow not real. I tried to form the words, but Tooren broke the mood.

"Are you ready to head back?" He'd brought the horses around.

We mounted and went back to the trail. As we rode, I kept glancing at Tess, trying to understand what just happened.

"Don't worry, Ranza. He'll show up soon." Tooren thought my silence meant I was worrying about my dad. In any case, he wasn't a skilled liar.

"Thanks. Well, maybe he decided to take another route. Maybe he went north, looking for whatever he's out there searching for, and he's returning or has returned by the northern route."

I lied too. I knew exactly where they had gone.

"Yeah. Maybe that's it," Tooren agreed.

The rest of the ride home was painfully quiet. I thought about Dad, about Tess, and about my frightening vision. Above all, I worried that I was losing my confidence. I was never one to feel weak, or to even show that I was afraid—ever. This felt so different. I was scared about Dad, confused about Tess, and frustrated that I'd let Dad go without me.

Bad as I felt, I wasn't about to share my private pain and fears with others. These were weaknesses that were best left inside. My ability to mask pain served me well, most of the time. Mom never liked it. She compared it to the same instincts that drove wounded animals to put up a false front in the wild. After all, an injured animal didn't usually fight as well as a healthy one. Most wild animals would do whatever they could to mask any weaknesses. If it was too hard, they'd usually go off alone and hide, hoping to survive long enough to become strong again. I always had this instinct. Where other children chose to run to their parents for comfort, I'd never let on to my fears, most of the time.

Right now, I just wanted to run and hide until my dad showed up. But I couldn't. I wasn't yet a wild animal.

RANZA
With Tess and the hunt team, pack horses laden with venison
Approaching Santa Rosa Nomás village from the west
Late afternoon, sun setting behind them

"WARMEST WELCOME BACK TO OUR HUNTERS, AND WE THANK you for the abundance of food that you brought home to us, your tribe." It was the council, performing the gratitude welcome that was reserved for those hunts that were more successful than usual. They could see, as we approached the village, that we'd filled every pack horse and had even had enough to drag behind on a litter.

I nodded for Tooren to do the honors.

"And we thank you, our village, for the honor of serving you." He bowed his head toward the council. The rest of us followed suit. Tess watched the ritual closely.

"You must get a laugh out of our strange traditions," I said. "I sometimes think about how we might look to outsiders. Pretty odd, huh?"

"No, I don't see it as odd. Do you remember how I greeted you the first time we met? I offered a similar bow, even though you tried to kill me." Laughing, she bumped her horse into Whisper. "And to make it worse, you said I look like a wild boar."

"No, I didn't mean that. You were a boar. I mean you changed. Oh, you know what I mean."

Tess smiled. It felt warm, from the heart. I started to feel good for the first time in two days. "Thanks for being my friend. I'm starting to feel a little better. It's just even though I know Dad'll be okay, I worry. He's not the fighter type. I hope Carter will be able to keep him safe."

Tess nodded.

"Welcome home, Rannie."

"Hi, Mom. Good to be back. Any word from Dad yet?"

"No. Nothing yet. I'm getting a meal ready for you and the hunt team. Why don't you and Tess let the others know, then come back and clean up, and we can talk about the hunt while we eat?"

"Sounds good. C'mon, Tess."

We headed out to the corral to get the others. However, as we walked over to where the horses should be tied, their places stood empty. No hunters, no horses, just Tess and me. The corral felt cold, ghostly, abandoned.

Confused, I commented to Tess how strange this was. But she seemed to be lost in her thoughts, looking off toward the trees at the edge of the corral, not saying anything, just staring. I tried to see what she was looking at, but everything was a blur.

Then, like the sunrise over the hills on a bright morning, things became clearer, and I saw him—the lion. This time the giant hawk was perched on his head. As soon as I saw him, the hawk lifted his wings and flew away. The lion looked into my eyes.

"They have him. He left a message for you. You are to find the message and do what he says."

The lion faded to nothing. I screamed. Tess grabbed me as I fell to the ground.

CHAPTER TWENTY-TWO

MARLON
   18 May 2249
   Prisoner of Barca Corporation
   Barcan BioSector
   Barca City
   Lights—harsh, blinding
   Sounds—loud, metallic, dangerous

I COULDN'T SEE PAST MY NOSE, WHICH BY NOW FELT TWICE ITS normal size and pushed sharply toward my left ear. It wouldn't matter if I could see, I suspected, because the lights shining in my face were so bright, so hot, that I was probably going to go blind in a short time because somehow my eyes wouldn't close. I wasn't sure why, but I also couldn't move either of my arms. They were pulled behind me in a painful twisting arc that made me believe one or both of them had to be broken. I wasn't certain, though.

The lights dimmed—all sounds stopped. There was something going on over my left shoulder, like people moving around without wanting to make any noise. They failed at that.

"He smells terrible."

It was a male voice, sounding as if my odor offended his presence.

"Take a deep whiff," I shouted, except the shout was more like a raspy whisper.

"Give him a reason to be respectful."

One of them touched the back of my neck with a shiny stick. My entire body was seized in a painful grip that felt like it came from inside. I could hear a mournful wailing sound that I realized came from my own throat. I could no more stop the scream than I could make them stop doing what caused the pain. It went on for a long time. My brain screamed, *Please let me die*.

"That's enough. He'll think hard before he opens his mouth again."

"Yes, Mr. President."

"Have the doctors look him over and make sure he'll be able to withstand what we're about to do to him. And make sure you have the guards clean him up before I come back."

"Yes, sir."

"Goh, activate."

I realized they must have damaged my brain, because as soon as the one called President, the one wearing what looked like a dress, spoke, the ghost appeared out of nothing. He wasn't really a man. This time I was sure I could see through him. Not like a window, but more like the fog. It was certain the ghost man was there in the room with us, but I guessed I could put my hands around the see-through throat and they would just pass right through.

"Ready, Mr. President." The ghost spoke.

"Keep a communication system close by to record everything that happens here for the next couple of days."

"Yes, sir."

In a flash, the dress-man President put his face next to mine, very close. I could feel his breath in my ear. He spoke in a deep, growling whisper, slowly and pointedly. "You will talk, Outdweller, and then you will die. Sorry, but I can't stay for the fun that is coming."

He left through a door that wasn't there before he approached it. This man could actually walk through walls.

"Aaaagh!"

Two black-uniformed thugs had grabbed my arms, clicked my wrists out of some locking device that held them, pulled me forward while keeping my arms twisted behind my back, then jammed what felt like the bones inside my shoulders back into place. My arms were suddenly no longer broken.

"Dislocation, Stinky. Works every time."

I had no idea what he meant. I just knew I was in intense pain and was being march-dragged across the room and around a corner, where a powerful jet of water slammed me into the wall. When I was drenched, they began to spray me down with some horrible-smelling oil that foamed when it touched my skin. Finally, they stopped, and one of them approached me with a long knife.

"Turn around, Stinky."

I hesitated. The guard grabbed my shoulders and dug his fingers roughly into the flesh, producing a pain that I'd never imagined. He flashed the knife past my eyes and down to my midsection. I waited for the end—the cutting. But it didn't come. Looking down, I saw the only thing the guard had sliced was my pants, leaving me naked and exposed.

"You didn't think I was going to actually undress you, did you, Stinky? I wouldn't touch you on a bet," he said, motioning to another guard at the hose. Another round with the water and oil, and I guessed they were satisfied that I was clean enough for their sensitivities.

"If you don't mind, I'd like some kind of covering. I wouldn't want any of you creeps to get too excited seeing me like this."

The attack came so fast I didn't see the knife as the guard pressed it against my throat. The terrible smell of something like decaying flesh poured from the guard's rotten teeth into my nose, making my gag reflex kick into high gear.

"And if you don't mind, you'd better start respecting your new home and those of us who would love nothing more than to push a little harder and slice right through that scrawny neck of yours."

I held the urge to shoot another smart-assed quip at him. I couldn't be certain he wouldn't just cut my throat.

"There's a uniform on the chair in the other room. Put it on and sit your ass down in the chair. And do it in a hurry. I don't like to wait." He spat at the floor drain, but missed. Wiping his mouth on his black sleeve left a streak from his elbow to his wrist.

I stumbled into the next room and picked up the uniform. The act of bringing my hands out from behind my back sent stabbing pain through my shoulders. Hooking my thumb through the waistband, it took a while to position the pants so I could push one foot at a time into the leg holes. I finally made it to where I could use both thumbs to pull the pants all the way on. Then, fighting the urge to scream, I forced my hands to somehow tighten the waist string and tie it in a clumsy knot. So much for easy things to do. The shirt glared at me, daring me to just try to put it on. It was a pull-on with no buttons.

I started by draping it partially open over the back of the chair. Things went bad after I'd worked first my hands into the sleeves, then my head into the neck opening. I found myself doubled over, jerking my head up and down in a desperate effort to drag the shirt over my shoulders. It all stopped halfway on, at which point I realized I wouldn't be able to finish the deed. I was stuck, leaning over, half in, half out of a shirt and no way to make it all work.

"Hey, Stinky. Need some help?"

Oh, no. this is even worse.

"Uh, no, thanks. I'm just practicing my technique."

He didn't ask a second time. He just walked over, grabbed

the neckband of the shirt, pulled me hard into an upright position, then roughly yanked the shirt on while I whimpered.

"Take him to the medical unit."

"Yes, sir." A guard locked my hands behind me again, reminding me of the pain in my shoulders, then dragged me out into the bright corridor.

As my eyes adjusted, I could see that the corridor only had walls on one side—clearly the inner side as the other was completely open to the bay far below, showing the bridges and beyond. I had to suck in my breath and step carefully or I might go over the edge of the walkway and fall, screaming, all the way down to the water below.

We came to a large doorway marked as *Medical Unit N18*. The guard pressed her ID card, hanging from her chest on a retractable string device, against the reader by the door. Nothing happened. She tried again. Same non-result.

"Stand right here," she commanded as she shoved me toward the bay, so far below. I thought quickly, *This is the opportunity to fulfill my oath to my people.* I jumped toward the edge and let out a gasp.

But I didn't fall. Instead, I slammed against the open abyss. My body hit and bounced back. I must have looked like an idiot. It wasn't open air at all.

"Are you serious? Haven't you seen an E-scape before? No?" She knocked hard on the middle of the bay below. Nothing moved. "It's artificial, like a hologram. Like Goh—the president's holographic assistant."

"You mean the ghost?"

"'Ghost'?" She laughed out loud. "That wasn't a ghost. His name is Goh. He is a hologram, like the view here, but more. Goh is an intelligent computer system. You know, computers that learn, just like we do."

She was speaking a new language as far as I was concerned.

She must have realized that I would never understand what she was saying, so she turned and knocked on the door—hard and fast—three raps. A voice commanded her to identify herself. She held her ID card up to a large device, and the door clicked and opened. We went inside.

"This is the prisoner President Hsieh has a special order in for." She directed this to the person at the main desk.

"We're expecting him." The man nodded, and two large men came out and grabbed my forearms. They led me to a small ante-room and immediately cut the clothes right off me again.

"You Barcans have a thing for cutting clothes off of people. Don't you think it's easier to just take them off?"

No reaction. They led me into what could best be described as the inside of an eggshell. Everything was pure white—no decorations, no furniture, no windows. I was made to stand in the center of the room and told to not move. Everyone left the room, and the lights started to dim. A small red dot of light opened above, shining a red circle on the floor around me that moved in tiny steps until whoever was guiding it was satisfied I was in the very center of the ring. At that instant, a clear tube-like device rose up from the floor, completely encircling me from head to toe. The tube lifted off the floor, suspending me in the very center of the room. All lights went out. Just as quickly as the room went dark, a series of brightly lit red lines began to trace me from all directions at once.

This was not light like I was familiar with—fires, torches, even the regular bright Barcan room lights. These were like arrows of light, growing and shrinking in length, drawing exact edges around my hands, fingers, body, as if some unseen artists were outlining every bit of my body.

The lights stopped all at once, leaving the room dark again except for the traces of color that my eyes seemed to be replay-ing. I felt the tube lower to the floor and soon found I was standing once again as the tube disappeared into the floor and the room lights came on.

An unseen door opened, and the guards reentered the room.

"Time to see your new home, for however long you're with

us. Just a hint: don't start making long-term arrangements. You won't be here long enough."

~

PRESIDENT HSIEH
   Office of the president
   Barca City
   GPS: 37° 33' 57.884" N 122° 11' 38.62" W
   Outside Conditions: light fog, temp 19.12
   Sustainability Factor: -12 (viral saturation)
   Interior Conditions: all systems functioning at peak

"YES, GOH. REPORT."

"Mr. President, the medical staff reports that the prisoner is damaged but is still in reasonable condition. It is their opinion that he can withstand level-19 interrogation, up to but not including electrical and water torture. Standing by for your orders."

"Alert Tom Sands to be prepared for the process to begin tomorrow morning at 9:00 a.m. I'll meet with Sands here in my office at 8:00 a.m. to review objectives and methods to be used in the procedure. That is all."

I'm going to enjoy this.

CHAPTER TWENTY-THREE

RANZA
  19 May 2249
  With Tess at Marlon's growing place
  Cool with no fog

DAD'S NOTE WAS WHERE I THOUGHT IT WOULD BE—UNDER the watering pot I had made him when I was just learning pottery.

RANNIE,

  If you've had enough time to look for and to find this message, it's clear that something has happened to us on the mission to Barca City. It's also important that if enough time has passed since we left the village without any sight or messages from us, we are probably not coming back.

  Tears can come later. You have a mission to fulfill. You need to step in and help Tess bring the magical plant to our people. Tess knows all you need to know about the plant—where it is and what it is. She'll be with you, and you must trust her.

  Rannie, I wish with all my heart that I didn't have to ask you to do this, but there is no one of our tribe whom I can trust with this more than you. Although I was clear that you were not to come with me, I know from what I learned from Tess that you are the one to bring this to the Nomás. And I know that Tess's magic will protect you. You must already know that Tess and I have talked about the plant and the mission, which must be fulfilled. And I know from Tess that you will someday lead our people. You will be great.

As for me, either Carter has performed his tribal duty and I am now with the ancestors, or I have been captured and I'll look for a way to take my own life to protect the tribe from harm.

Come get the magic plant and take your place among our people. I love you.

Dad

~

SOMETHING IN ME CAME TO LIFE THE INSTANT I READ THAT message. With other situations of this magnitude, I'd normally fall apart, sob, and become unable to breathe. That didn't happen this time. I could feel a change come over me as I read what Dad had written. Every muscle in my body tightened. I could see clearly. My movements became sharp, specific, and my thoughts centered on the task at hand. No need to look backward—that was finished.

My world had changed. Where it used to be "all about me," my feelings, my fears, my desires, my perspective had now shifted, and I knew it instantly. There was no room for self-pity. I was focused on what needed to be done, what I had to do as a leader and as the one called on by my dad to carry on this important mission. Everything was now up to me—me and Tess. When there was no possible way to argue reality, there was no argument. This reality said I could either hide from it and wait for the inevitable chaos, or I could step up and put it all on the line, become the leader Dad thought I should be.

I stepped up without hesitation.

"Tess, we're going to Barca City. Go tell the others from our team to grab some food, hunting clothes, weapons, and the animals. They're coming with us. Tell them to meet us here as soon as possible."

Tess gave an odd smile, as if to say she expected this change.

I went home to prepare.

"Mom, I'm going to Barca City to find Dad, Carter, and the plant." I grabbed the gear that was still packed from the hunt.

"Ranza . . ."

I stopped in midstride, turned to Mom, and put the gear on the floor.

"It's not up for discussion. I hope you understand, but there is nothing to talk about. I left Dad's note on the table for you." I paused. "Mom, it will be hard to read. Dad has either been captured or killed." I held her close, for only a moment, before stepping away. I had to leave before I lost my will. "Please wish me and the others luck."

My mother was shaken. Unmoving, mouth open, she just stood there.

"Bye, Mom." I hugged her again. She didn't move, unable to process what had just happened.

Niamh was lying down by the well when I reached her. I filled the water sacks, gave her a bowlful from the well. When she finished, we walked toward the corral. Tess and the others were there, mounted, and ready.

"I told them where we are going and why. They know the danger, and I've given each the opportunity to decide to stay here. No one has taken the offer. We're all ready."

I nodded and faced them all. "We're going to be journeying by land. You're probably wondering why I decided to take that route instead of going by sea, like Dad and Carter did. First, since Dad traveled there by water, the Barcans would probably expect us to do the same. They'd be watching for us. Also, we'll be able to have the horses with us if we need to move around quickly. Second, I hope to make friends at the Marin camp, a

Nomás tribe we've heard about that I hope will help us. They'll be important to us going forward, I'm certain. Third, the trip will be faster by land, and we can hide under cover of the forests along the way."

Tess smiled as if to say, "Well done."

I looked at each one of my crew and thanked them for their loyalty. Then, with nothing else to say, I turned and headed south, down the hill to the old highway. They followed in silence.

It was going to be an all-day ride. The horses fell into a steady gait. It drove me crazy. This pace would never be fast enough for me. I had to get there in a hurry. My head pounded as I tried without success to not think about Dad. Was he still alive? Was he being tortured right now? Had Carter killed him? The more my mind jumped from one possible scenario to the next, the faster Whisper stepped. Maybe she sensed that I wanted to pick up the pace. Before long, we were moving at a pretty quick trot. Then it felt like maybe a gallop would make sense.

"Ranza. These horses can't possibly keep up this pace all the way to Marin," Tess called out.

"I know, but I need to get there." There was a long road in front of us, and I didn't have time for it. We'd already been riding for two hours by this time, and we hadn't even passed the area called the Petaluma ruins.

Tess rode up to my side. Sensing her, I slowed a bit.

"Ranza, it won't do any good to get there earlier and have no strength left to fight our way into Barca, if that's what we decide. Sorry, but I need to say what I believe is best for us. You're the leader. We'll follow, but I hope I can offer my thoughts from time to time."

I pulled Whisper up. What Tess was saying made sense. She was right.

"I'm sorry. It's just that I'm so afraid for my dad. I don't even know what's happened to him, and it's tearing me up. All the same, you're right. We need to pace ourselves."

I clicked my tongue, and Whisper started up at the recent quick trot. I pulled her back to a reasonable pace, and settled in for the ride.

The trail followed an old highway that the ancestors had used to travel in their machines, or so I was told. We stayed a distance away from the path, riding the tree line to provide cover from the Barcans, should they be out looking for us. Also, the hard material of the roadway and the deep craters in the surface would have been too difficult for the horses to navigate. The grassy clay near the tree line was best for our purposes. No matter. It was a long ride.

The team was unusually quiet.

"Are you guys okay back there?"

Juvian was the first to answer. "Yeah. Although I think Shree could use a break. She keeps wanting to fly. Would that be okay?"

"Sure. Maybe you can have her look for any signs of the Barcans ahead."

We stopped while he removed the hawk's hood.

"Shree—danger, there." He pointed south in the direction of Marin. Shree wasted no time climbing and starting her circular flight. I liked to watch her rise and drop according to the heat in the air currents, as Juvie once explained.

I could almost feel Shree's joy as she danced in the sky, rolling, diving, floating with ease. I remembered the dream I'd had when I felt I was flying with Shree. I wished I could go there awake.

"Juvie. What's that? Over there, coming from the hills?" Something flew straight toward Shree in a way that reminded me of the Barcan drone.

Juvie saw it too. He sat taller on his horse, let out a high, shrill whistle, and pointed in the direction of the drone. The hawk wheeled in midair, saw the pending attack, and spun neatly out of the way just before the drone would have slammed into her.

The drone actually stopped and hovered in one spot, giving

Shree an opportunity to fight back. She dove at the machine, not realizing that the drone had several spinning blades that not only gave it flight but protected it from attack.

I screamed to Tess, who turned her eyes skyward. She wasn't able to quickly pick up on what was happening, though, and she hesitated too long. Without thinking, I raised my hand toward the hawk as my eyes focused on the drone and I called on Wakan Tanka for help. Almost instantly, the drone shut down, as if my own magic made it fall from the sky. Shree wheeled in midflight, headed on a sharp angle back toward us, and landed on Juvie's outstretched, leather-wrapped arm.

In shock, I turned to Tess with a look that was meant to say, "How did I do that?" She quietly smiled and whispered, "Later."

I was frightened for Shree. "Juvie, may I talk to her?"

"Of course, Rannie." He rotated his arm so the hawk could look at me.

"Hello, my friend. Thank you for putting yourself in danger for us."

As if she knew what I was saying, Shree closed her eyes momentarily as she bowed her head deeply until her crown rested on my shoulder. Rising again, her eyes looked into my own. My breath caught for a moment as I realized she was looking into my spirit, just as Tess and I had done earlier. I let out a short gasp as her thoughts rushed into my mind. Quickly I found myself floating above the fog, rising and falling, turning and diving, in a flight-dance just as I had seen Shree perform so many times. After what seemed like a long time, I felt myself leaving both the dream flight and Shree's spirit, coming back into my own thoughts. But Shree wasn't done with me. Looking into her eyes again, I imagined she spoke to me, like a human would.

"You saved me. I wanted to give to you what you asked for. You wished to fly with me again, like in your dream. I was happy to give that to you, friend Ranza." She turned back toward Juvie.

Juvie was moved. "I don't know how or what you did, but I'm

forever your friend. Whatever you need, I'll do it. You saved her." He couldn't find any more appropriate words, so he just stopped talking and leaned his head toward Shree.

Tess watched the scene with interest. "Ranza, that was special."

"Juvie and I have been friends for a few years. I've gotten to know him pretty well. He's a private person when it comes to anything but the hunt. Then he's all for the team. But you can probably see his affection for Shree goes way beyond the hunt. They're about as close as two friends can be. If something had happened to her, it would've hurt Juvie for a long time, might've even changed him somehow."

Off to the side, Tooren turned to Lantana. "Wow, that was really something, huh?" I heard him say.

"Yeah. You all are a great bunch of friends, and Juvie is a pretty loyal guy. I hope I can be his friend, too, but I get the feeling he just doesn't like me. And it isn't just Juvie. Except for Ranza, I feel like I don't belong with you guys. It's like I became one of you, but nobody likes that. I'm 'that annoying kid' to you and Juvie. I'm wondering when I get to be one of the team."

I saw Tooren shoot him a look.

"Seriously? I just came over to talk to you so you would feel included. C'mon, man. You haven't been here long enough to be complaining about how we treat you. Give us time, and we'll give you a reason to complain." He nudged Lantana's shoulder.

"Huh? You for real?"

"Hey, I'm just trying to lighten up the mood."

"So now I need lightening up? I must really be that annoying little kid."

I saw that Tooren was surprised by such candor from someone so young. I decided to let it play out.

Tooren gave Lantana's comment some real thought before answering the kid. "Ya know what? You *are* that annoying kid."

Lantana didn't know what to say, so he waited for Tooren to continue.

"You're that annoying kid because you're new to us—new to the team—and we didn't invite you. You were added to our team the day you finished training, no warning, no choice. Rannie told us one day that you were assigned to our group, and you showed up the next day. But now that we know you, and because you're a pretty good hunter and a nice guy, we should start over and try to think of the team as including 'that annoying kid,' and maybe you can stop whining so damn much." He laughed.

I heard what Tooren told the kid. I needed to treat these guys as a real team—not just "these guys" but as important parts of an important group who needed to mean as much to each other as they meant to me. Maybe they'd become a team after all.

I took advantage of the time to talk with Tess. I needed to know what we would do if we found Dad alive, if he was captured, or if he was no longer living. And I wanted a backup plan for each possibility. It felt like I was doing something instead of just feeling sorry for myself.

But first . . . "Tess, what was that back there? I waved my hand toward the drone and it crashed. Magic? What made that happen? I'm not magical. I'm just me."

"You are magical. Like it or not. It's part of what I've been saying about how we're a part of each other. Your magical part is starting to come out to allow you to use it."

"But what else can I do?"

"That's not for me to say. Wakan Tanka will show these things or not show these things, and only she decides how and when and why."

I could hardly deny that what I had done was some kind of magic. Maybe I could use it to save my dad. "I need your help on this magic you say I might share with you. So, what about Dad? What can we do to find and save him? And what kind of magical powers can we use to get him out of there? If they have him, and their city is impossible to get inside, what can we do? Do we have some magic for that?"

"We might, but we can't rely on magic to fix every problem."

"Okay, but why not? If you have magic, and you need it, why not use it?"

"Because you need to learn how to do things, how to lead, when I'm no longer able to give you any of my magic to solve your problems. If you don't learn, and there's no magic to count on, what then?"

"Give me your magic? So, it's your magic, and I don't have any of my own?"

"I'm not sure, but I think that's part of the plan. We're supposed to work together, me with my magic and you with your leadership. I am also not sure that you don't have magic of your own. I have to wonder. Think about this: did you have any magic before I came here?"

"No. I guess I didn't think of that. But you aren't leaving, are you?"

"Wrong question. Just trust I'll always be with you, in some way."

It gave me some small comfort and pissed me off at the same time. This was simply another of Tess's non-answers.

We rode on in silence. I tried to settle my mind, but it kept going back to my dad.

∼

RANZA
With Tess and team on approach to Sausalito
Dark
Light fog, cold

THE FIRST AND LONGEST PART OF THE JOURNEY WAS COMING to an end. As we rode through the dense forest and crested the final hill on the approach to the Golden Gate Bridge, we could see the peaks of nearby hills standing guard over the roadway.

Downhill, toward the bay, stood the ruins of the old Sausalito, where the Marin Nomás village was hidden in plain sight among the rocks and bushes against the base of the headlands. The tribe cleverly hid their boats, canoes, and nets among the long-abandoned boats and vehicles now strewn all along the bay edge, using dirt and distressing techniques to make their active boats blend in with the old, abandoned ones. You had to know which ones were usable, as you could never pick them out.

Entering the village at dusk, I wondered if we hadn't made a wrong turn along the way. There was nobody there. And there was no sign of life anywhere. Then I recalled what Mom taught me as a child.

"When you arrive in a village for the first time, you have to let the people know that you mean them no harm. The traditional way is to lie down on the ground, face to the dirt, with your arms outspread. Wait for them to come to you. Get this wrong, and you might feel the tip of an arrow as it enters you."

I ordered the animals to lay down and ordered the others to follow my lead. I dismounted, slowly rested face down on the ground, then waited for the others to follow. In very little time, I felt something sharp pressed into the back of my neck. I thought of the team and how they might react.

"Nobody moves. I'm okay."

A voice that sounded like it came from directly above barked a command. "Tell me who you are and why you are here. And make sure not to hesitate, or I'll kill you."

I did my best to keep my voice from shaking. Any sign of weakness would not be good.

"We are Nomás from the Santa Rosa area. I am Ranza, daughter of Marlon and Lora. We're on a mission to find my father, who may have been captured by the Barcans. We mean you no harm."

The voice laughed. "You mean us no harm?" The point pulled back from my neck. "Feel free to rise and look around you."

I rose to my feet and saw that we were surrounded by more

than fifty tribal members, each one holding a weapon—bow, knife, spear, sword—aimed at us.

"Tell me again how you mean us no harm. You bring a lion, a wolf . . . ," the young woman in front of me snarled.

Without warning, Tess began to glow. She raised her hands over her head and closed her eyes. A soft melody rose from everywhere at once. When she again opened her eyes, she lowered her hands in front of her, as if pushing something to the ground. As she did this, each of the Marin Nomás members dropped their weapons to the ground and let their arms rest at their sides. They stood speechless, as did we.

"As Ranza said. We mean you no harm, so, it is good that you have put your weapons down."

Their leader shook her head in confusion. "Who are you?" she asked.

"I'm called Tess. What I'll tell you is that I am with Ranza, the great Nomás hunter, and I am here to help find her father. We would ask also for your help. Ranza will tell you all you need to know, if she decides you should know it."

I glanced at Tooren and Lantana, who seemed to be having trouble processing what Tess had done. No wonder. Even I was impressed by this magic.

The Marins were clearly ready to do whatever we asked of them. Tess looked to me and smiled. I guessed that was my signal to talk.

"We know of the stories of your great skill as fishers, and your knowledge of the Barca City and the land around it. We need to learn how to get there and, if possible, inside the city."

"But why do you want to go there?" their leader asked.

I decided to push things a bit. "You ask me about our mission without even telling us who you are? Rude, don't you think?" I didn't smile.

"Please, I'm sorry. I am Cotana, tribal leader of the Marin Nomás village. We mean you no disrespect. You must truly be a great leader to have such a powerful one at your side."

"And you also have a powerful one at your side, Cotana," the young man standing next to Cotana said. He stepped toward Tess as if to challenge her.

"Coyote. Don't threaten," Cotana snapped at the young man. He continued to stare at Tess until Cotana walked toward him. I decided to intervene.

"Please, Cotana, Coyote." I guessed that was his name. "There is no need for that. We're here seeking your help and wisdom. Tess means you no harm. We offer you peace."

"I've learned that those who sit together and speak of peace soon find that peace," Cotana offered. "Can we sit in peace, Ranza?"

"Yes."

"Coyote, assemble the groups and have them light the fire in the grand hall."

Cotana signaled for us to follow as she led the way toward the hollows beneath the cliffs leading to the Golden Gate Bridge. By this time, most of our light came from the full moon rising over what looked like a mountain resting on top of an island toward the eastern side of the bay.

Sometimes, if the angle was just right and if the moon was extra bright, and for only a brief moment, the moonrise appeared as a giant bright ball in the sky. One could actually watch the moon move as it inched its way up into the sky, becoming smaller and smaller until it seemed that one had only imagined how big it was at the start.

This was one of those special times, and I couldn't help but stare at the sight.

"The moon has to be magical." I spoke my thoughts.

Cotana looked at me as if waiting for me to speak again. "What do you mean?" she finally said.

"What else in our world screams its entrance like the moon just did, gathers our attention, then settles back to rest, knowing that we are, for a moment, vividly aware of its presence?"

Tess smiled. "Well, many things do just that. We just take them for granted—no longer see them."

"Like?" I asked.

"Love," Tess replied.

I thought about that. "Ah. We are like nature in that regard, Tess."

"We're like nature in all regards, Ranza. Did you think people were somehow separated from nature—were above it, weren't affected by the same things that affect the tides, seasons, weather? People are only a small part of all of this. We're a tiny piece of nature."

Cotana, listening closely, seemed moved. She looked at Tess. "You're wise. You speak of things we never think about, yet these things make sense. Where did you learn this?"

Tess judged the young leader carefully. She must have felt Cotana would be okay with what she was about to tell her.

"You mustn't speak about what I now say to you. I'll tell you because you need to understand why our journey is so important." She paused, looked at the moon, closed her eyes, and a change seemed to pass over her, slight and so fleeting. "I'm of the spirit world. You saw a small display of my powers a few moments ago with the weapons your people willingly released."

"I was surprised, even a bit frightened."

"I won't harm you. As I am of the spirits, I am also of Ranza, and she is of me. I am here to help her grow into the leader that all Nomás will soon need if the tribe is to survive and if Earth herself is to be a place where we can continue to live. Ranza is the one. She'll lead all people—Nomás and Barcan alike—into a new life, one in which all care for each other and all care for the Earth."

Cotana looked at me, trying to see a leader hidden somewhere inside the normalcy. "She's like everyone else, so where is this leader supposed to come from?"

I wondered the same thing. Tess didn't answer. Instead she began to walk toward the group near the hills.

We were led into a very old and dark building that was called the hall. In a past life, it might've been a place where many came to eat, or a place where meetings were held. I could imagine many uses. Now, it was a crumbling ruin with cracked walls, broken and missing windows, and black crud everywhere—possibly from too much moisture and no sun ever entering the place. It was bad, but it was good for their purposes; they could meet there and not be seen from outside.

I took the opportunity to get Tess aside.

"You keep referring to me as the leader who will unite the people. Nobody asked me if I wanted to do that, and I haven't heard any Nomás tribal council suggesting me as a leader. Now you announce to the Marin tribe that I'll be their new leader. Why would you do that?"

"They need to know. We need them to support our mission. Not yet, but soon, you'll come to need their help in a big way."

"Why do you do that?"

"What?"

"You've spent weeks telling me that 'soon I'll know,' or 'soon I'll understand,' and yet 'soon' doesn't seem to come. I don't know anything. I am asked to believe you without any reason to. Why?"

"You will learn when it is necessary. This is a time to wait, but you already knew that."

"Yes, I knew. I knew because you keep telling me that same thing. It's getting to be annoying, and I'm starting to doubt it's true."

"I should be more careful in choosing my words. There is much more to come, so much more that even I sometimes wonder how it will all happen. If I were to reveal all I know at one time, it would be too much for you to accept. If I reveal parts of it to you, as time allows, then you might not reject the possibilities. So, yes, I need you to have a certain amount of faith. I'm asking you to trust me when there may seem little reason to do so. I promise that you'll soon know the missing and vague pieces. Can you trust that?"

"I'll try, but I can't promise. It's hard to believe in something like magic. But I'll try."

Just then, Tooren, Lantana, and Juvian joined us. Lantana seemed to be ready for some action.

"When do we find out the things we need to know for our trip to Barca?"

"We haven't even discussed any of this with the Marins yet. Why not wait and see?" I needed to put a collar on this one. I was hoping Tooren would take him under his wing and keep him under control, but it wasn't happening fast enough.

"So Tooren, did you and Lantana get to know each other better on the trip here?"

"Yeah. We had plenty of time to talk after we passed the Petaluma ruins. He's okay, but I'm gonna have to straighten him out a bit."

"Oh? Straighten me out? We'll see about that." Lantana was probably in no mood for playful banter.

Cotana and Coyote joined us near the fire. At their invitation, we all sat at the center of the room as Cotana passed a pipe filled with some pungent burning leaves around to the newcomers. Tess accepted and took a short pull on the pipe. Juvie, Lantana, and Tooren each drew long on the smoke, while I declined. Tess nudged me.

"This is part of their tradition. You should honor them by joining in the ceremony." She passed me the pipe.

"Oh, I didn't mean any disrespect."

Hesitating just a moment, I took the pipe and drew some of the strong smoke into my throat—and was immediately seized by a coughing fit that racked my body. I guessed that was funny, as the entire crowd laughed. Tess lightly touched my arm to let me know not to react.

"Thank you for honoring us with your presence." Now Cotana stood and addressed her people. "We're honored to welcome Ranza, Tess, and their team to our home. As we have come to know, Ranza is soon to become a great leader, and Tess is to guide her along the path. We offer to help them in any way we can, if they ask us."

I looked around at the crowd, all seated in small groups, shared pipes within each group. Cotana returned to her seat. Tess looked if to say that it was my chance to take the lead. I stood, unable to think of anything wise to say. As I did, however, I noticed that the fire had taken on a different glow, a sort of blue flame. From the center of that flame, the image of the lion spirit appeared, evidently only to me, as no one else noticed it. I wondered what it meant.

I'll ask Tess later. Now, I'm to speak.

"We're grateful for your welcome. I'm Ranza of the Santa Rosa Nomás tribe. I've brought with me the best hunters in our tribe: Tooren, Lantana, and Juvian." Each stood and waved in turn.

"The Nomás are, as you know, a peaceful tribe who seek nothing but to help each other and to help others when they're in need. Now we're in need. Recently, my village and my own home were attacked by Security guards from Barca City. They came into our village and sent a flying machine they call a drone to find us so they could capture us. It seems that they have a great need to find our people and destroy us. We were able to fight them off without letting them know we were even there. My lion, Niamh, attacked one of them and dragged him off. They had to go find their injured one and take him back to Barca City. But they'll return."

I looked at Tess, unsure if I should continue.

"Yes, tell them why we're here," she whispered.

"My father was contacted by a lion spirit. He was given a task that would make it possible for the Nomás and the Barcan slaves to live without fear. We would be able to protect our people, and yours, too, from the murderous Barca Corporation. My father traveled down to the San Mateo Portal to find that which the lion spirit described. Since he never returned, we believe he was either captured or killed by the Barcans." My voice started to shake, and I couldn't hide it. I looked down at my team. They had suddenly begun to giggle, an odd reaction to what I was saying. I looked questioningly at Tess and Cotana.

Coyote spoke. "It's just the smoke. They had more than they should've for the first time. Don't worry. It'll wear off. They might see things that aren't there, but it's harmless."

Was that why I saw the lion spirit in the fire a few moments ago?

I went back to what I needed to say. "We're going to San Mateo to find my father or learn what has happened to him. And we're going to find the thing that he went there for. We know nothing about the area, the land, and dangers. If we're going to have a chance, we'll need help from you. I'm hoping that we can have two of your scouts ride with us so we can get there and get out safely. I know it's much to ask, but we need help."

Cotana stood. "We'll do what we can. You're our people now, and we're yours. Who will volunteer?"

All fifty people stood.

"You see, we'll do whatever we can to destroy Barca. I'll pick the two best guides to ride with you. When do you go?"

"In the morning."

They'll be ready."

I looked again at the crowd. They made me proud to be among them. I looked down at my team once again. Tooren and Lantana were still giggling. Juvie was just sitting there, smoothing the head feathers on Shree.

Tess looked over the crowd. She was visibly pleased.

CHAPTER TWENTY-FOUR

Andy
22 May 2249
Outside—San Mateo Portal Sector
Barca City
GPS: 37°32'40.56" N 122°18'32.76" W
Outside Conditions: clear sky, no fog, temp 23.03
Sustainability Factor: -19 (heavy viral saturation)
Interior Conditions: no longer accessible

I'M SO SCREWED.

I hadn't expected to make it for so long. As far as I could tell, I'd been in the Out for almost a week. My head felt like my brain was swelling, to the point it was going to explode inside my head. I'd found clean water—a lake just over the hills away from the bay—so I'd been able to drink my fill and keep my thirst down to a minimum. Food was another story.

I'd found some berries growing wild in the ruins in the small sections called "houses," where the former society's families had lived alone, separated from each other, lined up one after the other like so many people-boxes. I was so hungry by the time I found the berries that I was willing to take a chance on their being poison. They weren't. I lived. But a few days of berries made terrible things happen to my gut. I needed to find something else to eat.

My legs were peppered with tiny, itchy marks down around my ankles that I'd started noticing the day after I woke up to find a family of little critters camping with me. Apparently they liked me so much they'd decided to adopt the hollow between my lower legs as their own bedroom. I wasn't sure what kind of animals they were—just furry nervous little things that wore their tails like a giant flag.

When it came to animals, my experience didn't leave me with any survival skills. I knew that only too well, as I hadn't been able to catch any animals the whole time I'd been in the Out. Bugs? Yeah, plenty of them. One made me throw up for a day. Another bit my mouth. Still others tasted so bad I'd rather have died than try to eat them again. I was so hungry right now that I'd even dive into a plate of the green crap they served in the cafeterias on the inside.

My memory kept flashing on how the bosses inside had made us take special classes to learn how deadly it was here in the Out —viruses and bacterial infections that would kill us, the dangers of eating certain foods like mushrooms . . . I'd heard there were plenty of safe mushrooms, but they never taught us about that. All they said was that mushrooms killed a person slowly and painfully. You died from the pain. I'd pass on them unless I got sicker. Then they might provide my only relief from this nightmare. I kept a bunch in my pocket, just in case.

I'm going to die. And probably soon.

Starving to death might be an easier way to go than to die from whatever was tearing me up from the inside out. Not just the headache. My throat felt like I'd eaten needles, and my whole body hurt. I'd been coughing and my nose felt like all the fluids in me were leaking out through my nostrils. Just climbing the hill to get to the water had become a major effort. I was no genius, but I knew when I was running out of time—and life. And I was scared, and I was pissed off. And so hungry

I knew what they'd done. They'd framed me. They made it look like I was trying to start a revolt, to get everyone to rebel against the Corporation. I also knew how they did it. They'd gotten that creep who called himself Jude to lie about me. They probably gave him some reward, or benefits, to get him to frame me, someone he didn't even know.

What I didn't understand was why. I'd never hurt anyone. I never slacked off. I was a good worker, kept to myself. Was I just at the wrong place, wrong time?

Oh, I'm so hungry.

But every time I try to eat, I just throw up.

Okay, Andy. Get a grip. Get up and start looking for food. You may die from whatever is making you feel so bad, but you will die sooner if you don't eat some food. Maybe you will die from throwing up. At least it'll be quicker.

Man, you're losing it. Get a hold of yourself. Get down to the bay. Maybe there'll be some fish, or other water animals that you can grab or trap.

Yeah. I was losing it. Losing my *life.*

I dragged myself down toward the water's edge as fast as my arms and weak legs would allow, which wasn't very fast at all. The closer I got to the water, the more my legs shook, the more my eyes blurred.

I don't think I'm gonna make it much longer.

I looked down to where my knees had sunk into the marsh mud saw what I thought was called a frog. He looked up at me as if to ask, "You gonna eat me?"

Yeah.

Then I stopped knowing things.

CHAPTER TWENTY-FIVE

Ranza
23 May 2249
With the search team plus Rik and Erlinda from Marin
Burlingame Ruins
Barca City
Clear sky, no fog

THE TRIP ACROSS THE BRIDGE WAS EASILY ONE OF THE MOST frightening things I'd ever had to do. But there was only one other way to get to the other side of the bay—to ride in canoes. And to my thinking that wasn't a choice. We needed our horses if we wanted to get there and back in a hurry.

So there we were, riding our horses across the old bridge as pieces of the roadway broke loose and fell to the depths below us. But, again, no choice. It was a scary ride, but it was better than sitting out there in the water waiting to be attacked by drones or worse.

"Slow, Whisper. Step carefully."

I'd half expected the decay. But the rotted and rusty machines filled with skeletons hadn't been a distinct thought until it became a reality every few feet across this bridge. I wondered what had happened to these people. Was it like the Elders said? Were they murdered where they sat, nobody even caring enough to save the spirits, to bury the dead?

Lantana's horse stumbled in a break in the road surface. Whinnying, the horse reared back to drag his ankle joint from the crack. The sudden motion jerked Lantana off the horse, and he dropped roughly to the roadway, landing next to a skull no longer attached to the rest of its bones. Surprised and obviously frightened, Lantana jumped to his feet, brushing his hands all over his hiding clothes as if he was contaminated by the specter of Death, having come in contact with the skull of an unfortunate victim of the Purge.

"Whoa, calm," I said. "We need to check your horse's leg. I hope he isn't lame."

Lantana was jolted back to the moment, suddenly concerned for his horse. Together, we went over the animal, looking for swelling and squeezing the joint hard to test for a pain reaction. It all checked out. Nothing broken.

"I feel like a jerk, thinking only about myself," Lantana said. "I was pretty shaken. I thought I was going to fall through the road. Then I saw this skull, and my mind kind of got weird for a moment. What was going on when that person died?"

"I'm not sure," I said. "We've heard about the slaughter, when anyone who refused to join Barca City was murdered. Some were burned alive, some poisoned by some kind of smoke, and some were shot with loud gun weapons and things called 'bombs' that destroyed everything in sight. Who knows for sure what happened. They're just a part of our story traditions and might all be far from the truth. Looking around here, though, I might guess they were poisoned or shot. No bombs, because they would have destroyed their machines, even the bridge itself."

My hunter instinct picked up on a new sound, like a buzzing

noise coming from the far end of the bridge. I knew right away it was the sound of Barcan drones.

"Quick, everyone, pull your hoods over your faces, lay down, and don't move. No noise either. That's the sound of drones. I'm hoping they won't see us. Tell your horses to wander away slowly. Niamh, Shree, move out from us."

Everyone dove to the roadway, and our animals were nearly off the bridge when the first of the drones passed over us and continued toward the horses to check them out—a good sign. It meant that the drones couldn't see through our hiding clothes. I lifted my head to steal a look at them as they floated above the animals. *Good*, I thought. *The horses are ignoring them, like they don't even see them.*

The drones must have decided these were just a pack of wild animals, and they flew off in the direction of the headlands.

I called for Whisper and for Niamh. Whisper led the other horses back to where we were still on the bridge surface. The team took a long time getting up to their feet, looking to see if the drones would return. I gave the order to mount up so we could head off.

"Rik, how much farther is it to the other end of the bridge?"

"It's not too bad. I believe in caution. So we should take our time to avoid any more holes in the road or broken rails that might cause us to fall over the side." He pointed to one of those breaks, very close to where we stood.

Okay, everyone. Let's head out." I clicked my tongue and Whisper started up while the others followed.

Riding from the north entrance of the bridge to the south was not as far as I'd imagined. At full gallop, we would have made the complete trip in just a few moments, not even long enough for the horses to break a sweat. But that was before the Purge—before the fires, before the bombs, the shootings, the poison clouds. The trip was dangerous. Any moment we might be discovered by the Barcans. Also, we never knew if a horse's hoof would puncture the surface or when we might hit a weak spot and slip over the side.

Mostly, it was frightening. Rotted old machines held the bones of the victims, countless skeletons possibly picked clean by hungry sea birds looking for an easy meal. Even the bleached bones of the birds could be seen inside the machines, next to the bones of their intended meals. These had likely died from the poison in the human meat they ate.

My imagination lit up with the frightening possibility that the Purge could happen again—to us, if the Barcans decided we were enough of a threat to them. I forced the thoughts out of my head, and we plodded on.

"Looks like we're on the other side. Rik, why don't you come up front here and lead the way. You said you've been here before."

"Okay, but I think we need to take a quick break here so I can tell you all what to expect."

Stopping anywhere near this Bridge of Death was the last thing I wanted to do, but I didn't want to override Rik's suggestion. We needed his experience to guide us.

"Good. Everyone, gather here and tie the horses to that tree." I found another large fallen tree that we could use for a bench. "Okay, everyone. Pay close attention to Rik."

The group was only too happy to sit and put their feet up for a while.

Rik began. "First, let me tell you about the animals here in the area. After the Purge, when most of the people were murdered and no one was left to take care of their pets, dogs and cats found their way outside and began to live as wild animals. We can expect to come across dogs that have become wild pack hunters. They have no fear of humans, and in packs they are deadly. We need to be ready to fight for our own lives. Cats are mostly too small to pose a threat. Besides, they'll be afraid of your hunt animals. But a large dog pack can easily bring down a human if they are desperate for food. Or a mountain lion." He emphasized the point by walking toward and standing over Niamh. "And they are all over the San Francisco ruins."

He let that sink in. After a pause with no one asking any questions, he began to speak again.

"Although there are some reported attacks from all over, I have never seen a dog. So we'll hope for the best. Now, about the humans. Remember, I said *most* of the people died. *Most* is not the same as *all*. There may have been survivors of the Purge. Surviving humans found their way out into the open, sleeping in caves, in underground train stations, in forests, and in abandoned buildings. Having no skills for hunting and likely few weapons, they may have become prey for the dog packs. There haven't been sightings for a long time, but just be aware of the possibility.

"Now, about our own food. We have plenty of dried fish, and Ranza, you still have some venison. Water is going to be rationed, and you must not eat any of the berries or mushrooms that you see along the way unless I check them out. Otherwise, we should be okay. That's about it."

I watched my team's faces. Rik's descriptions were pretty bleak. I could only hope the team listened and believed him. The reactions were what I expected. Tooren and Juvie listened closely, their eyes registering their concern. Lantana . . . Well, he was just being himself. At one point I saw him laugh under his breath as if to say that Rik's stories were a load of bear scat. *Well, puppy. I can't force you to grow up. You either will or you won't. I hope you live through the experience*, I thought.

Tess stood. "Of course, we want to also be ready for drones and possible Barcan Security along the way. Best to wear the hiding clothes for now."

"I agree with all that's been said," I added. "Now, let's be on our way so we can get there while it's still a bit foggy and we can stay as much out of sight as it will allow. Rik, lead the way."

We rode through the old military barracks high above the bay. The ground was lush and green, maybe a result of the combination of fog followed by rain followed by sun that we had experienced since we arrived in Marin. The ride was long but not uncomfortable. I asked the team to be on the lookout for anything like the flower we'd actually never seen. And I asked them to be on the lookout for my dad, on the slight chance he was still wandering around these hills.

I was about to ask Rik how long it would take to get to San Mateo when I was distracted by a low, sinister growl. Looking quickly around, I spotted one, then two, and then several more of what might have been small wolves. About half the size of a wolf, yet every bit as scary, they slowly approached us, tightening their circle from every direction, heads lowered, teeth bared, eyes on fire. They'd had us surrounded before we even heard the first growl.

The instincts of skilled hunters took hold, and we froze in place—all but Tess, who turned her horse to directly face the closest beast.

"Hold fast, Tess. These might be the wild dogs Rik was speaking of." As I spoke, I saw each hunter almost imperceptibly wrapping one hand around their own weapons, as I had also done. Tess stopped and held.

No sooner had she frozen in place than the dog facing her leapt into snarling attack, its jaw wide open as a wild scream exploded from its throat. It had leapt so high and fast, it was a breath away from Tess's throat when Rik's spear tore into one side and the point came out the other, killing the dog in midflight. We had no time to thank him before the rest of the pack went on attack. It was certain that we couldn't kill all of these monsters at once. Someone was going to get hurt, maybe even killed.

"Hey choon sh nee yo!"

This strange shout came from Tess. Before I could look at her, the beasts fell to the ground. They all sat, looked directly at Tess, lowered their heads, then ran away in all directions. The rest of us just sat atop our horses, dumbfounded, silent and unmoving for a few moments.

I opened my mouth.

"Don't ask," she replied to the unspoken question we all wanted to ask.

We rode in silence for a long time.

FROM THE MOMENT THE HORSES STEPPED THEIR WAY DOWN the hillsides of San Mateo, past the ruins of homes, toward the bay, I had a sense that any decision to turn back was now impossible. We were in this all the way.

As if to agree, the Earth began to hum—low and soft at first, an uninterrupted sound like a familiar meditation chant or the continuous hum of the cedar flute heralds at the Mourning Feast. The closer we came to the water, the more sinister and loud the Earth's warning, drifting into a deep, menacing growl. It wasn't natural, that much we knew. It couldn't be Mother Earth calling to us. This sound was something that none of us had ever heard before. It was unnatural, and it came from the south, toward where we knew Barca to be.

I was sure this was the sound of evil, coming out to warn us travelers away. But I would not be warned. I had to fulfill my mission: to find and free my dad before they could kill him then find the flower. *Nothing will keep me from finding my dad,* I thought.

We reached the bay's tide pools and headed south toward Barca. Walking our horses around the old airport, we passed a small island that had blocked our view south. As if a huge thunderhead had come upon us, we now stood face to face with what had to be Barca City, a monster of gigantic proportions that was the source of the evil hum. It blocked everything else and sucked the light out of the sky around it.

No one I knew had ever spoken of such a wonder. Sure, the Marins, the Bodega Bays, might have seen this. But in Santa

Rosa, we'd only heard of it by name, not by description. I hadn't known what to expect. And I hadn't imagined this. My mind couldn't quite grasp it all. It wasn't just large, it was otherworldly. Standing frozen in place, I hoped that what I was seeing was a specter—a product of my imagination. Yet it was real, and I was seeing and hearing it growl in all of its evilness.

"Tess, it's so unnatural, so sharp-edged and shiny. How can this be real? How could anyone carry material so high to build it up into the clouds?"

Barca stood in the middle of the San Francisco Bay. The front edge of the base held a rounded garden of trees, planted in neat rows, resting in a solid barricade that seemed to turn away the rising tide. The floor of the garden was covered in some form of grass, green and lush, with low, flowering bushes separating the trees. Such a natural landscape stood in contrast to the sterile, mechanical look of the rest of the city. Another garden, similar to the first, stood fifteen feet above the other and hung out from the face of the building with no visible support.

The main building, round and covered in some form of glass that reflected the light as a sparkling fire might, originated from the last row of trees and rose skyward. I counted windows to the sky. Sixteen stories. Secondary towers were attached to the main building and rose from either side, miles apart yet somehow connected to each other in a spiritual way. As if royalty lived in them, each secondary tower supported a godlike statue at the top of its floors. They fixed their gaze downward toward the water where entry into the compound was all but impossible in any case.

To the east of the main structure sat a magical place. Suspended above the water and connected to the main building by a moving walkway, a large flat platform extended in a circle. On the platform, I could see what might be people, their heads and faces covered in black as they attended to many aircraft. These craft were different from the ones at the old broken-down airport; they looked like giant birds with long, pointed beaks.

Every so often, one of these would float, as if by magic, straight up above the platform, then shoot forward like an arrow from a hunter's bow. It would fly ever faster and higher until we couldn't see it.

"We better get out of sight," Tess said. "If we're spotted, they'll come for us. Then our hopes of finding your father will be doomed."

We turned westward and headed toward the ruins of San Mateo as I wondered why she was at all concerned. After all, she was magical.

"Tess, why can't you just use your magic and get my dad and the flower. Then we could all just get out of this hellhole."

"I'm here to help you learn to lead your people, not to soften your path. A great leader must learn to make her own way." She turned toward the hills.

Without warning, I was lifted above her as Whisper reared back, startled by the body of what might have been a human on the ground. It lay in the weeds, moaning softly. I had an arrow out and nocked before anyone knew something had happened.

"No! Stop, Ranza," Tess shouted. "He's weak. You don't need to harm him."

"But, Tess. How do you know that? You are more than five horse lengths away, and whatever it might be is hidden by these bushes and rocks!" I approached the thing from the uphill side, giving me the advantage in case whatever it was decided to attack me. Heart racing, eyes looking everywhere, muscles tight and ready to fire, I dove through the air and landed directly above what appeared to be a boy, one about my own age.

He was sick with something that left him pale and covered in raised sores all over his skin. He shook uncontrollably as he tried to push himself up, but the effort exhausted him, and he melted back to the ground. He was ready to die.

"Stand back from him," Tess stated in a voice that I didn't recognize. It caught me by surprise, leaving me no option but to obey. I backed away from the boy.

Tess began to paw through the seedlings and weeds on the ground, looking for something specific. She was so focused she didn't even answer when I asked her what she was doing. After a time, she dug her fingers deep into the dirt, tugged fiercely on a seedling, and pulled it out of the earth roots and all.

Looking at the team, Tess gave an order. "We need a small fire," she barked. "Head into the forest over there." She indicated the uphill direction. "Make the fire small enough that the smoke will not be visible to them," she said, pointing at Barca City.

The mention of the giant structure to our south snapped us all back to reality.

"Tess," I protested. "Any fire at all will alert the Barcans that we're out here. We can't take the risk." A part of me was concerned about being discovered. Another part knew Tess was taking control of the team that I commanded. I didn't like this sudden shift in power.

"Tooren, take this root. Use your drinking cup and boil water." Tess was in charge at this point. "Make a tea with this root and bring it to me. Don't wait until it's strong. Hurry, or this boy will die."

Tooren didn't need any urging. He was off with the root before I could turn around to look at him. The rest of the team stood silently, watching the scene unfold and waiting to see what I would do.

"Tess, why do you help this man?"

"Because he's dying. Do you think because he's not Nomás he deserves to die? Ranza, all people are the same. Each of us has the same right to live as the next. This one is as important to the Nomás as you are, as your father is."

Rik was uneasy. "Can we catch this sickness?"

"No," Tess said. "I need you and Erlinda to start looking around for some strong sticks and some tule reeds from the water edge. We need to make a travois, a sled to take this man away to where we can try to heal him.

With nods, they left. The rest of the team and I watched while Tess knelt to assess the boy, who was clearly unconscious. Before long, Tooren returned with the tea in his cup. He gave it to Tess, who lifted the boy's head, dripping some of it into his mouth. He gagged a little when it hit his throat. Jolted awake, he looked at Tess through eyes that were mostly closed.

"Please, try to drink some of this. It will help."

The boy was eventually able to swallow half of the tea. It took only a few moments for the brew to provide the results. The boy opened his eyes.

"Who . . . I was . . . please . . ." He reached a shaking hand out for more tea. Tess finished giving it to him.

"You're quite sick," she told him. "I think we can help to heal you, but it might take some time. Just trust us. Where are you from?"

"I came from there," he whispered, pointing in the direction of Barca City.

"Tooren, Lantana, I need you to carry him deeper into the ruins. We have to hurry before Barcan Security spots us. Our hiding clothes can only do so much. They'll find us sooner or later. Make your movements slow and small."

The hunters didn't waste a second. They picked up the boy, one at his feet, the other lifting from his upper arms. They had him aloft and headed toward the forested ruins in a matter of minutes. I lagged behind as Rik and Erlinda returned with the supplies. They passed me by and followed Tess's instructions to fashion a makeshift travois.

When the rest of the team had disappeared into the deep forest, I surveyed the area. My hunting instincts told me to be on alert, watching for any movement that might give away Barcan Security guards. Satisfied we were alone, I raced off to catch up with the rest of them. Whisper needed no urging. She already knew where they had taken the boy, and she headed in that direction as soon as I mounted her.

Under the trees, Tess was bent over the boy, wiping his brow and humming a soothing mantra. As I approached, she looked up. "He's better now, but he doesn't have much time left before the disease is able to grab him again, and the next time it will kill him." She took me by the hand. "I think we can save him, but I need your help. Please stay here with him and keep him calm. There is something we all need, and it's not far from here."

Before I could answer, Tess was on her horse and had turned southward.

For the first time in a very long time, I felt poorly equipped for the task at hand. I looked down at this stranger and realized I had no idea how to help him if something went wrong. Seeing him as he truly was gripped my emotions. I saw the person under the disease, the boy—although I guessed that since he was about my own age he would be called a man. I felt his fear, his pain, and I wanted to help him. But I had no idea how to do that. So I followed Tess's lead and continued wiping his brow and humming soothingly.

Soon, as I stroked his forehead, he reached up without warning and grabbed me by the wrist. "Who are you?" he asked.

I easily unwrapped his weakened fingers. " I am Ranza," I replied. "We found you unconscious over by the water, and my friends and I are trying to help you. You have some kind of sickness. The real question is who are you, and where did you come from?"

"I don't know if I can trust you or not. So I think I need to not tell you anything right now." He looked frightened.

"I understand, and I'll respect your wishes," I replied.

Moments later, he must have had a change of heart. "I am A37921, sometimes called A37."

Tooren spoke up. "You have numbers for a name? A37-something?" he asked. "What kind of place has numbers for names? I don't think I believe you." He said this with his hand clearly holding the hilt of his long knife. He took a few steps toward A37, but I quickly leaned between them.

"Tooren, stop," I commanded. "He's too sick to be a problem

for us, so let's just give him some respect for who he says he is. Later, if we find out he is lying, we can deal with that. But for now, he says he is A37, so he is. No argument."

"My friends call me Andy," he added.

"Well, then, Andy is what we will call you. Now rest."

Tooren retreated just as Tess rode back over the rise.

"I didn't find it," she said. "What I was looking for must not be around here."

"And just what were you looking for?"

"The flower your dad came for. But for now, we need to hide. I saw a group of Barcan Security. At least that's who I thought they were, coming this way, and they—"

"What did they look like?" Andy interrupted. "Were they all in black, head-to-toe black, with black gloves, helmets, and face shields?"

"Looks like you're feeling better," Tess replied. "Yes, that was them."

"Barcan Outworld guards." Andy shook his head. "They'll shoot you the instant they see you."

"So," I snapped, "you're Barcan? Are you a spy?"

"Yes," Andy answered, "I am Barcan, but not a spy. Well, I was Barcan, until they banished me." He weakened.

"See, I knew he couldn't be trusted." Tooren leapt to his feet. "Let's kill him now and get out of here before these guards show up."

"Don't bother," was Andy's response. "I'll be dead in a day or two. That was their plan all along. In fact, they probably think I'm already dead."

Plan?" Tess asked. "What plan?"

"Okay," Andy said. "Yeah, I'm Barcan. At least I was. Someone framed me, made me out to be a traitor who wants to overthrow management. President Hsieh himself sentenced me to banishment to the Outworld. For us, it's a death sentence, as Barcans get some disease and die soon after we come out of the City. I'm pretty sure I have it now."

Lantana chirped, "He's trying to confuse you with these strange words."

I gave him a look. "Back down and be quiet." That made him stare at the ground and back away several feet.

"Why would they do that?" I asked. "What did you do to make them want you dead?"

"I wish I knew," he answered.

No sooner had he spoken than a rustling sound came from a stand of trees at the top of the hill to the west. This time, all of the hunters were quick to react. I drew back on my bow, Tooren began circling his sling, and Lantana had loaded his bow as he drew back, looking for a target.

Tess stood transfixed. Soon she opened her arms, palms outward, and raised them shoulder high as she called out to the sound.

"We know you, and you know us. Come forth and show yourselves. We welcome you, and we want to be with you." She bowed slightly toward the hill. As she did this, her clothing seemed to fade to white, as if it were changing color. "Bring us your gift, Great Buffalo," she whispered loudly. "Show yourselves to us."

We all, including Andy, froze in place. Unable to speak, and not understanding what was happening, Andy stared in wonder at the transfixed Tess, her long hair blowing as if some spirit wind had tossed it, her faced now aglow, her arms beckoning toward whatever she must be seeing.

As we watched, a large mountain lion, much larger than Niamh, showed himself from the trees. On his head I could see the beautiful red-tailed hawk that had come to me in my vision. I realized this was my vision come to life before me. Next to the lion stood a grand buffalo to whom the other animal spirits seemed to bow. Without knowing why, I also bowed deeply to the buffalo as the hawk took flight and began a lazy circle not fifty yards from where we stood. Shree, seated on her perch attached to Juvian's saddle, must have sensed that there was an important bird nearby. She was hooded, so unable to see. However, she, too, seemed to bow.

Tess raced to the spot directly under the hawk, bent down, and picked up a beautiful red plant from the ground. As she turned to the group, the plant burst into a brilliant red-orange flame that soon burned the entire plant to a small pile of ashes in Tess's hands. When Tess placed the pile of ashes on the ground in the middle of the group, the flower suddenly began to grow again, rising directly from the ashes. Tess bowed deeply toward the lion and the buffalo.

"We thank you, Great Spirit. You are Great Buffalo, Older Brother. We thank you for what you have given us."

With that, the buffalo, the lion, and the hawk were gone.

"Ranza," Tess told me. "Make a paste of the ash, and give some of it to the boy. Make him eat it. Quick, before they get here."

I did as I was told. Andy resisted, but he was simply too weak to put up much of a struggle. As soon as I placed the wet ashes on his tongue, his eyes widened, and his heart beat a little faster. With each successive taste of the ash paste, he seemed stronger. His sores started to vanish. Within a few minutes, he was on his feet. He looked like nothing bad had ever happened to him.

"Tess," I stuttered. "What just happened? Who was that? What's happening right now? This scares me. I'm confused. Tess, tell me, *who are you?*"

"I am your friend, dear Ranza. That is who I am. As to what just happened—" She softened. "We were visited by the Great Spirit, the one who owns us, the great lion. We've been given a gift. This gift is not for us alone. It will change this entire world, as you will see. This plant has magic, Ranza. This plant has a flower that can overcome even Barca. This is the magic your father came for. It's the flower that he was told to find. And he has found it, Ranza. He found it through you."

The mention of my father dragged me back to reality.

"My father." I turned toward Andy. "How long have you been out here? Did you hear of anyone from outside Barca being captured or . . . killed, before you came here?"

"There was a man," Andy replied. "Hsieh announced that an Outdweller was captured and would be interrogated, but he was very sure that this Outdweller wasn't a part of a community. He was thought to be just a straggler."

"You have to help me find him. There must be a way inside, and you'll help me find it."

Andy didn't have a chance to respond. We could hear, from the south, the soft hum of the headless horses of Barcan Security that told me a band of guards had made their way toward us. With a few quick words we formed a plan. Tess led the team up the rise and out of view while I remained behind, well hidden, to act as a distraction in case the guards headed in the direction of the fleeing group. From my hiding place, I could see that a handful of Barcan Security, now dismounted, had found the cup that Tooren used to make the tea. It was now a matter of time before they found my team. I stood ready to fire my bow, prepared to reload and shoot in rapid succession, hoping to take down the entire search party if need be.

What I hadn't counted on was that one guard had circled behind me and was now about to fire his strange handheld weapon at my back.

From somewhere deep in the forest, Niamh came crashing through the brush, grabbed the guard from behind, and snapped his neck with a crushing bite. The other guards, seeing this carnage, turned and ran toward their headless horses, hoping to make it back to the Portal before the lion came for them.

Niamh didn't even notice them. She focused all of her energy on me, wanting only to save me. Recovered, I raced up the hill with Niamh at my side, ready to kill again if anyone threatened me.

Together, me astride Whisper, Niamh close at my side, we climbed the hill in the direction that the team had just headed.

Every hunter knows that the prey, given enough time and circumstances, soon becomes the hunter. Although the guards raced away from me and my lioness, I knew that any moment they might just turn around and stalk us, moving in for the kill at their first chance. I knew enough to be ready. Although I needed to catch up with the others, I played it safe, zigzagging my movement so the Security guards wouldn't be able to predict where I'd be headed and, anticipating the direction of my team, be waiting there for them to arrive.

After riding some distance, I started to wonder if I might have gone in the wrong direction. Then I caught sight of Tess and the team not too far ahead of me. Calling out to them in the voice of a hawk, I was careful to keep moving in a zigzag pattern.

"Those were Barcan Security," Andy told us when I reached them, although we already knew this. "It was a small Outworld detail, but by now they've sounded the alarm to their station to dispatch a larger team of speedcycle enforcers whose only mission will be to kill anyone they happen to find out here. There's only a single Barcan alive out here other than the guards, and they don't care what happens to me. They're sure I must already be dead."

"But now you're not going to die after all," Tess told him.

I added, "What's a 'speedcycle enforcer'? Sounds nasty."

"Speedcycles are the things they ride on that let them move very quickly. This team after us now rode in on them."

"Headless horses? They're called speedcycles? Okay. Thanks for that. So now they have people called enforcers who will come here on speedcycles. Not good," I said.

"Right," Andy said. Now, we had all better get out of here or else no magic in the world can save us when the guards find us."

I was quick to take the lead, lest Tess maintain her authority. But I was only too happy she was with us. She'd saved us all more than once.

"Mount the horses and follow me," I commanded. "Andy, you can ride with Lantana, and do everything he tells you. Rik,

Erlinda, do as we do. We know how to hide, so there'll be no arguments. Andy, Lantana's going to help you hide with him." I didn't wait for an answer.

We headed into the darkest part of the ruins, seeking the thickest forest cover available. I selected a group of large buildings that looked like they might fall down if anyone pushed on them with any force at all. I guided Whisper into the largest building, found a series of halls and rooms that would suffice, then I told them all to dismount and send the horses away.

"Tooren, give the horses the command."

"Hide," Tooren spoke. As if of one mind, all four horses turned and trotted out of the building. Once they were outside, they sprinted to a full gallop and headed off in several different directions.

Each of us Nomás opened our daypacks and removed our hiding clothes. We pulled up the pants and foot coverings, tying them at the waist. Next, we pulled on the hooded tops—except Lantana, who handed a set to Andy, showed him how to wear the outfit, and put his own on only when he was satisfied that Andy understood. He thought he did understand, but when each of the rest of us had completed dressing in our garments, Andy was amazed and somewhat confused as one by one we vanish from sight. All he could do was stand there, dumfounded, and try to believe what he had just witnessed: people vanishing before his eyes.

After a few moments, Andy was further baffled when his own hooded garment seemed to float up and over his head, dropped down onto his shoulders, and Lantana's voice commanded, "Andy, pull it down to cover your body."

He did as he was told.

The sudden growl of speedcycles caught us by surprise. They stopped less than fifty yards from where we hid. "Command five, take that sector. Command four, search the hospital ruin. And I'll take Command two with me into that building over there." The voice was dark and distant. It sounded somewhat like it wasn't even attached to a human at all. But we all knew that it meant trouble for us.

I heard Lantana whisper to Andy to be silent. He told him that the guards would not see us and that silence would ensure our safety. He'd just finished explaining this when a handful of guards burst into the room, guns ready to fire at anything that moved, made a noise, or even trembled.

The lead guard motioned to the others which direction he wanted each of them to search. As I crouched there motionless, waiting, I thought of what Andy must be experiencing. He could clearly see the guards, as could we all. But they would pass him by as if he wasn't even there. I wished we'd had the time to explain to him how the clothing functioned.

The lead guard returned to the room, and I tensed as he walked straight toward where I knew Andy to be. If Andy was confused, if he didn't move, the man would walk straight into him.

I held my breath as the guard suddenly stopped. He stood, head cocked, starting in front of him. Then, with a wary expression, he reached out in front of his chest . . .

Nothing. There was nothing there. Andy had obviously moved. I let my breath seep out of me.

Unable to find anything, the guard finally stopped flailing long enough to hear his commander returning to the main room.

"Sir, we didn't find anyone. The building is secure."

"And you'd stake your life on it?" the commander queried.

"Um, yes, sir. We'd stake our lives on it," the guard replied, obviously hoping his inclusive use of "we" would somehow shift the responsibility away from him and onto the others.

The commander lifted a small box-like thing to his face and said, "Activate sector scanning for the outcast's microchip. Take your time and be thorough. He is here, somewhere."

Without acknowledgement, the leader turned and stomped out of the building. The others followed in a hurry.

When I was satisfied that the Security detail had moved on,

I lifted my hood and signaled to the others that it was now safe to remove the hiding garments. Quietly, they did so, and we all settled to wait out the search.

Nervous and unsure of what to do next, I absently pulled some jerky from my pocket. I tore off a piece and began to chew the salty-sweet meat. Just as I was about to put another piece into my mouth, I glanced at Andy, who was looking at my food like it was the best thing on Earth. I understood.

"Want some?" I whispered. I offered a piece.

Andy looked at the strange dark piece of meat—something he had probably never tasted—nodded his head, and reached for it. He bit off a hunk, as he had seen me do, and began to slowly chew the tough but delicious jerky. Before I could stop him, he had swallowed the piece whole and was already starting to bite off another.

"Hey, slow down," I laughed. "It tastes better if you chew it for a while."

Andy, looking a little embarrassed, offered, "Sorry, I've never eaten anything like this in my life." He bit off the second hunk and began to chew it slowly before smiling and nodding. "It does taste better this way. What is it?"

"It's called venison," I replied, not wanting to have to explain the whole hunting, field dressing, and cooking process to him. There were so many other things I wanted to focus on at this moment. My father was at the top of that list.

"Andy," I began. "You mentioned that someone was brought into the City from the Outside. Can you tell me anything about him? Was he young? Old? Did you hear his name? I need to know these things, Andy. You see, we think the Barcans took my father, and I hope he's still alive inside the City. Can you help me, please?" My eyes started to get wet.

"I don't know anything, Ranza. I'm sorry. I understand how you must feel, but all I heard was what Hsieh, the president of Barca, said the day I was arrested. He just made the announcement that they had captured an Outdweller and they we're going to interrogate to find out where he came from and if there were more like him. That day, they arrested me and pushed me out through the San Jose Portal. I'm not sure how long I was out of it when you found me, but they must have pushed me out three or four days ago. That was the day I heard about the capture. It was the end of my days as a Barcan."

He looked deeply into my eyes. I tried to open my spirit to him, allowing me to see his thoughts. And I knew he saw something there that he had never seen in anyone else's eyes. I am sure Andy saw fire. He saw the flame that burned deep inside me, drove me, and he was momentarily stunned. Because of our connection, I felt his reaction. He wanted to know me as a person. He wanted to get beyond all of this terror and meet me as one friend meets another. I felt that he didn't know how to get close to another person; all of this was new to him. But I knew he would do what I asked.

"Andy." I took his hand. "Can you help me? You know what it's like inside that horrifying place. You can tell me how to get around in there, how to find places, like where they would take a prisoner to interrogate him, as you said." Now the tears flowed freely. "Help me, Andy." Never before had I felt so helpless.

"Ranza, you have no idea," Andy answered. "Barca is not just a place. Barca's alive. You can't go anywhere, do anything, without the system watching your every move. Try to go where you aren't allowed, and you run the risk of being fried by automatic disintegrator or arrested or banished, like me. Everyone inside has a chip implanted in their body that is continually scanned. They know where you are and who you are, all day and every day. They probably know where I am right now."

As soon as the words came out of his mouth, the impact of what he said was obvious to all of us.

"A chip?" I asked. "That one guard said something about a microchip. What does that mean?"

"It's a tiny electronic device that sends out a signal every so often. Barca uses that signal to track us so they can know where we are at any time."

"Andy, does this mean that they are following you right now, trying to see where you go and if you are still alive?" Tess asked.

"Yeah. I'm certain of it," he replied. Realizing why we'd asked, his eyes widened.

Tess and I looked at each other. I spoke. "It has to come out." I reached for my long knife as I asked, "Where is it?" I headed toward Andy.

"You can't do that." Andy backed away. "You just saved me, now you want to kill me?" He was backed into a corner.

Tess raised her hand and walked slowly toward Andy.

"No, Andy. We don't want to kill you. We just need to remove the chip that they have planted inside you. Unless we do that, they'll find you, and they'll kill us all."

"Oh," he mumbled. "Sure. It's in my forearm, right here." He pointed at a tiny scar just below the crook of his elbow and held it out so we could see it clearly.

Now I was confused. I looked from Andy, his mouth open in a half smile, to Tess, her eyes fixed on Andy's face, and I just knew that Tess held some kind of magical power over him.

"Go ahead and remove it, Ranza," she whispered. "Andy won't feel any pain."

I moved toward Andy, expecting him to try to escape. He turned to me and smiled. His arm still extended, he gave me full access to the implant. Still unsure, I looked at Andy, eyebrows raised in a question, and asked, "Are you okay with this?"

"Yes, of course," was the reply. "We need to get this out before they come looking for me."

Given the go-ahead, I took Andy's wrist in one hand. As I pushed the knife blade tip into his arm, I expected him to recoil, but he did no such thing. In only a few seconds, I found the chip and pried it easily from his arm. Tess quickly prepared a poultice with some herbs and a cloth wrap, which she tied tightly around the wound. Andy smiled.

"Tess," I warned, "you have a lot of explaining to do." I took the implant to the entrance of the building, stopped, and whistled. In a moment, Niamh came running to me. I wrapped the chip in a small bag, which I tied to a string around Niamh's neck. Without saying a word, I waved her off and returned to the building.

"Okay," I began. "We need a plan. There's so much that we have to consider before we can decide how to proceed. First, we need to send this plant—" I pointed to the now flaming flower. "—back to our village, to the people who work for my father. They need to figure out how to grow more like it. Next, we need to find a way to get me inside that city."

Andy, staring at his bandaged arm, was the first to speak. "Ranza, you can't go in there. You'll be fried before you get five feet inside the Portal. You don't have credentials or a chip. You are, as far as the system knows, the enemy, and you are to be destroyed."

"You aren't going in there, Ranza," said Tess. "You have a duty to the tribe. Go in there, and they will catch and torture you. It would be only a matter of time before you gave up the tribe locations. I know how much you want to save your father, but he has probably, I am sorry to say, already taken his own life."

I felt the color leave my face. I tried to regain my composure. I knew Tess was right. Unable to argue the point, I turned my back and fought the tears that were sure to come.

"I'm sorry, Ranza," Tess added. "I know how much your father means to you. We all love him, but the tribe must come first."

My resolve was certain. I hated that I was willing to gamble with the security of the tribe for my own needs, and I wished that I could be stronger. Tess might understand, if she was able to see how I felt inside, but I also knew that I would never win any argument that placed the individual before the good of the tribe. I nodded, then turned my attention back to Andy.

Andy was beginning to come out of the state that Tess had

put him in. As his senses reawakened, I could tell he had a growing awareness of what we'd done to him. I felt his anxiety.

"Please don't be alarmed, Andy." Looking directly into his eyes, I added, "I only did this to save you from Barcan Security. They would surely have tracked you and found us all together. It was a matter of not very much time. Remember, you're an Outdweller now. You can't expect them to give you any special treatment while they're killing you." This last part caused Andy to smile.

"I get it, Ranza. It's just I can't remember how it happened that I found myself on the receiving end of your knife, and it didn't seem to bother me."

Nodding, I murmured, "Neither can I, Andy."

Turning to the others, I resumed command. "Well, if we're going to get this magical flower back to the tribe, we'd better get started. Andy can ride Whisper, and I'll run the perimeter in case those guards come back." This was a known hunting strategy, so none of the team thought it was out of place. "I'll keep Niamh with me to throw the speedcycle folks off your trail." Not waiting for an answer, I went to the door, calling for Niamh.

"Standard formation," Tess ordered behind me, surprising us all with her use of hunter lingo. "Tooren, you take the rear. Rik, Erlinda, Lantana, and Andy take the lead, and I'll ride the middle."

The team glanced at me, and I nodded. They quickly assembled, took their positions, and headed to the northwest corner of the San Francisco Bay, following the ancient roadways, careful to ride in the heavy brush to avoid detection. Tess had strapped the flowering plant to the rear of her saddle, checking that, in case it caught fire again, it wouldn't burn her or the horse.

I ran on the opposite side of the old roadway, slightly behind them, with Niamh behind me. From my position, I could keep a watch for Security if they approached the team. I was also hoping that the implant that now hung around Niamh's neck would still be in working order. Bit by bit, I slowed my pace, adding to the distance between me and the team.

"Tess, when we get to the longboats, let's wait for Ranza before we leave," I heard Lantana offer. Looking back, he wasn't able to spot me in the thicket across the roadway.

"I think that's the plan," Tess replied.

I wouldn't be coming any time soon. In fact, I had my own plan that didn't include going with them at all. Judging by the sound of the speedcycles racing up behind me, this plan was working only too well. I waited, crouching in the deep brush, for the right moment. When I was certain I could make out the blurry image of the Barcan Security guards headed my way, I gave Niamh a command.

"Niamh, circle left."

The lioness jumped into action as she sprang across the highway in direct view of the guards. The combination of the implant around her neck and the close proximity gave the guards a reason to raise their weapons, aim at the her haunches, and fire a shot that stunned her, right into her hip. Within a few seconds, she was on her side, panting heavily, with her tongue hanging out and down onto the pavement. The guards took off toward her.

"Hey," the first to arrive said. "Where's the Outcast we are looking for? The tracker shows him to be right here." He held the tracker in the direction of Niamh, and it began to chirp loudly. The closer it got to the lioness, the louder and faster came the chirp. The lead guard came to him and pushed him back from Niamh. He bent down, spotted the bag on the string around her neck, and yanked it off with a sharp tug. Ripping the bag open, he found the chip.

"So, either this lion ate the Outcast as he tied this bag around its neck, or someone wanted us to find it here. That would mean that the cat's a decoy to allow the Outcast to get away. Leave the lion, and we'll keep going in the same direction we were headed. They can't be too far."

On hearing this, I sprang out from my hiding place. "Hey.

You. Leave my lion alone." I grabbed my bow and drew the string back until my fingers touched my mouth, prepared to fire at the next Barcan who would touch Niamh.

The lead guard almost smiled, thinking me a foolish girl. He pulled out his hand weapon and aimed it at me, and I thought I was about to die.

At least I don't have to take my own life.

As the guard fired, I went down, gripped by paralysis, unable to move my arms and legs. In fact, I was unable to move at all.

Is this what dying feels like?

Two guards stepped to my side and easily lifted me to my feet, where I heard one say, "This should hold her long enough to get her inside the City, where management can decide what to do with her."

If I could have, I would have smiled. *It worked*, I thought.

CHAPTER TWENTY-SIX

*R*ANZA
23 May 2249
Guest of Barca
Main gate—San Mateo Portal
Barca City
Sustainability Factor: not relevant

I COULDN'T EVEN LOOK AROUND. I COULD ONLY SEE WHAT THE position of my body would allow. Nothing moved—including my eyeballs. And it was pretty frightening. I hoped whatever they did when they fired that weapon at me would wear off and I'd be able to move again. I wasn't even sure how I was even breathing.

"Hey, bow-and-arrow lady. We forgot to tell you about modern weapons. I guess you savages don't have a clue what hit you. Let's just say technology bit you in the ass. And it's the shits, isn't it?"

The one talking bent down to put his face right next to mine. As he opened his mouth to speak, I gagged from the horrible smell of rotten teeth. It was clear that the shiny face masks didn't keep stench from getting out.

I guess my stomach reflexes still work.

From a place I couldn't see came a sound so heavy, so loud and mechanical, I guessed that a large door or some kind of massive gate was opening into the Barca City complex. I felt my body being dragged forward. Soon I could see what looked like a giant cave opening—not like the caves near our Santa Rosa village in Sonoma, but man-made, like the rest of Barca City.

When it seemed we were inside, the cave closed, and I felt heat pour over my body as bright lights that hurt my eyes— terrible since I couldn't close them—crackled to life. My captors grabbed me roughly and pulled my clothing off like they were peeling a fruit, tossing the pieces into a bin that slammed shut and began to make a whirring sound. I felt the muscles in my neck as the pain told me feeling was returning. I was also regaining some control over my eyes. Looking carefully around so they might not notice, I could see they were also removing their own black clothes. I hoped they would put some cover on me, just as they did for themselves, but no such luck.

It was strange to see them without their scary black uniforms. They looked just like regular people. I decided to take a chance that they might be somewhat human.

"Hey, can I get some clothes too?" My voice sounded weak and scratchy, but at least I could talk.

The one I was sure was Stench Mouth spoke. "Open that mouth again and I'll shove something in it."

I guessed silence might be the safest approach.

They lifted me onto a table that had wheels and a thin pad on top. They must have thought I'd soon regain movement because they strapped my arms, legs, and waist to the table before rolling me into an unending hallway. That was where I first noticed the nonstop hum that came from nowhere and everywhere at the same time. It gave me the feeling that we were in a place that wasn't real, as if I'd dreamt the whole thing up. But the ache in my shoulders and the tightness of the straps told me this was all too real.

The guardians of Barca hell rolled me into a pure-white room that looked like it had no floor, ceiling, or walls. Just a white feeling all around. The table I was strapped to raised up to a standing position, then I was sucked violently into a clear tube and lifted high off the floor. Red and green lights flashed and flickered, seemed to touch every surface on my naked body. My mind spun out of control.

I think I've entered a different sort of life—on a different world.

Just as quickly as it began, it was over. They lowered me to the floor, unstrapped me, and handed me a gown that I was told to slip over my head for the next phase. Lights came on, and a door that wasn't there before appeared and opened. Two men came in and walked right toward me. One, a dark, thin man dressed in black with gold trim, spoke.

"I am President Hsieh, president of Barca. You will not speak to me unless I ask you a question. Is that clear?"

I nodded.

"You should be in full control of your body by now. True?"

Again, I nodded.

"Who are you, and where do you live?"

"I am Ranza."

"Where do you live, Ranza?"

"I am Ranza."

"Tom, it seems this Ranza wants to do this the hard way. Her choice. Have the medical team set her up for interrogation, like the other one."

The two of them turned and left without another word.

The other one? Could it be my dad?

～

MARLON
   Another guest of Barca
   Interrogation underway in Prisoner Examination Room #14

. . .

I was locked into this body device, unable to move an inch. My shoulders and legs had stopped hurting hours ago. That's what worried me; pain at least let one know their body was still alive. I could see out, but that was about it. Nearly every inch of me was encased in this tight body thing, even my face.

Just five minutes. That's all I need—five minutes of free movement. I'm certain I can do what I need to if I can just get out of this thing.

I heard the door open, but I couldn't see what was brought in. It was a person, I was sure of that. But man, woman, child? No idea.

"Hey, Stinky. We brought you some company. Too bad you can't see her. She's very easy on the eyes—a real cutie. And you should have seen her naked. Holy shit, I'd leave my wife for this one. But too bad. You'll never know."

"Yeah, I've smelled your breath, asshole. You should probably stay with your wife." What did I have to lose? They were going to kill me sooner or later, unless I beat them to it.

The guard must have done something. I felt clamps on my waist tighten so much I could hardly breathe.

"Yeah? Well, enjoy this little hug from me, Stinky."

I watched as they walked out, slamming the heavy door behind them.

"Hello?" I ventured. "Can you hear me?"

There was a long pause, then, "Daddy?"

The gates of hell opened to allow every form of evil, pain, and fear to visit me in the most horrific way. My Rannie, my baby girl, my life. "No!" Involuntary screams prevailed. "No, no, no, no, no, aaaaaughhhh!" I couldn't form words, just loud emotions. Fear like I'd never known, body and mind joined together in a scream-symphony that came from somewhere inside me. The smell of my own body shutting down threw me into a fit of vomiting that would have mercifully killed me, my face unable to turn away, had there been anything to throw up.

"Oh, Daddy. What have they done to you?" Sobs coming from somewhere to my left. She was losing whatever control she might've had. The recognition was enough to jolt me back to my own senses.

I'm her dad. I need to be there for her.

"Rannie. No. I'll be fine. Just the shock of hearing you in this hellhole," I lied. "I'm so sorry you're here, but we can work through this. First, never let on that you know me." I prayed Security wasn't monitoring the room and hearing this. "If these bastards ever find out who we are to each other, they'll use that in a terrible way. They'll torture one of us to get the other to talk. We don't know each other. I've led them to believe that I'm a straggler from the San Francisco ruins. You need to invent something similar so they don't guess. Please, honey. Please be strong. We'll make it."

The door opened.

"Time to find out who you are, Stinky."

"I already told you. I am just me. From nowhere. I don't know anything, and I don't have anything to offer you. So, can we please just be friends?"

He must not have liked that smart remark because he pulled off my headgear without loosening the straps. It was so unexpected I couldn't help but scream in pain. If I could see a mirror, I wouldn't have been too surprised to find my neck broken or an ear missing. I had no idea the horrific vision I must have presented to Ranza.

"Okay, so let's try again. Who are you and where do you live? Are there others, and how many? You have one chance to answer. Then we can start on this one over here and let you watch." He waited, I suspected, to let that sink in. "Yep, you guessed it. Heard every word, asshole, and your little baby girl here. Now, wanna try again?"

"Okay. Is this a game? Do I win anything?"

His gloved hand smashed into my already broken nose so hard that I might have blacked out. I had a sense of floating for a time before I found myself crashing to the floor under the weight of the massive body shell I was locked inside of like a clam. It was so heavy.

I felt someone pulling on my legs and heard a mechanical clanking sound. They might have been hooking me up to some kind of machine. I thought of what this was doing to Ranza, and I turned my head violently to find her. As my vision cleared enough, I could see her beautiful face—not the happy, smiling Rannie I knew but a face locked in fear, open mouthed as she studied what must be left of my own face. I guessed I wasn't too good to look at. I did my best to give her a gaze that said "Don't give in. Be strong." It seemed I got through to her; she looked away—half in disgust and half in an attempt to disguise the heartbreak that was emblazoned on her face.

"Up you go, Stinky." A machine purred to life, and I was soon being pulled upward, feet first, until my face was eye level with the others in the room. I gulped in air as quickly as I could. The guard came around to face me as he lifted my arms outward and flipped a toggle on the clamshell to lock them in place.

"Your fingernails are looking bad, Stinky. They need a trim." I could only guess what was next. He grabbed a handle that resembled a hook puller our fishermen used. He then picked up a glowing red disk from the table with the handle. He smiled. Without a word, he grabbed my hand and pushed the red-hot disk under my fingernail, then pulled it out, along with the nail itself.

My entire body was wracked with a pain I could never have imagined, while a frightening roar rose from deep inside me.

I managed to stop the scream, and I half smiled at my torturer.

"Is that it? All of the technology in the world, and that's it? You pulled out my fingernail?" Then I laughed out loud. I was desperate to show Ranza how we Nomás could rise above the most intense pain. She might need to call on that power herself.

Evil One took this as a challenge.

"Maybe we should show you how we get our ladies to talk. Wanna watch?"

"Sure—you're not able to get over on a grown man, so you need to pick on a little girl. I get it. Barcans are afraid of real men."

His face twisted. "Okay, you piece of shit. You win. I'll finish you off for the little lady's entertainment." He opened the clamshell, setting my arms and legs free, and I fell to the floor. I knew right away he would soon get one of us to talk. *It's for sure he'll torture one of us horrifically. I have to keep that from happening. No choice now.*

"Uh. I can't move my arms, my legs." I bent down at the waist.

"No problem. That goes away quickly. Soon you will wish you couldn't feel any part of your rotten body." He turned to get some other torture device from the table on the other side of the room, and I jumped at the chance to grab the red-hot disk puller, already loaded for another fingernail removal. I dove onto his back and jammed the searing disk into the base of his neck. I could feel the instant it embedded into his spine that it had done its job. His entire body went limp, and he stopped breathing. Knowing that I had very little time left, I turned to Rannie, mouthed, "I love you," then raced to the torture device table as another guard lifted his weapon to my face and pulled the trigger.

As my spirit floated upward, away from the horrors, away from my body, I watched as Ranza's breathing became shallow, gulps and coughs, as the horror of what she had just seen drove her spirit to the edge of insanity. A moan, dark and pain filled, rose from her and escaped into the universe, where it was heard by all as some unknown universal disturbance. Nature was alerted as her spirit left her physical being for a moment, so mournful it created a rift in time.

CHAPTER TWENTY-SEVEN

Tess

>*Leading team back to Marin with Phoenix Flower*
>*Presidio Base above Golden Gate Bridge*
>*Light fog, moderate temperature*

"Tooren, let Rik take the lead. Based on our first trip over the monster, I'm not willing to take a risk that any of my magic will keep us from falling through the roadway, and it's a long way down."

"Sure thing, Tess. Lead on, friend."

Rik slipped into the lead position, his horse instinctive and sure footed through the maze of broken cars, disintegrating road, and lonely, decayed lives. Nothing seemed to faze him.

"Rik, please be sure to keep a slower pace than you might normally. We don't have your experience to rely on."

"Okay, Tess. One thing, though. Your own horses will usually follow the steps of the lead horse without thinking about it. It's us humans who worry about our ability to move in line with the leaders." He winked at Tooren. Tooren just looked down.

I heard the last part of his reply as if it were an echo. I knew

I was heading into the spirit world. As in a dream, I found myself floating above the bridge. The fog lay dense at the top of the structure, leaving the two tall towers rising alone through the soft, white, foamy clouds like two distant castles ready to fend off any attack on the span. I wondered why they'd let the Purge destroy what was undoubtedly a beautiful thing.

"*Tess.*" I knew the voice right away. "*It is time.*"

"Yes, Wakan. I am ready."

"*You must tell the others to go on without you. You will return to your physical self and fulfill your promise. She waits, ready to accept her spirit self, although she is yet unaware. She will assume the leadership this day.*"

"Yes, Wakan. I am overjoyed to again serve mankind, the Great Ones, and the spirits."

I was once again on the bridge surface. Juvian was speaking to me.

"Tess. Are you hearing me?"

"Yes, Juvie. I hear. And I have something to say to you all: the time has come for me to leave you and fulfill my promise. You must continue on without me. Rik and Erlinda will return to their tribe in Marin, and the rest of you will take the Flower on to Santa Rosa. You will first divide the plant, cutting off one third of it—flower, stem, and roots—and leave it in Marin where it will be replanted. It will grow and propagate, creating a new crop of many such Phoenix Flower plants. These will be very important for what is to come."

"But," Tooren said, "what do we do with the part we take home?"

"You, Tooren, are to be the one who will bring it to the tribe. You will know what to do when the time has come. But you, Tooren, must be the one. Wakan Tanka knows your heart and has trusted you with this."

"But, Tess—" Tooren began."

"No, Tooren. I know what you fear. You have already lost Ranza, and now you will lose me. Life is loss. But you will not lose either of us for long if I am able to do what must be done. That's why I now must leave."

"Are you going back for her? I'm going with you," Tooren demanded.

"You can't. You must do as I have said."

With that, I was gone from them. I didn't leave in the bodily sense. I was simply gone.

∿

Tess

With Ranza, alone in the medical unit of Barca City

"Rannie. It's me. Look at me. Can you hear me?"

This was worse than I'd hoped. I wasn't sure she was even alive at this point. Standing there like a scarecrow, not blinking, not moving . . . I could see she was breathing, but no other signs of life.

"Wakan, what should I do? How can I make her ready?"

No answer. I needed to look within myself. I closed my eyes, slowed my breathing, visualized Wakan and the spirits standing around me. I listened, and I waited. Soon, I saw a vision. In the dream, I watched myself step closer to Ranza, closer and closer. We were face to face, nearly touching our noses.

I heard a voice in my thoughts. *"Don't stop."*

I knew what it meant, yet I had fear.

"I am with you. Take the step."

I knew it was Wakan Tanka, speaking to me through the spirits.

"Take the step."

One last look into Ranza's vacant eyes. *Is she there, or has she gone away? If I become one with her, will we both be gone?*

A deep breath now. I closed my eyes, and I walked forward.

We screamed, a long, pained shriek that was clearly two

singular voices moving closer in pitch and volume to each other. It went on forever. It seemed what felt like eternity before the sounds of the voices merged into a mirror-sound, each one matching the other, until they became one lone voice from two of us. It was good that the sound only existed in the spirit and not here in Barca.

We opened our eyes.

It was certain that part of me was Ranza and part of me was Tess, yet I couldn't tell which parts they were. And I felt those parts blending into a new soul, one from two.

"Ranza, I'm with you, and you're with me. We're now complete. We're now 'me.' Two spirits have become one for a time."

"Tess?"

"Yes," I answered, although we now spoke without words.

"Tess, where are you?"

"I'm here. I'm with you, a part of you. It's a time of knowing, Ranza. We're now one. You and I have become one spirit. I had to do this joining of spirits to go deep enough into your spirit to find you. Something has happened to you to make your spirit hide deep within yourself, your body. I have to bring you back, walk back to life with you. Come with me."

"Tess, my father . . ."

"I know. He's with the spirits now, but he'll always be near us, with us as we need. And you'll recall his wisdom many times as you go forward to create a unified tribe."

"Tess, I'm scared. Everything's changed. I'm no longer me, my dad's gone, the whole world I know isn't the same."

I wanted to let her know there was no reason for fear, no danger in our future, but it would be like lying to myself.

"We're very powerful right now, Ranza. Remember, we have magic. As we return to being Tess and Ranza, I will give you strength and wisdom, and I will make you aware of your own magic. We'll face dangers, but together we'll be able to complete our mission. Now, we need to separate our spirits. We'll be two again, learning to think and act as one. The final step's at hand. Are we ready?"

"I don't know how."

"Just open your heart. Accept me as a part of you, and I'll accept you as part of me."

We closed our eyes. When I opened them again, Ranza was next to me.

"What's all the damn screaming, you little shit?" It was one of the guards. He walked toward Ranza and put his smelly face in front of hers. Clearly, he couldn't see me, as he nearly walked right into me. I stepped back. "So, what's it gonna be, girlie? Wanna have some fun?" He grabbed Ranza's breast roughly and moved in as if to kiss her.

"I'm Ranza." She raised her hand out of the restraint as if it were paper and held it up next to his head. She began to glow. As his head began to shake violently, he shouted some profanity that I could hardly make out—just before he burst into flames.

I knew then that our joining had been successful. I had opened a door to her magic.

"I will leave you now, but I'll wait for you in Marin. Leave here, and you'll find Whisper waiting for you outside the Portal. When you need help, look inside yourself."

With that, I left her.

$\sim$

R*ANZA*
Facing Barcan City
Alone

I NEED TO GET THE HELL OUT OF HERE.

Looking down, I found I was still wearing the draped gown they had put on me when they inspected me in that white room. *Time for a new look.*

Remembering the black body suit, mask, and gloves of the Barcan Security, I was able to imagine myself similarly dressed. A moment later, I looked down and saw that the magic had worked. I was dressed like a Barcan Security guard. Now I could move around in relative freedom.

I hope this works.

"Where is your lieutenant?"

It was the voice I recognized as the person with the president man when I first came here. He couldn't recognize me behind the mask.

"He went to get the prisoner," I lied.

"Remove your mask when you address me, young lady. I'm your superior."

"Whatever you say, superior." I flipped the black mask off my face. His reaction made me laugh.

"You?" He turned red with rage. "How . . . ?"

"Magic. Wanna see some more?" I reached my hand toward him, and he slammed backward into the wall. I held him there from a distance. "Good trick, huh?"

He tried to speak but my mind grip had closed his throat.

"Do you even know what happened to the man in the medical room?"

I released his throat to the level of a whisper.

"Yes," he croaked. "They killed him."

"They killed him," I shouted. "In front of me, his daughter. They killed him. First, they tortured him, then they killed him." I was now screaming. "Did they have a reason to kill him?" I didn't wait for an answer. "No. But I have a reason to kill you, don't I?"

The man pissed on the floor.

"I'm not going to kill you. Killing for my own anger would make me a murderer. I'm no murderer. I'm a hunter. But I'll change you. Your life will never be the same. You'll never speak again to order the death of a person. You'll never again give your murderous advice to the Barcans. You've lost your voice. And if you ever harm another person, I'll know, and I'll return." I released my grip, and he fell sprawling to the floor. "By the way, what's your name?"

His mouth opened, his lips quivered, but no sound came. Tom Sands was unable to speak. I laughed.

I left that miserable slime there where he fell, and I headed out the door and into what was a long hallway dotted with signs and charts. I guessed correctly that these were layout maps to help people find their way through the sprawling Barca City complex.

The map closest to me showed a large red cross that I hoped showed my location. Using that as my starting point, I counted the number of hallways off the main one until it opened to a hall that linked to what appeared to be a main entry-exit to the complex.

That's where I need to go. I hope you're with me, Tess.

Above the map sat a large, flat, shiny thing that looked like a window into the life in Barca City. I concentrated as hard as I could on the panel. I imagined that I could make my own window say what I wanted it to. It didn't take much. Soon, I was looking at myself in my traditional clothing, filling every one of the panels I could see from where I stood. I hoped it was the same all over Barca City. Time to get to know Barcans, and time for Barcans to know truth.

"Hello to all Barcan people, both the bosses and the workers whom they hold captive. Yes, they hold you captive by lying to you that it's not possible to live outside the City. As long as you believe that, you're bound to live inside, at their mercy. And as long as you are bound to live inside, they control your every move. You must work for them, you must obey their rules, and they can simply kill you whenever they decide to, just as they tried to with one of your own called Andy. Yes, that Andy. You will recall that they falsely charged him with a violation of their laws, then they sentenced him to be exiled to the Out—a place where they say you will surely die.

"Andy didn't die. We have him, and we saved him with our medicine. And we can save you too. Those of you who believe can simply leave, and we're ready to help. But to those who are afraid, I can only hope we'll be able to prove this to you: you are no longer bound to stay here. You can leave whenever you wish. We'll find you, and we'll give you our medicine. Join us if you can. The way will open to you."

I could hear a loud rush of people coming my way, and they didn't sound too happy. *Maybe it's time for me to leave*, I thought. I closed my eyes and waited. When I opened them, I stood in the same Portal that I'd been dragged through on the way in. My glow came without any bidding, and it became incredibly hot in the Portal area. I focused on the gateway, pointed my finger, and the gateway rumbled\ outward.

Maybe that'll keep them busy for a time.

Again, I closed my eyes, and the spirit power that Tess had opened within me showed me where the team was. In a few heartbeats, I was on my way to them.

Without ceremony or warning, the Great One called out to me. *"You are now a powerful spirit, as granted by all the great spirits. You are now to be called Esperanza, the "hope" of all people. Esperanza, come to me in the place of your dreams."*

Without any decision on my part, I found myself in the cave where Tess and I had first met. I knew it was that cave the moment I saw the arrow I had loosed toward the boar-Tess, unleashing those events that had brought us to this moment. I looked around, but the darkness prevented finding Wakan Tanka, although I knew they were there. Awareness settled in as I recognized Wakan Tanka wasn't a singular deity but represented all of the great spirits in a single spirit known as the Great One, the Great Mystery, Not just the animals who spoke to me but the gods themselves. Each of the spirits gods were there in one—Earth, Wind, Water, Sun . . . So many I couldn't know or begin to count.

"Esperanza, we are here."

I still couldn't see them, but I felt them deep within my spirit.

"Mother, I have come to you. Tell me what you will."

"I first tell you, my child, that you are no longer the child you were as Ranza. The magic is complete, and there is no Ranza. You have become the powerful, loving, and wise Esperanza, leader of the tribes. As Esperanza, you will bring them together under one council.

"You must imagine a world in which the good of all is before the good of one. You will teach this generation of new Nomás how to live. They will teach the next, and they the next, as it should be. To do this, you must not turn to war. This would teach the wrong lesson. We know it will be difficult and will often seem impossible, but you are the one to make these changes. We are with you, but you must make it happen. This is a start, Esperanza, only a start. Be strong, but always know that even the strongest are sometimes weak. You are, after all, perfectly imperfect. You will have Tess to guide you for a time, then she will leave once again until the people need her."

Wakan Tanka allowed me to see all of their spirits as they were. I thought I could tell one from another, but their power nearly blinded me. Without warning, I was taken from their place, back to the cave.

∼

PRESIDENT HSIEH
  Office of the president
  Barca City
  On High Alert
  Update in progress

"MALLOY, WHERE'S SANDS?"

"He's right here, Mr. President." Lt. Malloy backed out of the camera shot. It took a few seconds for me to realize what I was looking at.

Tom Sands, the second most powerful person in Barca Corporation, sat crumpled in a useless heap on the floor, cowering in fear, his eyes vacant, his mouth wide open as if he couldn't believe what was happening to him.

"Sands. Get up, man. What the fuck is wrong with you? Malloy, have your people help Director Sands to his feet."

Immediately, a handful of uniformed Barcan Security tried to pull Sands up from the floor. He wouldn't have it; his body went limp, becoming dead weight.

"Goh. Replay video from the incident from every possible angle. I want to know exactly what happened and where the woman who caused this is hiding. Bring her to me right away." I turned back to the screen.

"I regret to inform you, Mr. President, that there is no video anywhere in the system that shows what might have happened to Director Sands. Further, the woman seems to have vanished."

"This entire complex is covered at all times by video scanners, every inch of it, and you tell me that we have no record of the attack that turned a fine, brave man into a pool of useless shit, and that the woman who likely did this has vanished? As if by magic?" I was screaming now. "Either find that woman or I will replace you and melt your circuits."

"As you wish, sir. I am not concerned for myself, only for your wishes. If you desire to terminate me, I'll comply. Thank you, Mr. President."

"You damned heartless pile of chips and silicon. Get out of my sight."

He did exactly as I demanded and faded to dark. I returned my attention to the screen.

"Lt. Malloy, report to Vonn Eriksson. He will assume all command of Security." I switched my communication screen to Vonn.

"As of now, you are director of Security for Barca City. Your first order of duty is to send that quivering mass of former humanity, Sands, to the psych ward. Maybe they can save his sorry ass. Next, you will post armed guard teams at every station, especially at the Portals. Anyone who tries to enter or leave will be terminated without question. Is that clear?

Yes, sir." He went into action.

Forgetting that I had dismissed Goh, I turned to give an order to him. *Leave it to that son of a bitch to be gone when I need him.*

"Goh. Get in here, now."

"Yes, Mr. President?"

"I wish to broadcast an urgent alert to all people of Barca. Set it up. How is my outfit? My hair?"

"Sir, I am not a good one to judge cosmetics."

"Right. Just get the camera rolling."

"All is ready, sir. On your mark?"

"Ready, start recording. People of Barca. We have just witnessed a criminal act of piracy. An Outdweller invaded our city and proceeded to cause chaos. She perpetrated an attack on our very own Director Tom Sands, leaving him in need of medical care. She murdered a prisoner we were in the process of interrogating in hopes of learning if there were any organized bands of Outdwellers who might pose a threat to every one of you.

"Obviously, there *is* a threat, a very dangerous threat. We've taken steps to prevent any further attacks. For now, Vonn Eriksson is acting Security director. He has strict orders to guard all entrances to Barca City, and as you can imagine, his orders are to terminate anyone who comes too close to the Portals. Take this as a warning. Do not enter any Portal access hallways until further notice. You will be executed on the spot.

"Finally, the criminal invader has eluded capture. According to initial messages from the sector, we have reason to believe that she has escaped through the San Mateo Portal, as the gateway has been compromised and is now open. We are in the process of repairing it, and the area is sealed so the contaminants from the Out can't get into the City, but anyone found within sight of the Portal will be terminated. We have no way of knowing if or when the criminal might return. We're going to remain on alert until she is recaptured or killed.

"Now, many of you have heard what the criminal broadcasted —that there is a way to leave the City and live successfully in the Out. If that were the case, why would she have to resort to wearing our guard biosuit with sealed face mask? Obviously, she also can't live in the Out without the breathing apparatus. The plague is real. We advise anyone who attempts to leave Barca City: if you are not instantly terminated, you will not last very long in that poisonous environment. Don't even try. It will be a terrible way to die, and you most certainly *will* die."

I nodded to Goh a sign to end the recording.

CHAPTER TWENTY-EIGHT

ESPERANZA
Spirit-traveling to the Nomás team heading to Marin
Marin Footing Overlook
Golden Gate Bridge

I COULD SEE THE TEAM PASSING THE NORTHERN UPRIGHT OF the bridge as they headed toward the overlook at the Marin side of the Golden Gate. I intended to arrive where they now stood, joining them without any noisy entrance, hoping to avoid frightening any of them. I didn't understand why I was stopped well above them, looking down. From my vantage point, I could see everything in the area—the team, horses, Niamh and Shree. I could see the entire span of the bridge, and I saw the devastation of the Purge in an entirely new way, all at one look. It shook my soul. I guessed that I was still in spirit form, as neither Niamh nor Shree sensed my presence. They would have if I were there in body too.

At that moment, I sensed movement and sound just below the eastern edge of the bridge.

Remembering the drones, I knew I needed to be down there,

on the bridge with the team, in a hurry. Just the thought was all it took, as I felt myself transported downward and my physical shape returning.

I arrived as if emerging from underwater. One moment I wasn't there, and then I was, coming into full view as my body left the ethereal and came into the living world with sounds, smells, and feelings intact. The team was caught off guard. I was there, and no one could figure out where I came from or how I'd arrived. I forgot I still had the appearance of the Barcan guard, so I must have frightened them. Odd, but none took up arms against this black-clothed stranger. I lifted the face shield off.

"Ranza, it is you, right?" Tooren was the first to speak.

Then Juvian, "Yeah, you look like Rannie, but somehow different."

Shree knew me. She leaned over and nudged me with her beak.

Finally, Niamh came from over the hill near us and pounced on me, sending us both to the ground. Shree leaned back to her perch.

After a brief tussle with Niamh, I stood up and allowed my friends to get a closer look at me. Tooren took the lead as he studied me from top to bottom.

"Yes, Ranza is here. She is a part of me."

"How did you . . . Where'd you come from? Did Tess break you out of Barca? What's wrong? Not sure what it is. Do you look different? Sound different? Act like a different person? I can't say what's changed, but I know that you're not the same Ranza we last saw in San Mateo."

Lantana saw it too. "You remind me of Ranza, but why are you wearing that Barca uniform?"

"No time to explain. We have a problem. I heard noise, saw movement over there, over the edge of the bridge." I ran in the direction of the movement. Leaning over the edge precariously, I jumped back. *A body?* Leaning over again, I could make out a human form, face covered in blood, clothes torn, wearing the unmistakable fabric of the Nomás hiding clothes.

"*Carter?*"

He looked up at me and moaned. It was him. No doubt.

"Juvie, Tooren. Help him up."

They were joined by Rik and Lantana. The four of them were able to grab Carter's wrists and pull him up enough that he was draped over the upper railing. With a hand wave, I helped him the rest of the way. Stunned, they all looked at me, confused looks on their faces as Rik and Tooren helped Carter sit up and rest his back against the bridge railing uprights.

"Ohhh . . . I fell over the side. Thought I would die. What happened?"

"You snagged in that wire netting there. It kept you from going all the way to the water." I checked his head wounds. He looked pretty good for a potential dead man. "Carter, where was my dad the last time you saw him?"

"Squinting, he examined my face, trying to recognize me. "Who?"

"I am Esperanza. You knew me as Ranza. Where was my dad the last time you saw him?" I pressed for an answer.

"Ranza?" Oh, I'm sorry. They got him. The guards got him. He wanted me to bring the flower back. I couldn't do what I . . ."

"I know. Don't explain. I saw him. He did fulfill his promise. Now he is gone. He is with the ancestors." I heard a collective gasp from the team. "Where is the plant, Carter?"

He tried to collect his thoughts. "It's, um, it's in my pack. Yeah, in my pack." He brightened, sat up a bit, and pulled the sack off his shoulders. Opening the flap, he looked inside . . . and sighed. "Not there. It's not there."

"That's good, because it probably would have set you on fire at some point."

Carter had a rough time understanding anything. "Set me on fire? No, it's a flower."

I saw he was still in trouble from the fall. "Someone give him some water and something to eat. Not a lot, just a bit for now." Rik handed Carter his water bag.

"Now, Let's get off this bridge." I mounted Whisper. "Andy, ride behind me, here, for now." He climbed up, and we headed to the Marin end of the bridge, turning into the overlook. I gestured for everyone to dismount.

"Please, sit down. I have something to tell you all." I waited for them to find seats on the stone wall. "From the moment Ranza and Tess met, it was made clear that Tess was sent to somehow complete me so I could become the leader that the Nomás people would need. Tess was sent to fulfill me, guide me to become Esperanza. The time has come."

"So," Rik asked, "why are you speaking about yourself as if you were talking about someone else? Why do you call yourself by a different name? I mean, you keep saying 'Esperanza' instead of 'Ranza.'"

"That's a good question for starters," Tooren echoed.

I could sense Tooren was having a hard time dealing with this news. He looked at me as if trying to find Ranza under the shell of this new Esperanza. He concentrated on my eyes, and I could feel him trying to penetrate my spirit, hoping to break through.

"Tooren, what are you feeling?"

"What do you mean?" He seemed suddenly embarrassed, like I'd caught him doing something wrong. "I'm not feeling anything. About what?"

"You've been staring at me. Is something wrong?"

He shrugged and looked away for a moment. "Wrong? What could be wrong? I mean, Ranza was just my best friend for so long. I cared about her. Now you tell me she's no longer Ranza, replaced by this new and improved version of herself, called Esperanza? Nope. Nothing wrong." He turned his back on me.

"You ask a good question. Ranza *is* me, but a *part* of me. I've gained much from the power of the Great One and by Tess's works. Wakan Tanka has gifted to me, and Tess has shown me how to use, the powers of the spirit. But I'm still Ranza. I'm still your friend. Please, Tooren, I need you to trust me. I can't explain all the details just now, but soon I'll tell you everything. Then you can decide if you really believe me. But for now, please trust me."

"The Great One . . . Wakan whatever you said . . . So you change your name, blame it on some mysterious spirit, tell us that you are changed . . . I understand that you have been through the worst pain you can imagine, losing your dad, but you can't expect me to just believe this amazing story without some reason to believe it. Let's just forget I said anything. We need to get going."

"Tooren, I didn't simply 'lose' my dad. I watched as they blew his face off right in front of me. Changed? Damn right I've changed. Maybe you don't approve of Esperanza, but you don't yet know the changes. I am still Ranza. I am still your friend. But I'll wait for as long as it takes for you to get settled with how everything has changed."

I turned back to the others. "Does anyone else have anything to say," I asked rather defiantly. Nobody moved or talked. I waited for a sign any of them would speak, but none did.

"Where there was Ranza, now there is Esperanza. This name means *hope*—hope for all. You'll help me rescue the slaves of Barca, and we'll lead them to a new life of freedom. Just as it healed Andy, ashes of the flower will keep them alive where they would otherwise die. We'll divide the plant between Bodega Bay, Marin, and Santa Rosa, and we'll learn how to grow more for our tribes in other places—Central Valley, Humboldt, and more.

"Once the workers believe they can live without the Barcan masters, they'll leave Barca City, join us, and live free. We'll build a new community, deep in the redwoods of Marin. This will be the new Redwood Nomás family. And we'll teach them to live in harmony with nature. We'll all live in peace, never taking the Earth for granted.

"But to do these things, we can't rely on war. Life is precious, even the lives of those who seek to harm us. We're all valuable, we're all important. Every person in Barca City can make their own decisions on how they want to live from now on. Those who want to join us will be given our help."

I turned to our ex-Barca member. "Andy, you know the design and layout of Barca City. Is your memory strong now?"

Yes, Esperanza, I can picture every detail in my mind. I could draw a map if you'd like."

"Yes, I'll need that. Make it happen as soon as you can. And now, I'll leave you all again. I'll visit the tribal leaders—Cotana in Marin, Ardon in Bodega Bay, and Lora in Santa Rosa—to introduce the future to them and to begin the process of unification that will soon include those from Barca into our global community. I'll rejoin you when it's time to free the Barcans.

"Tooren, after you stop in Marin camp, you'll lead the Santa Rosa people home, while Rik and Erlinda stay in Marin, where I will have spoken with Cotana."

They agreed, and so I left them.

∼

PRESIDENT HSIEH
Office of the president
Barca City

"YES, GOH. WHAT IS IT?"

"Sir, Director Eriksson requests an urgent communication be established."

"Set it up."

"I have, sir. Are you ready?"

"Yes, let him into my channel."

The screen came to life as Eriksson's face came into view.

"Mr. President, Vonn here."

"Go ahead, director. What's so important?"

"Sir, it's Director Sands. He has slipped into a coma. They

aren't sure why, and they can't tell me if this will resolve itself or if there is anything they can do."

"And you consider that to be important? I already replaced him. I replaced him with you. Are you telling me that you don't want the job?"

"No, sir. I am grateful to be selected and trusted."

"Then why the hell should I give a shit about Sands? He's served us well, but now it's time for a new strategy. And I expect you to deliver a plan by this time tomorrow, in writing and in person. Understood?" I didn't wait for an answer.

"Goh. Disconnect and call a board meeting to start in my office in fifteen minutes." I didn't wait for his answer either.

CHAPTER TWENTY-NINE

Esperanza
  With Cotana and Coyote
  Marin Nomás village
  Sausalito Ruins
  Bright sunlight, moderate temperature

"WHAT OR WHOEVER YOU ARE, BE WARNED THAT THERE ARE many of us hidden all around here, and each of us is capable of dropping you in your tracks." Cotana and Coyote were ready for a fight.

I lowered myself to the ground, face down, arms and legs outstretched. I spoke softly.

"Please don't be frightened. You know me. At least you knew Ranza. I am now, in spirit and in body, called Esperanza. No time to explain, but I have been elevated by Wakan Tanka, who has named me Esperanza, "hope" for the people. Tess has taught me to use these gifts for the benefit of all our people. I have been appointed as the one to lead all tribes into the future.

"First, I tell you there will soon be an uprising within Barca City, as many thousands of Barcan workers will rebel against their enslavement. I told them they can now survive outside the City, just as we do, because we have medicine to heal them when they get plague. The medicine is the ashes of the flower we now possess. The Marin Nomás will be given a piece of this plant to grow and breed. Rik and Erlinda will bring it home today. I'm here to ask you to appoint a team of farmers to learn the ways of this magical plant, to grow many from one plant. We will instruct you as to what to do from there."

"Yes, the fact is you remind me of Ranza, and I hear a familiar sound when you speak." Coyote stepped forward. "But in truth, why should we believe what you say? We've known you only a brief time since you've come into our community, and now you feel it's okay to tell us what we have to do?" Coyote was not about to accept what I said.

"You should believe her because I say to believe her." We each turned toward the sound of the voice to find Tess standing with us. Cotana bowed her head, recalling the fierce power of this spirit woman.

"Welcome back, Tess," she said. "We're happy to see you again."

"Thank you for that. But why do you not give the same respect to Esperanza, your new leader? You first doubt who she is, then you refuse to listen to her instructions. Don't you remember that I told you she has come to lead all Nomás tribes to a new unification? Didn't you believe me?"

Cotana was about to speak, but Coyote interrupted.

"Our new leader? Give respect to our new leader? No. I don't believe she's our leader. Who are you to tell us we need a new leader, and why do you think we would accept this girl as the one to bring us all together?"

Tess just looked at me and bowed her head almost imperceptibly.

I waved my hand at Coyote, and he stopped talking.

"Cotana, I am sorry this man-child has been so rude as to interrupt us when we were just beginning to get along so well."

Coyote opened his mouth, tried to shout, but couldn't find his voice. Enraged, he moved to come at me but found that his feet were fastened tight to the ground. He couldn't move from that spot. Now wild with anger, he began to flail his arms toward me. I felt he might hurt himself, so I commanded him to sleep. His eyes snapped shut, and he immediately fell fast asleep, standing up.

"Now, Cotana, as we were saying . . ."

"I'm sorry, Esperanza. I had no idea."

"No idea what? That I was powerful? That I am what Tess says—the new Nomás leader?"

"No, I had no idea Coyote would be so violent. I have never seen him this way."

"Easy to understand," Tess said. "Coyote had his hopes set on becoming the new tribal leader of the Marins."

Cotana reacted in surprise. "How do you know this?"

"I know many things, Cotana. And now, so does Esperanza."

"I need no convincing," she replied. "From the moment I saw the power in Tess, now in you, I have known it was not an earthly power. It comes from a greater source. I'm ready to do what you need of me.

I bowed my head slightly. Now it was time to be open with her. I wasted no time in bringing her current on the events of the search for the flower, my capture, Dad's murder, and our return from the journey. I also told her about my message to all citizens of Barca City that they would be welcomed to live with us as free people, and of the magical source of the cure for the plague. She had the reaction I'd expected—disbelief based on her inability to understand most of what I was telling her.

"Wait, Esperanza. You somehow put your face on the wall of every location in that entire city, and they could see you as if you were there with them? They could hear you as you spoke? How would that be possible?"

"I understand your disbelief. It's hard for me to believe it, even as I tell it to you now. But I ask that you believe it happened as I tell it, and I promise that someday you will also see the magic of Barca City. Now, here's what I need from you. I need the Marin tribe to take part in growing more of the medicine plants. Tess will give you instructions on how to do this. We will leave enough of the plant to get started."

Now I told her of the new tribe.

"Cotana, these new members of our community will need a place to live and to build their own lives, as you have here, as Nomás in Bodega Bay and Santa Rosa have also done."

"I understand."

"And there'll be so many of them. More, I think, than we've ever seen in one place before. If we're able to help them build this community, it'll be larger than all three of our current tribes together. This asks questions. First, where should we locate this community? Second, what will be the new tribe's contribution to the betterment of all? And third, what about basic survival needs such as their food source and shelters, and is there a large enough location that will grow as the community grows? This is so much larger than anything we have experienced before, so you can see the dilemma. I need someone who'll be able to find the best place for this community. This person needs to know the area well, have a leadership background, and commit to the future of the Redwood Nomás."

"Redwood Nomás." Cotana caught the reference. "It leads me to assume they'll be somewhere in the forests. So, we need to select someone who understands the deep woods."

"Well, I'm sure you know much of that, and what you don't instinctively know, you'll learn in a short time."

"Me? But I'm needed here in Marin."

"You're the one," Tess offered. "This is sure to become a very important task, and we— Esperanza, myself, and Wakan Tanka —have great faith in you,"

"But what about—"

"It's you, Cotana. The decision is made by the gods." I placed my hand on her shoulder and waited for her to look into my eyes. When we connected, I spoke to her through my spirit. No words, only thoughts and feelings. Speaking through the soul was the deepest form of connection. It enabled Cotana to see what my mind was seeing. When I was sure she understood, I broke contact.

"I'll do this, Esperanza. Please help me learn how to lead our people."

"That'll come, Cotana, in time. First, we have to help them leave Barca City without being slaughtered."

Cotana seemed to get lost in thought at the reference to the escapees being slaughtered. "How can we do this? They have such strange weapons, and we have spears and bows. Not much of a match, I think."

"Let Tess and me come up with that part of the plan, Cotana. We need to consider how to cripple Barca's ability to manufacture and ship their goods to other corporations all over the world."

"There are more like Barca?" Cotana was surprised.

"Yes," Tess replied. "There are many such corporations—former governments that control people in various parts of the Earth. And they all rely on the masses to perform the work needed to run the businesses, feed the workers, handle security, and do all the many thing a massive corporation has to do every day, all day."

"And," I added, "I understand each society treats its workers the same: like pack horses they can beat, starve, then toss aside when they're not happy with their work. The few at the top hold all power over the many, and they don't care how many are destroyed in the pursuit of wealth. We've learned much from Andy, a young Barcan man we rescued from the final stages of such a terrible death. He was exiled from Barca City and was quickly infected by plague."

"Where is this Andy?" Cotana was eager to hear more. "Is he healed now? Can I see him?

"He will be here shortly, with the others. He is one of us now.

His knowledge of the inner life of Barca is valuable. We'll use him to guide us as we help the workers who want to escape the hell they're trapped in. Tess will present him to the rest of your community, if that's okay with you."

"Of course. And Tess, will you also introduce Esperanza as the leader of the tribes of Nomás?

"Not yet," I answered. "I need time to show them they can trust me. I'll speak to them about our plans to help the Barcan escapees and what role they can play in that plan, but it's too early to discuss the unification of the tribes. And we who will lead need to become of one mind first." I said that as I looked at Coyote, still asleep on his feet.

"Now, it's time to see what we can do to calm this one down." I walked over to Coyote and put my face next to his ear. "Coyote," I whispered. "You have been hoping to assume a leadership role in the tribe one day. I'm afraid that will not be. You have great value to the Nomás, but your value can best be used in support of the leaders. For now, you will continue to support Cotana in all she does. This is an important role that will take advantage of your unique talents and knowledge. But you must commit to the tribes that you will never fail to show complete respect for the leaders of the Nomás tribes. You will place the good of all above the benefit to yourself. Do you agree?"

"Yes, Esperanza. I do."

"Then you may now open your eyes."

He did and found his feet were now freed from the Earth that held them. His voice had returned, and he used it well. "Esperanza, Tess, Cotana, what is your wish for me?"

Cotana spoke. "We wish that you would always be with us, as our trusted adviser."

"Then that is what I will do, what I will be. Thank you all for this honor."

"You may now go and gather the others in the hall. We need to be ready when the others arrive."

"Yes, Cotana. I will." He left to call the assembly.

Cotana gave me a look. "I think I like the new Coyote."

~

ESPERANZA
  With Tess, Cotana, and the hunters
  Meeting inside abandoned hall to avoid detection
  Marin Nomás village
  Sausalito Ruins
  Bright sunlight, moderate temperature

"WE'RE ALL GATHERED HERE IN THE HALL, COTANA."

"Thanks, Coyote. Esperanza, Tess, should I introduce you to the gathering?"

I took the lead. "Yes, thanks. Just a few words, then we can take it from there. And remember, nothing yet about the leadership changes."

We entered the hall, Tess in the lead, followed by Cotana and me, then the hunter team, including Rik and Erlinda. Tess, Cotana, and I went to the raised boxes that served as a platform, which enabled us to see out over the assembled tribe. Cotana took the lead position, centered between Tess and me.

"Marin Nomás, I humbly thank you for this time together. I am happy to welcome back the team from Santa Rosa from their dangerous journey to the San Mateo hills and Barca City. Yes. You heard correctly: Barca City. Please listen closely to them as they share their experiences with you. I welcome Esperanza to speak to us."

A tribal member shouted out, "You mean Ranza, right?" I was somewhat surprised that they remembered.

I stepped forward. "Yes, Cotana does mean Ranza. And she also means Esperanza. This is a name that indicates the huge changes I have gone through as a result of my experience inside Barca City." An audible gasp rose from the assembly. "Yes, I was held captive by the Barcans. I was beaten and abused by their evil Security. And that in and of itself was life changing. Particularly the experiences I endured at the hands of and under the command of their president, Hsieh. But I am sad to tell you that none of it compares to the horror I went through being forced to watch them torture and murder my father. *My father.* I went into a very dark place in my spirit when that happened."

I held silent for a moment. There wasn't a sound in the entire hall.

"You will remember Tess, daughter of Wakan Tanka, who again stands before you. I'm blessed that she was able to come to that dark place and find me. She pulled my spirit up and out of that horror. To that end, she has elevated me with the blessing of magic. I stand here a shaman, one who has powers. I will use those powers to fight with every breath against the evil monsters of Barca.

"Before I escaped, I was able to speak to every person in the miserable place that is Barca City. I told them of a medicine that we are able to give to them—a medicine that will allow them to live out here, in the non-Barcan world, without dying from any of the plagues. Your own Rik will show you where this magic comes from."

I motioned him forward. He brought the plant with him. It had recently blossomed, on cue, as if it knew what we needed. Rik raised the flower over the crowd. As he did, the flower began to glow, then suddenly burst into a brilliant red-orange-blue flame. The crowd gasped.

"As you see, this flower is like no other. It has burst into flame as if we put a candle under it, yet no one has any candle. It does this over and over every day, all day. Now watch carefully." Almost immediately, the flames went out. I picked up a handful of the ashes and sprinkled them back down to where there was no longer a flower. "The ashes are the magic. They can be made into a tea that, when sipped, passes healing to the one who drinks it."

One brave soul shouted out. "How can we believe you?"

Andy jumped to his feet. He looked to me, and I nodded approval.

"You can believe her because I am standing here. Now, you don't know me, and I sure don't know you, but you can put me to any test you like and I will prove to you that I am Barcan. My name is A37921, also called A37, also called Andy. I was born and trapped in Barca City. For whatever reason, I was framed, tried, and exiled from the city. After a week in the Out, I became sick. I have no way of knowing how long I was sick, but eventually I was dying. I knew I was dying, and I lay down in the wetlands near the bay, ready to leave this Earth. Tess and the others found me and they carried my body to a place where we wouldn't be found. She then gave me a paste made from these ashes. Do I look dead to any of you?" He moved to a group of Marin youth. "Look at my neck. What do you see?"

A young man answered. "I see numbers in your skin. It's A37921. It looks like it's printed into your skin."

"It *is* printed into my skin. I can't wash it off. Every worker in Barca has a number printed into their skin. It's how we know each other's names." Moving to a young girl, he bared his forearm and asked her, "What does this look like?"

"I dunno. It looks like you had a bad cut there once."

Tess stood next to Andy. "I can tell you what it is. That is where Ranza, now Esperanza, had to cut into his arm to remove a tracking device that all Barcans have buried in their arms. It can be used to track them down if they run. We didn't want Barca Security to find us when we saved Andy's life."

Andy continued. "Now, I ask anyone who still doesn't believe Esperanza to come here and see these things. If anyone is sick or has a problem with their body, please come here and try the ashes, if you're brave enough."

An old man stood. "Will it make me able to make love again?" The crowd laughed.

"No guarantees, sir," said Andy.

Another younger man stood. "They tell me I am dying. They say my stomach has an illness, and I'm in pain all the time. I almost wish I could end it all today, it hurts so much. Can your magic fix that?"

"We can try," I said.

He was helped over to us. I asked for hot water. A cup was placed in the fire, and water poured into it soon began steaming. Tess sprinkled some ashes into the cup and held it out for the young man.

"I don't know if it will help, but we can hope," I said. He sipped the tea. Then he sipped more, as if it actually tasted good. Finally, he finished the tea. We all waited. And we waited more. At last, the man stood again.

"I guess it either doesn't work on stomachs, or it's a fake." He turned to go back to where he was sitting. Two hunched-over steps later, he suddenly stood bolt upright and shouted, "What?" He spun back around, looked directly at me, and shouted, "It worked! My pain is gone. What in nature can cause this? It's magic." He began to sob out loud. Then he rushed to Andy and gave him a bear hug. "My brother, I haven't been without pain since I can remember. You saved me."

"No, the flower saved you," Andy said as he took his place with the team.

I moved to the center of the platform as the young man slowly walked through the crowd, speaking to any who would hear that this magic has saved his life. I waited for the loud murmur that rose from the crowd to subside. When it showed no signs of stopping, I realized I needed to catch their attention. I looked to Tess. Smiling, she held up her hand above her head while a bright light seemed to shine from her fingertips. The assembly went silent. All attention was on Tess. She lowered her hand and looked to me. I addressed the crowd.

"Are there any more who aren't ready to believe? It's okay. But I ask that you at least give us a chance to earn your trust. Doubt all you want. It's good to question things that you can't possibly understand. I promise there will come a time when you understand all of this. Just give us a chance."

I was prepared to go forward with introducing the plan, hoping to convince them we were legitimate, but I was not at all prepared for what happened. One or two at a time, the seated Marins silently began to stand. Then several at a time, until finally all were on their feet. As if on signal, each of them placed their hand flat on their forehead, the Nomás sign of respect that roughly translated to "I understand you." The gesture left me in awe. I returned the sign and spoke to them. "I'm humbled by your trust, sisters and brothers.

"Now, I need your help. Many people will wish to join us, to live as Nomás. These people are unlike any you've ever known. They've never been outside. They've lived in a closed world, never experienced nature, never felt the rain on their face in a fall morning. And they've never been able to make any decisions for themselves—no lifestyle decisions, no family decisions, no recreational decisions. They've never even had a choice about what to eat for the evening meal. That's preordained for them by their masters. I'm speaking of the Barcan worker slaves.

"There is so much to know about these people and why they'll be joining us. After I leave, I'll let Cotana tell you the story of what led to this. She'll be my contact. If you have any information that can help, or have any questions, please let her know. I'm sure when you learn about these unfortunate people, you'll be eager to do all you can to help. Again, I'm grateful. I understand you. Please understand me." Raising my hand to my forehead, I once again gave them the sign. Then Tess and I left the platform, motioning for Cotana and my team to join us outside.

"I'll leave now to visit the Santa Rosa and Bodega Bay tribes. You'll have much planning to do before you can let the Marins know what is about to happen, such as who will be your successor here, how many will leave with you to help build the Redwood community, and the like. I will be back very soon to help you with this planning. For now, Tess and I have much to talk about. I will see you soon." A smile and a hug let Cotana know it was time for her to leave us.

After she left, I nearly jumped on Tess in my excitement over what was about to happen. "She'll be perfect, Tess. I am so relieved to know your choice was right—relieved but not surprised. Now, I wish I could be as relieved at your having selected me to unify all of these tribes. Are you sure you made the best choice?"

"I made no choice. You were preordained at birth by the gods to be the one who will bring this about. It's not a selection so much as it's the way it is. It's simple, and it's unavoidable. If you or anyone were to fall off a horse, would you have to decide to fall either up or down? Of course not. It's the way it is. You fall down. Just as falling is that simple, the selection of who will lead the tribes into unification is that simple to Wakan Tanka. It's why you and I are here."

"It scares me," I admitted. "I have no idea what to do next, no sense of how to begin the process of unification. More than that, I have no way of knowing if anyone will even listen to me or follow my instructions. I might fail from the start. Help me, Tess."

"Of course I will. Starting right now. Let me ask you, what might be the first step in unifying these tribes?"

"I guess I would do what I've been saying: let them know about the plan, maybe visit the leaders and speak to them, like we just did with Cotana, right?"

"There is no right or wrong in this. You have to come up with your plan, then you have to do it. Things that help, keep them. Things that don't help, even make it worse, stop doing them. You'll figure it out, Esperanza. You are the one to make this happen. You will figure it out the way it works for you. But know that I'm with you."

"So, I'd better get going. Santa Rosa is a long ride."

"No need to ride. You have to cover a lot of territory in a

short time. You'll be able to use the magic for now, but don't abuse the powers I've given you. Magic can never replace the mind of a thinker. You have to use your mind, your thoughts and logic, to make this new world happen. Esperanza, you have to do so much more than magic alone can make happen. The ability to travel on the wind is no match for one who is able to take a seed of hope and grow it into a whole new society. Magic can't reshape the people, but the mind combined with the spirit can and will do that. Use the magic as a tool, but use yourself to recreate the world as you see it should be."

Her words were powerful. As she spoke, I felt strength flow through me.

"I have to leave now," I said. "Would you ask Andy to take care of Whisper until I return? And please let Niamh know I'll come back for her soon. She needs to protect the team."

"I am here for you, Esperanza."

∼

ESPERANZA
  Community well
  Santa Rosa Nomás village
  Santa Rosa Ruins

WHEN I SPIRIT TRAVELED, I JOURNEYED THROUGH A THICK, cloudy haze—not like the fog of the human world but more of a barrier between the spirit world and the corporal world. I couldn't see anything because there was nothing to see. I wondered if there would be a time when I didn't feel uncomfortable each time I left one place and then somehow traveled to another. I wished Tess had infused me with some level of comfort that made it okay to just pop in and out of places by magic and still be okay with it. What was most unsettling was that when I somehow returned to physical life in another place,

I passed through a world I've never been to before—not physical, not spiritual. It was more like a dream state where I could see people before they saw me.

It was different with Mom.

I saw her standing close to me. Although she couldn't yet see me, I felt she could sense I was nearby. It was odd that I still saw her as my mom. Yes, I knew that's who she was to me—Mom. But things were so different now, as if a lifetime had passed and we were starting over. I almost expected that as an elevated spirit I wouldn't have the same individual feelings as Esperanza that I once had as Ranza. But I did have those feelings. This was no stranger to me. Looking at her, I felt her as my mom.

It broke my heart that I had to tell her about Dad, and yet at the same time I was so happy to show her what had happened to me. I knew at the moment she didn't yet see me, but somehow she looked right at me.

"I don't know who you are, spirit, because I can't see you. But your aura is the most beautiful one I've ever seen. Please, will you show yourself?"

I didn't have to think about it or say any magic words. I could just feel that I was no longer only spirit. I was both spirit and physical. The moment I understood that, Mom gasped.

"I see you, but I saw your spirit first. How can that be?"

"May I call you 'Mom'?"

"Of course. Why would you ask me that? I'm your mother. Mothers always know their own. There's something different about you, but I am your mother, and you are my Ranza."

"We are called Esperanza."

"'We'?"

"I've been given a part of Tess's magical spirit, for a time at least. I honor that part of her by calling myself 'we.'"

"Ah. Esperanza. It means 'hope.' And what do you hope for?"

"It means that and more, Mom. We *are* hope for the people. For all people. We believe we are called on to lead the people to become one tribe, one people, who live much like the Nomás now live. Many will join us, and we will teach them that when we're one together, we become stronger than when we are many alone. You always taught me no one person is more important than all people, and no tribe is more important than its lesser member. We have become one spirit, Esperanza, to show that all will be one—one tribe. We believe this because we've been told by Wakan Tanka."

I was suddenly overcome by emotion—joyful and sad at once. "Oh, Mom, I'm so happy to be with you."

We hugged, hard and long. I broke it off gently. "Now I have to break your heart."

"No, you don't. I know about your father."

I could almost feel the pain reflected in her eyes.

"He's come to me twice since they murdered him. He promises to stay with me until the end of time. I'm heartbroken, but I'm so proud of him, and of you. I am so happy that they didn't also murder you, my Rannie. Your father, when he came to me last, wasn't able to tell me what had happened to you after he . . . after they killed him. And now to find you here . . . What greater gift can be given to me than the gift of eternal love and protection? And I'm so happy that you've escaped the death your dad had to endure. I haven't lost you. Either of you. Welcome home, Esperanza."

"Mom, I was there. I watched it happen."

She held me as if to tell me that she understood. But no one could really understand what it felt like to watch a father give up his life for the greater good—for my greater good. He'd sacrificed for the tribe, but mostly he'd died to protect me. That part of me that had been there, watching, wanted to run and hide from the evil in the world that before that moment I'd never knew existed.

"He was your dad. Of course he'd die for you. He must have known who you'd be and what Esperanza's coming would mean to all people. And more than that, what father wouldn't trade his life for the life of his child?"

She couldn't hide the tears. I saw through her façade and into her heart. Here was a woman in grave pain. And, to a degree, I was a cause of that pain.

Still, no matter how much I was devastated by our loss, I was here for a reason, I had to talk about the flower and the Barcan refugees who would depend on our people. I pushed my sadness deep down inside my spirit, where it would stay for now.

"Mom, did he tell you about the flower?"

"Only in very simple terms. Can you tell me more?"

"Yes. Tooren is coming back to the tribe with a gift from the Greats. It is the plant that Father sought. Great healing will come from this plant. Although there is only one plant, Tooren will know how to divide it for our people in Bodega Bay to have some. A small part of it has also been given to the tribe in Marin. Each tribe must produce as many sprouts as they can and as quickly as possible. We'll soon need many thousands of these plants to help those refugees who come out of Barca City.

"Each of the three Nomás councils will be responsible for growing and transporting the plants to where they need to be, making certain enough will be available to those leaving Barca, to save their lives. I'll explain all later. I depend on you, Mom, to organize this world-changing mission. Now I have to leave again. I'll come back soon. I know I haven't explained much, and I soon will, but believe that I need you now more than ever. And I love you."

Without explanation or goodbye, I held her, wrapped her in love, then left her.

CHAPTER THIRTY

President Hsieh:

29 May 2249

Office of the president

Barca City

GPS: 37°33' 57.884" N 122°11' 38.62" W

Outside Conditions: clear sky, very light fog, temp 23.13

Sustainability Factor: -19 (heavy viral saturation)

Interior Conditions: most systems functioning at peak

Reconstruction underway at San Mateo Portal

ALERT!—BARCA CITY ON LOCKDOWN—ALERT!

"YOU CAN GUESS WHY I CALLED THIS JOINT MEETING OF directors, department heads, and special advisers. In the time since the attack by the interloper from the Out, tension levels in nearly every sector have risen. The masses of workers actually believe that there is some magical way to survive in the Out, some way to cure the plague. This is a lie, designed to foment fear here in Barca, a feeble attempt to create chaos among our beloved citizens. The workers are already beginning to speak among themselves about an uprising, hoping to be able to escape

—hoping to abandon the benevolent City we've created for them here.

"These lower-class members of our society are limited in their ability to think. Reports from Security tell us that most of them believe the lies told by the intruder—lies that could eventually lead some to attempt to leave Barca City in the hope of freedom. Hope is a powerful lure for weak people, and it has its costs. In this case that cost will be their lives, one way or the other. In a desire to save the majority of our misguided citizens, I hereby declare that any Barcan trying to leave the city is to be publicly executed, on the spot, without any trial and without any defense. They try to leave, we kill them where they stand. Then we'll see how many are so willing to take the chance. We're forced to take this action in order to undo chaos ignited by the lying intruder. Our workers have never had to deal with such criminal tactics before, so naturally they believe what they hear. We have no choice but to shock them into reality. Public executions are the most powerful method we can use to save lives."

"But President Hsieh, is that the best decision?"

It was Margaret Showalter.

"Well, I am not surprised that you'd put up an argument. You're a financial wizard, Margaret. Does your expertise come into play in this case? Go on, share with us your wisdom."

"Well, sir, why kill them at all? Why not let them die in the Out and video-stream it as we've always done?"

"I almost expected you to ask that question. Try to imagine, in that head of yours, filled with numbers and very little imagination, the difference in dramatic effect between a slow, unattractive and natural death versus the immediate bloody impact on the psyche when watching your neighbor's head taken right off her shoulders. Now, Margaret, which would have the most impact on you? We can actually test the theory, Margaret. Which of your neighbors would be a good candidate?" *Let's see how this sentimental bag of bullshit who is, at least for now, the finance director, handles reality.*

"Sir, I don't know what to say. Are we killers?"

"We've always been willing to kill for the sake of Barca City. Fortunately, we've been able to let nature do the dirty work. But times have changed, haven't they? We stand at the brink of chaos."

Now I directed my comments to the group. "If even a small fraction of the esteemed workers of Barca Corporation attempt to leave, we'll have riots on our hands. Then, it won't matter how many we kill, it'll be too late to regain control. We have no choice. We must take control in a forceful, immediate, and direct manner."

"Sir, what about the rumor that there was another Outdweller captured in recent days?" It was Acting Security Director Vonn Eriksson asking.

"Vonn, you above all should know that we never discuss such things in open meetings."

"Yes, sir. Sorry, sir. I just thought as long as we are on the subject of Outdwellers—"

"Yes, you thought. You might want to let me do that and you can just do what I tell you to. Okay?" I didn't wait for his acknowledgment. The cat was out of the bag. "Now that he's brought that up, we did have another intruder. He was a male, about middle aged, and he was captured right outside the San Mateo Portal. Unfortunately, he decided that suicide was better than interrogation. We're trying to determine if he and the woman were somehow linked. You can imagine the importance of confidentiality here. If the masses learn that there might have been more than one Outdweller and that they might've been from some community of Outdwellers, it'll only make matters worse—much worse. Now, I charge each of you to be vigilant. Open your eyes and ears to possible revolt. It'll be there if you look for it. We must make several examples in the early days if we're to have the maximum impact on the masses. The rest of you are dismissed. Vonn, stay for a few minutes."

I turned my back on them, waiting until they left. Then I turned around again to speak to Vonn.

"Vonn, I am concerned about Showalter. I have a hunch she'll be a problem, the way she resisted my plan. I want you to do a thorough background check, dig up some dirt on her, really bad shit. If you can't find any, then talk to me. We may have to take a different approach."

"Yes sir. If it's there, I'll find it."

"That's all, Vonn."

He turned and left.

I wasn't yet finished with my own preparation. I walked over to my safe, allowed the facial recognition to scan my pupils, reached inside, and removed my laser sidearm. After I'd checked the charge level, I strapped the holster on my belt under my jacket.

Things might get dicey.

∿

Vonn Eriksson

With Margaret Showalter at informal meeting at executive park and pond

Domed roof garden

Barca City

Out Conditions: Fog and rain

Selected Holographic Conditions: Moderate temperature, mild sunlight, and occasional cloud images

Someone had made a good choice in the selection of the technologically contrived view from the executive park this afternoon. Yeah, maybe a touch too ideal for my tastes, with chirping birds and clouds slowly drifting by, allowing occasional brief glimpses of a bright sun peeking through the hills above Barca City. But the scene was historically correct. Homes and businesses thrived as part of what we imagined—and what history recorded—would have been life more than two centuries ago. Freeways below us teemed with just the right amount of traffic as the ghosts of the past made their way from one place to another. It was a scene that had probably played out tens of thousands of times each day back then, before the Purge.

Northwest of where I sat, antique airplanes lifted to the clouds and disappeared into the fog as the spirits of ancestors left their cares behind and headed out on some vacation, business jaunt, or just home.

The hillsides were filled with dwellings—tiny structures that were meant to provide a place for their owners to find solitude, tucked safely away from other citizens so they didn't have to look at them, listen to them, argue with them, love or hate them, all day and night, every day and night. They could be alone.

Alone. I wonder what that felt like.

I returned my attention to Maggie.

"He directed me to find out some negative information on you, as if to use it to destroy your reputation. Not sure why. Might be planning to get rid of you."

"Hmmm. Not surprised, the murderous bastard. So, what would you like to know?"

"There's nothing I need to know. You're probably the most genuine and bravest member of the team. I watch as you question his motives, knowing it'll likely cost you dearly, and I admire so much that you're willing to stand in the face of a tyrant. That tells me all I need to know. I'm your biggest fan. He picked the wrong guy to plot against you, Mag. Maybe we should turn the tables on him."

"My friend, how would you propose we do that? And be careful. This place, like the rest of Barca City, is monitored. For all we know he already overheard us and has sent his stormtroopers out to nab us for sedition."

"You forget, for the moment I run Security. I shut this sector down right before we came here. Changed the activation code too. No one'll be able to override it any time soon. So, I want to tell you, I do have a plan."

"Waiting to hear it."

"It starts with my belief that we're on a path that can only end in tragedy. Recall that Hsieh said the female intruder was able to blow open our Portal to make her escape? Well, what does that say about her ability to open a Portal to get back in or to hustle a bunch of our workers out, or both? And what if I have the ability to get a message to this intruder that tells her how to get the largest number of our people out without being noticed? That would piss him off, wouldn't it?"

"Vonn, have you been tapping into Hsieh's liquor safe?" Her expression indicated she wasn't kidding. "You're gonna get us killed with that kind of thinking."

"No." I shook my head vigorously. "I've thought this through. I've been able to look the other way all along while Barcan management gets rich and powerful on the backs of these poor folks, the workers. The moment he started ordering the deaths of anyone who wants to leave, I could no longer support him. I would be no better than a murderer. I need to fight this with all that I have in me."

I leaned in, looked her dead in the eye. "Help me, Mag. We can do this. Once enough of our people are free, they'll inspire more, and then soon everyone will rise up against that son of a bitch, and we can turn this world into what it could have always been—a place for the benefit of all, not just a bunch of elite creeps who get rich and powerful off the backs of the rest of the people. Hell, Mag, everyone calls them 'workers.' Let's call them what they really are—*slaves*. Does anyone care if they live or die? They're given a sentence of solitude; they're required go back to their quarters at night, alone, with no one to even talk to. Slaves. They get no pay. They have no freedom, and they're forced to work and live here under false threats and claims that have never been proven. The young women are required to serve the sexual needs of the males, without the right to have any real relationship, and when they get pregnant and have babies, the babies are taken from them right away and raised in youth camps like some absurd slave-replacement farm."

Margaret's expression wavered, and I hoped I was reaching her.

"Imagine, Mag, if you were one of these poor people, and you knew you would never have a better life. Not even for a moment. Slaves. Not people, not citizens, not workers. Slaves. Tricked into staying in slavery through some elaborate manmade twist of Barcan evolution: they can't leave or they'll die from some plague that we can't even see."

"Yes, they would die in the Out. Isn't that reason enough to stay and work here? No matter how miserable their lives are, death is not a pretty option, is it, Vonn?"

"You heard her, Maggie. The Outdweller. They've found a way to cure the plague. Assuming this is true, wouldn't that override your argument? It's possible they might have life and freedom in the Out. But more than that, they'd have something they never had before: choice."

"But how can we be certain that this cure she bragged about really exists?"

That's when I knew I had her. She was looking for a reason to say yes. "Well, if we can get proof that the infamous Andy lives, would that be enough for you?"

"Well, I guess it would. Yeah, so you have a plan. Question: you've done pretty well here in Barca City. Why would you want to risk all to overthrow Hsieh?"

"Simple—he ordered me to help destroy a woman I admire more than any other person just to protect his own position. He's murdered people to scare the slaves into obedience. Or have you bought into the ridiculous story about the snitch Jude deciding to jump from the hover-jet right before the vacation of a lifetime? Bullshit. He was pushed out of the jet. Think of how many management members have suddenly left their jobs after questioning Hsieh, never to be seen again. For shit's sake, Mag.

We need to look at reality. I have to choose which side to be on, don't I? I can decide to strengthen my position on the management team by selling you out, and selling my own soul in the process, or I can stand with you and finally do what I believe is the right thing. We have to take back our own lives before we can protect the rest of Barca City."

I was on a roll now and stood to pace in front of her as she watched me thoughtfully. "Just think about the tyrants of history who kept their lesser humans under penalty of pain and death simply through the strength of their lies—propaganda. If a lie is repeated often enough, people tend to believe it without question. Hsieh is a liar of the worst kind. He lies to the masses, telling them they can't survive outside his corporate benevolence. He lies to the board, telling them only what suits his own gain, and he lies to us, smiling to our faces while he plots to remove us if we merely commit the sin of questioning him. I've come to see that once we learn the truth against his lies, nothing else matters. The truth doesn't allow us to look the other way when lives are so easily destroyed."

"Nothing? Not even your own life? You know he'll kill you, Vonn. Just like he's killed so many others who went against him. Are you willing to die in the ridiculous hope that you can get rid of him?"

"Yes."

Margaret allowed a bit of smile come to her face. "Then, I'm in. What can I do to help?"

I paused. I knew too well that Margaret Showalter was the type of person who would put herself on the line for a cause she believed in fully. But it didn't make it easier to ask her to do what I hoped she would agree to. I looked at her, really looked. Here was a person who in another time might have run the world. She was strong, smart, driven, and, more than anything, principled. She was the right person for this job, but it would be so dangerous. My own weakness nearly convinced me to back down. And I would have, but this was a world-changing time, so we all had to be in up to our eyeballs. Who could live with themselves once this was out in the open and they were too weak to do anything about the tyranny?

"Mag, we need to go in all the way. We either take leadership roles and create a movement to take Hsieh down and free the people, effectively ending this tyranny, or we stand firmly behind him and try to convince ourselves we did the right thing. I've thought about this long and hard. If we become revolutionaries and we move against Hsieh, we might not live very long. On the other hand, if we stand behind this lying tyrant, what kind of life would that be? He's proven himself to be a monster without regard for people. As long as he thinks we're helping him stay in absolute power, we'll live. The instant he feels we're not adding to his self-proclaimed rule, we become short-timers in his world. So, damned if we do, damned if we don't. I'd rather go down with my honor intact. Put simply, I ask myself if I want to die as a hero or as a monster, like him. The answer is obvious. He has to go.

"The best way to undo his tyranny is to eliminate the source of his power. We free the people who build the products that create the financial success that keeps Hsieh at the top. Having no more slaves means no more products, and no more products means no more Barca. Once the people revolt and escape, he'll be the ruler of an empty kingdom. That's unless they kill him in the process."

"I'm with you. And I meant what I said before—what do you need me to do?"

"In the study of slavery in the United States, did you ever learn about the Underground Railroad?"

"Yes. That was the way the slaves were smuggled out from under their so-called owners' noses. Are you suggesting we establish a network to smuggle our defecting workers out of Barca City?"

"Not only suggesting it, I am asking you to head that up, be the driving force, recruit folks like us to help you, design the methods, keep track of how it progresses, fine tune it until we have a seamless path where those who want to leave are able to. This will quickly become a tidal wave of free people leaving Barca in such numbers that we cripple the entire organization, so it will soon catch the attention of Security staff. I can distract for a while, but I don't see Hsieh keeping me in this job very long. It's just not my skill set. Once he puts someone else in charge of Security, the pipeline out of here will be hard to keep a secret.

"But don't forget there will be many who are now in power who will turn against Hsieh and join our team. You'd be amazed at how many of the Barca power structure have told me they are ready to move against Hsieh. So, Mag, are you interested in the job?"

"Interested but scared. On the other hand, I'm terrified not to do it. I already told you, I am in. That includes this new wrinkle. Yes, I'm ready to take this on too.

The holographic environment changed to evening in the San Francisco Bay Area, sometime back in the 2000s. Lights flickered against a darkened sky. Somewhere near the Bay Bridge a stadium blazed light against the images of airplanes landing on runways that stretched from terminal buildings out into the waters of the bay. It was appropriately an unwinding of the day in the Bay Area, two centuries long past.

CHAPTER THIRTY-ONE

Ardon
  Leading a full tribal gathering
  Bodega Bay village
  Dense fog layer at the top of the headlands

SOFT WHITE PILLOWS OF FOG HOVERED OVER THE BAY, forming a ghostly ceiling over the gathered tribe. The campfire reflected off the fog above us; shadows dancing eerily above cast a spiritual ambience over the crowd. As tribal leader it was my honor to lead this gathering.

I stood, arms upraised, a greeting to our tribe. "Nomás people, thank you for this powerful gathering of our tribe. As always, we first ask the Great Ones for their guidance and wisdom, seeking only to know their bidding and not asking anything for ourselves. We pledge our very lives to the benefit of community, spirit, and Earth herself." Throaty flute music drifted over the gathering, seeming to come out of the softly lapping waves.

I watched Opatama struggle to his feet. He raised his arms

up to embrace the gathering. "Brothers and sisters, please join me in our prayer . . . Great Ones, you who have all of the wisdom, you with all the power, you who watch over the world and all of its treasures, please hear us, your people. We are not wise, and we do not know the words to speak that will reach your ears. We only hope that through your wisdom you will hear us and you will help us to be better citizens of this place, Earth. Soon we will smoke the pipe, hoping that you will open our eyes to your desire for us, letting us know what we must do to provide for all your children. As we have done for many, many, many long years, we seek your wisdom, firm in the belief that you will someday hear our plea and you will speak to us in a language we can understand." He paused for a few moments, then returned to his blanket, where the young men helped him to sit back down.

Without warning, a lightning bolt, so rare in this area, lit the sky, nearly blinding all of us. As my eyes cleared, I saw a beautiful woman floating above us, slowly descending to just below the pillows of fog. She held a strange plant in her hand, the flower of the plant engulfed in flames.

"The Great Ones have heard you, Opatama, and they have heard all of the Nomás people. They have sent me, Esperanza, to bring you the gift of the Phoenix Flower and to seek your help in bringing the magic of the flower to those who need it most: the captive people of Barca City."

"Esperanza," I asked, "you are so much like the one called Ranza, daughter of Marlon. Are you the same?"

"I am she, Ranza, daughter of Marlon and Lora. But I am more than that now. I have been given the gift of magic, a gift from Tess and the Great One, to use for as long as we need. To honor me, and to honor the gift from Tess, I have been given a new name. I am now called Esperanza, 'hope' for all."

"I do see Ranza's light in you, and I see the magic. Please, Esperanza, have you found Marlon and Carter? Are they alive?"

At the mention of her father's name, she who was Ranza

gasped and looked downward. "My father sacrificed himself to spare me. He gave his life to protect Ranza and all of us."

"And Carter?" Opatama asked. "Did Carter also die?"

"In a way, yes, and in a way, no. He lives, but he is changed from the Carter you knew. He may return to himself, but that is not what I came to tell you."

"Tell us what you need from us," I said.

Esperanza began to hum. Through the sound of her humming, I had a sense of words, not like she was actually speaking but more like we were understanding her thoughts. It was clear that she was laying out the future for the tribe and for those who would join us in a new-world society. We saw the magical flower as it dropped ashes to the ground; we sensed that people would harvest that ash to make tea, a potion that would be used to cure illnesses. And we had a clear understanding that we would be called on to receive these ashes, packed in skins, like we would package dried fish for storage.

Esperanza drifted down to the beach. When her bare feet touched the sand, it began to glow slightly, enough that I could see her clearly. What I saw both inspired and frightened me. Here was a woman who one moment looked like Ranza and the next like Tess. I took this as a sign that the magic from Tess was more powerful than I could have imagined. I was sure that combined spirits were present in this one person, Esperanza, and together they formed a magic spirit-woman of great powers.

"Ardon, take this plant and give it to your best grower, and have that person divide it and from one plant make two, then four from two, and so forth. Your tribe will harvest the ash for use here in Bodega Bay, to heal the sick, cure misery, and bring strength to the aged. As you use this medicine, there will be more ashes brought to you from the Santa Rosa people. This ash will be packaged for travel. You are to load your boats with it as soon as it arrives and then take it to the tribe of Marin. They will meet you on the shore by the nearest edge of the giant bridge. They, too, are a fishing village, yet they will be learning to hunt.

In return for the ashes, they will give you meat that you will bring back to your people as thanks for your efforts. The ash that you bring to them will be used to make tea for the newly arrived Barcan refugees, those who have risked their lives to seek freedom from the evil Barca slave masters.

"In time, I'll return to you to teach our people to build a new world. I know you believe our world is already perfect, but there is much that must change. Since before any of you can remember, we've lived in a world of isolation, content yet careful to live hidden from the evil of Barca, doing all possible to deny our very existence or be destroyed. Soon we will celebrate our world and the people in it. We will become one with the Barcans, who will join us as Nomás."

She bowed deeply to the tribe, rising slowly to the height at which she'd entered our gathering. I was filled with a great sense of love—love for her, for the Great Ones, and love for the Barcans, whom she promised would become one with us.

I sensed the sky changing, colors deepening against the fog, the sounds of the tidal waves caressing the shore in an almost musical way, and I felt we were no longer alone, that the Great Ones were above the fog, their all-seeing eyes watching us even though we couldn't see them. I knew they were there.

"All honor and respect to the Great Ones, and to you, Esperanza. We Nomás joyfully await your return, and we are ready to do whatever you ask of us."

Esperanza smiled, and we were filled with hope. Then she was gone, and all returned to as it was before she came to us.

Opatama was the first to react. "But, Ardon, we haven't even smoked the pipe. Did you see what I saw?" A murmur rose from the people.

"We all saw what you saw, Opatama. It was real, it was magic, and we each heard the words of the magic spirit called Esperanza. Our world will never be the same. I feel it."

I stood face to face with my old companion. "Opatama, friend, you spoke only a few moments ago, asking the Great

Ones to speak to us in a language we could understand. That was what Esperanza has done. Wakan spoke to us through her, and we understood her words. Our prayer has been answered, my friend."

Now I turned to address the hundreds of members of the tribe, seeing they were obviously frightened. "Nomás, there is no need to fear. Listen to Esperanza and rejoice. We celebrate our way of life, just as Wakan Tanka celebrates us. Celebrate others as you'd celebrate your own. Our primary purpose is in the belief that the common good comes before the needs of one. This is not a time for fear, not a time for hesitation. We will do what the Great One has asked of us."

Opatama grew rigid. He looked out over the crowd, but he directed his words to me. "Ardon, you are our leader. Of course we will do what you say, but I wish to speak."

"We're always ready for your wisdom, Opatama."

"Most of you have never witnessed magic before. You've never seen a woman floating, changing shape or face, carrying flaming flowers, and you have never seen lightning build a fire in the sky. So naturally you'll be ready to accept this magic as good magic, brought to us from the Great One. Not so fast." Now he looked directly at me.

"Yes, Opatama, go on?"

"There is little to show that this was a good spirit and not the trickster we hear so much about. There is evil in this world, for certain. You only need to look at the terrible evil in Barca, see the slaves, know that Marlon has been murdered just for living outside the dome of Barca City. And how can you explain what is called the Purge, leaving behind so many ruins and ruined people, if not to say it all came from evil? Why are you so quick to accept this magician as a good spirit sent by the Great One, simply on her word?"

I responded. "I have no proof, friend. I only have my heart, and it tells me that she is pure, that she is sent from the one who knows all." Looking over the people, I could see that this was not enough answer for them. They needed something more to believe in. I addressed them in a voice just loud enough to be heard.

"What's her message to us? Has she asked us to do any evil deeds? Has she not asked us to be true to our purpose? We've always placed the good of all before personal gain, haven't we? That's what Esperanza asks of us now. If she were evil, why would she ask only good of us?"

A voice bounced off the fog, and we all heard it, though we had no idea whose voice it might be. "Eat the ash, then I'll believe. If you believe so strongly, eat the ash."

I did not hesitate. Stepping to the flower, I reached for a pinch of the ashes from the sand below the plant.

"No," said Opatama. "It is not enough. You are young and strong. I am old, no longer healthy. My hair is gone, my teeth have left me, and I have pain in every place you might have pain. I'll take it."

I dove toward the plant, hoping to keep the old man from putting the ashes in his mouth, but too late. His mouth was full of dark ash before I reached him. I thought I saw a small change in him, something, but only a flash. Nothing exciting.

"Your eyes," someone said. "Your eyes brightened so much, like a young man."

I looked again, filled with amazement as I saw my old friend stand upright, no longer bent with pain. "Opatama, what do you feel?"

"My back pain has left me, and I can stand like a young man, much more erect, my bones able to move again." His voice filled with amazement. "I hear sounds like I haven't heard for so long. As if someone washed out my ears. I feel, if you can believe it, like a young man."

I knew what this meant. "People, the medicine is real, and it is for the good." Then I felt compelled to stop talking.

The fog glowed again as a voice came over us all. *The healing you see in Opatama is good, but it is not the highest purpose of the plant.*

You will, and should, use it for such purposes, but there is more. It is for those who might not yet live here in the natural world. The plant is given to you so that you can save them from the plague. Heal them against illnesses that they have never met before." The glow faded and we were again left to wonder what had just happened.

"Opatama, what do you say to this? It happened to you. What do you think it means?"

But Opatama couldn't speak. He only sat there, his eyes wide, his mouth open.

I knew he now believed. As we all believed.

CHAPTER THIRTY-TWO

PRESIDENT HSIEH
31 May 2249
Office of the president
Barca City
GPS: 37°33'57.884" N 122°11'38.62" W
Outside Conditions: clear sky, very light fog, temp 23.13
Sustainability Factor: -19 (heavy viral saturation)
Interior Conditions: most systems functioning at peak
Reconstruction at San Mateo Portal underway
BARCA CITY ON LOCKDOWN

THE PULSE OF THE CITY WAS PUSHED BY ELECTRICITY AND FEAR
—the electricity that made the hair stand on end and the fear of
the unknown. The unexpected had become expected. Would the
workers revolt? When would the workers revolt? When the
workers did revolt, would the Security teams actually do as I
ordered and kill them on sight? What would happen if they did?

I was pretty sure they'd do as I'd ordered. I was also confident this would have the desired effect of shutting down the
revolt quickly. It would be a blood bath.

I'm ready for it. Obey or be destroyed.

Barca couldn't be soft in this. Our future depended on obedience and compliance by our citizens. We would make it happen. That was the primary job of a president—to control the minds of the people.

I looked at my team, seated around the table in my board room. "Brendan, give me an update on the comm and visual systems. Have the changes been made?"

"They have, sir." Brenden Murphy was the perfect person to head our technology section—fast, efficient, and obedient. "The cameras and sound systems have been restricted to only those with top-security clearance. Only four people have the ability to broadcast over the system. Well, four people plus Goh. Yourself, Vonn, myself, and Margaret."

"Take Showalter off the approved list. Sorry, Margaret. I need to keep you under close watch. I'm sure you understand."

I didn't bother to look to her for approval. She didn't respond.

"Yes, sir," Brendan reacted. "I'll make the change right away."

"Then go now. Make the change. Vonn will fill you in if there's anything you miss."

Murphy left the room without a word. *Obedient, that one. Good.*

"Vonn, what's the mood among the workers? Are they starting to organize? Do they still believe they can leave Barca? Hope is like a forbidden fruit. Once they feel something might be possible, they lose all sense of fear. Hope takes over and they lose sight of everything. So, what's going on in the worker sections?"

"Truth is it's not pretty, Mr. President. There's nothing out in the open I can put a finger on, but everywhere I go I sense the people are hiding something. They smile that fake, toothy grin at me but look angrily at each other when they think I don't see. It's like they're sharing a secret in front of me."

"Go on."

"I have a few insiders set up to give me the real temperature of the sections. They tell me that things aren't great. But it's not in the ways we expected. We think about things like sedition, where the workers revolt with violence and take over the corporation, driving us out. These insiders tell me that the workers don't give a damn about us. They just want to get out of here, the sooner the better. They don't seem to care what we do after they're gone. But what's alarming is that they now believe it's possible to leave, and they're pretty much ready to go. And not just a few. They all want out. And it's anyone's guess when they might start acting on that wish."

"Sounds like we have a problem. When the people stop fearing the leaders and start looking for ways to take control of their own lives, there is only one sure-fire way to regain control over them. We need to arrest a handful of them and have a public trial for sedition. We will, of course, find them guilty, and they will, naturally, be executed in a most horrific way for public broadcast. Chop off a few heads, and watch how quickly the rest are ready to do whatever you ask of them. Human nature. Vonn, take the lead here. Use the insiders to name a half dozen of the rabble-rousers. Set up the trial. I'll name a judge and jury, and Brendan will establish the communications and direct the citywide show."

"But, sir, you're asking us to commit murder." Margaret spoke first, but from their expressions it was clear they all felt the same way.

"Are you questioning me, Margaret? You—"

Without warning, all of the broadcast screens came to life with a loud fanfare that signaled a citywide communication everyone in the city was required to watch. Onscreen, right in my face, was the living image of one we'd thought to be dead—Andy, A37. His presence was enough to send people into loud cheering. I could hear it on the citywide microphone system. It was also enough to send shivers down my spine.

"Hi. It's me, Andy. Remember me? I'm the one you all

watched get exiled to my certain death—the one Barca and the coward Hsieh doomed to plague a few weeks ago. And I'm the one who stands here not dead, not afraid, and very ready to help any or all of you to break the hold Barca thinks it has over you so you can come live with us in the Out. No more slavery.

"How did I get back in this hellhole? I have friends. Here is one of them. Her name is Esperanza, and she is far more powerful than any of the slime who run this place, especially the toothless lion Hsieh. Need proof? Watch this. Esperanza, what should we show them?"

I watched as the camera switched to an image of my face. *My face.* But how? The cameras in the office where I stood were all pointed at the floor. No matter. In a heartbeat, I felt my throat close, tightly. I wasn't able to breathe. My fingers scrabbled at my neck, but as quickly as it started, it stopped, and I fell to the floor, sputtering and gasping for air. I felt the veins on my forehead swell as the anger in me rose to a level I'd rarely felt before.

"I made the mistake of not ordering your killing, you bitch. I'll never make that mistake again." I pulled myself back to my feet. "Security, find them and cut their heads off where they stand. Make sure the cameras are on when you do it."

Andy was again onscreen. It was as if he looked right into my eyes. "Another idle threat, Hsieh. And a huge mistake. People of Barca City, as you wait for his order to be carried out—and it never will be—you will begin to realize that he holds no power over us. All he has is an imaginary power that is supported by his web of lies, starting with the lie that you can't survive in the Out. I stand here as evidence. Now I'll show you the rest of my surprise for Hsieh and his cronies."

The camera panned out to show six of Andy's former friends standing next to him.

"Please wish my friends a safe journey. They're about to leave Barca City with me to live in the Out as free people. We can be the path to your own freedom. Soon you will know how to contact us, but for now . . . be careful. Hsieh is evil, but he's clever. Don't trust anyone."

Cameras turned to the Portal door in the sector where they stood. Esperanza simply waved her hand, and the Portal opened wide, allowing the refugees time to leave without incident. After they left, the Portal gate remained open.

Silence reigned among my team as I ordered Security to close the Portal. When they reported back that the mechanism was somehow jammed open, I was forced to order the blocking of all entrance halls leading to the Portal. Barca City was no longer isolated from the Out, and chaos has been born. I took a breath to calm my anger before I turned back to the table.

"Vonn, and all of you, we are under attack. I declare martial law. Seal the Portal immediately and make the necessary repairs to keep these criminals out. Arm all staff with orders to shoot to kill anyone who does not obey your command. Those orders will be to maintain control over the people. If you feel the least threatened, shoot. If you believe anyone might be conspiring against us, shoot. Those are my orders."

"And," Margaret said sharply, "they are unlawful orders."

I wheeled on her. "I am the law, and you'd be smart never to forget it. That is the last time you will go against me, Showalter. Next time will not end well for you. Am I clear?"

Vonn stood and stepped forward. "Sir, you are not the law. You are the one who administers the laws, but laws are set by the board."

For just a moment I contemplated the fact that my acting Security director was defying me in front of my staff. He wouldn't be acting director for long. "Are you an idiot, Vonn? What the hell do you think martial law means? It means that I am the law, and you will do exactly as I say, no matter what. Clear?"

He just stood there, looking at me defiantly, and I caught myself about to arrest my entire team for mutiny. I thought better about this and decided to push that decision to a more secure time, after I'd been able to bring in a group of loyal players to take the place of these weakling traitors.

"Very well, then, Eriksson. I'll defer the action until after we've been able to present this problem and proposed solution to the board for their approval." I lied in order to buy time. I needed to come up with a plan. "I'll let you know when the meeting starts. In the meantime, get this city under total control. I hold each of you responsible for any escapes, attacks, or even any protests. Are we clear?"

Not a word.

"Leave my office now, and get to work on establishing control."

The exit doorway glided open, and they nearly fell over each other to get out.

CHAPTER THIRTY-THREE

ESPERANZA

With advance team from Marin setting up homes for newly arrived Barcan refugees
Council Rock—central meeting area
New Redwood Nomás village

"COTANA, I'M AMAZED AT THE PROGRESS YOU'VE MADE IN SUCH a short time. The new village is ready for the newcomers. Looks to me like we made the right choice in you as leader."

"I had so much help. Coyote, Rick, Lantana, and so many others worked night and day to build the bark homes and locate them in among the trees so they would just blend in and become a part of the forest. It was all Coyote's design. He came up with the idea of strapping sheets of bark together to look like large, fallen redwood trunks."

Tess was impressed. "Even I had some difficulty spotting the bark homes from the natural trees. Coyote showed me the interior of one he had just completed. There's more than enough room for a small group or family to live inside."

I wanted to check on the overall plan. "So, tell me, how will the people and their bark homes become an actual village?"

"This will become a cooperative village of both hunters and farmers, in the model of Santa Rosa. There's a variety of game all around us—deer, turkey, boar, and you've seen the stream just below here where salmon have been the dinner choice of the bears. There are plenty, so maybe they won't mind if we share them. For farming, we've located several treeless areas where we can grow all sorts of crops, including the Phoenix. There is so much land, we have set some aside for pastures where we can raise cows and sheep. Of course, we'll have to train shepherds to manage the herds and keep the predators away."

"Perhaps I can help train some lions for that purpose," I said with a nod to Niamh.

"Well, that would be great," Cotana muttered, "but I'm still not used to being so close to a mountain lion. But if you train them, I'm sure they'll be good."

"Now, let's talk about the newcomers and what you'll be dealing with," Tess said. "As much as your team has been able to quickly adapt to life inland, in the forest, these people have never even been outside, never touched anything of nature—no soil, no fresh water from a stream, and, if you can imagine, they've never eaten any real food. Their diets are pretty much chemical based. Now, how will they be able to process natural foods? What will happen the first time they realize the bread is made of ground plants and the meat is, well, you know. And what would possess them to cut open a fish to savor the insides? Beyond the thought of this, will their bodies reject the nutrition we take for granted?"

"Yeah. I see. But what did you do for Andy? Didn't he do well on our diet? He certainly loves a good portion of jerky or a hot piece of meat fresh from the coals. If he was able to adapt, won't the others do likewise?"

That was the first time I saw Tess struggle for an answer. She looked to me.

"Well, in fact, we started him out slowly—grain for a day or two, then plant foods, then mild venison jerky. After a week, we let him try stronger foods—smoked boar, for example. He had some mild discomfort with that one, but he grew to enjoy it. I suggest you try the same plan with the newcomers. Now, tell me about your organization."

Cotana hesitated. I sensed she had some concerns about how she was establishing order and who would be her core organizational team.

"I wanted to ask you about that. I know that you, Esperanza, have to set up teams in all our tribes, and I understand that you need to put some key people in each location. But I . . . I want Andy to be my second. He's well known to the newcomers; he understands their concerns, he feels their fears, and he's admired by everyone. The newcomers need someone they can look up to, right away. You said it yourself: they have so many changes to deal with. I just think he would inspire them."

"All that is true," Tess said. "What do you think, Esperanza? Can you afford to do without him somewhere else?" She smiled.

"What you ask is a lot, Cotana. I'm not sure. Do you really feel you need him here?"

"Oh, yes, I do, but if you need him somewhere else, I will look for someone else."

I smiled at her. "Actually, we all agree. Tess and I were hoping you would select him. He's a perfect person for such a critical job. You have my blessing. What about Coyote? How will he take it?"

"Actually, it was his idea, and Coyote has asked to be allowed to establish our security. We'll be lucky to have him in that job."

"Then all is settled for now. Cotana, I am so happy that I can count on you to build and grow this new tribe. I know Wakan Tanka is also pleased. So, show us around the Council Rock and meeting places you are so excited about."

I turned to Tess, only to find her eyes closed and her head bowed. After a moment, she opened her eyes and spoke.

"I'll go now, for a time. Esperanza, if you need me, call out to my spirit. Cotana, we are blessed to have you."

We both touched our foreheads, then Tess left.

CHAPTER THIRTY-FOUR

Margaret Showalter
  20 June 2249
  Leading refugees out of Barca City
  A little-used classroom, fifteenth floor (Portal level), San Mateo Sector
  Barca City
  GPS: 37°33'57.884" N 122°11'38.62" W
  Outside Conditions: clear sky, very light fog, temp 23.13
  Sustainability Factor: -19 (heavy viral saturation)
  Interior Conditions: some systems functioning at peak, some systems beginning to fail
  BARCA CITY CONTINUES ON LOCKDOWN
  Update: 717 refugees have been publicly executed
  -500 shot with laser weapons
  -217 beheaded
  All executions have been broadcast over citywide communications network

I TOOK ANDY ASIDE. "WE CAN REPORT TO ESPERANZA THAT Hsieh's theory—that mass executions and forced witnesses to the carnage will quickly stop the chaos—has proven to be a false vision. Panic has fostered gloom all over the city, with more and more people desperate to get out while they still can. Just the sight of you standing before them, alive and well, has destroyed the propaganda Barca has depended on to keep the people in line. Now having begun to believe in freedom, these people will not be stopped, not even under the threat of death."

I faced the group of refugees.

"Who among you are former Barcan managers?" Not a hand was raised. "And if I promised that there would be no retaliation?" A few hands were lifted slightly, still afraid that those here would turn on them. "Know that you have no power over others from this point on. You are no better or worse than any of us. In fact, you might even say that you have a debt to repay, and you will repay it by a promised example of your life of humility and service to your fellows. Do you all agree?" Every hand-raiser nodded in agreement. "Then, lower your hands and offer it to your new friends as a sign of your respect for each other."

There was only a brief moment before all of the refugees were embracing each other in friendship. It was a good start.

"I'm Margaret Showalter, the finance director for the Hsieh regime. That marks me as the closest person to Hsieh that you will ever meet. Yes, I have been a part of his demonocracy for some time now. As such, I might be hated and distrusted by you. I get it. I'd probably not trust me either if I were you. I expect that, and so I've brought someone who will vouch for my intentions and my promise to help."

I reached out to Andy, who stood next to me hooded and anonymous, as a signal that he should show himself. As the hood dropped, he stood tall and said, "I am Andy, the former A37291. You all know me and have seen my face, heard my voice. You know I have been in the Out for some time, and you now witness that I am still alive, healthy, strong. You'll experience this same thing when you accompany us. Margaret is famous to those of us in the Out. It's because of her willingness to risk her own life that she offers you this path to freedom. My friends who left with me the last time I returned here with Esperanza are positioned along the way. They will lead you, one leg of the journey at a time, to your new home, and you'll take this path starting now.

"You're here because you've agreed to take this dangerous step to a new life. You've been sworn to secrecy and to take this journey. Therefore, none of you are going to be able to back down from this point forward. We can't allow any risk of discovery in the event you return to the inside and are forced to divulge who we are and how we operate. Does anyone have any questions?"

None were asked. I thanked Andy as he pulled the hood back up over his head again, as if it would prevent his own discovery.

"Now that the issue of backing out is settled, let's get started."

"Wait. Are you saying that we have to leave right now and can't change our minds? Isn't that a form of taking away our newfound freedom?" I didn't recognize the questioner, but it didn't matter.

"Yes and no. I'm saying yes, we leave now, and none can back out for the sake of all other's safety. And I am saying no, it's nothing like taking away your rights to free choice. As you'll recall, when you asked to be a part of this, the risks were all explained in great detail. And you'll also recall that the person who interviewed you made it clear that this was an absolute agreement that could not be broken for safety's sake. Correct?"

"Yes, but—"

"Then you leave now." Leaving no room for discussion, I walked to the small ordinary door at the rear corner of the room and entered the correct code into the pad. The familiar click told me that the lock had opened.

"On the other side of this door is a dark and sometimes dangerous passage that's used for access to various systems within Barca City for maintenance and repairs. It's dangerous because there are many stairwells on either side of the hall that are not protected. Nor are they well lighted. Some of us have very dim lights attached to our helmets that will provide enough vision to get us through, but you need to stay close together to take advantage of the lights. And silence is a strict requirement. Systems are in place to monitor any unusual sounds in the corridor. One loud cough can get us all captured. And capture means . . . Well, you know what capture means. Ready? Let's get moving."

Andy held the door open, and we began the journey.

A young man to my left stumbled right away. "Sorry," was his mea culpa. Then he proceeded to do it again five steps later.

"Stop, everyone," I said. "Close your eyes and don't open them until I tell you to. We're in grave danger of being grabbed by Security. While you let your eyes adjust to dark, I'll give you a little image of where you're going and how you'll get there." I paused for total silence.

"First, we'll make our way to a little known and rarely used access gateway, quite close to the San Mateo Portal. This Portal is known to management as Dead Man Alley. It's given that name partially in jest—a disrespectful nickname for the actual path the dead of Barca City are taken on to the crematoriums on the other side of the old airport—but you needn't bother with the details. Just know there are as many ghost stories about this place as there are people who would like to see Hsieh in jail.

"Once you exit the city through the Portal, we'll be met by a team of guides from Nomás. They'll be headed by one named Tooren, a fabled hunter and close friend of Esperanza. He's been chosen to head up the Freedom Express program. Tooren and his friends have helped many of us to escape to a new life of freedom in the Out.

"Tooren's team will guide you north to the first stop along the way, where you'll be handed over to one of Andy's friends, and the first leg of the journey will be completed. Your destination is Redwood Nomás village, halfway between here and the

Bodega Bay fishing village. In the redwoods a new village is being built that will protect you from the ever-searching scanners of the Barcan drones. You will see things along the way that you have never even dreamed. It is called nature, and it is all wonderful, from what I have seen. Now open your eyes."

A collective sigh told me they were now able to see well enough to proceed. We headed toward the Portal without further incident.

"This is it. Once you pass through this doorway you'll be in the Out, no longer in Barca City, and you will have your first breath as a free person. It will be a terrific feeling. On the other hand, the legend of the plague is real, so there is a very slight possibility that you may be infected the moment you step out into the natural air. We've prepared a cold tea from the ashes of the Phoenix Flower for you to drink before going out. We've found that it's not only effective as a cure, it can also help prevent any plague from infecting your body in the first place. Drink all of it when you receive it."

Andy walked over to one of the trash containers. Its lid was secured by a lock. He placed his thumb over the lock, and the tumblers clicked once, the lock opened, and he lifted the lid. Quick and silent, the team guide dipped a small ladle into the vat, lifting enough tea for one person to take. Each of the refugees in turn quickly drank its contents.

"You can't get sick sharing the ladle," Andy reassured them. "The tea takes care of that too."

Now, I thought, *they're ready*. "My wishes go with you. Now, be on alert. Andy, travel safely."

Silently, I hurried back to the stairwell.

CHAPTER THIRTY-FIVE

Tooren
With Andy leading the refugees out of Barca City
Outside the San Mateo Portal
Barca City
GPS: 37° 33' 57.884" N 122° 11' 38.62" W
Outside conditions: clear sky, dissipating fog, temp 24.00
Sustainability Factor: no longer relevant

I'D PLENTY OF TIME TO THINK ABOUT OUR STATUS, WAITING for the next group to leave Barca City. I wasn't surprised to learn that the lockdown continued in Barca. Word had spread about mass killings of groups of would-be refugees who'd tried to leave Barca City on their own and were apprehended trying to open the main Portal gates. Our mission has entered critical phase to avoid more slaughter of innocents.

It had been a long, cold, and damp night spent in the rushes here near the Barcan San Mateo Portal. I was amazed at the size of this monster every time we came close to the giant closed city, built for the sole purpose of keeping people in so they could be exploited forever. It strained my neck to try to see the whole thing from this close. I could hardly see from one end to the other, from the water line to the ornate statue-encrusted skyline. Those statues added a measure of fear and evil power to an already frightening façade.

"Rik, take five guides with you and make sure the barges are still ready to load the moment we arrive with the people. We'll have to move as quickly as we can to avoid discovery, though there isn't much chance anyone from Barca will be looking for us. From Showalter's messages it's pretty clear those Barcan Security who haven't already defected have more than enough to do with the uprising under way. Just stay there and send one messenger back to give us the ready signal."

Rik nodded. "You five, come with me. No, wait, you with the weapon, stay here with Tooren. He might need you more than we will. Can I just take these four?"

"Yeah, fine." I turned to the guide carrying a bow and arrows. "You know how to use that thing?"

He turned away, drew a shaft, nocked it, aimed and fired, all in a split second. The arrow pierced the skull of a lurking Barcan agent right between his eyes. He fell silently to the ground, buffered by the fallen leaves below.

"So, your answer is yes?" Saying this, I had already drawn my own arrow and had it nocked and ready, scanning the area for any more agents. We couldn't find any. Our attention was drawn to the sound of the lower Portal door opening, where we found Andy ready to lead the refugees out of their hell.

"Andy, we need to stay alert for any more Barcan Security. If they know for certain we're taking these folks out of Barca, our underground effort comes to a bloody end. Do you have a count of those coming with us this trip?"

"One hundred seven. Do you know how many that is? Remember the hundreds I taught you?"

"Uh, yeah. That's more than the last group. They were only in the tens. Five tens, right?"

"That's right. This group is about twice as many as last time. Do you have enough boats to carry them all to Marin?"

I had to think hard about the numbers he was teaching me. It made me feel small and weak to not know something Andy knew so well. On the other hand, I'd like to see him track and hunt a buck using just his wits and a bow and arrows.

I had to answer him. "Well, last time we had two boats, and today we have four. Last time we had plenty of room for more, so I think we can handle them all. Otherwise, some can stay overnight near the airport."

"Impressive. I'm surprised by the logic you used to come up with that. Good work."

Why does he talk to me like I have no brain? I'd challenge him to a hunt, or to try to make a bow and some arrows, or to identify what kind of animal had made the stinking pile of scat on the trail, but I didn't think Esperanza would like that. Just the same, I had no idea what logic he was talking about, so I just smiled and started helping the refugees through the door.

"How were they, Andy?" He knew what I was asking.

"Well, all good except one who was questioning his right to back out at the last second. Might want to have a close talk with him, try to find out if he's a spy or just a troublemaker. You'll know him. Margaret marked him with her handprint. It's on his right shoulder where she touched him with the marking fluid. I can take him on my boat, or you can handle him during the crossing if you prefer."

"I got this." I was concerned about this type of report. We couldn't be too cautious. One spy could jeopardize the entire population of Nomás villages, including our newest village in Muir Woods. I'd given my word to Esperanza to protect the villages at all costs. I intended to keep that promise.

From the signal, I could tell the group of refugees had all been brought out and were ready to go.

"Everyone, listen closely. We're about to take a long journey. The first part of the trip will be pretty easy for you in some ways.

We'll load into long boats. All you'll need to do is board, then sit quietly while we travel up the bay and across the Golden Gate. Never mind what any of that means. You'll see soon enough.

"Now, in another way it might not be easy for some of you. Having never traveled by water, some people experience a sickness for a time. That can be uncomfortable, but it passes quickly, and you'll be fine." I was lying.

"The next part of the trip is a bit more difficult. We'll ride horses from just under the old bridge all the way up the hills to our new village deep in the dark redwood forest, about a half day's ride. Since none of you are experienced riders, you'll spend the night in Marin camp so you can rest, then we'll head out in the morning, riding in full daylight."

I could see the worry come over them. "What are horses?" one asked.

Oh. I didn't think of that. "Horses are large animals that walk on four legs. They can travel quickly. We sit on their backs and ride them to where we want to go."

"But we don't know how to do that."

"There's no need for concern. We'll take care of you every step of the way. Our horses have been trained for new riders, and they'll be gentle and careful all the way."

As I spoke, I walked in between the refugees, looking for one particular person. It didn't take long before I spotted him—a man with a faint red handprint on his right shoulder.

Movement in the direction of the shoreline caught my eye. It was the guide sent by Rik to let us know the boats were ready.

"Let's head down to the water. Stay together, and keep out of sight. There could be more of those Barcan agents out here, and they might be hiding anywhere."

We lined the refugees up in small groups. "Everyone, look at the person next to you and remember their face. You're responsible to let us know the instant any of your teammates can't be found. We're in this together. Take care of your friends."

We moved downhill toward the landing spot only a short

hike away. I made sure to walk close to the marked man. I'd make sure he and I were on the same boat for the trip to Marin shoreline.

"Isn't this exciting?" I wanted to start the conversation in the right direction. "I mean, to even think about leaving Barca and living in the Out. It has to be like a fantasy."

"I can't make myself believe it yet," said a young woman.

An older man joined in. "I believe it. I just hope nothing goes wrong before we get to safety."

"Safety? Who sold you that myth? Do you really believe a bunch of wild hunters can protect us from Barca Corporation? Right. Keep thinking that." It was the marked man.

I decided to press him. "So, if you don't believe we can protect you, why are you here?"

"Sounded good at first. But when I thought it through and wanted to back out, I was told it wasn't going to happen. That I was committed and couldn't back out. Who knows what you'd do to me if I tried."

"Yeah. I know exactly what would happen, and I understand why. We don't know you from the start. Who knows, maybe you're a spy. Maybe you just wanted to back out so you could go back to Hsieh's minions and tell them how our escape system works. How do we know you really aren't a spy?"

"So, what are you going to do about it? You can't prove I am, and I can't prove I'm not a spy. So, what's the next step?"

"Pretty easy," I said. "We let Esperanza decide. She can look inside your spirit and tell exactly who and what you are. For now, any move to put us in danger will be dealt with in a fast and final way. Get my meaning?"

"Yeah. I get it."

"And you're to stay right beside me for the whole trip. Understand?"

He didn't respond. Just stared at me with what could best be described as total resistance. I was worried about this one. I needed to check him out a bit.

"Andy, do you know this one?" He joined me and looked the man over thoroughly.

"Nah. Can't say I do. He's not familiar to me. Why?"

"Margaret had a suspicion about him—marked him. See?"

"'Marked' me? What do you mean 'marked'?"

"Quiet. If we want you to know, we'll tell you. Andy, let's see if we can figure this guy out. Ask him about his life as a slave worker."

"Fuck you," the man snapped. "You have no right to question me. I'm going on the trip, like we agreed, so get out of my way, and let's go."

"What was your work sector? Your number? Where did you live?" Andy was in this guy's face. It was clear Andy wasn't about to back down.

"What was yours, dead guy? You should have died already. What gives you the right to question me?"

Andy closed in and caught the man by the shoulder. The marked man turned away, but Andy was too fast, grabbing him roughly to turn him back. He locked on to the man's wrist and pulled it out so I could see that there was a fresh line of glue-repaired skin where a medical incision had been made.

"A tracker," I snapped. "You're a damned tracker. Margaret warned us to look for this type of cut. Means he had a tracking chip implanted in his arm. And from the looks, it's a fresh implant."

Andy backed off a step. "Well, Tooren, I think we have an answer."

"Yeah, I believe you're right." Turning to one of our security team, I ordered the man to be restrained until we could get him in front of Esperanza or Tess. Andy, on seeing the security member reach for the man, released his hold. At that moment, the spy wheeled around, grabbed the security guard's hip knife and raised it, ready to lunge at Andy. The man had no idea just how quickly a skilled hunter could nock and fire an arrow. I placed it right in the middle of his brow before anyone could even react to the threat. The man hit the ground like a rock.

"Okay, let's get him buried. Remove the chip first, and toss it into the water." The security team was already on it. "Two of you stay behind to finish the job. The rest of you get your people ready to go. Wait a moment, so I can try to calm their fears. From their perspective, I might have just murdered that man."

I waved for everyone to come as close as possible so I didn't have to shout.

"I know what you just saw must have been frightening, and you might not be able to figure out what happened and why. We learned that the man was wearing a tracker chip to allow Barcan Security to follow us electronically. When he was caught as a spy, he tried to kill Andy then run away. I couldn't let either of those things happen. First, Andy is one of us, and we protect our own. Second, if he had escaped, we would soon be facing an attack from Barcan assassins. I want you to know I would do the same again to protect you. You are also our people now.

"Now, because of the tracker, it's certain Barcan Security are already on our trail. We bought some time by getting rid of the chip, but they'll be here soon. Let's get going before they arrive."

The dense fog wrapped us like a cold, wet blanket—enough cover to keep us hidden but so much that we missed our mark by a distance and had to backtrack to find the barges. I hoped in silence that it wasn't so thick out in the bay that we might miss our mark again and end up in the middle of the ocean. But not much choice; we had to leave right away.

As we reached the barges, our boat handlers saw us coming and pulled the tules away in one sweep so we could see them. The cover must have worked as planned, since there were no drones scanning the area. It was possible, too, that the rebellion, now catching the attention of the Barcans, had forced all focus away from the Out and onto the very real dangers under the dome covering the city.

To get underway required all of us to help push the flat-bottom barges off the weeds and then hold the craft so it wouldn't float away before we had a chance to board. Those manning the tillers stayed aboard in case the barges did start to float off, so they could try and maneuver the crafts closer to shore long enough for everyone to get on.

I had imagined it would be a simple operation to gain floatation then push or pull everyone aboard, but I was wrong. I hadn't taken into consideration the reality that these people had spent their entire lives in a fortress over the water without ever actually touching the water themselves, much less learning how to swim in it or even move around enough to drag their legs over the side of the barge and onto its deck. Some of what transpired were comical escapades, where people kept almost clambering aboard before falling unceremoniously into the water headfirst at the last second. A few of these incidents were dangerous and might have become deadly if not for the skill and determination of the crew.

One moment in particular shook me to my core. A young lady somehow slipped headlong into the water at the precise moment the barge drifted ashore, pushing her completely under the silt, unable to move or breathe. The man on the tiller immediately sensed the danger and countered the wave skillfully, dragging the tiller through the water at the exact angle needed to push the barge the opposite direction so we could free the girl before it came crashing back onto her.

As difficult as it was, we somehow managed to load everyone into the two barges and push off toward what we hoped would be the Golden Gate on our way to Marin. The fog was much thinner out on the water, enabling us to spot the bridge structure almost the minute we left land. With such a clear view of the bridge, we had no trouble finding our way north, across the bay, to Marin. We had no trouble, that is, except for the poor landlocked folks of Barca City, who had never been on a raft, much less a barge in the middle of a bay that was somewhat encircled in fog. It was too much for some of their stomachs to handle, and they spent a fair amount of the trip leaning over the sides of the barges, throwing up into the water. It was not a pleasurable sight, to say the least.

With the help of the crew on the tillers and the luck of the fog, we made it to the other side of the bay pretty quickly. I easily understood why the passengers were able to disembark much faster that it took them to board.

A team from the Marin Nomás were there to greet us and to guide us to the next stop—the Sausalito Ruins.

CHAPTER THIRTY-SIX

PRESIDENT HSIEH
   23 June 2249
   Office of the president
   Barca City
   GPS: 37°33' 57.884" N 122°11' 38.62" W
   Outside Conditions: cloudy sky, deepening fog, temp 19.32
   Sustainability Factor: -19 (heavy viral saturation)
   Interior Conditions: system-wide failures caused by deferred mainte-
nance due to staff defections:

   - environmental systems overloaded
   - food service functions sporadic
   - medical support running at half capacity
   - security systems almost nonexistent

   Reconstruction at San Mateo Portal
   Martial law imposed due to rebellion underway

· · ·

Everywhere I turned, it seemed I was seeing the ghost of someone hiding, lurking in my safe zone, ready to come at me if I let my guard down for even a nanosecond.

There was no one left to trust—not that I ever did trust anyone. More than half of the Security staff had turned to the side of the rebellion, wanting little more than to see me hang, to fling open the doors of every Portal to allow the people to go to the Out and let the dreaded Out come into our glorious, cherished castle.

Spineless pukes, every damned one of them. Not one of them would be anything without me.

I'd pulled them out of the gray masses of the workers, handpicked them for greatness. Now they'd turned against me. No guts. All they needed to do was follow orders, kill the damned rebels in their tracks, zero tolerance. But they were cowards. They chickened out. And the lowlife workers had seen their cowardice, and they knew they could count on the cowards to help them escape. Now the whole place might fall. Barca City, the greatest accomplishment in centuries, going down in defeat.

Well, not with me, it won't.

"Goh. *Goh*! Where the hell is that piece of crap?"

"Here, sir. At your side."

"Goh, communicate with the Flight Port. Have my private jet made ready right away. Have them set course for Toyokohama. I'll transport to the deck in five minutes, as soon as I can get there."

"I am afraid that's not possible, sir."

"What? Don't you defy my direct order."

It's not that I'm disobeying an order, sir. It just can't be done."

"Explain."

"Sir, the transport tubes are blocked beyond repair. You will have to walk to the Flight Port yourself. Estimates to climb down thirty-seven flights of stairs, then walk the corridors to the Flight Port indicate it will take approximately forty-five minutes.

And that estimate will be meaningless in the event you are discovered alone in the halls by the rebels. You'd last eighteen approximately seconds according to—"

"*Enough.*"

"Sir?"

"You are telling me there is no possible way for me to escape this place?"

"None that I can calculate, sir, but I will continue to adjust my algorithms to see if—"

"Stop. Help me to come up with a plan to negotiate my exit in the event the rebels are in charge. And have Vonn Eriksson report here immediately."

"Yes, sir."

I took the time to relax as best I could and to try to come up with a reasonable plan. I needed to think. "Hsieh personal log entry. Note date and time. Category—Rebellion. Begin recording."

Taking a breath, I collecting my thoughts. "What do I know so far? It's for sure we are in a full-on rebellion. The masses are attacking the leaders on every front. Team leaders murdered. Board members pushed out of the Portal without even a hearing. And traitors leaving the City by the thousands. What I can count on—at least I think I can—is that what remains of Barcan Security is still behind me. I've been given reports by Goh that the guards are still executing traitors in the halls, marking their doors so they know who is a traitor and leaving the doors of others unmarked. The City system has marked those known to be faithful by adding a code to their chip so we can scan a group for traitors. If I can assemble these loyal people into a single military force, we can actually retake the City, sector by sector, until we overrun the entire complex and regain control. Then we can deal with these traitors with force."

I stopped. The rest would have to wait. "End recording. Goh, open all channels and train the cameras on me."

"Yes, sir." The cameras lit up, and screens flickered on all over Barca City. I stepped up to the cameras.

"People of Barca City. This is your president. I have thought long and hard about what I might say to you at such a momentous occasion. What I keep coming back to is this: you don't deserve any explanation. You, the rebels, will soon find out how good you had it here under my protection. You, my former allies and staff, watch me and learn what true courage looks like. I condemn you to your own hell."

I reached down to my desk and lifted the President Jackson pistol. "A very brave man originally owned this pistol. I have kept it as a reminder that it takes extreme courage to change the world. I have done what I needed to do to make our world more powerful, richer, efficient. Your cowardice in the face of a minor uprising is disgusting. I intend to use this gun to bring an end to the most cowardly of my former staff. Oh, yes. I have spies everywhere, and I know that this one in particular is a leader of the rebellion. And I will broadcast the execution so that none of you continue to believe in this false Moses. Stay tuned." I gestured with pistol in hand. "Goh, stop recording."

"Yes, sir."

Vonn Eriksson came into the office. "Mr. President, you wanted to see me?"

"Yeah, Vonn. Report on Security. What's happening out there?"

"We're fighting the good fight, sir. The rebellion has traction, but certain sectors show promising signs of peace. There's even an offer in compromise coming out today from Science and Development."

" Compromise? Offer in compromise? And you called that a promising sign? Bring me the head of the leader of that sector, and I'll show you what a compromise looks like. Vonn, you're getting weak. What the hell is wrong with you? Show me the visuals."

"Yes, sir. But you won't like what you see."

"Show me, dammit!"

"Yes, sir. Goh, play the security visuals numbered 30625SEC."

"Yes, Director."

What he showed me on screen could only be described as a bloodbath. In the first sector we viewed, workers were beating Security forces with anything they could get their hands on—chairs, tools, broken pieces of machinery. It was only a matter of minutes before the sector was overtaken by the former workers and the Security forces were taken prisoner. The second and subsequent sectors showed even less promise. The fighting had already stopped, and it was easy to gauge the outcome. Workers, newly emboldened, were winning their fights.

"Vonn, why aren't they using their weapons?"

"They no longer work, sir. The workers somehow figured out how to disable charging stations system wide. When the guards strapped on their weapons this morning, they had no idea they were useless. Pretty clever, don't you think?"

"'Clever'? You want 'clever'? Here is something 'clever' for them to chew on. I know, Vonn, that Showalter is connected to this. I want you to capture her so I can execute her right in front of the entire City. Take out their leader, then we'll see how fucking 'clever' they are. And for measure, I'm going to use the Jackson gun to blow her brains all over the camera lens."

I held the gun up so he could admire this ancient tool of destruction.

"Amazing, sir. May I see it?"

"Sure, but handle it with respect."

Eriksson took the antique pistol in hand. He noted that the hammer was cocked.

"Is this thing loaded?"

"Oh, yeah. Loaded and ready to fire."

"Wow. Then you wouldn't mind putting your hands behind your back while Goh cuffs you?"

It took a second for his words to register. "What? What did you say to me?"

He aimed the pistol right into my face. "Goh, please bind the prisoner."

"Yes, sir." Goh's chest plate lit up as he turned toward a robot standing dormant in the corner. "Secure President Hsieh for prisoner transport."

The system, under Goh's manipulation, sprang into action directly behind me and grabbed my arms roughly. Before I could even fathom what was happening to me, it had clamped wrist cuffs tightly onto my arms.

"You reprogrammed my assistant?"

"Mr. President, I hereby relieve you of command, and I place you under arrest for the crimes of sedition, murder, and tyranny. You will be tried immediately following the complete surrender of the City into the hands of the people."

I was dumfounded. "Vonn? You are part of this? Why?"

"I was always a part of this. I would never support a murderer who would enrich himself on the backs of enslaved people. People whose very birth was inspired by need. Need more workers, make more slaves. I was always against you, but I finally decided to take you down when you ordered the mass killing of those people whose very reason for living was to do your bidding, fulfill your orders, add to your power. And, I might add, I admire Margaret Showalter more than any other human. She puts her morals and her honesty above her personal benefit. We call that 'principles.' Something you know nothing about. Just so you know, I disabled all weapons and chargers last night. Kind of handy to be the head of Security, wouldn't you say?"

"I'll see you burn for this."

"Perhaps." He called for Security. "And perhaps not. Take the prisoner to the lockdown."

"*I'll see you dead, you weak piece of—*" My mouth was clamped shut by a face-block device.

∾

VONN ERIKSSON
   23 June 2249
   Offer of Peace

"GOH, OPEN ALL CAMERAS FOR TWO-WAY VIEWING."

I was able to see into all sectors, and all sectors were able to see and hear me.

"People and forces of Barca. The former president, Hsieh, has been taken into custody. He is to be tried for his crimes when all sectors surrender and peace returns to Barca City. As you know, many sectors have already fallen to the people, and Barcan forces have surrendered. I am going to offer to all Barcan management and forces an opportunity to end this madness peacefully.

"As you may or may not know, Margaret Showalter and I have been a part of the uprising. She has been helping evacuate those who wish to leave, and I have worked undercover to create a rebellion force made up of many former slaves and former Security forces. This organization is to remain in place to develop a peaceful transition to a fully democratic way of life here in Barca. You will all have a say in how we live and in how we move forward from here. It'll be tough, but not as tough as a life of slavery. This is a one-time offer to all. Surrender now, and we will accept your surrender without consequence. The true evil has been eliminated, and the rest of us will learn to live in harmony.

"If you agree to this surrender, hand your weapons to the rebel leaders now. And then the leaders, accepting your surrender, will signify by lighting the green light over their sector cameras. Once all sectors have gone green, we will begin the transition."

Almost instantly, sectors began to show green, indicating that the war, for them, was over. When all sectors had become free, I made the next announcement.

"People of old Barca, welcome to the new world—a world

that will be called Nomás. This former Barca City will be the new location of the Inworld, home of the Barca Nomás people. And you will be known as Indwellers.

"It is also important that you know that you are free. This freedom allows you to live In or Out, your choice. You will be given the medicine of the Phoenix that will enable you to travel freely outside these walls. And for this, we thank you and we thank Esperanza, Tess, and Wakan Tanka, three spirits you will soon come to know.

CHAPTER THIRTY-SEVEN

Esperanza
  Blessing of The Redwood Nomás village and ceremony to welcome Cotana as tribal leader
  Great Tree circle and ceremonial fire
  Redwood Nomás village
  Midday
  Clear sky, cool, no fog

I LOOKED STRAIGHT UP TO SEE SHREE IN HER MAGICAL, JOYFUL sky-dance, her shrill screeches lending sound to the happiness of the entire tribe as our people assembled here as the Redwood Nomás community for the very first of what would be an annual Unification Ceremony.

Already seated here before the Great Tree and Council Rock were the leaders of the four tribes—Santa Rosa, Bodega Bay, Marin, and now Redwood. I had asked Coyote to lead the Marin tribe in the Sausalito Ruins, and he accepted that request. Seated next to Lora, my mother, was Tooren, my dearest friend. He would be the tribal leader in Sonoma, home of the Santa Rosa tribe, my birthplace. Ardon would continue to lead the fishing village of Bodega Bay, with Opatama as his second.

On my signal, Cotana took her place at the center of the Council Rock, standing on it just tall enough for the gathered Nomás and former Barcans to see. She began the ceremony.

"Welcome to all Nomás. The good of all before the good of one." She waited for all to take a seat on the ground, on a fallen tree, or on a rock. She then signaled for Coyote, Tooren, and Ardon to take their positions, standing between the Rock and their own tribes, able to pass Cotana's words on to those too far away to hear.

"We will soon hear from our great Esperanza, but at this moment, she wishes that you accept her mother and offer her your support for her new role as the spiritual adviser to all Nomás people. Lora, please stand here so that all can see you."

As she stood and made her way to Cotana's side on the Council Rock, a deep and low rumble filled the air. It was the entire crowd as they whispered at first, then chanted, "Nomás, Nomás, Nomás . . ." ever stronger until the whisper rose to a shout. The sound of many thousands of us speaking our tribal name in unison was almost too much for the senses. Many cried, some laughed, all were touched deeply.

Lora waited a moment for the sound to soften. It didn't. Looking at me, she smiled, then raised her hands above her head, palms outward. The sound stopped almost immediately. She spent several moments looking out over the assembly as if she wanted to look inside the heart of every Nomás seated there. In due course she smiled to all, nodded once, then said, "Esperanza is with us. She has come to us today to bless the world with hope."

There was another groundswell of emotion, but before it could take hold, the sky filled with a soft, brilliant fog. A hush came over the crowd.

"Now, as spiritual adviser to the tribes, I welcome our new members—there are so many of you—and I bless the new tribal leader Cotana." Everyone cheered. "I know that you have so much to learn. A new life isn't natural, so you have to learn to work at it, learn how to be your own leader of your life. The tribal leaders are here to help, but you are now in control of your destiny. You will create your own way. Make it a great one, to thank Wakan Tanka for this gift of freedom. Now, we bow down to our own Esperanza—Hope for the Nomás."

As she backed away and I rose, I was startled to be greeted by total silence. Not a chirp, giggle, cheer. No sound at all. I walked to the Council Rock, stepped up, hugged my mother, and turned to the crowd. It was then I noticed that every single person was actually bowing to me from the waist. I felt a flood of emotion as tears ran down my face and I recalled all that we had to endure to come to this moment. I wasn't able to speak for some time. Finally, I found my voice.

"You are my sisters and brothers, and I hold you all here, in my heart." A thunderous cheer came up from the ground and swarmed me. "I give you one thing that you've never been given: I give you hope. You are no longer alone. You are Nomás. We are one tribe. As Nomás, you are forever protected. The good of all before the good of one.

"I bring you great news. The tyrant Hsieh has been arrested and will never again hold dominance over any other person. Next, we will help those in Barca who wish to leave and live out here with us. Those who wish to stay will soon form their own tribe, known as Barca Nomás. They will establish under guidance a set of guidelines such that the principle of the good of all before the good of one is upheld. Then we will welcome them into the Nomás culture. But today is a new beginning for all of us here, in Santa Rosa, Bodega Bay, and in Marin. This is the day we commit to unification of all Nomás people under a single culture—the Nomás culture.

"Now, I have a surprise for you. So many of you have heard of the one who saved me, the one who elevated me, so that we could overcome the evil of Barca. Tess is here with us."

From behind the Great Tree, Tess walked slowly, head bowed. She wore a brilliant white dress with the symbol of a buffalo calf across her front. A soft, throaty hum came from her as she walked around to the front of the tree and stepped onto the Council Rock. She finished humming, raised her head to look at the people, and raised her arms to the sky.

"Great One, we thank you for this day and for these people." Now she opened her arms as if to hold all of the tribe. "Now we pledge our unity as Nomás. Please repeat, 'The good of all before the good of one.'" She waited for it to be done. "Now I tell you what I have learned this phrase means. I learned this from Lora, from Esperanza, from Ardon, Tooren, and Cotana. And I learned it so fully from Marlon, father of Ranza, husband of Lora, who lived and died with this pledge. He gave his life for his people. He gave his life for Ranza, now Esperanza, to give her the power to be our hope. He gave his life for you, every one of you. It was his sacrifice that made your freedom even possible. That is what is meant by 'The good of all before the good of one.' And so, to seal your commitment to unity, I ask you to say, as one, his name: Marlon. Say 'Marlon.' Say it again. And again. And as you say his name, know that you are making a pledge to be like Marlon if you are ever called to sacrifice your wants and needs for the good of all."

The crowd continued chanting my father's name. I was so moved, it brought me to my knees.

Now Tess raised her hands again, and the people were silent. "You will do this every year. This is to be called the Unification Ceremony, and your tribal leaders will hold these ceremonies in each tribal council. I bless you before I leave you. You will see me again, when it is needed."

She stepped down to the ground and knelt beside me. Helping me to my feet, she whispered to my spirit. "I never gave you my magic, Esperanza. It was yours all along. Use it wisely."

Then she left. No one saw her go but me.